DISCARD

SLEEPING LATE ON JUDGEMENT DAY

A Bobby Dollar Novel

TAD WILLIAMS

DAW BOOKS, INC.
DONALD A. WOLLHEIM, FOUNDER
375 Hudson Street, New York, NY 10014
ELIZABETH R. WOLLHEIM
SHEILA E. GILBERT
PUBLISHERS
www.dawbooks.com

First printing, September 2014
1   2   3   4   5   6   7   8   9

DAW TRADEMARK REGISTERED
U.S. PAT. AND TM. OFF. AND FOREIGN COUNTRIES
—MARCA REGISTRADA
HECHO EN U.S.A.

PRINTED IN THE U.S.A.

I started the Bobby Dollar story by dedicating it to my friend David Pierce, who left us. Since then, I have lost a few more dear ones, and our field of science fiction/fantasy has lost quite a few as well.

Mortality is pain, but it's also perspective. We miss you all, you writers and artists and creators, and I still really miss Dave, but that's the terrible, beautiful conundrum of our lives: We can't love without someday learning about loss.

ACKNOWLEDGMENTS

My book, my rules. And the most important rule is—acknowledge, acknowledge, acknowledge! Because one of these doesn't get finished without many people's help.

My dear friends and editors, Betsy Wollheim and Sheila Gilbert, have been very important to the creation of this book (as they have with all the others, too). Blessings upon them.

My excellent agent, Matt Bialer, has held my hand (metaphorically, mostly, because he's in New York) through many crises and freak-outs. Blessings upon him.

Marylou Capes-Platt has performed another little miracle of copyediting, giving me lots of corrections and suggestions without ever once making me want to bite myself savagely. That's impressive. Blessings upon her.

My wife, Deborah Beale, as always, has been there for me and with me at every step of the process. I am lucky to be married not just to a wonderful person, but to an excellent editor/publisher as well. (Hint: I am not a bigamist. They are the same person.) Blessings upon her. Always.

My dear friend Lisa Tveit, the Queen of All Online Stuff, has continued to make it look as if I know something about the modern world. My gratitude is endless, as have been her efforts on my behalf. Blessings upon her.

And my dear friend Ylva von Löhneysen has helped me out with many important questions related to German. Plus she's just cool. Blessings upon her as well.

Thanks also to the Bobby Dollar Army, as drawn from the splendid Smarchers of tadwilliams.com and the fine Facebook folk of *tad.williams* and *AuthorTadWilliams*, and the kind folks on Twitter, who have been cushioned slightly from the Full Tad Madness by the gentle selectivity of my life-partner at *MrsTad*. Blessings, blessings, blessings.

In fact, if it weren't for readers, I wouldn't be writing—I'm a storyteller, not a hermetic scholar — so blessings on all of you reading this as well. Thank you—and keep it up, please! At this rate, you'll have finished the whole book before you even know it.

prologue

I HADN'T ATTENDED a trial in Heaven before—not in person. They don't happen that often, for one thing.

But wait, O wise angel, I hear you say. *How can there be trials in Heaven?*

Which is a perfectly good question, because once you've made it to the Big Happy you should be golden, right? You've been judged righteous or you wouldn't get in, and after that you're doing the work of the Highest, so how could you go wrong?

Well, first of all, there's the whole Free Will thing—people and angels have to be free to make mistakes, or else we live in a clockwork universe where everything's predetermined and perfect. Most of the time Heaven does seem like that, a flock of serene shiny creatures living in complete harmony, a hive of buzzing happiness and shared purpose. But we all know that in nature, no matter how well any system works, there's always a couple of dumbass birds heading north for the winter when everyone else is flying south, or one dipshit salmon belly-surfing down the rapids, yelling, "Whoo, yeah! Check me out!" as he smacks face first into the more sensible fish swimming upstream to spawn. The fact that these unrepresentative idiots freeze and plummet from the sky or die without issue isn't the point—the point is Free Will, and apparently we angels are capable of poor impulse control just like everybody else. Thus, there *are* trials in Heaven, and I was about to attend my first.

Although "attend" is a bit misleading, I admit. It wasn't really my first, because I'd been aware of several other trials. Here in the Happy Place you can know about important things like that and even follow them closely without actually being present, although it's hard to explain, because—duh—it's another Heaven thing. Imagine sitting in a crowded bar when the playoffs are on and a local team is involved: you don't have to stay glued to the screen to know what's going on in the game; you can pick up what's happening in a dozen different ways. And that's how I'd done my trial-watching in the past.

But this trial was going to be different, and so I had secured myself an excellent seat, front row center. The poor bastard angel on trial was going to face the full weight of Heaven's judgement, and the entire Shining City was full of anticipation. The Hall of Justice sparkled and throbbed with the light of watching angels, angels who wanted more than just a general feeling about this trial, who wanted to experience it up close and personal. I thought I even saw my boss, Archangel Temuel (who us angelic grunts usually called "The Mule") not too far away.

The crowd of the Saved, jostling each other in the massive shining hall despite being only semi-tangible (another Heaven thing which doesn't really translate), began to murmur with anticipation as the jury appeared, a row of blooming angelic flames that represented the great and the good—in fact some of the very greatest and goodest that our Third Sphere had to offer. I recognized them all.

"*We Are Convened In The Sight Of The Highest To Do Justice.*" These words came from the diamond-faceted white light that represented Terentia, a powerful angel who was acting as master of ceremonies. The other four heavenly judges, Karael, Raziel, Anaita, and Chamuel watched silently from beside her, their flames lined up like a menorah on Hanukkah Day Five. "*God Loves You All,*" Terentia added, then turned her attention to me. "*Angel Advocate Doloriel, You Are Accused Of Conspiring Against Heaven's Laws. In Addition To Several Crimes, You Are Also Charged With The Sins Of Wrath, Pride, Envy, And Avarice, All Most Dreadful. If You Are Found Guilty, You Will Be Cast From Heaven And Into The Unholy Pit, There To Dwell In Suffering For Eternity. Do You Have Any Questions Before We Begin?*"

So, yeah, the reason I had such a good seat was because I was the one on trial. And if you've got questions, believe me, so did I— probably the same ones, in fact, beginning with "How did I get here?"

and "How do I get out of here again?" But for reasons I'll explain as I go, I didn't think it would do me any good to ask.

"Look, you've already decided what you're going to do," I said, with what I hoped came off as a tough, cold-blooded calm I sure didn't feel. "Let's cut to the chase, because we all know the fun part is going to be the sentencing."

But wait, I hear you say. *How did you wind up on trial in Heaven, Bobby Dollar? How could such a thing happen to you, one of Heaven's most beloved and respected angels?*

Oh, yeah, that's hilarious. Kick a guy when he's on trial for his immortal soul just to get a cheap laugh, why don't you?

You really want to hear how I wound up here? I guess it started with a dream I had.

one

just an angel

THE WOOD was stacked higher than the heads of the catcalling spectators. On top of the mountainous pyre, the prisoner sagged against the stake like something unreal, a discarded shop-window dummy or a forgotten toy. The condemned wore a soldier's gleaming armor, but the slightness of the figure told a different story. This was a woman about to be burned. This was St. Joan.

She lifted her head and looked out across the crowded town square. Our eyes met. I saw the pale white-gold hair, the eyes red as blood, and my heart went cold. This wasn't the Maid of Orleans, it was Caz—*my* Caz, my beautiful demon-woman, the creature who had both captured and endangered my soul.

Someone set fire to the stacked wood. The kindling caught first, freeing wisps of white smoke that quickly rose and spread around her feet. Within moments the flames began to climb the sides of the pyre, painting the rising smoke with sunset tones. Caz struggled against her bonds, more and more desperate as the fire rose.

I couldn't move. I opened my mouth and tried to call to her, but I couldn't speak, either. I was frozen, helpless. When she needed me most, I couldn't do a thing.

"I can't reach you!" she cried, coils of smoke climbing her writhing body like snakes. *"Oh, Bobby! I can't reach you!"* Then her words turned to shrieks.

Flames leaped high into the air, until I could hardly make her out through the shimmer of heat. Her struggling figure, the smoke, the buildings in the background, all bent and wavered as if under water. Then, through the rising, spreading cloud, I saw a clutter in the air above her—winged shapes, dropping from the sky.

Hallelujah! The bells of the town began to clang, ringing out the song of redemption. *Hallelujah!* The winged ones swept down through the smoke—angels, angels coming to save her!

But then I saw the shapes more clearly. Maybe it was the warping of the heated air, but these supposed rescuers looked grim and terrible, eyes lightning-bright, wings black as burnt paper and glowing at the edges as though fire were their natural element.

Angels, I wondered, *or demons?* Coming to save her—or drag her back to endless torment? Paralyzed, silent, I could only watch as the bells grew louder, louder.

Hallelujah!

HAH-lay-loo-yah!

HAH-lay-loo-yah!

I lurched upright, my blanket tangled around me. The room was dark except for a little bit of streetlight creeping in between the cheap curtains. No flames, no smoke, but my phone kept beeping out that horrible joke melody over and over.

HAH-lay-loo-yah!

My phone. It was just my phone.

Yeah, I thought through the pounding of my heart and the slow gathering of my confused thoughts. *Fuck you, Handel—and your fucking Chorus, too. And fuck whoever in Heaven decided to use it as our ringtone.*

After knocking half the crap off my nightstand, I found the phone and then the "talk" button. The hosanna-ing finally stopped.

"What?" My pulse was banging like I had stumbled off a cliff into empty air. "This better be good or someone's gonna die."

"Someone already did." It was Alice from the downtown office— our local branch of Heaven's management. "You've got a client, Dollar." She gave me the details like she was reading a shopping list. "Go get 'em, cowboy. And maybe you wouldn't be such a grumpy piece of shit if you didn't drink yourself to sleep."

She hung up before any witty replies occurred to me.

"I can't reach you!" Caz had cried in my dream. And I couldn't reach her, either, because we were separated by much more than distance. One of us was in Hell. The other one only felt that way.

As I lay there waiting for the morning's first flood of black hopelessness to pass, I heard a scuffling noise on the other side of the wall near my head. I'd noticed it earlier when I was going to bed, and had put it down to rats, or possibly one of the neighbors in the adjoining apartment scraping something off the wall. This time it went on for a while, a repetitive *skritch-skritch-a-skritch* that quickly got on my nerves. Finally I thumped the wall with my fist and everything went silent.

I wasn't crazy about my new digs in the downmarket Tierra Green apartments, but things and people that wanted to hurt me kept finding out where I lived, so lately I hadn't been able to stay in any one place for long. And I *hate* moving.

Between my girlfriend-on-fire nightmare and the noise in the walls, it took me a good minute or two dunking my head in a sink full of cold water before I could calm down enough to get my mind to focus on work.

Angel advocate, I reminded myself. *Somebody needs you.*

The client was only a short distance away, out on the Bayshore freeway, but even after I got out of the apartment I couldn't find my car for about ten minutes. Not, I hasten to say, because I had come home drunk (although I might have been a tiny bit fuzzy around the edges) but because after recent experiences with a murderous semi-zombie named Smyler, I'd started leaving my ride in a different place every night.

I felt like I'd only managed about ten minutes sleep, but it was almost dawn, which meant I'd slept a decent amount: I'd passed out almost directly after getting home. Again, not because I'd been drinking, although I'd probably had a few beers with dinner. (I've been trying to cut back lately, in fact, be a little more responsible.) No, I was falling asleep at odd hours and forgetting where my car was because I'd been sleeping so badly. And I was sleeping badly because I kept dreaming about Hell. See, I'd just spent what felt like half a year there, and it was exactly as bad as you'd imagine. No, worse. It's not something you just get over in a night. Not to mention the fact that the whole reason I'd gone there had been to free the demon-woman I loved, Casimira, the Countess of Cold Hands, and I'd failed. Badly. Thus, your pal Bobby's apparently permanent sense of insufficiency, and ugly dreams nearly every night.

This had been a new one, though, and worse than usual. Usually I just dreamed of Marmora, the fake Caz that the archdemon Eligor had used to sucker me like the smallest small-timer you can imagine, and how she had transformed from Caz into liquid nothing in my arms. Sometimes I also dreamed of the horrible things I'd seen happen to Caz while I was being tortured by Eligor, her boss and ex-lover, although I was convinced most of those things hadn't actually happened to her. (I really needed to believe that.) So what had been different about this dream? Caz told me once that when she herself was being executed, she had thought of Joan of Arc, so it only made sense my subconscious would add that nasty wrinkle to the regular pattern of nightmares.

But there had been something different this time—something deeper that I couldn't grasp, almost as though she had truly been trying to communicate with me. But how, why, or about what, I had no clue.

I found my boxy old Datsun at last, down an alley off Heller Street that I only barely remembered choosing. It was late November but dry and clear, so traffic wasn't too bad even this close to downtown; it took me less than a quarter of an hour to reach the accident scene, just a little way south of the Woodside Expressway cloverleaf. Some kind of minivan with writing on its side lay upside down and badly damaged at the end of a trail of wreckage. Black and whites and emergency vehicles had parked all over the shoulder, lights whipping blue and red. The only body was on the ground, covered with a bloody sheet, and nobody looked like they were in much of a hurry.

Angel time.

I left my car on the shoulder about a hundred feet past the accident and walked back through the ice plants. None of the cops gave me a second look as I approached, but that's pretty much how it is: when angels are working, especially at a death scene, we just don't get noticed. Of course, the cops and paramedics were going to see even less of me in a second. When I was within a few yards of the body, I stopped and opened the portal of bright but unsteady light we angels call a Zipper.

Yes, that's what we call them. Spare me the crude jokes, because believe me, I've heard them all, mostly from other angels. The Zippers are just an opening we go through to do our work. They're holes in

Time, and everything on the other side of them is kind of a bubble made of that single moment.

The sounds of the freeway died as I stepped through. On the other side, the emergency vehicles and the passing cars, and even the people, had all frozen into place as if a billion gallons of clear plastic had been poured over everything—cops halted in mid-gesture, lights frozen at different stages of illumination, an entire universe gone silent as a tomb. Other than me, the only thing moving was a guy in work clothes walking in and out among the motionless cars, pounding on windows, trying to get one of the drivers to notice him. They wouldn't, of course, because he was outside of Time and they were all still inside it.

He saw me coming and ran toward me. He had a thick mustache and dark skin, but all I could really focus on were the terrified whites of his eyes. "Help me!" he shouted. "I have had an accident!"

"Gurdeep Malhotra," I said. "God loves you."

"Who are you?" he asked, stumbling to a stop.

"I'm Doloriel, your angelic advocate." I gave him a moment for that to sink in. "I'm afraid you didn't survive your accident."

He stared. If blood had still been flowing in his veins, I'd have said he went pale. As it was, he seemed to lose resolution for a moment as the shock washed through him. "But . . . but I can't! My son! It's his . . ." He shook his head slowly. "My wife! Will I never see her again?"

"There's a lot I can't tell you," I said as kindly as I could. In fact, there's a whole lot I don't know myself. "But first we have to prepare you for judgement. That's my job. I will do everything I can to defend you. I know you were a good man." (I didn't really know that yet, but it never hurts to calm a client down so you can work with them.)

He was still staring at me. "But you . . . you are an angel? How can this be? I am not a Christian!"

"That's okay, Mr. Malhotra. I'm not a Christian angel. I'm just an angel."

The judgement didn't go as fast as I would have liked. The prosecuting demon was a little upstart named Ratpiddle, the sort who thinks he's going to win every case with some amazing Perry Mason move. He dragged out every transgression the poor dead guy had ever made—a reckless driving where the officer hadn't even ticketed him!—and tried to create a picture of a life of unconcern for others, despite the fact that this morning Gurdeep had only been hurrying because he wanted to wrap his son's birthday presents before the kid got up for school. That got to me, and I'm afraid I referred to the prosecutor as, "scum scraped from the restroom floors of Hell," which, although reasonably accurate, was not strictly collegial. Anyway, luckily for me and Mr. Malhotra, the judge was a stolid ball of radiance named Sashimiel whom I'd argued in front of dozens of times; she wasn't prone to getting excited because some prosecutor was trying to make a reputation. After a decent interval she simply cut Ratpiddle off in the middle of some new detour and declared judgement in favor of my client. Whoosh! Gurdeep Malhotra was off to whatever happens next. (Despite the fact that the same thing must have happened to me, too, I don't remember any of it, so I'm afraid I can't fill in the blanks.) The judge poofed back to wherever Powers and Principalities go between judgements, Ratpiddle disappeared in a smoking snit, and I was free to get on with my day.

two

old friends, new fiends

WHEN I got back to the so-called real world from the timelessness of Outside, it was a bit before nine in the morning. See, just because we step outside it doesn't mean Time actually stops. I think it's something to do with us earthbound angels wearing mortal bodies. As soon as we step back through the Zipper we catch up with the difference between Outside and the real world—in this case, a couple of hours or so. I'm not really a morning guy, but the thought of crawling back into bed to dream about Caz again depressed me, so I headed across the waterfront to Oyster Bill's, a bar that serves food, sort of. I have a soft spot for the place, and I've been going there as long as I can remember, which I suppose proves I have more loyalty than sense. In fact, if I weren't already dead, that could be my epitaph.

I was polishing off the last of the starch-and-grease mélange Bill mischievously refers to as "breakfast" when an old rummy wandered in from the street and started making his way down the counter, discreetly panhandling (because Bill doesn't like begging in his bar—he thinks it lowers the tone of the joint, which is about the cutest thing I've ever heard). Most of the other customers didn't talk to the guy or even acknowledge him, waiting until he got the point and walked away, but when he reached me I fished in my pocket for some loose bills. The old fellow had rheumy eyes and hair that stood up like it had been fashion-moussed back in the 80s and never touched since. He also smelled like he'd been drinking something you aren't supposed to drink—Aqua Velva, perhaps, strained through an old shirt.

I put the money in his hand and said, "Good luck. God loves you." I didn't say it very loudly, because being polite in Oyster Bill's is a bit like visibly limping past a pride of hungry lions, but he seemed to hear. He smiled toothlessly and patted my shoulder.

"Thank you, friend," he said, slurring less than I would have expected. "I'd like to give you something for your kindness."

"No, really, you don't need to . . ."

He reached into his pants pocket and pulled out a creased, once-white sheet of paper that had been folded like a letter. He handed it to me like it was worth something, which was another kind of sad. "Promise you'll read it. Promise you'll think about it. God knows you and wants you for His great plan." Then he shuffled off and out onto the esplanade.

Okay, yes, it was a tiny bit ironic for a wino to be assuring an angel that he's wanted for God's great plan. I glanced at the piece of paper, but it seemed to be more political than religious. The headline was something about "Someone in the White House wants you destroyed!" I almost left it on the counter, but for all I knew the old duffer was watching me through the window from outside, thrilled someone had actually accepted one of his crumpled handbills, so I stuck it in my pocket before I headed out.

I still didn't want to go home, but ten in the morning was way too early to go over to the Compasses and get blotto in the company of sympathetic co-workers, so I decided I'd try my buddy and co-angel Sam, who I hadn't heard from in the last couple of days. (Sam had inadvertently got me into most of the shit I was currently wading through, so it speaks volumes that I still considered him my bestie.)

I hate walking and talking on the phone almost as much as I hate people who walk and talk on the phone, so when I saw an empty bus bench on Parade Street—usually full of brown-bagging office workers, tourists, or those ubiquitous, slightly ratty-looking, downtown young people whose dogs always wear bandanas—I grabbed it and got out my phone. In the process the rummy's screed (which really sounds like a horror movie now that I think of it—*The Rummy's Screed! Return of the Rummy's Screed! Curse of the* . . . okay, you get it) fell out of my pocket, so as I listened to Sam's phone ringing on the other end I looked it over again.

There wasn't actually a whole lot on it. At the top, in big blocky handwritten letters it said, "Someone in the White House wants to destroy you!" with a picture of the building in question floating in the clouds. Then it said, "You have enemies. Don't you want to know about them? THEY know about YOU!" Beneath that was the mandatory bible quote found in so much of your finest crazy-person literature:

Ecclesiastes 9:12

For man also knoweth not his time: as the fishes that are taken in an evil net, and as the birds that are caught in the snare; so are the sons of men snared in an evil time, when it falleth suddenly upon them.

Down at the bottom a group of slightly odd things had been cut out of magazines and taped to the original before it was photocopied. The first two were a picture of an angel and another of a donkey. The angel bit was an interesting coincidence. I glanced at the donkey, wondering if that was meant to indicate the Democrats, the current White House occupants. Sam's phone kept ringing. At last I hung up, but something else was bothering me now.

Then it hit me. Donkey. *Mule.* Archangel Temuel, my supervisor.

Two more pictures were at the bottom of the handbill, a clock out of a child's picture book and a cartoon of a garden bench. That seemed another long coincidence, since I'd met the archangel on a bench in Beeger Square a few times in the past. And if it wasn't a coincidence, I was being ordered to a meeting.

I trotted over to the square but saw no sign of the fragrant old man on any of the benches. Could it really have been Temuel? Our archangel liked disguises, especially when he was being secretive, and it was entirely possible he knew that everyone in my department called him "The Mule." Also, "White House" wasn't that different from "the Big House" and other things we angelic grunts called Heaven. But did I need a message to tell me people in Heaven were out to get me? Shit, I knew that already. *Temuel* knew that I knew that already. So either it was what I'd thought in the first place, a slightly coincidental piece of mail from Farthest Crazyland, or my boss had come all the way to Earth to meet me so he could warn me I was in even deeper trouble than I thought I was. And I'd missed the meeting.

I looked at the piece of paper again and this time I noticed that the hands on the clock were pointing to eleven. I checked the time on my phone. Nine-forty. No wonder there was no sign of Temuel—I still had almost an hour and a half to wait. So apparently I was going to the Compasses after all, because I sure as hell wasn't going to sit in windy Beeger Square for all that time. Besides, I wasn't going there to drink, just to kill time until I could find out if this was a real communication, so it didn't really count.

How often have you held a piece of paper in your hand and prayed that it belonged to a real drunk smelling of real, rank sweat and old aftershave instead of being a message from an archangel?

First time for me.

When I got to the Compasses, the place was all but empty—just a couple of angels I didn't know too well, French Didi and another guy, sitting in one of the booths emptying a bottle of wine between them like it was ten in the evening instead of ten in the morning. They only looked up long enough to nod, then went back to arguing about Formula One racing. Like I said, I didn't know them, and Formula One isn't really my thing, so I almost walked out again. I bellied up to the bar instead and asked bartender Chico to slide me a beer.

Yes, I know I said I was cutting back. See, vodka, that's drinking. Beer—well, beer is just getting the inside of your mouth wet.

Anyway, as Chico pushed the bottle of Negra Modelo over to me, he said, "Looks like all you special cases are coming home to roost today."

"Who else beside me?"

"What am I, your secretary? Go look in the back room."

I figured it must be Sam, who had already made one dangerous (and as far as I could tell, completely pointless) return to the bar, where he'd been treated like a returning war hero by the rest of the Whole Sick Choir, but what he was doing in here at this hour was beyond me. The idea made me very nervous, and it wasn't because it was so early. Because of his known involvement in the Third Way, Sam was seriously *angelica non grata* with our bosses in Heaven.

The back room at the Compasses is actually a little alcove on the way to the restrooms—what the Brits call a "snug." I pushed aside the curtain and found Walter Sanders huddled over a mug of beer.

Yes, *that* Walter Sanders: the angel who had been stabbed by a crazy dead guy who I'd assumed was trying to stab me, just when Walter was about to tell me something important. (I now felt pretty sure Walter himself had been the target, to shut him up.) Then he had disappeared completely. The last time I'd seen Walter he'd been in Hell wearing a demon-body, working on a slave ship. The last thing he'd done had been to point a finger at Anaita, one of my most powerful angelic superiors, as the person behind the Third Way (Heaven's currently Most Wanted rebels) and much of the rest of my recent troubles. And Hell was where I'd left Walter Sanders, too, which meant I was more than a wee bit surprised to see him sitting there in an overcoat, nursing a drink like any other Compasses regular.

"Walter!" I threw myself onto the bench across from him. "What the hell—pardon the expression—are you doing here?"

His first response had been a flinch, but when he saw it was me, he smiled. It was a tired sort of smile. "Hey, Bobby. Good to see you. I'm back."

"Fuck, yeah! I noticed. But how? When? What happened?"

"Still not quite sure. Last I remember, you and I were walking down the street, then . . . nothing. When I got rebodied, I found out I'd been gone for weeks! Pretty strange. A little hard to . . . to get up to speed again." He laughed unconvincingly and sipped his beer. "But it's nice to see a familiar face."

All the questions about to pour out of me suddenly clogged my brain like a dammed-up stream. It took me a couple of seconds to work through what he'd just said. "Hang on. You don't remember anything? Since you were stabbed?"

He shook his head. "Not a thing. I hardly remember the night it happened, either. I just remember you were there. I hope it wasn't too tough on you, Bobby. I know you tried to get me help."

I could only sit, my beer untasted, and stare at him. What was going on? Had Walter been mind-wiped after being sprung from Hell? Or was he just being cagey—too smart to start blabbing in an angel bar about the kind of things that had really happened? I took a deep breath, tried to keep my hands from shaking, and made appropriate small talk while we drank our beers, although I didn't want mine now at all. When I'd drunk about half, I put it down and announced that I had to go. I asked him if he was walking and if he wanted company, but Walter only shook his head again in that sort of dazed way.

"No," he said. "No. I'll be honest, Bobby. It's my first day back and this is about all the talking I can handle today—I saw a couple of the gang already, earlier. I'm . . . I don't know . . . tired. Really tired. I'm just going to finish this, then I'll call a cab."

I was feeling a little desperate. "Okay. But you're sure there isn't anything you want to talk to me about? Doesn't have to be tonight. Any time is fine. Because you wanted to talk to me that night. You had something to tell me."

He gave me a strange look. "There *is* one thing, actually. Does this mean anything?" He pulled out his wallet, fumbled for a moment, then produced a piece of folded paper. It was a leaf from an executive calendar, one of the note pages without a date, and it said, *"Talk to D about A -?s"*

My pulse sped a bit. "Is this your handwriting?"

"Yeah. But it's from before the stabbing, and I don't remember what it's about. I just realized "D" might be you. Ring any bells?"

"Could be." Damn straight. *Talk to Dollar about Anaita asking questions*, that was what it meant. "Appreciate it, Walter. I'll give it some thought. Feel better."

When I returned to the bar, Chico looked at the half bottle I put on the counter. "Sick?"

"A little," I said. "Unsettled" would have been a better word. Because I knew that was all I was going to get from Walter Sanders. Whatever had made him want to talk to me on that fatal night was gone, burned out of him by the machineries of Heaven. But thanks to the note Walter had made to himself before he was taken off the board, I wasn't going to waste any more time wondering whether I was right about that supreme bitch-angel Anaita. From now on, as far as I was concerned, she absolutely *was* out to get me.

Which still left me with the unpleasant fact that somebody much more powerful than me wanted me silenced, if not utterly obliterated.

As I came out of the Compasses, wishing I still smoked, something scuttled under a car at the edge of my sight. Normally I wouldn't have paid any attention, but Walter's return—or at least, the return of part of Walter, just not the part I needed—had me more than a little on edge, so I looked carefully. After all, if knife-wielding Smyler had come back and decided I was Bobby Bad Angel again, I didn't want to be caught by surprise. From the split-second view I had before it vanished down a storm drain, whatever it was didn't look much bigger than a cat, but cats didn't run like that, legs splayed out, bellies almost on the ground.

If I hadn't known better, I might have said that what scurried silently back into the darkness behind a dumpster had, just for an instant, looked like a spider as big as a bicycle wheel. But that could have just been my eyes playing tricks on my twitchy, extremely stressed brain.

three
archangelic aftershave

I COULD SEE the crusty old man all the way across Beeger Square. He had the bench to himself, which wasn't much of a surprise.

"You've got the smell down." I seated myself, but not too close.

Any doubt I might still have had vanished at his shy smile. "Good? I didn't overdo it?"

"You sure didn't underdo it." I stretched my legs out. One useful thing—nobody was going to sit down here and interrupt us. The aromatic top notes of aftershave-strained-through-a-sock nestled atop a deeper tang of rancid sweat with just a fruity hint of human urine. "I was just in the Compasses. I saw Walter Sanders."

"Ah," said Temuel.

"Yeah—'Ah.' What happened to him?"

"He's back to work. Back to normal."

"Bullshit! That guy's been cored like an apple, memories lifted right out. And it's because of me, as we both damn well know. Because he knew something about why this shit is happening to me." *Something about Anaita,* I wanted to say, *that hellbitch everyone else calls an angel.* But Temuel had made it very clear in the past that he didn't want to talk names. "Last time I saw Walter, he was working on a slave ship in . . . well, let's just say a very unpleasant place. Did you spring him?"

No eye contact this time as Temuel watched some pigeons fighting over a tortilla chip. "Your information was acted on. Walter . . . Advocate Angel Vatriel . . . was returned to active duty. That's all I can tell you."

Which was clearly a big yellow Dead End sign. "Okay, let's try something else. If it's not about Walter. then why did you want to talk to me today? Why hand me your little mystery rebus?"

He gave me an irritated look. The cross-hatching of purplish veins on his cheeks and the bridge of his nose were as realistic as his odor. "Because I can't talk to you in Heaven. And I can't be seen talking to you anywhere else. But you need to know that things are bad, Bobby. Some important people Upstairs are losing patience with you."

It was still odd to hear him use my Earth-name, though outside of Heaven he hardly seemed to use anything else, which puzzled me. I still wasn't entirely comfortable with this "my supervisor, my secret protector" bit either, although without him I'd never have got to Hell and had a chance to rescue Caz. Not his fault that hadn't worked out, at least as far as I knew, but I still had too many unanswered questions about Temuel for my liking. "What does that mean? How bad?"

"Bad. It wasn't easy covering for your long absence. And it's not just the Ephorate asking questions, now it's other higher-ups, too. You don't have any idea how hard it is to keep something from Powers and Principalities."

I was getting tired of being made to feel guilty. "So why do it?"

"What do you mean?"

"I mean, what's in it for you, Archangel? Why should you lift a finger to help me? Why risk your own soul? Because you like me? That seems strange, because nobody else does."

"I do like you, Bobby, I suppose." He gave me a grandfatherly look, or it would have been if the grandfather in question were a piss-soaked degenerate. "But of course that's not all that's going on. Of course not. Karael, Terentia, Anaita, they're all much, much more powerful than I am—and they're not even part of the High Host, His most important servants. They're just Third Sphere like the rest of us, watching over Earth. There are powers above the Powers, you know." He spread his blackened, crack-nailed fingers as if to illustrate the universe as a string game. "My goodness, it goes up and up and up!"

"Yeah, I get it, I don't want the higher-ups thinking about me so much. So what am I supposed to do about this unwanted attention? Get down on my knees and stay there?"

"That wouldn't be such a bad idea, at least for the moment." He was stern again, an Old Testament prophet in a grimy pea coat. "Just try to keep a low profile for a while, will you? Don't ask for time off. Don't draw attention. And *stop moving around*, for goodness' sake. You've had several apartments in the last year, not to mention your tour of various unsavory motels."

"I could have stayed in better ones if Heaven paid us anything decent to live on." As you can guess, I wasn't the biggest team player even before all this nutty Third-Way, angels-and-demons clusterfuck got going. "Look, I know you're trying to help me. I get that, and I'm grateful. But you know why I had to move all those times, right? You remember the various things that were trying with extreme prejudice to kill my ass?"

"Yes, but that doesn't matter to Heaven, because it doesn't happen to the other advocates. It's you, Bobby. You're a magnet for trouble, and even the Powers that want . . . even the Powers that don't have anything against you are beginning to wonder why your name comes up so often."

"Yeah, I get it—don't make waves, don't do anything weird. But it's the weird that keeps coming after *me.*"

Disappointment, this time. I was getting the full treatment. "You know there's more to it than that."

And he was right. Yes, crazy shit does keep happening to me, but a big part of that is because instead of minding my own business, I go over to crazy shit's house and say, "Hey, wanna come out and play?"

"But the stakes are too high for me just to quit," I said. "You know why I went where I went. To that place." *To Hell,* I meant. "And why it didn't work out."

"Don't tell me anything." Temuel lifted his hands as if to cover his ears. He looked like that Munch *Scream* painting. "Just, please, whatever else you do, stay out of trouble. Stay visible to the folks upstairs. Stay in one place. And do your job, your *real* job. I'll help when I can." And then he abruptly got up and walked away across the square.

You know your life is pretty screwed up when even the winos turn their backs on you.

four

too hot

I WOKE UP twice in the night, the first time because I thought I heard something tapping at my window. I took a flashlight and my gun, just to be prepared, but found nothing. The second jolt into wakefulness a few hours later was for no reason I could put my finger on. Still, as I lay there listening to the silent darkness, I couldn't help noticing a very bad smell, as if a large rat had gotten into the apartment heating ducts and died.

Wouldn't that be just my luck?

I woke for the third time about five minutes before the alarm went off, and lay there thinking about some of the bad decisions I'd made in the last year. Then my phone rang. It was Alice, of course, with her usual impeccable timing. She had work for me, an eighty-eight year old lady who had just died in the Orchard District west of Spanishtown. I had time only to chug a cup of reheated coffee before going out, and my head felt like it was full of wet grit.

It could have been worse, I guess. The job itself wasn't too bad. Everything about the deceased's life proved to be ordinary and even praiseworthy, and I saw her soul off to Heaven about eleven o'clock (or at least that's what it was when I returned to Earth Time).

Since I had nothing I immediately needed to do, I parked at the San Judas Amtrak station—what some old timers in Jude still referred to as "the Depot"—then walked through the Station Arcade, first built at the beginning of the Twentieth Century, when the railroad station was the heart of the city. I badly needed some stimulants and there's a coffee place there I like, not because they serve anything other than the high-priced stuff you can get everywhere else these days, but because the manager or somebody likes jazz, and it's usually playing on the sound system.

In fact, I have a soft spot for the arcade in general, and not just because of the coffee joint or the spectacular glass and iron fretwork roof that runs from the station all the way to Broadway. Walking along one of the upper levels beneath the high atrium ceiling, looking down on all the busy shoppers, reminds me in a weird way of Heaven. Of course, unlike the Happy Place, retailers at the Station Arcade have splashed corporate logos on everything, undercutting the Edwardian grace of the building just a teensy bit, but I still enjoyed it. I *like* people, see, I really do. I just don't like them much close up.

The coffee shop is called Java Programmers, which I assume is a tech joke of some sort, but I forgive them because of the background music. I ordered regular coffee, a chicken salad sandwich, and some kind of non-potato chips (a mistake I will not make again because they tasted like baked sawdust). The sound system was playing something modern, a saxophone duet. As I chewed and sipped and listened, I tried to get my head around what I was going to do next.

Don't get me wrong, it was nice to be back to work and living the old, familiar angelic life, something I'd doubted I'd ever see again when I was slogging through Hell. On the other hand, I was only having this brief vacation in normality because I'd managed to avoid being ripped to bits, shot, or stabbed several dozen times by folks who, as far as I knew, still wanted to do all those things to me. Several loose ends from that Hell trip were still dangling, the two most important being Caz, the woman I loved, who remained a prisoner in Hell, and Anaita, the powerful angel who kept trying to off me for no reason I could discover or even guess. You'd have thought I'd stolen her designated space in Heaven's executive parking lot.

The whole mess seemed to revolve around a bargain that important angel, Anaita (masquerading as angel Kephas) had made with Grand Duke Eligor, the big-name demon who was holding Caz prisoner. Eligor had received an angel feather from Anaita as a symbol of their bargain. Actually, the feather was meant as blackmail fodder, to keep her quiet if their deal to create a home for the Third Way experiment fell apart. The feather had eventually come into my possession (don't ask unless you've got a free week or so) and after I got back from Hell, I'd tried to trade it for Caz's freedom. Eligor tricked me: he got the feather, but he also hung onto Caz.

But just when I had begun seriously wondering whether angels could commit suicide, my junior angel friend Clarence had asked me what Eligor contributed to the deal as *his* marker—in other words, what had the demon swapped for the feather? This had never occurred to me, and with this realization I found a reason to go on. See, if I could get my hands on Eligor's marker—which I was pretty certain had to be one of his horns, since I'd seen that he was growing one back when Eligor accidentally showed me his real (and really scary) face—it would be worth just as much to him as the feather, and I could trade it for Caz and get the swap *right* this time.

But here was the problem: I didn't *have* Eligor's horn, and I didn't have the slightest idea where it might be. I was going to have to figure out where Anaita had stashed it, then steal it from her. Oh, and get away with it, without either Anaita or any of my other bosses finding out or, in fact, learning *any* of the stuff I'd been up to lately.

Easy, right?

As I finished my sandwich and sawdust chips, I watched a bunch of teenagers dicking around in front of a video game shop across the way. Something about the way one of them was spinning around, smacking his friend with a wool scarf, reminded me of Mr. Fox, the dancing maniac I'd met near the beginning of the whole wretched Third Way mess. Foxy had helped me by setting up an auction to sell the feather. I never intended to sell it (at that time I didn't know I actually *had* it) but I wanted to find out what it was that everyone thought I had, so I decided to get a bunch of crazy people in to bid on it.

Well, it seemed like a good idea at the time.

As with so many of your hero's thrilling adventures, the auction ended with a bunch of nasty folks trying to blow me to pieces with dangerous weapons, and then a giant Babylonian Demon Whatsit—a *ghallu*—shredding my car into metal scrap with me and Sam inside it. But thinking of Mr. Foxy-Foxy reminded me that he knew the kind of people who were interested in things like a genuine angel's feather. Which made him a logical candidate to know things about a Grand Duke of Hell's horn, too. It wasn't a perfect fit—Fox had only known about the feather because word leaked out that it had been stolen from Eligor—but he might be able to point me to someone who could give me a few leads. I certainly needed *somebody's* help, because right now, I was as empty as the giant cardboard bucket whose contents I'd just downed—what passed for a coffee cup these days.

So: not a plan, maybe, but at least I had a caffeine buzz going now, and a next step: ask Foxy.

I was so close to downtown I decided to leave my car in the station lot and just walk. The weather was pretty nice—November in Northern California is like September most other places—and I didn't mind stretching my legs.

I passed several of the city's cherry-picker trucks: the public Christmas decorations go up in Jude right after Thanksgiving. You know, in case someone didn't know it was the holiday shopping season, despite every store in the city draping itself in tinsel and pumping in canned versions of "The Little Drummer Boy" and "God Rest Ye, Merry Gentlemen."

Downtown Jude has really grown a lot in the last ten years. I admit to being just enough of an old-timer now to find some of it a bit irritating. They were pretty careful not to muck up the historical buildings at the heart of things, but everything else seemed to be painted these toytown colors that really didn't work for me—big swathes of yellow and purple and blue, bright colored awnings, lime-green lamp posts. Sometimes it looks like the whole downtown has been turned into a daycare center for overgrown children. I guess that's progress of a sort. I'm told that in the 70s and 80s it got pretty grim in the old part of town, nothing but bums and liquor stores and strip joints, but I've lived downtown since I got out of the Harps, and I'm enough of a romantic to say I might have preferred the old version to living on *Sesame Street*. And now I hear Jude's chamber of commerce wants to rename the old part of downtown "the Pioneer District." Shudder.

As I slowed down near the entrance to Beeger Square, to let a large family cross the intersection in front of me, I noticed that a couple of guys I'd seen earlier were still walking behind me and that they'd stopped too; they were now having a discussion in front of the showroom window of a baby needs store called Small Wonders, pointing at things and animatedly discussing them. The pair looked a bit like Mormon missionaries, young, clean-cut white guys wearing boring suits. I suppose they could have been a couple of young fathers-to-be, but the act seemed a little forced, and something about their suits and black shoes didn't look quite right. Cops? The po-po did seem younger every year, at least to me. Or were these guys something more sinister?

I was tempted to lure them into an alley and scare the shit out of them, but for all I knew they really were just a couple of kids looking for people who needed the word of Jesus. It would have been bad enough terrorizing innocent Mormons, but if they were undercover cops, things could get complicated. Besides, I had something to do and didn't want to be observed, so I strolled into Beeger Square, doubled back behind one of the food trucks that swarmed to the square at lunch and dinner times, then slipped into one of the public restroom kiosks. I stayed there, savoring the smells of human failure for several charming minutes, then stepped back outside. No sign of the missionaries, so I headed out to the street corner where I had first successfully summoned Foxy Foxy, everybody's favorite dancing dealer in stolen supernatural goods.

When I reached the intersection of Marshall and Main I climbed onto the nearest pedestrian island, pushed the "WALK" button, then pretended to wait for the light. Nobody seemed to be looking, so I drew a line down the air and one of Heaven's patented Zippers sprang into being. As the first group of pedestrians gathered around me I waited, then as soon as the light changed and they stepped off, I leaned in and softly called Fox's name into the glowing crease that only angels and a few other select folk could see.

He had appeared almost instantly the first time, so I looked around. The usual river of cars was inching past, but there was no sign of Mr. Fox—and believe me, he's a hard guy to miss. I waited a minute or so, then was just about to try it again when I noticed something flitting at the edge of my peripheral vision on the far side of Marshall Avenue, a white shape like a very tiny, very agitated ghost. When I focused on it properly I saw it was a handkerchief being waggled up and down from behind a wooden hoarding where construction work was going on. I waited for the light to change, because even an angel doesn't want to get his earthly body ground to hamburger in the middle of a busy street, then I wandered over.

As I reached the plywood hoarding, defaced with an entire catalogue of graffiti, I saw the hand emerge again, sans handkerchief, and beckon me toward the shadows at the edge of the building area. As I got closer, I could make out a familiar silhouette.

Mr. Fox, or Foxy Foxy, or whatever his name really is, looks like a cross between Dick Van Dyke in "Mary Poppins" and the host of a really weird Japanese game show. He wears baggy suits and floppy scarves, and he also happens to be an albino, I think. I say "I think" only because he might be something that just *looks* like an albino human. If you want to get past making snap judgements, hang around with Bobby D. for a while and meet some of the people I know. Seriously. It'll cure you of the tendency very quickly. One of the nicest people I'd met in the last few years was about ten feet tall with a giant axe wound right in the middle of his skull. He looks like he should be making sandwiches out of kindergarten students, but he's actually a sweetheart. Too bad for him he lives in Hell.

Anyway, back to Foxy. I could tell immediately that something wasn't quite right, because even though it definitely was him—same corpse-white skin, same cat-yellow eyes—he wasn't dancing. At least, not the way he usually did—constant swirl of motion, bending, spinning, a bit of soft shoe, jazz hands and big finish! That kind of thing. Instead he was staying in one place, and the only consistent movement was a nervous shuffling of his feet.

"Mr. Bob!" He smiled but it wasn't the most convincing thing I've ever seen. "So nice to see you! Too bad can't talk now!"

"What do you mean?" I looked back in case he'd seen something I hadn't, but we were well out of the flow of foot traffic, mostly hidden by the construction scaffolds and the plywood wall.

"Oh, you know, Dollar-man—lots of work! Foxy Foxy always on call. But I see you real soon!" He was already backing deeper into the shadows.

"Hold on. I need to ask you a question. About the auction at Islanders Hall. You remember that, right?"

He laughed—a trifle bitterly I thought. "Oh, yes! Very exciting! Many shootings! Completely not bad for business, Mr. Bobby."

"Look, I'm as sorry about that as you are. You should have seen how I spent the rest of that evening." That had been the Babylonian Demon Whatsit I referred to earlier, which had not only killed my car, but had destroyed half the Compasses when it followed me and Sam there. "But I need to know who was at that auction. More specifically, I need to know who might be interested in certain kinds of articles. Not the one I was selling that night, but something . . . um . . . similar."

Now the fidgeting became a full-force tap dance of agitation. "So sorry, Mr. Dollar Bob. Don't remember any of it! Don't remember anyone there! Don't even remember what you are talking about—suddenly it is all oh-so-distant." Now he really did back away, still jiggling like a man who badly needs to urinate.

"What is this bullshit, Fox? You're the one who came to me in the first place, remember? You're the one who said you'd be happy to work with me anytime."

"Oh, and I would, I tell you true! But right now? No. Simply too hot. Too much bad stuff. Sorry!"

"What do you mean, too hot? What's too hot?"

"You are. Whole thing. Mister Foxy can't get involved. Way too big for poor little Fox Man."

I didn't like the sound of that at all. "Just tell me what you know."

"Can't. Talk to you soon, Mr. Dollar Bobby. I'm sure everything will go super swimmy great for you. No problem. Just . . . just . . ."

While I waited for him to finish that sentence, a car horn blared a short distance away. I jumped, but it was only a cab driver honking at an adventurous pedestrian who had decided to explore the zone outside the crosswalk. When I looked back, Foxy Foxy had vanished like a New Year's resolution in February.

Did I like this idea of myself as a doomed target that even crazy semi-people would avoid? I did not. Fact is, if I hadn't been all the way across downtown from my car, I would have sloped right back to the Compasses and had myself a shot or two of tell-Reality-to-shut-up. But I didn't want to get a work call while I was still a sober fifteen minute walk away from my car, let alone a more lubricated twenty-five minute stumble, so I turned my back on the big bayfront skyscrapers and started back toward the railroad station. I kept an eye open, but this time I didn't see my friends in the missionary suits, or—and I was even more grateful for this—any giant might-be-spiders lounging under parked cars, either.

We should always be thankful for the small, good things.

Back home to my only-slightly-squalid Tierra Green apartment. Just as I got through the door and reached for the lights, something furry ran across my feet. I admit that, in the mood I was in, I might have been a little wound up, which probably explains the fact that I jumped and bellowed in surprise so loudly that the upstairs neighbor started pounding on his floor. It also explains why I didn't see more than the last little bit of whatever it was that scuttled out the open window of my second floor walk-up. What it *doesn't* explain, though, is why the thing on the windowsill appeared to be a hairy, skinny, gray and black arm with a shriveled little bruise-colored hand at the end of it, like an un-mummified version of the Monkey's Paw. But before I had a chance to make a foolish wish, or even to start shouting again, the clutching fingers let go, and it dropped out of sight.

I rushed to the window, of course, but saw nothing in the alleyway below but a couple of recycling bins too small to hide even the most modestly sized ape.

Maybe I was catching all the crazy floating around. Maybe it was just post-traumatic shock. I still slept with my gun underneath my pillow that night.

five

haunted

"SERIOUSLY," I told Clarence the junior angel as we waited to order, "it's starting to freak me out a little. It's been going on for days. First, there's something scratching in the walls. Oh, and an intermittent smell of rotting meat. *Love* that. Then there's the Monkey's Paw or whatever that was."

"Monkey's Paw?"

Clarence brushed some lint off his sweater as I explained about the little gray hand on the windowsill. The kid had upped his game a bit lately, clotheswise—more GQ preppie, less Your Dad On His High School Debate Team. He was even rocking some cool wire-rimmed glasses, plus he had let his hair grow out a bit and had the floppy, *just got off my sailboat* look going on.

He was also, at least at that moment, wearing the facial expression of an astrophysicist who is listening to an anal probe hysteric explain why aliens are real. This pissed me off a bit because pretty much all the stuff I've told him has turned out to be true.

"Yes, it was a *hand*, damn it," I said. "Don't look at me like that. With little fingers and a little tiny thumb."

"Maybe it was a raccoon."

"Fuck your raccoon. Besides, there's more. Last night, I start hearing something bump against my window while I'm lying in bed—like a really big fly, you know how they do, but this sounded *huge*. I kept trying to catch it, but every time I get up, I find nothing. Then, when I checked in the morning, I saw a kind of slimy smear on the outside. Like something really disgusting had been pressing its nose against it."

The kid was still doing the slow nod. "So, you're being stalked by Mormons, monkeys, and whatever the thing with the wet nose was— some kind of ghostly Irish Setter?"

"Yeah, see how funny you think it is when *your* apartment turns out to be haunted. Oh, wait, it is—by old people." Clarence rented a room in some rich folks' house. *Living* rich folks.

"Burt and Sheila are really nice, actually."

"I'm sure that my visitor is a really nice cursed Monkey's Paw, too. Kind to children and dogs and shit like that. But I still don't want it hanging around my apartment when I'm not there, especially since the Mule told me I'm not allowed to move somewhere else, which would be the obvious solution. By the way, thanks for your words of support, Junior."

"Look, I'm not making fun of you, Bobby, I just don't know what to say. This is still a bit new to me, all these demons and monsters and stuff." He stared at his menu, which he had been doing a lot since he'd come in. "Speaking of new to me, I don't know what any of this stuff is. Seriously, I don't recognize anything. Do they eat actual food in Indonesia?"

"Kid, kid. If you're going to start hanging out with the big boys like me and Sam, you have to start eating big boy food. You live in San Judas, one of the best restaurant towns in the world. We've got people selling gyros and Vietnamese-Mex and even chicken and waffles out of street trucks! Not to mention a zillion different interesting ethnic restaurants like this one. You're going to be dead a long time—hey, you might have been dead a long time already, for all I know—so you might as well branch out."

"Yeah, but do I have to start with Indonesian? Look at what they're eating over there. Rocks and bark!"

I shook my head. "First off, this isn't Indonesian, it's actually Javanese food. Java is only one of thousands of islands in Indonesia. Like all Boston clam chowder is American food, but not all American food is Boston clam chowder. Second, what those folks are eating is *nasi gudeg*, and it's really good. The rock, as you so ignorantly called it, is a marbled, hard-boiled egg. The stuff it's sitting on is not bark but *gudeg*, which is made from jackfruit."

"Yeah? How about the fried washcloth?"

"Buffalo skin. Probably from a cow, actually. No, it's *good*. Stop making faces. Just let me order lunch for both of us and try not to hyperventilate."

While we waited for the food and Clarence watched various menu items go to nearby tables—the kid's expression was like someone forced to watch ugly people have sex—I brought him the rest of the way up to date. Well, not about Anaita's involvement: Clarence was still new to this whole disobeying-the-bosses thing, and Anaita was seriously high in the hierarchy. I wasn't ready to drag him in that deeply. He listened, but he also seemed distracted, like there was something on his mind. He kept saying things like, "You know, Bobby," and then kind of trailing off as though he'd chickened out on whatever he'd been about to say. Whatever it was, I figured he'd bring it up when he was ready, and besides, I had worries of my own—not just unexplained things-going-bump, but Foxy Foxy and his very obvious case of The Fear.

"Who is that Foxy guy, anyway?" Clarence asked. "How did he find out about your feather in the first place?"

"I don't know, but once it had been stolen from Eligor I'm sure the word got around, and locating odd items for interested buyers seems to be what dancing Mr. Fox does."

He frowned. "So the feather means Kephas made a deal with the Grand Duke of Hell." "Kephas" was the angelic pseudonym Anaita had used setting up the Third Way.

"Eligor is *a* grand duke," I told him. "I think there are a few." But only one whose heart I personally needed to tear out of his immortal chest and squeeze like a ripe tomato, and that was Eligor the Horseman.

"But why would a high angel like Kephas do that?"

"Because no one could open up a new territory like this Third Way place without both a major angel and a major demon signing off. That goes all the way back to the Tartarean Convention." I saw what looked like our order being lifted onto the pass-through, so I signaled the waiter to bring me another Bintang. (I said I was cutting back and I meant it. Bintang beer doesn't have a lot of alcohol in it. Honest. But you need something cold and wet to wash down the peppers.)

"Yeah, I get that, but *why?*" Clarence asked. "The two of them made this big bargain and opened this new territory, I understand that. And I get that . . . Kephas wanted it for this experiment or whatever." He had hesitated oddly before using Anaita's pseudonym. Did he have suspicions of his own about the identity of Sam's mystery angel? "But why would Eligor go along with it?"

"Actually, that's a good question, and I don't know the answer. So the angel would owe him a favor, maybe. That's got to be useful if you're a major player in Hell. The rivalries those guys have with each other are as bad as anything they feel about us."

"Still, it seems weird." His look of dissatisfaction turned into something altogether more perturbed as the waiter thumped a bunch of plates down on the table. "You ordered rocks."

"Eggs, kid, eggs. And I don't care if you sit there and starve, but if you keep me from enjoying my food I'm going to skull you with one of them, and it's going to hurt."

As we ate, I thought about what Clarence had said. I was beginning to think he was right: if I was going to find the horn that Eligor had given as a marker on the deal, it might help if I understood the deal better.

"Maybe it's time I let Sam show me his new place." I shoveled in a last wiggly fork full of *bakmi Jawa*. "There might be something about his Third Way that would put the whole thing in a different light. Because right now, I'm stuck." The Third Way was what they called the alternative to Heaven and Hell that Anaita had put together. Sam had jumped ship to work for them, so he clearly thought it was a good idea, but I still didn't entirely get the whole premise. I mean, yeah, Heaven and Hell are moribund and old-fashioned—why wouldn't they be after eleventy-nine gazillion years?—but I wasn't sure that creating a competitor for the two of them was a smart thing to do. After all, Heaven has a long memory and Hell has lots of lawyers.

"Where is Sam, by the way?" Clarence had tried a few things, but mostly he had been pushing his dinner around like a ten year old pretending to eat enough to earn dessert. "I thought he'd be meeting us."

"I left him a message and asked him to, but maybe something came up." At the table behind Clarence a couple of very American-looking teenage girls were sitting with their parents and an older Asian lady who was probably their grandmother. The girls looked about as happy to be here as my guest did, rolling their eyes at every new dish that came to the table. "But one way or another, I've got to get hold of that devil horn. It's my only bargaining chip."

To get Caz back, I could have said, but didn't have to. Clarence knew. He'd been in the parking garage with me when it all went sour, when Eligor went home with the angel's feather and I was left with nothing but a couple of gallons of dissolving fake Caz. Clarence and Sam had basically carried me home that night, then poured me back out of a vodka bottle a couple of weeks later.

The girls at the next table were ignoring their parents completely now. As the adults conversed quietly in what was probably some Indonesian dialect (if you think I know the difference between Balinese and Javanese you've definitely got the wrong angel) the girls giggled and squealed in English. "She *says* she's getting an after-school job!" pronounced one of them with disdain.

"As a slut!" said the other. They both collapsed into laughter again. The parents and the old woman didn't even look at them. They may not have understood English very well.

The grown-ups probably don't know much about what their kids are getting up to here in the Land of the Free, I thought.

This sparked an idea, which distracted me enough that I missed part of what Clarence was saying.

". . . Because if this Kephas stashed the horn in Heaven somewhere, you'll never find it, Bobby."

"No, I don't think that's where it is." But I was focused now on what the girls behind him had said—*after-school job.* "If you had something that belonged to an important demon, the last place you'd want to stash it would be Upstairs. Talk about something sticking out like a sore thumb! It would be like trying to hide a chunk of uranium in a Geiger counter factory."

"So you think the horn's somewhere here on Earth?" He snorted. "Should be easy to find after narrowing it down so far."

"Sarcasm is like training wheels for the humor-impaired," I informed him. "You want another beer?"

"No, thanks. I've got something to do in a little while." Suddenly he seemed to go a bit cagey. "But thanks. The buffalo washcloth thing was actually pretty good."

"You're a miracle of tolerance, Junior." I flipped some money onto the tray to cover the bill and the tip. "I just thought of something I have to do, too."

"Oh." He looked disappointed. "I thought we might hang out a bit longer."

"Why?"

"Nothing." But he looked like it had definitely been something—the kid wore a mild but distinct air of disappointment. "I just wanted to talk to you about—never mind, it doesn't matter. It can wait."

"Good. Because I just realized I have another resource besides the fabulous Mr. Fox who can give me some information about auctions—especially auctions for exotic objects, like angel feathers. And possibly demon horns, too."

There are very few activities that are going to make a guy look and feel more like a pervert than driving slowly past a Catholic girls' academy when school lets out, examining all the young women. (You have to look closely, because the uniforms make them look alike, you see. Honest, there's a reason I was doing this.)

I finally spotted her and eased up alongside the curb. Luckily for me, she was walking by herself. I had a suspicion she did that a lot. I rolled my window down.

"Hi. Can I buy you a milkshake, young lady?"

She looked up with a slightly unfocused expression, as though she needed to see me before knowing whether she was being teased or actually threatened. She pushed her glasses up her nose, then smiled.

"Mr. Dollar! Hi. What are you doing here?"

"Like I said, Edie, buying you a milkshake—if that's okay. Can you spare me fifteen or twenty minutes?"

"Sure. Do you want me to get in?"

"Probably give people the wrong idea. The SJ Creamery's just around the corner and down a block. I'll meet you there."

Because of slow traffic from all the people picking up their daughters, Edie actually reached the place before I did. I settled in on the other side of the booth, facing her and her enormous backpack. Despite her youth, Edie Parmenter was one of the most acute sensitives in Northern California, and her after-school job had nothing to do with rolling burritos or stacking jeans at the Gap.

We both ordered chocolate shakes. I was still fairly full from lunch, but it's hard to turn down a serious milkshake, and that's the kind they made there. "It's weird to see you here, Mr. Dollar," Edie said. "Not bad, I mean, just . . ." She laughed. "I totally didn't expect you."

"Me and the Spanish Inquisition," I said. "Sorry—old joke."

Edie gave me a stern look. "I know about Monty Python, Mr. Dollar. My dad quotes them all the time."

"Ow." I leaned back. "How's life? How's school?"

"Tenth grade completely sucks, but at least I don't have to board at school this year. But I have to say I don't think nuns make the best science teachers. Like, Sister Berenice was telling us the other day that humans only went to the moon to try to find God. And this other teacher told me that God hates San Judas because there are so many gay people living here."

"Yeah, especially around the downtown fabric stores," I said. "That's a real problem for Heaven. Armageddon is supposed to start right here in the Pioneer District."

She looked at me carefully. "I get it. You're joking. There's nothing wrong with gay people."

"I agree. Not to mention that anybody who pisses off nuns is okay with me." I paused while our shakes arrived, nodded thanks to the server, then unsheathed my straw. "Hey, I wanted to ask you something, Edie. The last time I saw you—remember?"

"Islanders Hall?" She pushed back her glasses again so she could see to force her own straw into the thick shake. "The auction, yeah. That was totes scary! All those people shooting! And you knocked me over on my bike."

"It was quite a night, all right. But I wanted to ask you to tell me what you remembered about it. Mostly I want to know who else was there."

I had picked the right girl. Edie reeled off a list—Japanese Crowleyites, some Jesuits, Scythian priestesses (Foxy had called them "Amazons," I remembered) and more. But none of the names sparked any new ideas. I asked Edie in a roundabout way if she'd heard anything lately about a horn that might have the same kind of value as the feather, but she only shook her head.

"Oh, no! That feather—that was crazy! I've never heard of anything like that before. Not since then, either." She paused for a moment, sorting something out in her mind. "The person who sent me that night, well, that person (she was walking around the pronoun, I noticed, protecting her client) wanted me to describe everyone else who was there, too, just like you."

"I don't want to get you in trouble, but can you tell me anything about your client? Anything at all?"

She put down her milkshake. "You know I can't do that, Mr. Dollar. It's bad business."

"I get it. Drink up, I understand. Okay, here's another question. I have a real need to find out some things, and that night and the people who wanted the feather make a good starting point. Any chance your client would talk to me?"

Edie's eyes went big. "I don't think so."

"Well, do me a favor. Contact him or her and ask, would you? Tell them it's important to me and that I'd make it worthwhile to them."

She still looked worried. "I don't know."

"It can't hurt to ask. You've known me for a few years now, Edie. Have I ever lied to you about anything? Done anything crooked?"

"You hit that guy in the face that one time."

"Are you talking about the jamoke who was trying to sell that bogus relic of Le Saint Prepuce? Come on, that was gross, and he totally had it coming. Let's be fair—he threatened to pull a knife on me."

She giggled. "Actually, it was pretty cool. Like a movie." She slurped up the last of her shake and sat back, studying me through her slightly crooked glasses. She could have been Encyclopedia Brown's cooler sister. "Okay, Mr. Dollar. I'll check it out with my employer. How do I reach you?"

I wrote down my cell number on the receipt and pushed it across to her.

"I gotta go. I've got a crap-ton of math homework. Thanks for the milkshake!" She slid out of the booth and out the door, trundling her backpack on wheels behind her, just another tenth grader who could read ancient Akkadian and tell a genuine Stone of Giramphiel from a realistic fake at twenty yards' distance.

Just as I was pulling up next to my apartment, my phone rang. This time it was my frequent co-conspirator, Sam. Finally.

"Sorry I couldn't make lunch today, B. Things to do, people to irritate. What's the good word?"

"The good word is *gudeg*, boychik, and you missed it."

"Yeah, I know. Next time."

"But I still need to talk to you. The shit is getting thick around here. And now, on top of everything else, my apartment is haunted." I gave him the five-cent tour of my recent spectral happenings.

"Are you sure it's not just a couple of your one-night stands still knocking around the place?" he said. "Judging by your past habits, I wouldn't be in a hurry to call an exorcist."

"Yeah, well, fuck you too."

We passed a few more lazy insults and agreed to make a new lunch date in the next couple of days. As I went up the stairs toward my second-floor rooms, I was feeling like I might actually be making some headway with the four or five thousand critical issues hanging over my head. Then I got to my apartment, and even as I reached into my pocket for the keys, I noticed that the door wasn't entirely closed.

You know how those alarms blare when a sub starts diving? That's what I felt up and down my spine—*danger, danger, danger!* I left the keys where they were and pulled out my gun instead, then ducked down and slid through the door as quietly as I could.

I didn't have to go far. Two young, pale guys in suits—yep, the same two I'd seen following me downtown—were pulling stuff out of my cheap pressboard book shelves, making a big old mess in the process. Worse, they had actually painted a big ragged swastika on the wall above the television set.

"Freeze!" I stepped in, gun up and braced, and swung it back and forth between the two of them. Both were young, probably mid-twenties. One had dark hair, one had light, but both were as Caucasian as Betty Crocker's firstborn. They looked like student athletes, maybe a little older, but certainly less than thirty. And though they were equally wide-eyed as they looked at my gun, neither of them seemed particularly frightened, which was not a soothing thing. These weren't just thugs or thieves, although I was pretty sure they were both human.

"So," I asked, "you Jehovah's Witnesses need to supplement your income these days, huh? You're not going to get much for those old issues of *Car and Driver*." I gestured to the swastika, but didn't take my eyes off the men. "Or are you something else? The local Neo-Nazi Welcome Wagon?"

One of them started to lower his hands, but I gestured angrily for him to put them back up.

"If you just tell us where it is," he said in a calm voice, "there'll be no need for trouble." He sounded American, that's all I could tell you.

"And if you lie face down on the floor with your hands where I can see them, I won't have to send you to Jesus with a bunch of holes in your face," I pointed out.

Several things happened in the next second or so. I heard a noise behind me, then something hit me hard on the back of the skull. I staggered, and the only shot I took went wide and high of both the guys in suits. I fell forward onto my hands and knees, my head suddenly feeling like a broken cabin window at thirty-five thousand feet, all my thoughts rushing around and being sucked out into darkness. Also, and I realize I wasn't a very reliable witness at that instant, but I swear that the swastika painted on my wall ran away.

As I crouched there in the silence following the echo of my shot, swaying, trying to find the strength to get up, I heard my upstairs neighbor start pounding on the floor again, as if a gunshot was no different than playing the stereo too loud. Then somebody kicked me in the head—yes, the same, hurting head—and I went off to sleepy-bye land, which was very, very dark.

six

black sun

YOU CAN tell it's not a good day when you get coldcocked, and then you regain consciousness and they're still hitting you.

Two guys had my arms, one on either side of me. I couldn't see them very well through the blood running down into my eyes, but I was pretty sure it was the two missionaries, because the guy in the black t-shirt currently punching my face was a new player in the game. He was a muscular, bald-headed thug a little shorter than me, with forearms like premium hams. Unlike the other two, he seemed like someone who hit people for money. Instead of just beating my face into hamburger, he was working the body as well, softening up my ribs (well, turning them into the bottom of a snack bag, to be precise) and then going back to the head every now and then just when I started to be able to think straight. He'd already opened cuts above my eyes, judging by all the blood, and my nose cartilage definitely felt bendy and wrong.

He paused when he saw me looking at him.

"Okay. Now we can get down to business." Bald Thug looked like he might be local muscle. I couldn't swear to it, but I thought I might even have seen him in Oyster Bill's once or twice, on the ass-end of a Saturday night. He finished up with one last, solid punch into my breadbasket, doubling me up.

"How'm I . . . s'posed . . . talk?" I grunted, trying not to puke Javanese food all over my shoes.

"Shit, I don't care whether you talk," said B-Thug. "Just point. Where is it?"

Man, I was getting fucking tired of that question. I'd gone through a long stretch earlier in the year of being asked that by an animated corpse with a long knife. That had been about the feather. Since Eligor had taken the feather back, I was pretty sure this was about the horn. That worried me almost more than the beating, because there was no way anyone should know already that I was looking for it. So I played dumb. "Where's what?"

He hit me again, a quick, straight right that split my lip and sent a generous dribble of blood down the front of my shirt. "Don't bullshit me. Where's the thing? Some important people want to know—*now*."

"Whatever it is, I don't have it."

An open-handed shot from his left rocked me back. I couldn't help wondering where my gun was: I'd dropped it when I first got hit and I couldn't see it anywhere.

Who were these people, why did they want Eligor's horn (if I was right about what they were hunting) and why did they think I had it? I was pretty certain they were all human, which meant they might be uninformed enough to think I really was holding out on them, and *that* was a scary thought. The young guys on either side of me, although hanging on to my arms with grim determination, didn't look or act like pros, but Bald Thug definitely seemed capable of killing me, or at least killing this particular body. I really hate dying at the best of times, and at the moment I wasn't absolutely certain that my bosses would give me a new body afterward.

I let myself go slack so that the two guys holding me had to pull harder to keep me upright. While I pretended to a moment's grogginess—even more believable if they didn't know I was angel-strong, because their muscle guy had absolutely knocked the crap out of me—I glanced at their positions on either side. As I did, I couldn't help noticing that one of the missionary boys' had an unusual tattoo on his wrist. I couldn't make out the whole thing, but it was enough to catch my attention.

Then, as they set themselves to haul me up straight again, I smashed my foot down on the instep of the guy on my right, then back-kicked the other guy in the shin. Even as they both let go, howling in pain, I lunged forward and rammed my head right into Bald Thug's gut. I drove him backward, doing my best to knee his face as he fell. I didn't catch him solid anywhere, but I knocked the breath out of him long enough to throw myself onto the floor. I scrambled to the couch as fast as I could, because I could already hear B-Thug climbing to his feet behind me. If I'd been planning to make a run for it, I wouldn't have made it. I wasn't, though. I was just trying to get to my sofa gun.

What, you don't have a sofa gun? I thought everyone did.

I kept mine under the cushions where they came together in the middle, a place nobody ever sat (mostly because I almost never had any visitors). It was my good old S&W five-shot revolver, a piece I'd semi-retired. It was about as reliable a gun as you can find, excellent for stashing in a couch against a sudden need. I yanked it out, rolled, and there was Bald Thug still a couple of feet away, stock still now and staring at the muzzle that I was pointing between his eyes.

"Down on your knees," I told him. "Hands behind your head. Yeah, you've been here before, haven't you?" I moved back a little so I could keep all three of them under the gun, but I kept talking to the pro. "I'm not going to punch you just because you punched me, Slappy—I'm not the vengeful type. But if you *or* either of your buddies move, I'll immediately blow the whole middle part out of your face and then figure things out from there. Clear?"

Thug nodded, hands still behind his head, so it looked like he was doing yoga or something.

"Good." I stared at him for a long second or two, then turned to his partners. "Okay, boys, pull up those sleeves. I want to see what's on your wrists. No, the other wrist, shithead."

As I suspected, they both had the tattoo, which I could now see in full:

"What the hell does *that* stand for?" I asked. Neither of them would meet my eye. "I strongly suggest somebody tells me what's going on and who you three are before I get any more irritated." Strangely, it wasn't just the muscular pro who looked like he was going to keep his mouth shut, but both missionaries, too.

I turned to the one on my right. "Hey, I could shoot you in the balls. That might loosen you up a bit, unless you're extra-brave." I swiveled the gun to the other missionary. "Or I could shoot you both in the gut, and you could watch each other bleed to death, all the time thinking how much easier it would have been just to answer my questions—especially after you broke into *my* place and painted a fucking swastika on my wall, then beat the shit out of me." But I noticed there was nothing on the wall now, as if my hallucination of it running away had been real. "Where did it go, anyway? Did you wipe it off?"

Weirdly, both the younger guys only looked more frightened when I mentioned this. The muscular, bald guy just shook his head. "They're not going to talk," he said. "They're crazy. And you don't have the stones to get anything out of me."

I walked to the nearest missionary, the dark-haired one, and put the snout of my .38 up next to his eyeball. He was clearly nervous but held his water pretty well. "Is that true, kid? You'd really take a bullet instead of just having a friendly chat?" He only set his jaw. I was beginning to wonder what I was going to do with them. I couldn't be sure one of them didn't have a gun—shit, they probably all had guns—so I didn't know how long before one of them did something dramatic and the serious shooting began. Not that things would go all that easy even if they were all unarmed.

The dark-haired guy, up close, may not have been the sort of mayhem machine that B-Thug was, but he and his blond partner both looked pretty fit, and they certainly weren't panicking. They were both clean-shaven and had similar haircuts, trimmed high on the neck and sides, leaving nothing around their ears or the back of their heads but precise stubble. They looked military, but if so they must have been from the Northern Finnish Irregulars or something, because they didn't have a square inch of tan between them. The pair looked like fanatics—and that was the problem. The more I watched them, the more I got the sense they weren't going to tell me anything useful until the pain got very intense. After spending a long stretch in Hell, I wasn't sure I wanted to do that, even to these deserving shit-stains. But what else could I do? Just shoot them? Yeah, and then have to get rid of three bodies in downtown St. Jude. I could have called the cops, but these guys weren't ordinary criminals, and I might attract more attention than I wanted if I tried to have them arrested for burglary. Maybe I could have called the Compasses to see if anyone there wanted to help me find out who these guys were, but at the moment I was even less willing to share my private business with my co-workers than with the police. The more I thought about it, the more I could see only one practical solution.

While I still had the gun next to his eye, I quickly pat-searched the dark-haired guy, whom I decided to call "Timon," and then did the same to his fair-haired partner, "Pumbaa." To my surprise, neither had a gun or any other weapons to speak of, although one had a can of pepper spray in his pocket. I impounded it, then gestured the two of them toward the front door.

"Go, and just keep going. Get the fuck out of my place. I'm going to have a little chat here with your friend." I waved the gun toward Bald Thug, who was watching with the cold, calculating eye of an ambush predator. "When I'm done, there won't be much left of him, so don't bother hanging around. And if I see either of you again *ever*, I won't waste time with another of these informative chats. I'll just blow your brains out."

Timon and Pumbaa both looked at me, then at each other. It was obvious what they were thinking.

"Yeah, you could try it," I told them. "But I promise I'll blow at least one sucking hole in each of you before you get near me. You may be some kind of fanatics, but no matter what you think, you're not super-heroes. You go anywhere other than out that door, and you'll be carrying your intestines with you."

They didn't turn fast enough for me, so I pepper-sprayed them both lightly in the face and shoved them out the door with my foot as they gagged and gasped. As I turned my attention back to Bald Thug, I heard them stumbling in the hall and then clattering down the stairwell, still choking and cursing.

B-Thug stared at me as the noise of their exit slowly died away. He shook his head. "Big play. But you're not going to get anything more out of me, so you might as well just shoot."

"Look, chummy, I let them go because you're right—they're obviously crazy. The kind who'd rather be martyrs. But you're not." I stepped a little closer, still not getting too near him; I never let my gun waver from the center of his torso. The .38 was loaded with some of my gunsmith friend Orban's special handloads, good for a close-up weapon with a short barrel. They'd make a mess of him if he tried to jump me. "I'm betting you're just earning some money. You're a pro— you've got no loyalty to those guys."

He actually smiled. It was weird to see, since it obviously didn't mean the same thing as when an ordinary person smiled. "Don't lecture me. You don't know shit about me—or about them." His mouth twisted. "You have no fucking idea who they work for, or what those people can do. They are into some totally sick shit, and it's all *real*. I would rather have you shoot me any day than have them come after me for talking out of school."

At that moment, I heard footsteps in the hallway outside. When the door suddenly swung open I was already turning toward it, certain that the Happiness Twins had nerved themselves to come back and try again.

Sam stood in the open doorway, confusion on his big, familiar face, waving his hand vigorously to fan away the last of the pepper spray.

"Hey, B, my eyes are burning—" was all he had time to say, then Bald Thug swept my legs right out from under me with some kind of kick, dropped me on my ass like it was the first day of karate practice. Then he was up and running. He hit Sam like a fullback on a dive play, and even though my buddy was taller and at least the same weight, he was staggered by the sudden impact and fell back into the hallway. B-Thug was out the door past him and down the hall while Sam was still trying to pull his gun, and although I got up and made the doorway a second or so later, B-Thug was already in the stairwell, so I had to let him go. If I missed him I might wind up putting a bullet into one of my neighbors' apartments, or even into one of my actual neighbors.

Not that they were going to be my neighbors much longer, I felt pretty sure—some tenant must have called the police by now. Even in this part of Jude, indoor gunshots were unusual. Sorry, Temuel, but it looked like I was about to be driven out of another shitty apartment by work-related mayhem, whether the folk Upstairs liked it or not.

"What the genuine fuck . . . ?" said Sam. He grabbed me and kept me from collapsing. I seemed to be dribbling blood everywhere.

"Oh, yeah." I paused to listen. Our Bald Thug was not a small man, and I could hear him caroming down the stairs like a two-hundred-fifty pound pachinko ball. "Yeah, you definitely took the words right out of my mouth, Sammy-boy."

Sam opened the windows to ease the lingering sting of the pepper spray, then kindly filled a towel with some ice for me. Since I didn't have a towel big enough to cover all the bruised areas, I concentrated on my face. While I lay on the couch, revolver still in hand in case any of my new friends came back, Sam scavenged the pantry for something non-alcoholic to drink and finally found one of the warm cans of Vernors that I kept around just for him.

When he popped the tab, tiny little bubbles flew out the hole like angry wasps. Sam took a long swig. "Ah," he said. "The Scotch Bonnet pepper of ginger ales. Nice fit with your new air-freshener." He pulled up a chair beside the couch and handed me my Belgian-made .45. "Found it on the kitchen floor. Somebody probably kicked it out of the way."

I gave him a quick rundown on what had just happened, along with the rest of the recent news, including the Spook Train ride I'd been on even before I'd found B-Thug and friends in my apartment, scratchings and spiders and disembodied monkey-paws. "Which reminds me," I said as I finished. I didn't want to come off all suspicious with my only real friend, but the timing of his arrival had been strange. "What the hell are you doing here?"

"I was in town, and since I missed the lunch . . ." He got distracted by the design of the missionaries' tattoos that I'd scrawled on the back of a Chinese delivery menu so I wouldn't forget. "This is the ink they had, huh? Never seen it. Looks kind of Eastern—Indian, maybe."

"Yeah, but they sounded like local junior college students, and they were dressed like the kind of guys who travel in black helicopters."

"You always meet the most interesting people, B. Then they try to kill you." Sam frowned at the drawing. "We should look this up online."

"If I knew what it was called, I would. But since I don't, I have other ways to get information." I took a picture of the drawing and emailed it to my friend George, aka Fatback, researcher par excellence. "Shit," I said, catching a glimpse of the clock. "He won't even be human for hours."

"Don't be a hater. You and I haven't been human for years."

"You know what I mean." My main researcher happens to be a were-hog, which isn't all that common, whatever some single women may tell you. "While he has pig-brain, he's not going to be able to do anything."

"We can wait. What were you planning to do this evening, anyway, sport? Your face looks like ground beef, and from the way you're breathing you've got a couple of cracked ribs, too. I recommend you settle back, hold that ice against the meatloaf on the front of your head, and let me bring in something to eat." He held up the menu with the tattoo scrawl. "How about Happy Buddha?"

"I just had Asian food," I said. I felt my jaw and groaned. "But you get what you want. I think it's going to be nothing but broth for me until at least tomorrow."

At about eleven I realized I couldn't remember a single thing Sam had said in the last half an hour. I needed to crash so badly I couldn't hold my head up. I told Sam he didn't have to watch me all night.

"Naw, I'm staying. What if those assholes come back, B?"

"Fine," I said. "But I'm not moving off this couch because all my bones are broken. You can sleep on my bed."

He got up to examine the tangle of not-washed-lately sheets. "Never mind. I'll sleep in my car downstairs."

"Don't be such a pussy. Just pull that stuff off and get my sleeping bag out of the closet. Or there's even some clean sheets and blankets in there, I think." Actually, I wasn't too sure of that at all.

"Yeah, I'll take the sleeping bag. Can't be any worse than some of the places I've slept." He leaned in through the bedroom doorway and called out, "Don't take that as a challenge, you weird organisms that live here in Bobby's filthy room."

"Fuck you, Sammy." I sank back into the couch and pulled the blankets up, but I wasn't ready to relax. I really wanted a drink, but I wasn't going to ask my teetotal buddy to pour it for me, even though he would have. I got up and staggered across to the cabinet where the vodka bottle was and brought it back to the couch. "Don't wake me up for anything short of Judgement Day."

But I didn't get to sleep anywhere near that long. Sometime between eleven and midnight my phone rang.

"Hi, Mr. Dollar? It's me, Edie. You said to call. I hope it's not too late."

By now my entire skull felt like a flower pot that had been dropped from a third story balcony, so I just said, "No, 's fine."

"Okay, that's good. Doctor Gustibus says he'll talk to you."

"Who?" I wasn't entirely awake.

"Doctor Gustibus? You know, the guy I was working for at Islanders Hall? He says he'll talk to you if you want. At his house. I'll give you the directions if you have a pen."

Sam was snoring contentedly in my room, so I got up and walked my throbbing head around until I found something to write with. "Shoot."

When Edie had finished and hung up, I stared blearily at the scrap of paper to be sure it made some kind of sense, then I put it in my wallet and slid back into dreams of marching columns of Disney cartoon characters, who each stopped to punch me in the head before goose-stepping past. There were a lot of them.

Man, that was a long night.

seven

world's edge

THE PHONE woke me again about quarter to five. It was a client.
Well, to be more precise, it was Alice informing me I had a client.
Alice has been working for the main office as long as I've been an an-
gel. She's efficient (in an at-least-the-trains-run-on-time sort of way)
but she has a voice that could strip paint and the personality of an itchy
Komodo dragon. Choosing her to be our dispatcher, like the Hallelujah
Chorus ringtone, shows that somebody in the heavenly hierarchy has
a third-grade sense of humor.

"Don't you ever sleep?" I asked her.

"Can't. I lie awake feeling bad about having to wake up hungover
bums like you."

See? The milk of angelic kindness positively drips from that woman.

Sam was asleep on top of my bed, sprawled like an elephant seal on
the sand and making similar noises. I took a quick shower, doing my
best not to scream when the soap got into all the scrapes and cuts, then
rang my friend Fatback to see if anything was happening on the research front.

"Morning, Mr. D!" He sounded quite cheery for a man who was going to turn back into a brainless beast in a man's body at any moment.
"I'm just sending out that stuff you asked about."

"Thanks, George. Anything interesting?"

"Nothing out of your normal range of weirdness. That design's called
the *Sonnenrad*, the sun wheel. It's always been big with racial pride

groups in Europe, but the occult boys in Hitler's SS picked it up, too, and it's associated with some of their black rituals. That means modern neo-Nazis love it, of course, and there's a pretty nasty group these days named the Black Sun Faction—"Black Sun" is another name for that Sonnenrad design. I can't find much about them, but they look spooky."

"Cool, I'll read it all through when I get a chance. Bill me, yeah?"

"Don't worry, I already did. I'm saving up to get this new Swedish eye-tracking software. My voice-control stuff is too old and slow, and it makes too many mistakes."

Just to clear up any confusion, George Noceda—at least the George I talk to—has problems using a keyboard because he doesn't have hands, he has trotters. That's because he's a pig. Pig with a man's brain by night, man with a pig's brain by day—pretty much the shittiest kind of were-pig you could be. The reason why is a long story, but basically he got hosed by Hell. "Hope it works out for you, buddy."

"Very kind, Mr. B. I'd better get off the phone—the sky's getting light. *Vaya con dios.*"

"You too, man." And I meant it. I wouldn't have wished George's curse even on Donald Trump, and George is a really nice guy.

The client I'd been called to argue for was a nice old lady named Eileen Chaney who had just died in Sequoia General an hour before I got there. When I stepped Outside she was patiently waiting for me, and seemed completely unsurprised by any of what was going on, except that I didn't have wings.

"Haven't earned them yet," I said, which might not have been the exact truth but was at least simple.

"I'm sure you will, young man." She took my hand and gave it a squeeze. "You have a nice face." Okay, so death hadn't improved her vision, but I still resolved to do my best for her. Turns out there wasn't much to do. Mrs. Chaney had nothing shocking in her background, Hell's prosecutor was comparatively new and only offered the most perfunctory case against her, and so the whole thing was over in what felt like half an hour.

When Mrs. Chaney and the judge disappeared, I was left alone with the prosecutor for a moment. Except for the whites of his eyes, this demon (who went by the charming moniker "Shitsquelch") looked like a statue carved out of a giant peeled purple grape. He stared at me with unhidden interest.

"I've heard about you, Doloriel," he said.

"Yeah. People get bored, my name comes up."

"Seriously. Some of the folks on my side really don't like you. Like, they've got plans. If I were you I'd get into a different line of work."

"If you were me, your friends would have killed you a long time ago," I said.

While he was puzzling that out, I split. I was afraid he might ask me for my autograph or something.

It was about seven-thirty in the morning when I got back to the apartment house, an ugly time of the day for any sane person but especially for someone with as many sore parts as I had. I parked across the street and looked around carefully before leaving the car. In the building lobby I ran into some neighbors, two young women who lived down the hall. We'd seen each other a few times but never spoken. I thought they were probably a couple, because I only ever saw them together. One was tall and lithe and dark, the other only a little shorter, red-haired and impressively muscular without being particularly big. They were dressed to go out running. I stepped aside to let them by, and the redhead stared at my face.

"Oh! *Z vamī vse garazd?*" she said. Sounded like Russian. "Are you quite right?"

I assumed she meant, "Are you all right?"

"I'm okay, thanks. I was mugged."

"*Bozhe mĭĭ!*" She said something else that I couldn't understand to her dark-haired friend, who shook her head gravely. They walked past me with sympathetic looks on their faces.

"Take careful!" the tall dark one told me as they went out. She too was pretty obviously another non-native speaker.

Sam was gone, off to save the world or buy more ginger ale. I was on my own. I tried to catch up on a little sleep but I was too wired to relax, not to mention my ribs and skull felt like they'd been run through an industrial stamping press, so I got up again, swallowed about eleven ibuprofen, and checked out the directions Edie Parmenter had given me the night before. Her employer, this Doctor Gustibus, lived a good distance out of the city, over on the coast side of the hills, but I didn't mind a little thinking time.

As I headed toward the freeway on-ramp I called Alice and asked her to take me out of rotation for a couple of hours while I handled some personal business.

"You can call it what you want," she said. "Me, I'd just be honest and say 'Staying home to watch game shows and jerk off,' but I'll pretend if you want."

"It's a complete mystery to me why people so often use the words 'vicious bitch' to describe you, Alice."

She hung up before I'd finished being rude. I hate that.

I do like driving, especially when I don't have to worry about a call from work. I followed the Woodside Expressway up and over the hills toward the Pacific, rising from oak scrub to redwood forest. When the sun got high enough it burned off some of the morning mist. It was not what you call a gorgeous November day, at least by Northern California standards, but it was nice enough. This time of year the golden light we get in October turns a bit brassy, and it's almost silver by December. Today it was still on the buttery side, but there was a distinct nip of winter in the air, that cold twinge of mortality even an angel can feel, the chill that can make you shiver even in direct sun.

As I slalomed through the hills, I took inventory.

Anaita had made some deal with Eligor, and (as best I could tell) they had exchanged Feather and Horn to seal the bargain. Eligor had lost the feather for a while, but now he had it back, thanks to me, Barnum's favorite angel. (I call myself that because apparently there's a sucker born every minute even in the afterlife, and I'm the afterliving proof.) The horn, however, the other marker of their bargain, was still hidden.

And now, to add to the fun, some neo-Nazis and local criminal scum had apparently banded together to find the horn—reasons unknown—as well as work in a few beatings for me when their busy schedules allowed. I had no idea how these guys fit into things, but lots of folk had been interested in the feather when I had pretended I was going to sell it. It was possible some of the bidders at the Big Feather Auction had been fronts for the Black Sun or were connected to them some other way. I hoped Edie's employer could tell me more about those organizations than just their names, which was why I was driving all the way out to the coast. If I didn't get anything useful out of this

Gustibus, I'd be back to square one again. And I didn't have anything in square one except empty space.

As I crested the hills, the fog began to turn into drizzle. I put on the wipers and turned up the CD player, one of the few additions I'd made to the extremely old Japanese car I was driving. Charlie Patton's blues took me through the rain and back into the light as I reached the shining, wet expanse of Highway 1 on the far side of the mountains, where I headed north.

The sky was streaked with clouds, although blue was trying to push through. The ocean itself was a steely gray, and there must have been some decent surf because I saw cars parked in several places along the shoulder and people in wetsuits heading down to the shore with boards.

Edie's directions said, "Before you get to Half Moon Bay, turn left at the flying horse." I wished I'd double-checked with her before leaving, because she hadn't specified whether this marvel was a street, a restaurant, or an actual horse with wings. As I got close to Half Moon Bay, I slowed down a little. Luckily it was only a bit past noon, because the visibility gets really bad later in the afternoon as the sun drops toward the ocean and shines straight into your eyes. I passed a few restaurants and bars with picturesque names, but none of them were anything to do with horses, feathered or otherwise.

I was just a few miles south of the golf course and thinking seriously about turning around when I passed out of the latest sprinkle of rain. As wipers swept the last drops from my windshield, I saw it. It really was a flying horse—not, I hasten to say, a live one, but one of those old gas station signs, although in this case you couldn't see anything but the red Pegasus, and not much of that because it was leaning against a tree about ten yards off the highway, half covered with underbrush. I couldn't help wondering why nobody had snatched it and sold it to some collector.

Highway 1, or at least that section, was still a pretty basic old road: you didn't need to wait until the next exit to get off. I turned in front of the rusting horse and onto a dirt road that I wouldn't have noticed otherwise—really not much more than a two-wheel track. I followed its curving course in the general direction of the Pacific, which sprawled across most of the horizon except for the spit of land I was navigating. I wound through a stand of very old eucalyptus trees; the scent that wafted through my opened windows was like the world's largest cough drop. Then the road climbed, and I could see that I was approaching the top of the promontory, which was all evergreens, pines, and cypresses tangled together. There was no sign of a house.

But when I got to the edge of the promontory, I found that the road didn't end there. Instead, it narrowed even more and wound down the front of the tree-covered bluff. After following a bend and finding myself looking down a steep sandstone cliff to the ocean and white-frothing rocks below my passenger-side door, I finally saw the house, tucked into the hill just to my left, and facing the water.

The building didn't seem strange at first, just a large, three-story white house with a high A-frame roof pressed back into the hillside, totally hidden from the highway by the trees. But as I got closer I saw that there were quite a few other buildings on the property, including a group of perhaps a dozen smaller houses—cabins, really—set out in straight lines on a level further down the hill.

I parked on the gravel drive. No other cars, which I hoped didn't mean this Gustibus guy had decided to run down to Pescadero for a crate of artichokes or something, and I was going to have to come back another day. It was cold by the front door, with nothing between me and the late autumn wind off the Pacific, so after I banged the heavy iron knocker I pulled up my jacket collar while I waited.

I was beginning to wonder if I'd been right about the emergency artichoke safari when someone finally opened the door. It was a woman, two hundred years old if she was a day, wearing a long, tent-like black dress, like a mourner at a RenFaire funeral. Her black head-gear was flat on the top, with a veil hanging down all around that left only her face visible. She looked at me as though she didn't meet many actual people.

"I'm here to see Dr. Gustibus. My name is Bobby Dollar."

She nodded. That took so long I thought halfway through I was going to have to oil her like the Tin Woodman. "Come vith me," she said, then turned and shuffled away. Another one with an Eastern European accent. Was this Act Out Your Favorite Hammer Horror Movie week or something? Had I missed an announcement?

We went through a short hall and the old babe in black knocked and opened a door before stepping aside to let me enter. The room was really something. Not architecturally or anything—it was a big old plain barn of a place on the inside and looked like the last serious work done to it had been a century ago—but because of the books. I'd never seen anything quite like it. All through the main room, which must have been a good forty or fifty feet long and more than half that wide, and whose ceiling was clearly the second floor ceiling in the rest of the house, shelves lined the walls almost to the very top. A huge variety of makeshift ladders stood against the shelves, some nice ones with wheels that had been built to go with the shelves, others crude products that looked like they'd been thrown together for dunking suspected witches. At the center of the room stood a huge refectory table, also covered in books, and various other surfaces had been similarly buried. The few spaces not covered by books were crammed with other things—bones, jars, painted stones. Except for the obvious fact that some of the volumes were extremely old, the whole place looked like a second-rate museum had staggered in here and thrown up.

At the far end of the room, in front of a modest fire burning in a fireplace as big as my bedroom—the kind of fireplace you cooked whole cows in and then fed them to your knights and squires—stood a figure dressed in what I thought at first was a white lab coat (but which on closer inspection was some kind of vaguely Eastern-Guru thing, all loose-fitting linen); a figure that I could only presume was . . .

"Doctor Gustibus? Hi, I'm Bobby Dollar. Edie Parmenter told you I was coming, I think."

He carefully marked his place before he set the heavy book down, giving me time to look him over. Gustibus was certainly one of the more interesting people I'd seen lately (outside of Hell, of course, where they play a high-stakes version of "interesting"). He was tall and slender, and—speaking of Hammer Horror—he looked a bit like a middle-aged Christopher Lee, with bone structure for days. His long, white hair was pulled back in a ponytail, and he had a tiny tuft of white beard on his chin.

He looked past me to the doorway where the old woman was still waiting and said, "Thank you, Sister," in a voice like a veteran actor, all stretched vowels and precise consonants.

"Sister?" I asked. "Your sister?" Because she looked too old to be his grandmother, let alone his sister.

He showed me a wintry smile. "No. Sister Philothea is a nun. *Was* a nun. It's complicated. For all of them." He followed up this confusing explanation by extending a long, pale hand. "I am Doctor Karl Gustibus. And you are Doloriel. I've been waiting a long time to meet you."

It was a full second and a half before what he'd said hit me, but when it did it was as though Bald Thug had just slugged me in the breadbasket again. "Dol . . . Doloriel? I'm sorry, but my name is Bobby Dollar."

"Yes, Mr. Dollar. I know." He still wore that little half-smile, but his eyes seemed as cold and remote as stars in the night sky. "But I know your other name too. And I suspect I know why you're here, as well. You've been having a little trouble with the folks in Heaven lately, haven't you? A little . . . unpleasantness." The smile winked off. "Or, knowing some of the players at least a bit, I'm guessing it's rather a *lot* of unpleasantness."

I couldn't think of a single thing to say, and that doesn't happen to me much. So I grabbed for my gun.

eight
braincramp

I POINTED THE Belgian automatic at his chest. Alarms were going off in my head, telling me I'd walked right into some kind of trap like the greenest rookie angel who was ever sent out to find a halo-stretcher his first night at Camp Zion.

"Pardon me," I asked, "but exactly who the fuck are you, and how do you know any of that?" I'm afraid I wasn't as calm and cool as I'd have liked to be, so if you're my biographer, please fix that part.

Gustibus didn't jump back or freak out, but he did look like he took the gun seriously, which was a relief: half the bastards I've drawn on lately didn't even seem worried. That's what happens when you hang out with demons and loonies, I guess. "Please point that somewhere else," he said. "You don't need it here."

"I'm only going to ask one more time. How do you know that name?"

"I know lots of names. It's what I do." He gestured to the books that covered every surface and nested along the walls in thousands, like sea birds on the cliffs. "I am a student of sorts, Mr. Dollar. A researcher, like your friend Mr. Noceda, who is always interested in what the infernal powers are up to. The difference is that I have instead devoted *my* time to a study of Heaven and those who rule there."

He knew about me, *and* he knew about George the Info Pig. What was up with this guy? I didn't get it, but I couldn't just keep waving the gun at him when he wasn't doing anything except cooperating.

Unfortunately, there's no cool way to put your gun away again. I thumbed the safety on and slipped it back in my pocket. "Okay. But keep talking."

"I've been wanting to meet you for a while, actually. When Edie said you wanted to ask me some questions—well, it seemed like Fate."

That made me itchy. "Why did you want to meet me?"

"Let's not hurry ourselves." He walked past me to the window and stood looking out at the ocean. "Did Edie tell you anything about me?"

"Not a thing. Just your name and how to get here."

"She's a good girl."

I didn't know what to say to that, so I just watched him. "Look, are you going to give me any information about the auction at Islanders Hall?" I said at last. "That's why I'm here."

"Oh, if that's all you want, I'll be happy to do it. But I can tell you much more. Why don't you sit down?"

There was no obvious seating area, just a few chairs scattered around the room, all covered with old volumes and strange objects. Gustibus scooped a few books off the nearest, moved those to another, equally cluttered surface, then gestured. "Please, don't wait for me. I never sit."

This guy kept coming up with things that just shut me up. I wasn't used to it. I sat.

"So?"

"I'll happily tell you about all the other participants in your auction for the angelic feather, although I'm surprised you didn't keep your own notes."

"It got a little busy there," I said, thinking of Eligor's soldiers and the huge, burning thing called a *ghallu*. It had indeed been quite a night.

"Fine. Then as a gesture of good faith—" He proceeded to name everyone who'd been there, including several Edie had forgotten, and to give me a quick capsule biography of each. None of the names or facts gave me any new thoughts on where Anaita might have hidden Eligor's horn, so I asked him about the Black Sun Faction.

"I know a little about the Black Sun, yes," he said. "They are all human as far as I know, but a most unpleasant group of humans. Several murders have been ascribed to them, as well as countless arsons, robberies, and other crimes. They are political fanatics, the truly dangerous kind. But they were not at the auction or connected in any way, as far as I know."

"How about Foxy, then? Mister Fox, the guy who put the auction together—do you know anything about him? Who is he? *What* is he?"

Gustibus showed me a slight smile. "I'm fairly certain he's exactly what he says he is. A fox."

"Um . . . does that mean you find him sexually attractive? Or that he's actually a small doglike predator with a bushy red tail?"

"Not an ordinary fox. A fox spirit. From Japan, originally, but you know how crowded that country is. I'm reasonably certain he immigrated here a dozen years ago or so."

"A Japanese fox spirit who deals in stolen supernatural goods from a street corner in downtown Jude?" I shrugged. "Why not? Nothing else makes any sense, so why should he?"

I assume my expression was pretty easy to read, because Gustibus smiled again. "But as I suggested, Mr. Dollar, I can tell you more useful things than that, especially in your current situation. Shall we bargain?"

"Bargain?"

"Oh, come. I'm a collector. I don't give things away."

I adjusted my position so I could reach my gun quickly if I had to. "And what do you want in return? Don't tell me—it begins with S and ends with O-U-L."

He shook his head, his expression like I'd just broken wind. "Please. I'm not on that side. I'm not really on either side, although both have more power over me than I'd like." He lifted a fat folio off one of the windowsills and held it out, spread open. The page on top was covered with spidery lines and tiny little notes. "Please, come closer so you can see."

I edged my chair forward, still not sure of him and not wanting to be within arm's reach. Not that Gustibus seemed particularly dangerous—actually, he looked a bit like some kind of skinny, Buddhist-Druid version of Santa Claus—but he was tall and his movements suggested he could be quick when he wanted to be.

I squinted because I was still a couple of feet distant. "It looks like a map of San Judas."

"Actually, it's a map of the whole peninsula south of San Francisco, down to Alviso. Do you recognize any of the names written on it?"

Now I really had to squint. I gave up at last and got off the chair. The map had been divided with blue pencil lines into little territories. Right over downtown Jude, at the center of the map, in a blue square labeled, *Masonic Lodge*, and then below it, *Now Compasses—taproom*, was a list of names. Nahebaroth was the first one—my old off-and-on sweetie Monica Naber's real name. Beneath were was a couple of dozen others, including Sammariel and Doloriel—yeah, me. I looked up at Gustibus, surprised at how hard my heart was beating. "We're all on there."

"You certainly are. That represents years of work. And if you notice the names grouped around the bar on Parade Street called *The Emergency Room*, you will notice that they are members of the opposing tribe."

I looked. The crabbed black letters listed *Smearhawk*, *Rotwood*, *Weepslug*, and several others that I recognized, most of them infernal prosecutors. There was even a note for Shitsquelch, the fanboy prosecutor I'd met that morning. "I don't get it. What is this?"

"What is it? History, Mr. Dollar. Some men spend their entire lives studying just the Battle of Bosworth Field or Marathon, others take a larger view and make the entire War of the Roses or Peloponnesian struggle their area of interest. But the struggle that fascinates me is ongoing. It is the war between Heaven and Hell."

"You're a historian?"

He shrugged. "Of a sort. It's a field of study pursued by a small number of researchers, all of us with far more to do than we can ever hope to accomplish. But the quest for knowledge does not relax its standards because of the inadequacy of its devotees."

I was really beginning to wonder who this guy was. I'd never heard of him, and yet he'd apparently been around for a while. Was he human or not? "So what could you possibly want from me?"

Gustibus actually looked surprised. "Why, information, of course. What else? I have had very few chances to interview any of the actual combatants in this eternal struggle. In return for answering my questions, I can help you find what you're seeking."

"And how do you even know what that is?"

He put the folio back on the windowsill and picked up a little bell with a handle, then shook it briskly. "I know a great deal, both about your struggle with Eligor the Horseman and your current problems with—let us be discreet—*certain of your own comrades*. I assure you my methods are nothing sinister. I seek out and buy information—some of it in the form of the books you see here," he waved his hand, "but also intelligence that can only be discovered thanks to modern technology." He gestured again, this time at a pretty nice desktop computer perched at one end of the refectory table. "But I do not simply gather information, Mr. Dollar—I study it."

The door of the huge room opened, startling me a trifle, and another little old nun came in. I only knew it wasn't the same one because her headgear was different, more of a straight wimply-veil thing that fitted close to her head.

"Sister Kassia," Gustibus said, "Will you bring some refreshment for our guest and myself?"

She nodded and tottered out again like something brought only partially to life by an underachieving mad scientist. I was too nonplussed to think of anything to say about all the things Gustibus had just told me, so instead I asked, "What's with all the nuns?"

"This property was a Russian convent when I bought it in 1947," my host said. "The building itself was deconsecrated, but for various reasons having to do with politics and other things, many of the nuns had nowhere to go. I let those who wished to stay remain here. They help me around the house, they tend the gardens—we grow most of our own food. We have received a few novices over the years, but most of the original group have died. I'd say there are only a dozen or so left out of what was once a congregation of nearly a hundred."

So he'd bought the place in 1947? That was well over sixty years ago, and he didn't look like he could be any older than that himself. Who was this guy? I didn't get a Hell-vibe off him, but that didn't mean much. You almost never did, unless they wanted you to. Maybe Gustibus was like my gunsmith friend Orban, who claimed to have lived centuries by the simple expedient of refusing to die.

I meet all kinds, I'm telling you.

Sister Kassia came back sooner than I would have expected, and set out a tray with a pitcher of ice water, a large bunch of grapes, some bread, and a wedge of white cheese.

"Try it," urged Gustibus. "It comes from our own goats."

I took a little, just to be polite—it was actually pretty good—and poured myself a glass of water. After popping a few grapes, I took my chair again. "If we did make this bargain, what kind of . . . information do you want? I mean, I don't know you well at all, but to be honest, there are a lot of things I couldn't or wouldn't tell you even if I did." Why should I trust this new guy Gustibus? I still didn't entirely trust Clarence, even though he was another angel and Sam liked him.

"I don't want names," Gustibus said. "As you can see, I have my own sources for those. But what my sources can't tell me is what it is actually *like* to be an angel of the Lord. I would like to ask you questions about your experiences, your day-to-day routine. In return, Mr. Dollar, I promise I will give you information that will help you— perhaps even make it possible for you to locate the rather unique horn you're looking for."

It was the first time he'd mentioned the horn, and the first time I'd had solid confirmation that Eligor's token really was the thing everyone was interested in. I was relieved to know I'd been right, but I still took a moment before replying, since sharing with someone I'd just met felt like stepping off onto something shaky. "The horn, right. Do you know where it is?"

"No. But I can give you a few suggestions that may save you a great deal of time."

"Such as?"

"I hardly think it fair that I show you mine before you show me yours." The wintry smile returned; he'd amused himself. "Surely we can find some way to help each other?"

By now, I was beginning to almost like the guy, although I wasn't any closer to trusting him. He clearly knew things about me and the other angels that most people didn't know. "Any chance you could tell me a little bit more about yourself, Doc?" I asked. "Where you came from, how long you've been doing this, stuff like that?"

He smiled. "It will be a long time before you've earned enough credit for that, Mr. Dollar. But maybe someday."

"Okay, then we'll play it your way for now. How about I give you some of what you want to hear first, then you can return the favor? After that, we'll swap back and forth."

"Excellent. Tell me about your own experiences, please. Did you first wake up in Heaven or here on Earth?"

So I related the basics of my angelic life, starting with my first memories of waking up in Heaven, then continuing through my training in Camp Zion with my old sergeant Leo, and on through the early days of my work as an advocate. I stopped well short of the current mess, with no further mention of Eligor and nothing about my trip to Hell, or, most especially, of course, about Caz. I was economical with names and locations in general, and I kept the recollection to broad strokes, but otherwise told the truth as I remembered it. Gustibus made no notes, but I had a feeling that would come later, and that he wouldn't have forgotten much.

"Excellent," he said when I stopped. "And much of it quite informative. I know of Camp Zion, of course, but I have had little chance to hear about the Counterstrike Units from anyone who actually served in one." His smile this time was less cheerful. "I have spoken with a few who received some rough treatment at their hands, however. Do you remember an armed encounter with Hell's forces at a place on the bay called Guadalupe Slough? I believe your unit, the *Lyrae*, were involved."

"Smugglers had a warehouse, and we hit it," I said. "Nasty fight. It was a few years before my time, though."

"Yes, you're right. I had the occasion to speak to a gentleman who went by the name of Eduardo Stayner, at least in human circles, although he was better known to many as Freezegripe, a lower-order demon. He was on death row at Folsom Prison for his later role in a botched hijacking that had killed two Brink's guards, and since he was confident he would receive a new body after he went to the gas chamber, then go right back to work for the same infernal masters, he felt comfortable telling me about the firefight at Guadalupe Slough. Your *lochagos* Leo apparently shot him in the face during the raid, and he was still somewhat perturbed about it. He'd healed, but the scars were still very prominent."

"My heart bleeds for him."

The smile again. "As did mine. A thoroughly unpleasant fellow. But he was the first live contact I'd had in a long time with any of the Opposition soldiers, and because I'm a good listener he told me a lot more than he intended."

"Well, that's interesting . . . sort of," I said. "But it's not really what I was hoping for when you said you thought you could help me."

"It's more interesting than you suspect. You see, a lot of what I'm going to tell you now first came from Freezegripe, although I've been able to confirm most of it from other sources." Gustibus was still standing—apparently he truly didn't sit—and now he walked to the window and leaned against the sill. Outside the sea had gone dark as the afternoon drew on and the overcast thickened. I noticed for the first time that not only was my host dressed like a hipster monk, his feet were bare.

"I suggest you pour yourself a glass of water, Mr. Dollar," he said. "Now I have a few stories to share with *you*."

I'm glad he suggested the water, because within a few minutes I was learning things that not only made my hair curl and my brain cramp, but also made the inside of my mouth feel very, very dry.

nine
buddhist druid christmas

GUSTIBUS SAID, "I can tell from the way you talk about San Judas
Tadeo that you care for the city very much, Mr. Dollar."

"Really?" Nobody had ever accused me of that before. I mean, yeah,
I guess I have a sentimental fondness for Jude, sort of along the lines of
what you might feel for an alcoholic parent who loves you but keeps
setting fires by accident.

"It is clear. But the problem is, you are not taking a long enough
view."

"You just talk, Doc. I'll listen."

Again the slight smile. He wasn't so much cold or aloof, I had decided, as a bit otherworldly. I still wasn't positive he was human, at
least the ordinary, mortal kind.

"Very well," he said. "Let me give you an example of what I mean.
Back in the middle of the nineteenth century, at the height of the Gold
Rush, the Barbary Coast of San Francisco was a worldwide hub for
adventurers and fortune-seekers. One fellow, a gambler and occasional
saloon owner—the deeds to these places were passed back and forth in
innumerable games of chance—was a man named Portugee Jake. He
was a famously dangerous fighter, and was said to have shot more
than a few men dead with the pearl-handled Colt he always wore. He
eventually went into whisky and made an immense amount of money
selling to the other saloon owners, and the tales of the wicked parties
he gave at his mansion on Nob Hill were legendary."

"I said I'd listen, but I don't see the point."

"Stay with me, Mr. Dollar. Perhaps you'll be more interested if I tell you that not only was Portugee Jake a noted shot and a man with, what was called at the time, "a vast catalogue of vices," he was also known far and wide as an exceptional horseman."

"Ah," I said. "Horseman."

"Just so. In any case, Portugee Jake disappeared during the Great Fire of 1906, and although he does not surface again in the histories, I can tell you that a large portion of the assets he collected in San Francisco eventually made their way into the portfolio of a man named Cyrus Van Leydeken—"the Major" as everyone called him, owing to apparent service at the siege of Fort Canosa in the Spanish-American War. Major Van Leydeken went into the arms business, but instead of building his business in San Francisco, he chose instead to head south to the small but growing municipality of San Judas."

"Was this Major Van Whatsit guy by any chance an expert horseman, too?"

Gustibus nodded. "He certainly owned them and cared about them a great deal. One of his horses nearly won the Preakness, and his studs created much of the Bay Area's prize stock. He built a large mansion on several hundred acres of rolling hills in what is now Atherton Park and became one of the founders of the modern city of San Judas.

"Then, in the 1930s, Van Leydeken died—or so we are told. His son, who had apparently been overseas, arrived to take up the family concern. His name was Jasper Van Leydeken, and the resemblance to his father as a young man was said to be uncanny. The second Van Leydeken spread the family fortune into many other areas, including the early foundations of the aerospace industry—what would someday earn the area the name of "Silicon Valley." Late in his life, apparently, the son also began a partnership with something called the Vald Family Trust—a name I'm sure you recognize."

"Oh, yeah."

"When Van Leydeken was gone, the company was administered by lawyers for both families until eventually Kenneth Vald stepped in. One of the businesses he built was Vald Credit, as you probably know, since VC Inc. continues to dominate the local economy to this day."

"So what you're telling me is that my least favorite demon, Eligor the Horseman, has been here in this area since the nineteenth century. Okay, I get it. But what does it mean to me?"

"It means you're asking many of the right questions, but you have to think bigger. And longer." He paused. "I myself wonder why Eligor found San Jude such a pleasant base of operations. He has several other identities and fortunes in other parts of the world, but he has spent a great deal of his earthly time here. It might be something as simple as enjoying the mild California weather—he certainly spent a great deal of the Renaissance in Italy's similar climate—but I suspect there is more to it than that. What it is that drew him and others here, though, I still can't say."

I was trying to wrap my head around all this, but I have to admit it was making me feel stupider rather than smarter. "Okay, but what . . . ?"

"What does it have to do with you? I am coming to that, Mr. Dollar. Patience. First, let's put a few more names on the table. I am told that the matter of this upstart Third Way has occupied Heaven's attention lately. As William Blake wrote, 'A robin redbreast in a cage, Puts all Heaven in a rage.' Well so, apparently, does building a new cage for the robins that your employers consider to be their personal property, because Heaven is, quite plainly, in a rage. Well, most of Heaven. But it is those few who are *not* who interest us." He poured himself a glass of water, but didn't drink. "The reason, I suspect, that you are still struggling to get answers is that you are too close to the problem."

"Meaning?"

"Meaning that you must distance yourself, both historically and in other ways, to truly understand the situation. At the moment you fear one enemy even more than Eligor—isn't that true?"

This guy seemed to know everything. "I guess that's fair to say."

"One of the very ephors who judges your behavior. An angel of high standing—a Principality, in fact."

He was good, that was pretty clear, or at least his sources were. "Yeah. And I suppose you can name that angel in three notes or less."

"I believe I can. Anaita, Angel of Moisture."

A sudden superstitious reflex made me pause, as if naming her might cause her to appear. "Go on." It felt more than a little crazy to have this odd man I'd never met before today telling me things about my own life, things no ordinary person should know. It was a bit like opening a fortune cookie to read, "Your boss will send you on a business trip to Houston, your youngest child needs dental work, and on Thursday you will receive a tax refund check for three hundred and forty dollars."

"Here again," he said, "you do not have the necessary perspective. What do you know of this particular angel?"

"Not much," I admitted. "She's powerful. She's old."

"Here is something else to consider." Gustibus finally took a very small and precise sip of water. "She was not always an angel."

"*What?* You mean she used to be an ordinary person? A mortal?"

Gustibus shook his head. "That I couldn't say. But long before she was considered an angel, she was a goddess."

"A goddess? You're kidding, right? You mean like Pele, the Volcano Queen, or something? What the hell does that even mean?"

"The world of the immortals is more complicated than you can imagine. She's had many names, but Anaita—or Anahit, or Anahita—was her name when she was a goddess, too. The ancient Persians revered her."

I had to get up for a second to walk around. Bad enough I had an important angel trying to kill me, but a *goddess?* "How does someone get promoted from goddess to angel? Is that even a promotion?"

Gustibus puffed out his thin cheeks and then sucked them back in again. He did it a couple of more times, and I was just wondering if I was about to hear his mating call when I realized he was laughing. "Oh, I like that, Mr. Dollar. Very good. I don't know exactly how it came about, but I can assure you that the entity known as Anaita of the Third Sphere was once known as Anahit, Goddess of Moisture and Fertility. That was several thousand years ago, of course. I'm sure you know that many of the great lords of Hell were once considered gods or goddesses, but how this Anaita 'changed teams', if you'll forgive the analogy, is a story still undiscovered, although I very much hope to unravel it someday."

"Okay, so I'm in even worse shape than I thought. I'm not sure this does me a lot of good."

"You were being patient, Mr. Dollar. Please keep listening. Whether she is goddess or angel is not so much the issue—she is what she is. But it does point up the fact that you are dealing with immortals or near-immortals, and you must stop thinking in the same human way."

"I'm pretty certain I used to be human myself. That might have something to do with it."

He waved his long hand, dismissing my remark. "I'm sure. But you need to think about these unanswered questions, because at least one of them may help you with your most pressing problem. The first two questions—who wanted this Third Way? And why? And here's another, just as important: If Anaita and Eligor collaborated to open this new territory (and if they hadn't there would be no feather and no horn to concern you) how was that collaboration arranged? Remember, these beings are the equivalent of high government ministers of two warring nations, except *their* respective masters have been at war for uncountable millennia. They cannot simply drop in to each other's offices for a chat. In fact, if they were even seen in the same general location, it would be cause for gossip and speculation among both immortals and mortals alike."

"You're saying that whatever deal they made . . . it probably didn't happen right off the bat."

"Exactly, Mr. Dollar. Whoever made the first overture would have moved with incredible caution. What if he or she misjudged the other? Making bargains with the enemy is a capital offense for both parties. And here's another question whose answer might help with our earlier queries—who seems to be in charge of this Third Way?"

"Well, from what my friend says, it's Anaita—or Kephas, as she called herself while she was setting this up. Certainly I've only ever heard him talk about instructions coming from Kephas, no one else. I haven't heard that Eligor's had a single thing to do with the place. Which means it was probably her idea. That means she was the one to approach Eligor, not the other way around."

Gustibus nodded. "Now you're thinking in a useful way. Remember, these beings are immortal, but in the real world their power is more limited. They cannot simply wave their hands and have things happen—at least, not very often and not without a great outlay of their own energies. Because of that, they tend to use local resources when possible. How did I know that Portugee Jake and Cyrus Van Leydeken and Kenneth Vald are all the same entity? Simple. I followed the money, Mr. Dollar—I intend no humor, by the way—and it showed me that while the identities changed, the money that allowed those identities to thrive in our world all came from the same source of funds over the decades, since I first found Eligor's footprints on California soil, as it were. Now we must follow another trail, also hidden but equally visible to logic, and ultimately that trail should lead to Anaita and perhaps the answer to your problem." He took another sip. "But first it is your turn again to answer *my* questions. Unless you still doubt that I can be useful to you."

"No, sir. Fire away." This was one of the weirdest days I'd spent on Earth, but I had finally begun to get the swing of how this Gustibus guy worked, and I wanted more. It had never occurred to me that Grand Duke Eligor could have been in San Judas so long, and I realized there were a lot of things like that I hadn't even considered.

I let Gustibus guide me through what he wanted, which was a (still carefully self-edited) version of my last year, including the specifics of my beef with Eligor. I left out my relationship with Caz and my trip to Hell again—there were some things I just wasn't ready to discuss with strangers, even useful ones—but Gustibus seemed to know most of what I'd been doing anyway, at least in general terms. When I surprised him, he would say, "Really?" and nod with approval. He did it a lot as I described my doings with the ephors, the angelic fact-finders who had been on my case for a while.

"Excellent," he said after I'd answered his last question. "Oh, this is a pleasure, to speak to someone on the inside with eyewitness information."

"So you've never been to Heaven?"

He looked genuinely sad. "My information comes from other sources. I have spoken to angels besides you, but only in very guarded conversations, swapping one bit of pertinent information for another, equally isolated piece. In fact, I hope we can do this again sometime, you and I."

"Yeah, it's possible." I'd been collecting informants myself ever since my Counterstrike days—George, the ghostly Sollyhull Sisters, and a freaky piece of work called the Broken Boy, just to name a few—but this guy was entirely different in what he knew, and you can never have too many good sources.

He took another sip of water. "So now we return to your current situation. You are under investigation by your superiors, with an unconsummated bargain of some kind remaining between you and Eligor the Horseman—this I infer from your obvious desire to find the horn, plus the many things you have pointedly not told me, despite the your willingness to share the other details of your story. More crucially, you are apparently also a target for Anaita, which complicates matters, because Anaita has something you seem to want very much—Grand Duke Eligor's horn."

"Okay, you proved it. You're smart. Are you going to tell me where it is?"

"Oh, no, Mr. Dollar. No, I'm afraid I don't know where the horn is."

"But you said . . . !"

"I said I'd help you. Listen to me carefully, and I think you'll agree that I'm keeping my side of the bargain."

"I've had my fill of bargains lately, to be honest. They seem to keep blowing up in my face."

"Well, we will complete ours now, in any case," said Gustibus. "Honor demands it. I said you needed to take a bigger view, and now I will explain. Eligor has been here and active for more than a hundred years. Anaita needed him or someone like him so she could accomplish her aims, namely opening a new haven for human souls after death. The whys and wherefores of it still remain to be understood, but we do know one thing—if she needed Eligor, the former goddess is likely to have been the one who made the approach. We also know that something about San Judas appeals to Eligor, and it is his main base of operations."

I finally grabbed the thread. "So she probably came to him here. On Earth. Most likely in San Judas."

"I think it likely," he said, nodding. "And it would not necessarily have been recently—remember, these beings play a long game."

"But even if I know how they met, that doesn't tell me anything about where the horn might be."

"Perhaps not. But don't be too sure until you actually learn the truth about the first meeting. I can tell you as a scholar that you must follow the questions rather than try to jump straight to the answers. How long has Anaita had a presence here? And what is that presence? That is the next thing you must find, I feel certain. With luck, it will lead you to further answers."

"It'll lead me to lots of further questions, I can pretty much bet on that."

"Then if you're at all like me, you will be a very happy man."

Clearly I wasn't much like him—I didn't want another damn question to answer, let alone thirty or forty of them—but I had to take what

I could get. Some of the things Gustibus said had definitely set me thinking in new ways. Of course, if Sam had been there, he would have said, "And thinking is what always gets you in trouble." But he always said that about me not thinking, too.

"Why do I get the feeling," I asked Gustibus, "that you could figure out the rest of this in about half an hour?"

He smiled. "I'm honored you think so, but I've just presented you with the results of a great deal of consideration backed by years of study. Don't overestimate me. I am only, as I said, a researcher. A scholar, to give it an old and honorable title. I have no urge or ability to travel in some of the places you've visited."

An oblique reference to my trip to Hell, perhaps. I could tell he either knew or had guessed something about it, but I also figured it might buy me some other useful stuff from him later on, so I wasn't giving that story away for free.

Another of the little old nuns, or maybe the previous one, stuck her head in.

"Supper is almost ready, Dr. Gustibus," she said.

"Ah. Would you like to join me, Mr. Dollar?" he asked. "We are having kale from our own garden tonight, and some lovely carrots and steamed, late-season cauliflower from a local farm. I do not eat meat."

"No, thanks. One more question, though—where does your name come from?"

"Gustibus?" He nodded again, slowly, as if this was another deep philosophical question. "It was not my given name, but when I was younger and first involved in my field of scholarship, I chose a Latin name, since Latin was the primary language we used in our studies. My given name meant both "taste" and "tongue" in my original country, and since I did not think "Doctor Tongue" suitable, I used the Latin translation for "taste." And of course—" he paused before the punch line, "—it allowed me to remind my friends and fellow scholars, *There's no disputing Gustibus!*"

He waited for me to laugh. I smiled weakly.

"*De gustibus non est disputandum,* you see," he said.

"Ah," I said.

He looked disappointed. "I admit it is a somewhat dry joke, but it is my own."

He didn't come out to see me off, maybe because I hadn't gotten his joke. The last I saw of him, he was standing at the window again, staring out at the dying light and the throbbing Pacific Ocean. Outside, I found the fog had come in to lie across the roads. I almost drove off the edge once, but I eventually got back to Highway 1, and soon was sliding through the misty evening hills, Dexter Gordon's *A Swingin' Affair* playing quietly on the stereo.

The more I thought of what Gustibus had said about Eligor and Anaita, the more I began to feel how hopeless it all was. As if being an angel wasn't complicated enough, I had somehow managed to fall in with gods and monsters.

And seriously piss them off.

ten

four arms, no waiting

I FULLY EXPECTED to find an eviction notice on my apartment door when I got home, or even a couple of police officers wanting to talk to me about guns being fired, but to my surprise I found neither.

I should have moved out right then, I guess. After being haunted, then getting my shit all beat up in my own living room, I sure didn't feel quite the same cozy way about the Tierra Green apartment (in fact I'd never felt cozy about it to begin with) but I was under standing orders from Heaven not to move again. Plus, I was sick and tired of people (and non-people) just waltzing in and out whenever they wanted to. Instead of throwing all my stuff in the trunk of my car and heading for the nearest Econo Lodge like a sensible person, I stopped at a hardware store and got a chain to put on the door and a couple of window locks. At home I busted out my screwdriver and installed them all. I was doing it mostly to slow down my new friends from the Black Sun. The nastier things I come into contact with from time to time weren't going to be kept away by chains or locks, but at least I'd hear them getting in.

When I was done and had eaten the last of Sam's Chinese food order directly out of the fridge, I called George, aka Fatback. Javier, the old family retainer and pig-keeper, picked up the phone because at that time of the evening George was still a human with a pig brain wallowing naked in mud. (I never call George "Fatback" to his face, by the way. It's not my nickname for him, but I didn't know his real name until I actually met him, so it still slips out from time to time.) I asked Javier to let me ring through to his boss's answering machine, then I updated my list of things I wanted George to find out.

After that I called Sam and left a message for him as well. It was strange, not automatically trusting Sam the way I used to, but even after all the secrecy and weirdness about his new allegiance, he was still my closest friend, and he'd risked getting shot at my side a few times recently when he hadn't needed to. Also, I'd decided that whatever my personal reservations were, I really did need to see this Third Way place of his. If one of Anaita's pet projects was trying to murder my soul, it probably behooved me to know a little more about her other hobbies.

Oh, and I stashed my sofa gun again. Not in the sofa this time, of course, in case the Black Sun Faction came back. Despite the locks I'd put in, I wasn't that opposed to seeing them again. After all, I still owed Bald Thug a serious beating, and I'm not really a forgiving kind of guy.

I must have fallen asleep on the couch because that's where I was when the noise at the window woke me up. It wasn't anything ordinary like a branch scratching at the glass, or leaves being blown against it by a stiff breeze, but what was truly strange was that it didn't really sound like anyone trying to break in, either. It was the same bumping I'd heard before, over and over but with no discernible rhythm, like your drunk cousin dancing at a family wedding. I got up but didn't turn on any lights, and I took my automatic with me.

Whatever was outside the window, it wasn't trying very hard: the awkward thumping barely made the glass shiver. Then, just as I had almost crawled close enough to see what it was, it stopped. I put my face close to the window, but I couldn't see anything beyond it except the dim, shadowy outlines of buildings and the street.

My first impulse was simply to crawl back to the couch, because whatever it had been was probably a brain-damaged bird, and didn't seem big enough to do any harm anyway. Also, I was back on the heavenly job clock—I could get a call any time. But things had been freaky enough lately to make me more careful than usual, so I got a flashlight out of the kitchen drawer and returned to the window for another look.

Whatever had bumped the window had left little smeary marks on the outside, like the track of a snail on his first acid trip, but the largest part of them were translucent blots, as if someone had pressed a small round thing like a ping pong ball, sticky with slime, over and over against the glass. I had no idea what it meant, and I didn't like it.

Of course, true to the infamous Dollar Luck, as soon as I'd stretched myself out on the couch again and covered myself with my jacket (because who wanted to walk all the way across the apartment to the bed?) my phone rang.

It was Alice, dear sweet Alice, of the dulcet tones and liquid nitrogen blood. After she'd expressed disappointment at not waking me up, she told me I had a case in Spanishtown. It wasn't a nice one either, some kind of domestic dispute that had ended in a killing.

Heigh Ho, Heigh Ho, and it was off to work I went.

Unluckily for the victim (but luckily for me) my dead client was the brother-in-law of the shooter, a nice guy who had tried to interfere with the beating of his sister, the killer's wife. The lucky-for-me part was that I didn't have to plead the case of the killer, a guy who'd shoot his own brother-in-law so he could get on with smacking the shit out of his spouse. The brother-in-law had been a perfectly nice, hard-working guy named Mejia, a construction worker, and I had no trouble getting him accepted into the Big Happy, but he had real trouble going, still worried about his sister. I'd seen police cars at the residence when I got there and could tell him, without breaking any rules, that I was pretty sure his brother-in-law had already been arrested and was on his way to jail. This was enough to convince Mr. Mejia to step into the light.

As I came back through the Zipper into the blinking blue and red glare from the cop cars that were currently turning Macdonald Street into a carnival midway, my phone rang again.

"Bobby?"

"George!" I looked at the time out of habit. A bit after one in the morning. "So you got my message . . ."

"Look, uh, I just wanted to let you know that there's some pretty weird stuff going on around here, Bobby. Weird stuff."

"What do you mean?"

"I don't know. Noises. I thought it might be rats up in the attic of the barn, but they're too damn big, Bobby. It's been going on for a couple of days, but Javier sent his son up and there's no droppings, nothing. And Javier said he's seen some stuff around the property, too. Something pretty big, in the bushes, and something running under the main house, all hairy."

So whoever they were, my enemies were watching Casa Fatback, too. I felt pretty guilty about that, since I was willing to bet it hadn't started until I first asked him to check up on the Black Sun stuff.

"Yeah, that was when," he confirmed. "That night. You think it's those guys? But they're just a bunch of Nazi punks!"

I didn't want to tell him exactly what Gustibus had said about them also being murdering robbing arsonists—no point in worrying him more, because he already sounded pretty freaked out—so I said, "Yeah, well, you know I run in some strange circles. Have Javier hang out with you for the night. If it's still happening tomorrow, I'll come up and have a look around." Not that I was going to accomplish much when I couldn't even keep the whatever-they-were away from my own apartment.

My promise seemed to make George feel a little better. We were getting ready to hang up when I remembered something that had come to me while driving through Spanishtown, one of my favorite districts, and thinking idly about how the past shaped the present. Gustibus had said that in her goddess days, Anaita had been worshipped by the Persians. Maybe that was a starting point for some of the questions I needed to answer.

"Hey, is there some kind of Persian cultural center in San Jude, George?" I asked.

"Persian? Like Iranian?"

"I guess. But the people I'm thinking about—the person I'm thinking about in particular—would look a bit farther back in history. So I'm particularly interested in Persian stuff. Libraries, archives, historical stuff. Newspaper and magazine articles, too, I guess."

"Don't know—that's a big search area. I'll check. Anything else?"

"Just the stuff on your voicemail. Have Javier make sure all your doors and windows are secure, okay? And call me again if anything else happens."

"You're a good man, Mr. D, even if you aren't really a man."

"That's what *she* said, George my friend. That's what she said."

At least I could make him laugh. That had to be some help on a bad night, right? Because otherwise I felt pretty fucking useless.

*   *   *

I wasn't sleeping all that deeply, because subconsciously I was probably listening for that weird noise at the window again. When I came very sharply awake at 4:19 in the morning I heard noises, all right, but they definitely weren't the same as the muffled thumps I'd investigated earlier. No, this was the scraping noise again, the one from the earliest days of my "haunting", but this time it sounded like it was inside my apartment. My heart was beating pretty darn fast.

Barefoot, gun in one hand, flashlight in the other, I went looking for my nighttime visitor. At first I thought the sound was coming from my bedroom because it seemed to get louder as I got nearer, but by the time I reached the bedroom door it sounded like it was behind me. But once I had crept back to the living room the noise was behind me again.

The hall closet. Mine was a shallow affair, just about big enough to hang a few coats and pile up other stuff that was only needed every now and then, umbrellas and gloves and hats. A healthier guy than me could probably have hung his expensive mountain bike on the wall in there.

I paused beside the pocket doors and held my breath as the scraping noise started up again. It had been bad enough as a mysterious noise in the wall; up close it was much creepier. For a moment something primal in me, something that must have predated angelhood and almost everything else, told me very urgently *don't open that door.* But whatever version of me that might have been, some child frightened by a bedtime story or by a stern sermon about what happens to sinners, it didn't have anything to do with who I was now. Scared by noises in the closet or not, it was my job to open that door. So I did.

As soon as the door started to slide I heard a scrabbling, then a thump and quiet clatter, as if something had fallen into my pile of umbrellas and cold-weather gear. I yanked the door the rest of the way open and shined my flashlight inside.

Nothing.

Well, not quite nothing, I saw a moment later. At the top of the closet, on the side wall over the shelf above the coat rack, a board had been dislodged and pushed to one side. It was far too small an opening for an ordinary human to get through, but I had been in the business long enough to realize ordinary humans weren't usually my biggest worry.

Well, I thought, *at least I know how the fuckers are getting in.*

A movement that might have been coats and other junk settling at the bottom of the closet caught my attention, and almost without thinking I flicked some of the clutter out of the way with my foot. I had about a half-second to see something crouched in the corner, something the size of a small dog but with long, hairy legs. Then it leaped past me and skittered off toward the living room. I probably made some noise when it jumped. Might have even shouted a bit.

Since it was running from me, I decided I had the advantage and went after it. It stayed just out of my reach and mostly out of my sight, a gray-black shadow with spidery legs, dashing from hiding place to hiding place while I scrambled after it, always keeping my gun in front of me. We made a lot of noise—at one point I tipped over the couch in a failed attempt to trap it in a corner—but nobody pounded on the ceiling, or the floor either, for that matter. The neighbors were either deeply asleep or had moved out, or just given up.

Or maybe they hadn't: just about then, someone started knocking on my apartment door, firm and loud.

I had a moment of indecision, as you can probably guess. If I ignored whoever was at the door, it might be the police, and they'd kick it in. Then again, it might be the neo-Nazis, and if I opened the door the party might *really* get going. Or it might just be some of my suffering neighbors.

The thing had disappeared into the living room again, but the hall closet was now closed, so it wasn't getting out that way. I decided to chance a quick trip to the door.

To my surprise, what I saw on the other side of the spy hole was not anyone I'd expected but one of the two young women from down the hall, the taller one with short dark hair. She looked very intent. I opened the door a crack.

"Excuse," she said, trying to see me through the narrow opening, "but so loud noise! Just come home and . . ." She spread her hands. "Worried."

"Sorry, sorry," I said. "It was a mouse—squeak squeak, right? It surprised me, and I tried to catch it." I faked a laugh. "You know . . . chasing it, knocking things over, *bang, bang, bang!*"

"You are sure?" She bent and took something from her pocket, scribbled something on a small piece of paper. "Here, phone to call. I am good with mouses. Call if I and Halyna will help you."

Yeah, I thought, *you'll just* love *helping me exterminate a nest of devil-spiders*. But I opened the door a little wider to accept her number. It was, even for me, a pretty weird way to meet women.

I heard the slightest whisper of movement behind me, then suddenly a knot of hair and legs pushed between my ankles and shoved itself into the space between door and frame. I tried to lean on the door to close it, but the young woman's arm was still there, and I didn't want her to have to make her way in a big bad foreign city minus a limb. While I hesitated, the thing I'd been chasing squeezed out at the bottom. Like a cat, it was clearly able to go through much smaller openings than it appeared to need.

"Oh, no, your pet get away!" she said, and ran after it.

This was rapidly becoming a very bad scene. I chased after her, but she was already following whatever-it-was down the dark stairwell and into the entryway where all the recycling bins had been piled to go out to the curb. The outer door was shut, though, so the thing had nowhere to go. The neighbor woman stopped and looked around, but it was pretty clear to both of us there was only one place it could be.

"Behind," she said, and before I could stop her she leaned over and dragged the plastic bin out of the way, exposing my uninvited visitor as it froze in the glare of the flashlight.

It was *horrible*.

The resemblance to a spider was obvious, because the thing had four long, hairy, black and gray limbs that joined in the middle as if they had a single common joint. It had no eyes I could see, or mouth either, but the worst thing about it was that each of those legs—arms, I guess you'd have to say—ended in a small, mottled human hand. A child's hand.

As I stared in shock, it scurried behind one of the remaining cans.

"It go nowhere," said the young woman. She sounded astonishingly calm, under the circumstances. "Now you move other." She pointed to the can. I must have looked at her as if she were insane, because she said, "Really. You move it."

I pointed my gun, then reached out with the flashlight hand and grabbed the handle of the recycling bin. When I yanked it away, the thing cowered back from the light again, but my neighbor had been right—it had nowhere else to go. It backed against the wall, then climbed slowly upward a few feet, clinging like the spider it resembled. It flexed in the cradle of its long, jointed arms, ready to run again or perhaps this time to attack.

Now I knew why there had been a swastika on my wall. And why I'd thought I saw it run away. I pointed my gun at it, trying to keep my hand steady. It had been a very, very long day.

"No," said the woman. "Not that—no loud."

Then, in almost a single movement, she pulled a gleaming combat knife out of her sleeve, one of those nasty little ones that look like plastic-handled toys but will cut through a lead pipe, and shoved it right into the place where the four legs came together in a knot of muscle. The blade made a wet, cracking noise going in, like someone disjointing a roast chicken. The thing hissed and the arms thrashed, but she had pinned it against the wall.

As if all this wasn't surprising enough, the writhing monstrosity began to smoke. The young woman pulled her knife out and let it fall to the floor. Within moments nothing was left of my four-legged visitor but a greasy smear on the old linoleum and a stink in the air like extremely rotten fish.

"Silver work good," she said, wiping the blade of her knife on the side of the recycling bin. "And for neighbors, better too. More quiet. Oxana I am. You come to our apartment, drink tea and talk, yes?"

"Yes," I said. I mean, it was 4:30 in the morning, and we had just killed a hairy swastika in my apartment lobby. What else could I say?

eleven

tea and shurikens

HALYNA, OXANA'S redheaded roommate with the muscles, was already up and heating the kettle in their studio apartment. She had pulled her hair back into a tight braid, but was still apparently wearing what she slept in, a man's long t-shirt with the arms cut off so high that I had to keep looking away when she bent over, because the bottom of the armholes reached down to the base of her rib cage. Just in the interest of fair reportage, Halyna had very neighborly-looking breasts and an athlete's extremely muscular stomach.

Oxana went off to do something in the bathroom, so I sat on a rolled-up karate mat on the floor. The place didn't really have much other furniture, just a low table and a pair of military-style bunk beds standing against the wall. If these women were a couple, they were a slightly odd one, but it was easier to examine furnishings than to keep looking away from Halyna's armholes, so I went on with my observations. Only the walls of the apartment showed any sign of personality but, other than several pictures of young women with weapons, most of the things my neighbors had taped to their walls were posters and newspaper headlines in what looked like Russian, so I didn't learn a lot. There were, however, lots of weapons around—a fuckload of weapons, to be more precise—and not just in the pictures. Some leaned against the wall like farm tools in a barn; some, as with the throwing stars, had been hung on stick-up hooks from the hardware store. A few more rolled mats and many more sharp things lay strewn around the room. I saw long throwing axes and machete-length knives and even baling hooks, as if these nice young women sometimes liked to load and unload hay. More mats stood rolled up along the walls, and I realized that they probably kept the floor clear for sparring.

Halyna came out with three glasses of milky tea and set them down on the table along with a plate that contained what I swear was a McDonald's apple pie cut into three pieces. They were rolling out the red carpet for me.

Oxana came back. She was at least as attractive as Halyna, but I thanked the Highest that she was still in the baggy tracksuit she'd worn to my door. A guy can only take so much before his mind starts wandering into non-helpful avenues.

"Okay," said Oxana as Halyna set out the tea glasses. "You are probably with questions."

"Yes, I am probably with questions. What was that thing, how did you know silver would kill it, and who the hell are you two?"

Oxana took a piece of the apple pie and ate it quickly enough to suggest she was actually hungry, which—after finally meeting the thing that had apparently been crawling around my apartment lately, was not so true of me. She licked her fingers carefully before answering. "It called Nightmare Children. Silver not kill it, but does back-sending it."

"Back sending?"

"Send it back," explained Halyna. "To the place it is coming from." She had better English than her roommate. "To the dark place."

"Keep going," I said. "Who are you?" I swept my hand around the room, indicating the mini-armory they had assembled. "What's all this for?"

"Protect," said Oxana. "We protect."

"Who? From what?"

"From enemies. Protect what they would destruct."

"We are Scythians, you see," said Halyna, more than a little proudly, as if that explained everything. I didn't even recognize the word at first—she pronounced it *Skeet-ee-ahns*. "Also some are calling us Amazons. They were our ancestors."

Click! Finally, something made sense.

"Amazons—Scythians." I nodded. Foxy Foxy had said something about that, I remembered. "You were at the auction for the feather, weren't you? At Islanders Hall?"

Halyna shook her head and blew on her tea. "No. Those were sisters of ours, but they have gone back to Ukraine. Now our turn to be watchers. To be protectors."

I tried my own tea. It was a little sweeter than I liked, but after the night and morning I'd had it was quite acceptable, thank you. "Begin from the beginning," I said. "Why are you Amazons, exactly?"

It took a while to get the story, because Oxana's English was a bit confusing and both women were prone to introducing bits of Scythian philosophy whenever possible. The upshot was that a group of Ukrainian women, including these two, traced their history back to the Amazons of the Greek myths, who—they told me—had been one of the Scythian tribes of Asia Minor back before Christ became Flavor of the Millennium. The ancient Amazons, Halyna and Oxana assured me, had been women warriors who rode beside the men into battle, and were buried with their weapons when they fell. Halyna and Oxana's Amazons, however, were a modern day cult of sorts (my word, not theirs) who had developed an entire code of life, were obsessive about self-defense and martial arts, and whose Amazon-ism was all wrapped up with Ukrainian nationalism and religion and a complicated dislike of Russia—*and* to my surprise, an even more profound dislike of Persia. Not Iran, the present-day version—it's pretty damn easy to find people who don't like Iran—but Persia, like the Persian Empire. Like, way more than two thousand years ago.

"But it doesn't exist anymore," I pointed out.

"Not true," said Halyna. "Some bad parts is . . . are very much alive."

They told me about the Scythian way of life—compounds in the forests of the Carpathian Mountains south of Lviv that were half summer camp, half bunker, with no men to distract from the intensive schooling and training.

"Training for what?" I asked. "And how did you know about the whatever-it-was, that *swasti-kid*?" My nickname for the hairy horror with children's hands puzzled them. "Sorry, what did you call it? Nightmare . . . ?"

"Nightmare Children," said Halyna. "We know because we have fought with them before. They are favorite tool for work of the Black Sun."

Click! Click! Second thing that made sense. "And how do you know the Black Sun? They're not Ukrainian, are they? I thought they were American."

"They are from many places," said Halyna. "And they are wanting Anahita's treasure. We want to take it for us instead. They will use it for bad things. We will not."

Anaita. Click, click, click. The whole thing now actually began to come together, at least in a welcome-to-my-world sort of way. Unfortunately, since Anaita's treasure was Eligor's horn, these Amazons and I wanted to get hold of the same thing. And apparently so did the Black Sun Faction and their thugs and their unpleasant, faceless hand-spiders. But I needed that horn to get Caz back. I couldn't let anyone get in the way of that. "Really? Anahita's treasure, huh?" So these Amazons knew about it, too. Had I been the last to figure it out, or had my initial guess somehow tipped off everyone else? "And what will you use it for?"

"For destroy her," said Oxana. She didn't sound like she was kidding.

"Okay," I said. "We *do* have a few things to talk about, don't we?"

Later, after they had given me a bit more background about themselves and what they knew about the Black Sun, I asked them, "So how long have you two been living here in this building? Have you been watching me long?"

"Watching you?" said Halyna. She frowned. "No, watching *for* you. To make sure they did not take the treasure from you."

"But I don't have it."

"Now we know," said Oxana. She was eyeing the last, uneaten piece of the apple pie. "Not know when we start."

"Four weeks ago," Halyna explained. "Some people move out, apartment is open. We come in then, tell manager of apartment we are waitresses. Waitresses come in and out, all time, late hours all normal, you see? Nobody notice."

I waved to Oxana to eat my share of the pie. She did, quickly, as if worried I might change my mind. "I noticed you two," I said, "but I certainly wouldn't have guessed you were anything more unusual than foreign. But if you were throwing this stuff around in here, all these weapons and weights, sparring and spear-fighting and whatnot, I'm surprised your neighbors didn't have a fit. The people in the apartment above me bang on the floor every time I make a noise." Although they hadn't made a peep today while I was chasing the swastikid all around the place, knocking over furniture, which was a bit odd.

Halyna looked puzzled. "Nobody is above you."

"What do you mean? Jeez, I've heard them pounding away up there like Max Roach having a seizure."

She shook her head. "Nobody. We ask manager because we think it will be best place to listen, maybe." Here she actually blushed a little, only visible because her skin was so pale. "Maybe put a listening machine. Device. You know. But manager say empty, yes, but going to be painted soon, nobody rent."

"Nobody come in since then," Oxana said. "We watch everything so close."

"We're talking about the same apartment? The one directly above mine?"

They both nodded. I wondered for a moment if painters, who in my experience usually had loud boomboxes playing Lynyrd Skynyrd and liked to play catch with aluminum ladders, would knock on the floor to complain about noise below. I suddenly had a bad feeling.

"Wait here," I said. "I'm going to my apartment to get something. Back in a minute."

I went home and picked up my lock-picking tools, my gun, and of course my phone, because in my business an obscenely early hour of the morning is no defense against the call of duty, or more specifically, the call of Alice. Then I invited the Amazons to come upstairs with me. Halyna clothed herself in jeans and a jacket, which made it a lot easier for me to concentrate. We went quietly up the stairs—nobody else seemed to be awake yet—and I put my ear to the door of the apartment just above mine, third floor, second apartment from the stairwell. Nothing. I knocked, and we waited. Still nothing, but I thought the echo had a slightly hollow sound. So I went to work.

Twenty-five seconds later or so—most apartment locks are absolute shit—I carefully pushed open the door while standing with the Amazons to one side in case somebody started shooting. Still nothing but silence, so I ducked my head and went in, gun in hand.

It was silent but for the buzzing of flies, and it smelled like death—not the recent kind, salty with spilled human fluids, but like an unplugged refrigerator someone forgot to empty. It was also dark. The light switch didn't work, but there was enough gray dawn light leaking in through the blinds to show that the apartment was indeed empty. I could, however, see a few signs of recent occupation. Apparently the last tenants had been a family. Either the Mansons or the Addamses, to be specific.

The beige walls were scrawled with painted symbols—I hoped it was paint, but a lot of it looked like dried blood. None were in any language or alphabet I recognized. The carpet had been cut to ribbons and folded back, and someone had made a kind of campfire out of an iron pot set in the middle of the room. Ashes and pieces of burnt wood still half-filled it, and the pot itself sat at the middle of a crude version of the Black Sun symbol, drawn on the wooden floor with what looked like smears of gleaming fat. The flies that had risen into the air at our entrance now settled back down onto the sticky scrawl and continued with the business of being flies.

Oxana was holding her nose. Halyna had pulled the neck of her t-shirt up over hers. "Foo!" said Oxana. "Very bad!"

"You damn bet this is very bad. These fuckers have been living right over me, probably since before you moved in. No wonder my apartment is haunted!"

As we stared at the ghastly scene something vibrated my pocket. I looked at my phone. It was Alice. "I have to take this," I said and stepped into the hall.

It was a client, of course. Heart attack at a gym over in Mayfield.

"Sorry," I told the women. "I have to go. Business. We'll talk later, right? Tonight?"

Halyna and Oxana nodded. They were looking at the wall inscriptions with carefully noncommittal expressions, but Oxana was still holding her nose.

"Just close this apartment up and stay away. And please don't move out of your place before I get back, okay? We still have a lot to talk about."

"This was meant to send death," said Halyna, frowning. She kneeled beside the iron pot, then lifted out one of the chunks of pale, burnt wood. "This not wood. This is a bone. Children's bone. They try to kill you."

"Then they're going to have to send more than one inky-dinky spider," I said. But I wished she hadn't told me. Because I was pretty sure she was right.

On the way out I called somebody I knew to send over a cleanup crew, the kind of angels who make unpleasant messes disappear. There was no way I was coming back to my apartment knowing all of that was still spoiling in an empty room upstairs.

It's pretty depressing dealing with a forty-something guy who just keeled over dead on the elliptical machine, leaving behind a wife and kids he loves, even if he gets a heavenly invitation at the end of it. I mean, I know that's good, but even if his family believes in an afterlife, they're still going to miss him. Anyway, the job kept me occupied until later in the morning, at which point I grabbed some breakfast at a coffee shop and drove around for a while, trying to figure out what to do now. This new stuff was crazier than the old stuff, and the old stuff had already been pretty crazy. Neo-Nazis sending headless spiders with children's hands after me. Angels who were ancient goddesses and still the subject of grudges thousands of years old. Real live Amazons. I mean, if weird was money, I'd be Bobby Million Bucks, not just plain old Dollar.

The Black Sun wouldn't come back, of course, at least not to that room, especially since the cleanup crew had been and gone while I was out. I took a brief, nose-clamped look just to check, but the place looked clean and ready for occupation. I unclamped. It smelled like it had just been painted. Yes, some of Heaven's employees are a lot faster and more efficient than Yours Truly. Still, when I let myself into my own place, I couldn't help feeling like I could still smell decay from upstairs wafting through my air vents. I also knew there were going to be questions from Heaven about what the cleaners had been getting rid of, and why I knew about it.

But I couldn't deal with any of that stuff right at that moment, because I was stressed and completely exhausted from lack of sleep. I righted the upended furniture and cleared away some old socks and empty cans and bottles at the same time—a frenzy of cleaning that lasted at least a minute and a half. Then I stretched out on the couch, put on some quiet music to cover the midday noises from the street, and let myself get tugged down into unconsciousness.

And yes, the chain was on the front door again, the panel in the closet had been nailed back into place, and my gun was very, very close to my hand.

*   *   *

I woke up because somebody was knocking at my door. It could have been Girl Scouts with my seasonal Thin Mint assortment, or Amazon Scouts with more fast-food pies, or even Black Sun Scouts with a shipment of Blood Libel Mallomars, so I checked the spyhole before opening.

It was Clarence. Since he was one of the few people I didn't think wanted to destroy me at the moment, I let him in.

"Hi, Bobby," was his unambitious opening.

"Hi, yourself, Junior. What the hell are you doing here?"

"Hey, that's nice. I drop by to see you and that's what I get?"

"The only times you've ever come to see me is with Sam. Is Sam with you?"

He shrugged. "No."

"Then why are you here?" It came out more unpleasant than I'd wanted. I was losing patience with visitors, known and unknown, and I was still stupid and cranky and felt like I'd barely slept. I looked at the clock—past 5:30 in the afternoon. Getting dark soon. Maybe it was time to rise up after all. "Sorry, it's been a tough day. Come on in. Can I get you something to drink?"

He stepped in, but not too far in. He'd seen the place before, so it wasn't disgust keeping him out, and in fact it looked better than usual after the tidying. "I can't really stay, Bobby. I just wanted to see how you were doing. You haven't been down to the Compasses lately. Did you know about—?"

"Walter Sanders," I said, cutting him off. "Yeah. And he doesn't remember anything useful." Clarence knew some of the story about Walter, like the fact he'd probably been stabbed by someone who wanted to get me, but he didn't know I'd seen Walter in Hell, or that I was now convinced that Anaita had arranged it. Until I knew for certain who among my angelic comrades was really working for whom, I was keeping a lot of this stuff to myself. "What about a drink? I have milk. Still liquid, even."

Clarence made a face, but he still didn't come all the way in. "Really, I can't . . ." The kid seemed a bit nervous, actually. "My ride is waiting downstairs. I just wanted to say hi."

Before I could respond to this preposterous statement—who would come all the way to my apartment and walk up the stairs just to say hi? To *me?*—a car horn honked outside. Wondering if it really was Sam and this was some elaborate maneuver to trick me into going out, I went to the window, unlatched it, and leaned out. There was a fairly pricey-looking recent model car double-parked in front of the building. (I had no idea what kind of car it was. That's my gripe with the modern ones, they all look the same—like running shoes for giant robots, every damn one of them.) The person standing next to it, who had presumably leaned in to honk the horn, saw me and waved. He was vaguely familiar, good-looking, blond, and wearing what looked like an expensive cable-knit sweater.

"Oh, hi!" he called up. "You must be Bobby. Can you tell Harrison to hurry, please? We're already late for our reservation."

"Harrison" was Clarence's official earthly name, short for Haraheliel. His co-workers just called him Clarence because we were jerks.

I smiled, sort of, and nodded to the man before withdrawing. I did not wave. I never wave.

"Harrison?" I said. "Your ride wants me to tell you . . ."

"I heard." He was scowling like a scolded child, but there was something else going on, too.

"Who is that, anyway? I feel like I've seen him somewhere."

"That's Wendell. He's one of us—an angel, I mean, an advocate. He works up in San Francisco, mostly around Cow Hollow and Dogpatch." Now the kid actually colored, reddening from cheeks to forehead. "We're kind of seeing each other."

"Okay." I didn't know what else to say. You think with an afterlife as fucked-up as mine that I have any inclination to judge anyone else's? Hell, I don't even have the *time* to judge anyone else. "But I wish you wouldn't have brought him here."

"Bobby, I told you—he's one of us!" He stopped, and I could see him going pale, the beginnings of anger. "Or are you trying to say something else?"

"Shit, kid, I don't care if you date buckaroos or kangaroos. But I don't like everyone knowing where I live, even if they're on our side. Shit, *especially* if they're on our side. I can't really trust anyone right now, and it's been a bad couple of days."

"Really?" Now he felt bad for me, which made me want to hit myself in the face, but someone else had already done that. "I noticed the bruises and cuts. What happened?"

"Look, don't keep your friend waiting. We'll get together, and I'll tell you about it, but not tonight."

Eventually I persuaded him to go back and join Wendell and his stylish sweater, but even after everything else that had happened to me recently, it still felt a little strange. Clarence had never come to my place on his own before. Was it really that important to let me know he was gay? I'd already half-guessed. Or was something else going on?

Great, I thought. *Now I don't even trust the guys who I'm going to have to take into battle with me.* And that was bad, because I was pretty certain into battle was just where I was going—and soon.

twelve

melted frog seeks melted mate

I HAD ONE more client after Clarence left, a woman who breathed her last in a hospice in the hills, a peaceful exit after a long struggle with cancer, and although there were a few issues with the woman's past, the prosecutor could deliver nothing serious enough to keep her from reaching the bosom of Abraham (or whatever exactly it is we help people reach).

Honestly, I wish I did have more answers for you. I wish I knew more about how things work. That would make a much more informative story, especially for those with a theological turn of mind. But I don't. I'm an ordinary angel—a grunt. There are lots of us. Some of us live on Earth and wear mortal bodies and try to defend people's souls against the lies (and sometimes unpleasant truths) of Hell. Beyond that, I just don't know much. I mean, I regularly see the joyful saved both in Heaven itself and the Fields outside, but I can never get a clue to what they're thinking and feeling: it's like trying to talk to one of the people working at a theme park when they're in character.

When I got home from the job, I put on some music, opened a beer, and began studying a bunch of information Fatback aka George had sent me. Nothing in the material was all that startling, but my porcine pal's covering email provided some unwelcome news:

Bobby, here's a bit more on the B. Sun and a lot of material about Persia. Honestly, I could dump hundreds and hundreds of articles on you about

Persians in the Bay Area, but I'm trying to weed out the stuff you don't need. If I'm getting it wrong, let me know.

You'll have to do it by email, because I'm going out of town. I can't take this place anymore, I don't know what's going on, it's like living in that Amityville movie, so I had Javier and his sons clean out the trailer and they're going to take me to go see this special vet I know near Visalia, where I can lie low. I'll only have my portable equipment, but I can still help you out if you need it. But I just can't stay here. I'll be back in a week or so, I think.

So even the swine were starting to desert the sinking ship. Not that I blamed George at all, after having seen one of the things that was actually haunting my place, but I was beginning to get a bit paranoid. First, dancing nature spirit Foxy Foxy wouldn't talk to me. Now George had been chased off to some luxury pig spa in Tulare County. Even Clarence the Junior Angel was acting a little loopy. What next? It's not like I had a lot of friends in the first place.

There wasn't too much new stuff in the Black Sun files George had sent, just more bits and pieces about what was turning out to be an ugly organization even without the neo-fascist politics. Everybody seemed to agree that they were one of the "New Nationalist" organizations, but their membership seemed to come from many different nations, and they seemed to get nationalistic only about countries with a lot of white people in them. The local Black Sun Faction was predominantly American, with ties to the Aryan Brotherhood prison gangs, but a Norwegian guy named Baldur von Reinmann was one of the up and coming leaders of the American branch.

Baldur wasn't the guy in charge of the whole Black Sun, though. Even Fatback's multiple sources couldn't agree on who that was. The most they could come up with was that some shadowy guy who called himself "The Imperator" had been the power behind the organization since the fifties, which made him pretty damn old.

I also found suggestions in George's material (because, remember, he fishes in some weird backwaters) about the Black Sun's distinctly dark-magic interests, and even a couple of vague references to the swastikids (or "Nightmare Children" as everyone else seemed to call them, despite my name being better). Some sources went so far as to suggest that the N.C. were not the worst critters the Imperator and his friends might employ on "traitors, unbelievers, and other mongrel-loving scum," as one charmer—his online name was "Hammer of the Jews"—posted on an obscure racist message board. These were only rumors, of course, and to my irritation not a single one seemed to suggest anything about what to do when an infestation of swastikids hit your apartment. Killing them one by one with a silver knife, as Oxana had done, was appealing but seemed like it could get pretty tiring.

Enough with the neo-Nazis and their ugly little allies. I moved on to the Persian stuff, quickly grasping why George was frustrated with such broad parameters, but I did learn a few things about Persian-Americans. They were also called Iranian-Americans, but a lot of them preferred the first, not only because it separated them from the current Iranian government but also because it underlined their ethnic pride. Not everyone in modern Iran is Persian, see? The US has the most Persians anywhere outside of Iran, and now your history lesson is done. Oh, except that many, if not most of them, came into the US in the early 1980s when the Ayatollah and his crazy Islamic fanboys took over.

But most of what George had sent me was even less informative, primarily social news about various civic functions highlighting Persian-Americans. Occasionally a crime or some other big news threw a spotlight on some facet of the community that didn't get discussed much, but mostly it was a parade of difficult Middle-Eastern names without much context and therefore without much use. I did see a few names crop up over and over again and decided that what I needed to do was pick an arbitrary date, probably 1980, and look for names that came up again and again after that point. I could do some of that on my own, but I was going to have to hope George could manage some of it while he was getting his Swedish back-bacon massages and sea-weed trotter-wraps, or whatever this special pig doctor did to make him feel fresh and happy.

I wandered out to get dinner and bring back another six-pack. When I returned to the apartment house it was getting dark. The Amazons had left a note on my door that said, "We go out but we call you later," which was nice of them.

A check around my place with a flashlight found nothing swastika-like hiding in any of the corners and the loose board in the closet still firmly nailed into place. (And backed-up with about fifty feet of duct tape, just for added certainty. Those four-armed crawlers might be able to travel the dark dimensions, but I felt sure even they were no match for enough duct tape.)

I needed to share these new wrinkles with Sam, so I called and left a message and hoped he'd be back from the Third Way soon. Then I watched a bit of a Warriors game, but the basketball season was too young for me to care a lot, and there were too many new players this year I didn't know very well. Propped up on the couch, the TV rattling away in the background, I found myself getting sleepy and let myself drift.

Yes, I had my Belgian automatic right next to me. Loaded with silver slugs, too. I'm casual, but I'm not entirely stupid.

I woke up to that sound again—not the quiet scrape of creepy little children's fingers in a closet, but the thump-thumpity-thumpty-thump of something bouncing haphazardly against my window.

It was a different window this time, in the bathroom, and it was hard to reach because I had to half-lean on the sink while standing on the edge of the tub. The glass was that kind you can only see through a little, like a bunch of little round funhouse mirrors, so I couldn't make out what was out there, except it looked about the size of a sparrow, but it certainly had the same disturbing habit of going *thump, thump, thump*. There was no way I could get the window open fast enough to lean out and grab anything that wasn't already both extremely stupid and bleeding to death, but I eased up the window a few inches—the bumping stopped—and then turned off the bathroom light and re-treated to sit on the closed toilet seat with my toothbrush glass in my hand.

Whatever-it-was came back a few minutes later and began bumping again, this time on the upper part of the window. I waited as patiently as I could, and considering the thing couldn't have been much larger than a finger puppet, while I was full size and combat-trained, I was surprisingly nervous. Because it wasn't natural, see. I know that sounds odd coming from an angel, especially one who's been to Hell, but you don't expect anything in Hell to be normal. In your own apartment, you expect normal. You *need* normal. So I sat there and tried to keep my breathing even, and eventually the thing bumbled its way down the window and then flopped onto the windowsill where it bounced around for a moment, wings buzzing. It was no bird, or bug, that was for sure—even in the dim bathroom I could see that it was too big to be an insect, and its wings were too small for a bird. I waited until it had bumped along a few inches, then I shot up from the toilet seat and clapped the glass over it.

It didn't even fight, that was the strange bit. A bee, a wasp, you put a glass over them and they get angry. This thing just kept diddling along, as though its mission in life was to bump against glass, but whether inside it or outside it didn't matter much.

I got up and flicked on the light. If I'd been hoping it was a crippled bird, I was disappointed. It wasn't a bug either—I'd been right about that. But even in the bright light from above the medicine cabinet, I still didn't know what exactly it was. Except that it was extremely and obviously *wrong*.

Quick description: Imagine a small frog. Now imagine that frog owed money to the Mob, so they took it out back and gave it a severe beating, deforming its face so that it almost looked like a tiny, ugly dwarf, and also breaking several of its bones that later healed back crooked. Now imagine the frog instead of being a healthy shade of green or even brown was mostly gray and blue and extremely slimy. Oh, and don't forget the dragonfly wings in a lovely shade of translucent crimson, and the three eyes, also red, glowing like the LEDs on your DVR.

I stared at the thing I'd caught for a long time, wondering if I should just go find a hammer and beat it to jelly. It clearly didn't belong on Earth, but if it was some kind of spy or assassin creature sent by the Black Sun, they seemed to have chosen badly. After throwing itself against the inside of the glass for a while, it just squatted and let its wings curl. Its mouth moved oddly, as though it was having trouble breathing, and it occurred to me I could just let it suffocate, or even hasten the process by sticking a lighted candle in there or something. Yes, I know that sounds cowardly, but if you'd seen it you wouldn't have wanted to touch it either, even to kill it. Trust me—you'd have moved out of the apartment and called in an airstrike. I mean, it was *ugly.*

At last I got a round chunk of cardboard that had most recently been part of the packing for a frozen pizza, then slid it carefully under the glass. The thing didn't really have feet, more like a pair of mushroom stems that might have been made from slug-muscle, but it didn't seem too bothered by the cardboard and just stepped up onto it as it slid underneath. Then I took the whole weird package to the living room.

I put a heavy book on top of the glass, then went to see if the Scythians were back and could identify it as one of the Black Sun's special friends, but they were still out, although it was now almost ten at night. I went back to my place, half hoping that the thing had knocked over the glass and managed to escape the apartment so I wouldn't have to deal with it, but the horrid little lump was still sitting on my cheap coffee table, staring back at me with three eyes' worth of incomprehension. I'll say this, it didn't seem particularly malicious, but even if it had been wearing the face of a famous Hollywood star, it wasn't going to get many dates.

It was making the mouth movements again, which made it look more than ever like something crooning invitations across a dark swamp—melted frog seeking melted mate. Taking pity, I lifted the bottom of the glass just a little to let in some air, and when I did so, I heard something thin and squeaky coming from inside the glass.

Words. I swear by the Highest, actual words. In English. I could make out only one, "*revenge*," but that was enough.

What the hell *was* this thing?

I went to the kitchen and rummaged around until I found the strainer I'd used the last time I cooked anything for myself, which had been spaghetti. The answer to your next question is: Probably about fourteen months earlier. I brought the strainer out, put it over the glass, then rattled the whole thing until the glass tipped over.

It certainly didn't hurry, but eventually the flying frog-thing bumbled out of the sideways glass into the larger enclosure of the strainer. It settled its grotesque little body again, blinked all three eyes, and said, "*Dearest, dearest Bobby . . .*"

thirteen
the great dictator

WHEN I heard that ugly little creature say my name, I jumped
back about three feet, then threw my jacket over the whole mess,
the strainer and the upended glass and the nasty little blob itself. I
could still hear its tiny, whiny voice under the jacket. My heart beat so
hard it felt like it was going to break my rib cage. No, not just because
an ugly little Hell-bug was sitting on my coffee table and knew my
name. I was freaking right out because despite its high-pitched, ragged
tones, an odd combination of helium and horseradish, the cadence and
the phrasing were all too familiar. The voice belonged to Caz.

A moment later, and almost as shocking and sudden as that recognition, I suddenly wondered if this was somehow my Countess of Cold
Hands herself, escaped from Hell after being punished by Eligor. I jerked
the jacket away. The thing was still droning on. If it was Caz, she sounded
like an answering machine message that was starting to wear out.

"... *hope you've stopped shouting at this thing by now. It's not me,*" the
little horror was saying. "*It's a nizzic, a minor demon—a message carrier.
Don't worry how I got hold of it, or how it got out of Hell to reach you. Now,
if you got yourself that drink I suggested, sit down and get comfortable. I need
to tell you several things.*"

I was too stunned to do anything but slump onto the couch and
stare at the winged gob of phlegm as it parroted back the message my
beloved had somehow taught it.

*   *   *

"The first is that I lied to you. Don't feel bad, I lied to myself, too. It's only now that I know you're safely out of Hell that I can tell you that whatever you wish to call it—need, obsession, insane attraction, love—well, I also feel it, Bobby. I have since the first. But everything else I said is true. It doesn't matter what we feel, because everything else is against us. And I mean everything. I won't torment you with thoughts of what could be, because they can't. But I won't cheat you out of the most important part any more. Whatever it is you're feeling, Bobby, I feel it, too. I cannot imagine not seeing you again. But that's exactly how it has to be.

"Eligor is finally satisfied. His cruel trick worked. He got the feather back, he made you suffer, he made me suffer and even had the extra pleasure of making Marmora, the drowned girl, suffer as well. But knowing you, you're determined to get some kind of revenge.

"You must forget about it. As things stand, he'll probably leave you alone now. You can't hope to survive his full attention again. But I will survive, Bobby. I will go on. I am not some mortal woman, some comparative child, who cannot live with pain and difficulty. I will survive. I shared the best moments of my life and myself with you. That will keep me during the times ahead.

"I love you. There. I'm sorry I never said it to your face. Now, please, forget me."

When it finished reciting, the nizzic sat there slowly, blinking all its eyes but otherwise motionless as a lump of particularly dirty wax or a dead mouse that had been under the couch a long, long time. After a few moments it started over again from the beginning of the message in the same disturbing, not-quite-Caz voice. I listened to the bits I'd missed when I'd covered it with my jacket, none of them particularly important (except that they were more words from the woman I loved and who I sometimes thought I'd never hear or see again, and so each was as precious as a diamond). But as it got back onto the part I'd already heard, I decided I'd had enough. It was like listening to Caz down an old-fashioned long-distance line as she demonstrated the effect of multiple strokes on human speech. I threw my jacket over the little horror again.

But even though a part of me was grateful (no, ecstatic) to hear from Caz, and thrilled by the substance of the message—she did love me! She did!—I was also feeling a slow burn that was beginning to heat up.

It was Eligor's name that started it, or rather it was the way Caz had suggested that now was a good time to slink off into the undergrowth so Eligor the Horseman would forget all about me.

He was in a good mood, she said. The monster who had tortured both Caz and me, not to mention brought untold horror to human lives for countless thousands of years, was in a good mood. Yeah, that cheered me right up. And if I was really, really lucky, he was bored with torturing and humiliating me. I mean, yeah, he was still holding prisoner the woman I loved, probably raping and tormenting her, but I wasn't supposed to dwell on that.

I'd thought for a long time that there would be nothing higher on my bucket list than squeezing the black, sticky blood out of the Grand Duke of Hell's black, sticky heart, and that was still true. If I had been given a choice at that moment between destroying him and destroying Anaita, even if it meant she'd get me for sure . . . well, there would have been no contest. Eligor was an obscenity. The entire universe would benefit from his sudden and hopefully violent retirement.

But Eligor didn't matter right now, because there was literally nothing I could do about him. I'd already made my way through Hell once, suffered hideously, and found that, just as I'd suspected, I couldn't stand up to him for even a second. And I'd paid for that stupid decision with more hours of horrifying pain than any being could suffer anywhere else in the universe and still be able to renew his magazine subscriptions. But what mattered was that the bastard still had Caz. Anaita had Eligor's horn, and I didn't have a chance of getting her without it. I'd failed with the feather, but I knew Eligor would swap my beautiful Countess for the horn without a moment's hesitation, because it would lift a big weight of concern for him. Without the horn, nobody in Heaven *or* Hell could ever prove that he'd made a deal with an angel. He might not give a shit about Bobby Dollar, but he was scared to hand any advantage to the other Hell-lords, fat slug Prince Sitri and Grand President Caym and the rest.

So despite the craziness, the joy, and the bitterness that were all burning through me after hearing Caz's voice, nothing had actually changed. My only hope for a happy life—shit, probably my only hope for life, period—was to get that horn somehow and then force Eligor to give her back to me.

I went and fixed myself that drink Caz had suggested. I could hear the winged snotbag muttering away underneath my jacket, and it occurred to me that I might be able to use the same creature to send a message back to her. I had no idea if it would actually work, but as someone once said, *Fortune favors the brave.* Sam usually added, *"And stomps on the stupid,"* but I don't think that's entirely true. I've done all right so far, and nobody's ever called me smart without tacking "-ass" onto the end.

I polished off the vodka-tonic pretty quick, then lifted the jacket. The nasty little thing was trying to fly again but of course not succeeding much, just bumbling around against the metal cage of the strainer while repeating its message like a broken toy. I lifted the strainer and reached in, and was surprised by how hot the thing was, like Silly Putty sauteed in butter. I dropped it, almost sucked my fingers until I realized what I'd be putting in my mouth, then grabbed a kitchen towel and tried again.

"...Don't worry how..." it was saying as I lifted it up, but it was squirming a bit, too.

"Shut up," I explained, and gave it a nasty squeeze, but not so roughly that it would pop or anything.

"...Got out of Hell..." it said quietly. I squeezed it again, harder.

"Shut *up*, you flying turd!"

After a few rounds of this merry game, the little blotch finally got the hint and stopped muttering Caz's message. It sat in the towel, three red eyes staring at me, looking like something that a dog had eaten and then put back into play. I leaned in close to feel the heat coming off it. *"I'm going to get you out,"* I said as slowly and clearly as I could. *"Pack a suitcase. I don't know how long it will take, but I am going to get you out. I swear by the Highest."*

The nizzic stared at me, but I had clearly convinced it not to make any noise at all. I gave it the message again, this time with another squeeze, then again and again. After about the fifth time it goggled its eyes, opened its mouth, but instead of repeating what I said, it let out a belch like the tiniest corpse-fart you can imagine. It was still enough to make me lean back, eyes watering.

"All right, you little fuckstick," I said. "You want to play with the big boys? You want to step to me?" I wrapped it in the towel like putting Frances Farmer in a straitjacket, then carried it into the kitchen. "Last chance. Repeat after me. *I'm going to get you out...*" But the nizzic only looked at me without a glimmer of understanding, like the world's smallest complaints department employee, so I opened my refrigerator and shoved it into the freezer, towel and all, and went back to pour myself a second drink.

Five minutes later I opened the freezer door. The thing was lying on its back, gasping like a landed fish, and something steaming hot was running out of its mouth and earholes and nostril slits. I held it while it shivered and crawled around in circles on my hand—it was much easier to hold now—and then gave it the message again.

It didn't do anything useful, so I put it back in the freezer.

This process went on for about an hour. I put the sports news on the television and tried to make myself relax, but it didn't work. Too many crazy things had been happening lately—armed Amazons, weird warnings, Dear John snotgoblin messages from the woman I loved, not to mention Nazi thugs and demonic arm-spiders, all shoving to get onto my calendar. I was tired, confused, and mad as hell. I was *pissed off*.

After I took it out for maybe the fourth time, the nizzic seemed to be getting the picture. It lay panting in my hand, sucking back in the hot liquids it had sweated out in an attempt to keep itself from freezing, and when I tried my message again it actually opened its mouth and croaked, *"I'm going . . . I'm going . . . I'm going . . ."* I thought it was just being melodramatic until I realized those were the first two words of my message.

That was all it would give me, though, so I shot it a stern look. "Any man don't keep order gets a night in the box," I warned, then I shoved it back in the freezer, but I didn't leave it in too long this time.

I had downed maybe four vodkas by the time the turdball finally managed to repeat the whole message to me. I'm sure Caz had some better way to program the ugly bastard, but we all make do with what we have, and I was determined to let her know not only that I had heard the message, but that it didn't change anything important. I was a little wobbly on my feet—I haven't been drinking that much lately, as I think I said—but feeling more than a bit triumphant when someone knocked on the door.

I wrapped the towel around the flying hobgoblin so I could peek out and see who it was, then opened the door. Sam walked in. He looked me up and down and said, "You look weird. What's that in your hand?"

I looked down at the squirming kitchen towel. "Hang on," I said. "I'm almost finished here." I opened the towel and the nizzic sat up, still shivering, its wings like crumpled cellophane. "What do you say, you ugly little fartsparrow? What do you say?"

"I think you need professional help more than you need a new pet, but I'm glad you're trying to give your life meaning," said Sam.

"Shut up," I told him. "Any man talking loud gets a night in the box."

"Oh, lord, it's the *Cool Hand Luke* thing." Sam shook his head and stared at the nizzic. "What *is* that?"

"Hold on. Like I said, I'm almost done." I made the tiny monstrosity repeat the entire message through without mistakes, then took it to the window and stuck my hand out. It sat there on my palm for a moment, then spread its wings and buzzed off in awkward circles like a dangerously overloaded helicopter.

"So this is how you spend your evenings now?" Sam asked. "Professing your undying love to random snotbugs?"

" 'S not a snotbug," I said grumpily, then laughed. " 'S not. Snot. No, 'sa snot*goblin*. Incredibly huge difference."

"Shit, B, how many drinks have you had?"

"Hardly any. Four. Maybe seven or eight if you count beers. Doesn't matter. That was from Caz. She sent me a message."

"And spared no expense, clearly. Whatta gal!"

"You . . . are an asshole." I knew there was something I wanted to talk to Sam about, but damned if I could remember. Actually, I realized, I was pretty much damned no matter what. I laughed again.

"Coffee," he said. "You'll still be an idiot, but you'll be an alert idiot." He helped me up and kept a firm grasp on my elbow as we went down the stairs to his car, one of his usual selection of ultra-boring rides. Sam always drives cars that look like the government gave them to him. Not the CIA-sniper-rifle, high-tech government, either. I mean he drives shit that makes him look like he works for the post office or the Bureau of Prisons.

We wound up in a twenty-four hour joint down on the Camino Real at the edge of Spanishtown. After I'd had a couple of cups of coffee I began to feel like maybe life wasn't so bad after all, so I told Sam everything that had happened—Caz's nizzic, the Black Sun Faction and their swastikids, the Amazons, and even about my warning from

Temuel. Then the alcohol started to wear off and all I had was the caffeine. I was seriously wondering which of the other customers I should strangle to burn off some of my irritation with the world when Sam came back from a trip to the restroom.

"They say man proposes, God disposes," he told me, squeezing in behind the table. "But seems to me like I have to do most of the disposing. Man, I think I just pissed out several gallons in there. I'm serious. Like a racehorse."

"Not really interested," I told him.

"Actually, I've got something I need to tell you about." Sam checked his coffee, which had gone cold, and waved for our ancient waitress to freshen it up.

"What's that?" Maybe some food would help me, I decided. I was really jittery now. Maybe some pie.

"You asked me if you could come to Kainos."

"Kainos?"

"That's what we call the place. You know, the Third Way. You said you wanted to check it out."

"Hey, don't make it sound like I saw the light or something. This isn't a conversion, man, I just need to make a fact-finding trip."

"Well, that's the problem, B. You're not going to be making that trip. Things have changed."

"What does that mean?"

"That the operation has been shut down, more or less. Kephas just told us that we're not bringing in any more souls and that from now on there won't be anyone going in or out except for me and the others who've been helping—the rest of the Magians."

Magians was the name Sam's group of angels had taken in their quest to find suitable human subjects willing to risk their souls to join the Third Way after death. "So you're saying I can't get in?"

"I have no idea what kind of controls or whatever Kephas has, but I'm pretty sure you'd be noticed if you even tried, which would put me square in the crosshairs. Remember, Bobby, unlike you I don't have anywhere else to go if the shit hits the fan."

I felt weird, exhausted, and wired at the same time, and even if it wasn't making me feel cheerful anymore, I'm pretty sure the alcohol was still fucking with my judgement. I probably shouldn't have broached the subject, not then, not there, but I was beginning to feel I needed to know where everybody really stood—who was truly on my side.

"Sam, I gotta tell you something. I know who Kephas is. And you know what? It's your Kephas who's out to get me."

He just stared at me for a long time, then picked up his spoon and stirred his black coffee for another lengthy interval. "Talk," he said at last.

And I did. You have to remember, I'd been holding this in a long time, ever since the dead murderer Smyler told me that Kephas was *his* boss, too, and Walter Sanders passed along something that made me realize that Kephas was probably Anaita. I had to explain the whole thing to Sam, of course. I'd held back a lot from him, how I'd met Walter in Hell and the whole works, and it took a long time to bring him up to date. Meanwhile, Sam just sat and sipped a little coffee and said nothing at all, but I have to say the vibe he was putting out was not a harmonious one.

I was praying that when I finished he'd do something good, slap my shoulder and tell me he was with me to the end, or come up with some better explanation that made sense out of everything, but instead when I stopped talking he just kept looking at me for a few seconds, then said, "You done?"

I said I was.

"Good. Because I have to say that's the biggest bunch of horseshit I've ever heard, and I've been shoveling the stables of untruth for many, many years." He leaned back. "Look at you, Dollar. You're a fucking wreck. You're in love with a woman who was burned at the stake and admits herself she deserved it. You went to Hell for her, for Heaven's sake! You've pissed off one of the heaviest hitters on the Opposition, you got the Compasses torn to pieces because of it, and now you're trying to tell me that the thing I've worked on with all my heart for years is just some scam. In fact, you probably think it's just another plot to get you. Do you think I'm in on it too, Bobby? That because I kept some secrets, I'm your enemy? That I'm working with Kephas to get you?"

"No, Sam, don't be stupid . . . !"

"Stupid? Shit, don't just look at yourself, *listen* to yourself. You move every few weeks, you've got bullet holes in your apartment wall, you don't sleep, and you've got all your bosses pissed off at you, not to mention the hordes of Hell. But instead of just making a clean break and coming with me to Kainos, you've been determined all along to do it your own way. Well, old chum, I hate to tell you this, but your way sucks."

While I was still sitting there with my mouth hanging open like a gaffed fish, he stood up and threw a five on the table for his coffee, then tossed a twenty in front of me. "Get yourself a cab, man. I don't want to spend any more time with you right now. If you weren't covered in bruises I'd be tempted to take you outside and pop you one in the nose."

He took a couple of steps and then turned around. "I get it that you're miserable. I get it that you think the world is hopelessly fucked, both the human world and the world we live in. Shit, I more or less agree. But that doesn't mean I have to go down and roll in it with you. You may be right about some of it, even, but that doesn't mean you're right about all of it. And at the moment, I don't care about *any* of it."

"Sam, I'm sorry . . ."

"Tell me some other time, maybe I'll listen," he said, walking away. He was in such a mood that he accidentally dragged his coat across the plates of the two people sitting in the booth next to ours. Sam's big, though, and when he's angry only the suicidal would jump up and start something. They didn't even start talking about what a jerk he was until the glass door had closed behind him.

After he'd gone, I just sat staring at my coffee, watching it get cold. The waitress wandered by a couple of times and offered to freshen it up, but I just waved her away. I didn't want any more fucking coffee.

fourteen
other people's problems

I DIDN'T GET much sleep that night, but for once it wasn't because of bad dreams. I had the distinct feeling that a noose was being drawn tight around my neck, tighter by the day. I had one hope, and that was to find the horn and get it away from Anaita. But meanwhile I was losing friends and allies right and left.

I didn't think Sam was gone for good—not really. But I wasn't used to him being that pissed at me, and I still didn't know all the facts about his arrangement with Kephas. On top of it all, I still had a few trust issues with him. After all, he'd lied to me from the beginning about the Third Way, and that was something I hadn't believed could ever happen. Shit, maybe he'd known he was working for Anaita all this time. Maybe the bluster was all faked. I didn't even know how to think about that, it seemed so impossible.

But if I couldn't call on Sam, who did that leave for Team Bobby? Foxy Foxy had made it clear he wanted nothing to do with any of this—I believe the good old phrase "scared shitless" applied, if you could say that about a Japanese nature spirit. Clarence was a maybe, since he still hadn't entirely cleared himself after starting out his career as a spy and trying to arrest Sam. (Of course, I'd clocked him on the skull with a gun butt, so it wasn't like I'd been a great mentor, either.) George the Internet Pig was out in the Central Valley somewhere, the Sollyhull Sisters would have been out of their league completely, and the Broken Boy was more broken than usual after answering my last set of questions. Which left me what? Two Amazons I'd just met and my guns-and-cars supplier, Orban—in other words, two women who didn't speak great English yet and an immortal Hungarian who never would. Anyone else? Dr. Gustibus, but he was too weird an unknown to count on.

Of course, I'd almost forgotten my old friend G-Man, aka Garcia Windhover, the wannabe-gangsta idiot kid who thought he was one of my operatives. He'd do anything for me, despite his complete and utter lack of qualifications or even rudimentary intelligence. His English wasn't too good either, even though it was his first language. Sure, I could always bet my immortal soul on G-Man—or just shoot myself now.

I wrestled with some heavy questions that night, things that could affect not just my afterlife, but perhaps even the balance of Heaven and Hell. When at last I gave up on any really solid sleep and made myself some coffee, I had come to at least one major decision, something that scared me badly, but which had to be done.

It was time to sell my car.

"You are not serious."

It was always hard to tell with Orban whether he was asking a question, making a statement, or talking to someone else entirely, because he didn't make a lot of eye contact and was usually surrounded by bearded men who wanted his attention, a bit like Snow White during dwarf mating season, so I waited until the latest group of armament mechanics had eddied away. Orban repeated his earlier remark, which proved he'd been talking to me all along.

"Wish I wasn't," I said. "I love that car like an ordinary man loves his mother. More, because that car never gave me liverwurst for lunch or made me wear hand-me-downs to school. But I need the money, and I honestly don't know if I can ever drive it again without feeling like *America's Most Wanted*."

Orban walked with me to the garage, and pulled the tarp off my muscle car, my beloved AMC Matador Machine. The coppery paint job and the black and white checkerboard upholstery were so beautiful I almost cried.

"It is certainly an ugly fucker," he said, "but the engine runs like a dream. Nice, new four-oh-one."

"Don't remind me." Why did everyone have to talk shit about how my car looked? Didn't anyone in this town have any art in their souls? "I still owe you ten. How much you think you can get for it?"

"If I can find a blind man who likes to drive fast, maybe twenty-five total." He squinted at me and frowned, which made him look like an Eastern-European Popeye the Sailor. "How bad are things? If you really want to sell, I can give you another ten now if that will help."

"It would. It really would." I was already beginning to think strange, un-Bobbylike thoughts about holing up in the woods with a bunch of guns and growing a beard. (Or maybe getting a job with Orban, since that's how everybody he employed already looked.) But I definitely wanted liquid assets, and fast.

Because of his business, or more specifically his brand of customers, Orban was always handling cash, which was well known among the drug dealers and smash-and-grab robbers who tended to patronize him, both for guns and well-armored vehicles. But even so, nobody had ever tried to rob him. This probably says almost as much about Orban himself as about the dozens of well-armed guys who worked there and were pretty much on the premises all night and all day. Orban claimed he'd been the designer for the cannons at the siege of Constantinople. Don't bother to Google, I'll tell you—AD 1453. He might be nothing more than a formidable liar, but considering that my own girlfriend had been around that long, I was more willing than most to accept that as possible. He also claimed he had simply decided not to die, and that was why he hadn't. If you spent a half hour with him, especially if he was giving you one of those looks of his, you'd probably take his word for it like I did. He isn't a big man, but he has presence like a porcupine has sharp stuff.

In his office he counted me out a hundred Benjamins and I signed off on the pink slip. Then he broke out a bottle of wine, and we had a drink. Here's another Orban tip: never tell him the Hungarian stuff he drinks tastes like cow piss. He claims it's called Bull's Blood, but I think that's a translation error.

I promptly gave him a couple hundred back for his guys to paint the ancient Datsun I'd been driving for a while, another Orban special. I would have liked a fresh start and a new, never-seen car in case I had to disappear, but I settled for having the old car sprayed an unexciting black. I'd throw some dust on it when it dried.

While they were taking care of that, I wandered down the Salt Piers to a little burger joint and had a late breakfast. While I waited for my hash browns, sausage, and eggs, I went through Fatback's Persian stuff again, then emailed him with directions on narrowing the search. Seagulls fought loudly on the railing outside the window. It was hard not to imagine that the crows who came to pick my bones when Anaita was done with me might sound a little like that.

As I drove back across town, Sam's words were still stinging. Was he right? Was this all happening just because I was a stubborn asshole? I mean, nobody was arguing that I *wasn't* a stubborn asshole—I lost that debate a long time ago—but had I really brought this all on myself? After all, it was Sam who had first stuck the feather in my pocket (more or less—inside the pocket had actually been inside a different part of time) and got me into this mess. Not that I was holding it against him, since it had led to Caz. Of course it had also led to the giant Sumerian monster trying to kill me, and Eligor having a personal grudge against me, and me going to Hell. Actually, I *was* holding it against him. Bastard.

Even after an hour or more under the hot lights, the car's new paint job wouldn't really cure for a month or so, but it was already dried shiny, so I turned off on the way back and drove along a couple of sandy dirt roads I knew that ran near the bay. Yes, I was pitting the new paint, but "new" wasn't the point. "Different" was the point, along with "unremarkable." I had several important things to do and I wanted to avoid attention.

I had decided that no matter what Heaven thought about it, I had to get out of the Tierra Green Apartments. Too many bad things had found me there. I had already packed a suitcase earlier with all my most crucial stuff. I wasn't taking much with me, because I didn't want it obvious to either my enemies or my bosses that I had moved out, so I was leaving most of my crap in the old apartment. My new place? Well, let's just say I'd had an idea.

Once I got near downtown I called the cellphone number Halyna (the Red Amazon) had given me. I hadn't talked to them since the Night of the Swastikid, so I was surprised and pleased when she actually picked up. I told her I needed her and Oxana to meet me, told them where and what to bring, said I'd see them in an hour, then hung up.

Once again I was back in the middle of town with some time to kill, but I wasn't going anywhere near the Compasses, especially in the Datsun. If the place was being watched, as it probably was, I might as well just share pictures on the internet: "Here's my car's new paint job! LOL!" Instead I parked in a municipal lot and went into a bar I'd never visited. The tavern was called The Bung, and it was about as classy as you'd guess from the name; the kind of dark, depressingly quiet place where you could get completely shitfaced in the middle of the day and nobody would look twice. But all I wanted was a beer and some quiet to study the Persian stuff again, and even the beer was just a hair of the dog for my vodka-aching head.

I still had some shit to straighten out with young Clarence, Mister Hey-Guess-What-I'm-Gay, Mister Hey-Just-Dropped-By-Without-Calling, but that would have to wait for another day. And of course there was still the matter of those Black Sun charmers, especially the bald one with the big, bony fists who'd had so much fun with my face and ribs. Normally I would have already found those bastards and set their families on fire, but these were busy days.

As I looked through Fatback's files again, I became more and more certain that there were four or five names in the Persian material that were real possibilities as a San Judas identity for Anaita, so I emailed George to focus on those. Then I just sat back in my booth and sipped my beer while some guy at the bar complained about his ex-wife. It was strangely soothing, listening to other people's problems.

Evening was creeping over the city as I walked into Hoover Park. The lights of the tall towers downtown had mostly come on, so I was surrounded by bright windows that hung in the sky like square stars. I made my way to a bench on the southern side of the park, which I'd picked because the Amazons could walk there from our apartment house without too much trouble.

Ten minutes later I saw them, carrying duffel bags and looking pretty much like any number of other semi-homeless young people. I waved them over.

"Let's take a walk," I said.

We made our way to a more isolated part of the park, out by one of the children's play structures. At this time of the day the only people in sight were a young mother with a couple of cranky, runny-nosed kids, but they were already packing up to head home. As I watched them walk off down the path I asked Halyna, "Now tell me again what you two want. Exactly. And why you helped me."

She looked a little surprised by the question. She looked even more surprised when I pulled out my pistol. "What is going on?"

"It's nothing. The technical term is 'due diligence.' Oxana, you sit down too."

Their eyes were wide, but to their credit neither of them looked anywhere near close to panic. I wondered how many bad situations they'd already seen in their short twenty or so years on Earth. "Why is this?" Oxana asked, pointing at the gun.

"Because I need answers, and this time I need real, truthful ones. First your people, you Scythian Amazon whatevers, wanted the feather, and now you're trying to keep the horn away from the Black Sun. How do you even *know* the Black Sun? How do you know any of this and why do you care?"

"We know because the bitch Anahita has been our enemy for hundreds of years," Halyna said. "She made her Persian servants steal our sisters and put them in slavery."

"When?"

"When? When all the Persians obeyed her. Worshipped her."

"You do realize you're talking about more than two thousand years ago."

"We not forget," said Oxana.

"We were raised for not forgetting," added Halyna.

"And how do you know about the Black Sun and their hairy pets?"

Halyna nodded. "Because after the feather and the auction, Black Sun got interested in you. But we know them already because they are in Russia too, and Russian Black Sun hate us Scythians. They call us race-traitors and whores." She smiled. "Oh, and lesbians of course, but some of us are not so bothered by that. They try to get into our camp, we kill one of them. After that, it is war between us."

"So they don't work with Anaita?"

"No. I don't know why they care about the horn, except that it is a powerful thing." Halyna shrugged. "We don't care about horn, except to hurt Anaita."

"So you're out to overthrow a goddess. An angel. You do realize that's not going to happen, right?"

Oxana was still looking worriedly at the gun, but Halyna seemed to have forgotten it. I made sure both of them had their hands in view, and that neither of them could reach me easily. I have pretty fast reflexes, especially compared to a normal human, but I had seen the sharp things these ladies practiced with, and there were two of them. Also, I was reasonably sure neither of them had drunk between seven and many alcoholic beverages the night before.

"We fight a long fight," Halyna said, a curl of red hair lying across her forehead like a bloody weal. "We keep her from winning. That is our victory. Our leaders tell us that because we don't have the feather, we cannot hurt her, but if we get the horn we will hurt her in a different way. She will lose power."

Well, Anaita would lose power over Eligor, that was certain. And if Eligor went down, he'd try to take Anaita with him—the grand duke was thoughtful that way. I hoped he had the clout to at least raise some very serious questions among her angelic comrades in Heaven if it came to that.

"So it was nothing to do with me? Why were you living in my building?"

"To watch you," Oxana said. "Not hurt you."

"Because lots of people know you are the man with the feather," explained her comrade. "Now they hear you may have the horn. Very big news with some people, especially some bad people. We think Black Sun may come, so we watch for them. They must not get the horn." Halyna shrugged. "That is all. We do our job. We work for our people."

"And all your people want is the horn—but here's the problem. I can't let you have it. Do you understand? I need it more than anyone else does. But I can promise you this, if I do get it, your Anahita won't like what happens. And we can all agree that we don't want those goose-stepping Black Sun bastards to get it either."

Halyna turned to Oxana and they had a quick conversation in Ukrainian. I kept the gun up, but I didn't point it straight at their faces anymore. Sometimes courtesy is as important as actual trust.

"Okay," said Halyna at last. "Is okay. You promise, we believe. Not give the horn to Anaita, everything okay. We can work together."

"Not just work together," I said. "Go to war. Are you ready for that?"

Oxana nodded eagerly. "We have been in war all our lives. This war. Same war. Against the Persian bitch."

"Okay," I said. "One last thing." I turned my gun around and handed it butt-first to Halyna, who took it with a look of surprise.

"Why?" she said, eyebrow lifting. "Not loaded?"

"Oh, definitely loaded. Go on, look." I waited while she examined it and saw that it was jammed with shells. "Silver, too. I've had to give up lead almost completely."

Halyna handled it for a moment, then pointed it at me. She looked quite capable of pulling the trigger if she chose. "Why do you give this gun to me?"

"Because I'm tired of not trusting people. Honestly, from here on in I don't think I'm going to have time to do a lot of background checks. So if it's really me you want, just shoot me now. I'm too tired for all the usual skullduggery."

Halyna looked at the gun, then at me. "What is . . . 'skullduggery'?"

"Never mind—let me rephrase it. I'm too tired for the same old shit. Are we on the same side? If we're not, then just put two in my skull, and I'll see what comes next."

Halyna stared at me for a few seconds, looked briefly to Oxana, who also seemed quite prepared for anything, then handed me back the gun. "Same side, Bobby Dollar."

"Good. Bring your stuff. We're going to take a ride."

See, Caz's message-via-demon-crudlump hadn't just reminded me about Caz and how I felt about her, because to be honest I never really stopped thinking about that part. It had also reminded me that she and I had both flirted with disaster even before we met—the Countess more than me, considering she had stolen Eligor's most prized possession. So why hadn't the grand duke just grabbed her and taken her back? Because for part of the time *he didn't know where she was.* That was the important part.

I drove the long way around, making sure no one was tailing my new/old Datsun. We drove through the harsh neon glare of Whisky Gulch and into a neighborhood tucked behind the stately homes along University Avenue. The Amazons were puzzled when I pulled into the driveway of an undistinguished apartment building, but they were positively astonished when I slid into one of the parking spaces and got out to punch a code into a panel disguised as a utility meter, and then the entire back of the garage opened up so we could get into Caz's secret apartment hideaway.

Being back there was definitely a mixed blessing for me. It was a great place to hide, because as far as I know nobody on either side knew about it. I'd told Eligor everything he wanted to know (because I was being tortured, kids) but as far as I remembered, he'd never asked about Caz's hideout. Believe me, I'd have happily spilled that information to keep myself out of the burning flames for an extra minute, but it just didn't come up. Those who have not spent days feeling the skin singed off their body, regrown, and then singed off again are not allowed to comment on my lack of silent courage. No, seriously, shut the fuck up. You don't know anything.

Anyway, I was talking about mixed blessings. Caz's place was a hell of a lot nicer than my now-empty apartment, but it was also the last place she and I had spent any safe time together, and the night we'd had there—well, night and morning and not much sleep during either—had been without doubt the single best moments of my life. I'd known the code since our night together, but I'd never even considered using it before this because I knew it would be painful to return. And it was.

The Amazons loved it, naturally. They had been living like gypsies for the whole time they'd been in America, and I had a feeling the Ukrainian Amazon compound in the Carpathians wasn't any bower of delight, either. (Actually, from what they'd told me, it sounded like Single Sex Sadist Camp, but ever since I got out of the Counterstrike units I've had an aversion to discipline, as well as an even bigger aversion to segregation of the sexes.) But now you would have thought Halyna and Oxana were on vacation. They ran around looking at everything, fiddling with the television, touching the costly fabrics that draped the rooms, opening and smelling all Caz's perfumes (just the scents gave me a sharp pang in the heart) and marveling at the expensive clothes in her closet. I hadn't showered in about two days, so while they were having a half-serious pillow fight—I'm telling you, it was like taking teenagers to a holiday cabin—I went in and sluiced the dirt and sweat off me.

Later I went out and fetched some dinner from an El Salvadoran place around the corner. The Amazons had never had *panes rellenos*, and looked at me like I was a magician after they took their first bites. (The little local joint turned out to be pretty good.) We shared a few beers, and then I gave them the bedroom—I was just able to deal with being in the apartment, but I didn't think I could handle Caz's bed, too—and set myself up on the couch with all my case notes, some paper, and a pen. I sat up late drawing little lines and arrows, trying to create a diagram that made sense out of all the connections and all the crazy shit that had been happening, something that would give me some perspective on what was going on and where I had to go next. What I was really doing was keeping my mind busy as a defense against early-onset craziness.

I woke in the middle of the night, having dozed off sitting up. As I made myself more comfortable, I heard noises from the other room. At first I thought from the thumping noises and occasional cries and grunts that the Amazons were sparring, but I realized after a while that they were almost certainly involved in a much friendlier interaction. It went on for a while. A long while.

Ah, the irony. Hidden away from the world, rejected once again by the woman I loved, alone with a couple of hot young Amazons, and I was the guy out on the couch, listening in like a sad old pervert. Not that I had any choice about listening. But even if I had been interested and they had been interested too, I was still a man in love, and I had to stay true to something, even if that something was only self-denial.

Can't say I enjoyed it much, though.

fifteen
fun in america

WHEN MORNING came, I left the Amazons sleeping the sleep of the semi-innocent and wandered out of the apartment into the meticulous brick courtyard, trying to see how far I had to go to get a cell signal. Caz's apartment was shielded against cell calls to prevent the location being traced, which was good for discretion but bad for communication, and I had no idea how trustworthy the landline was these days. Turned out I had to walk a couple of blocks before I got any bars, and the reception still wasn't great, but considering the guy I was calling had once used my phone (with help from our bosses) to keep tabs on where I was, I wasn't too unhappy.

"Clarence," I said. "Are you alone?"

"Bobby?" He yawned. "I hope so."

"You sure you don't have a little Wendell or a Wendell-surrogate of some kind stashed away there under the counterpane?"

"What's a counterpane? No, there's no one here."

"Ignorant youngster. We need to meet up, and I'm not driving all the way to your place. So get a cab or something and meet me in twenty minutes at the diner where you met the Sollyhulls—remember the ghost sisters? I thought so. And make sure nobody follows you." I hung up before he could protest. I didn't really care about driving that far, but I'd gone to all the trouble of painting my car to look different, so I wasn't going to blow it by driving up to some known place and displaying it to anybody who might be watching.

I picked up some coffee at the local forked-mermaid franchise and a couple of vaguely healthy-looking muffins for the women. When I got back, Oxana and Halyna wandered out in t-shirts and underpants, so I adopted a stern, paternalistic air to disguise the fact that all this free-range femininity was starting to get to Yours Truly, who, except for a couple of stolen hours in Hell with Caz, had been living a monastic life for months.

"Okay, women-friends of complete equality, come and get some coffee into you, and then let's make a shopping list."

"Guns?" asked Oxana brightly.

"Bigger knives?" Halyna suggested. "I had a boovy knife, but I lost it on the bus."

I figured out after a moment that she was talking about a Bowie knife. Those usually run about eight inches of blade or so, so it must have made quite a clunk falling out of her duffel bag. "No, not weapons. That comes later. Today I need you to find yourself some disguises. Nothing too ambitious, just a couple of wigs and some civilian clothes so you don't look quite so much like an Estonian punk rock band."

"You don't like this clothings?" Oxana pulled up her sleeveless t-shirt, exposing way more of her underwear and flat, tan stomach than I really wanted to see. After all, I may not be human, but I'm still only human.

"Not for the kind of stuff we're going to be doing," I said, looking resolutely into her eyes instead, which were also kind of fetching. If I hadn't seen all the weapons in their apartment or the way she stabbed that hairy little monster, I would have pegged her for a poli sci major who was also a cheerleader, which probably demonstrates which way *my* fantasy life is inclined. "Let's make a list."

When we were done, I gave them some cash and drew a map so they could find their way discreetly to the other side of the freeway. Ravenswood was a pretty small part of town, especially the shopping district, but I figured they could find what they wanted in thrift stores. Then I taught them the combination for the apartment and reminded them not to bring anything or anybody home or I'd have to kill them. Daddying done, I set them free like the fierce Ukrainian she-creatures they were, to romp among the used pantsuits and granny scarves.

I got to the diner early, checked it out, then parked the car and walked back from a block or so away. It wasn't all that nice a place, but I hadn't been there for months, not since the Sollyhull Sisters had given up haunting the place and moved somewhere else, so I figured it wouldn't be on any list of my main hangouts. Plus, it had a back door. I like those.

While I waited for Clarence, I sifted through the latest information my porky source had sent me. There was some good stuff in this shipment, so even though George was almost certainly squatting naked in mud at that moment, aware of nothing more complicated than a strange aversion to applesauce and sauerkraut, I sent him a thank you he could read later. As I did, I noticed that he'd appended a little note to the information he'd sent me.

Hi, Mr. D! Guess what? I have worms! Ascarids, I think they're called. They're really bad for pigs but I don't think I have that serious a case. The vet here is great and they really respect their patients' privacy. I'm supposed to take something called Mibendazol (sp?) to kill the worms. And the food here is great!

I was so glad I hadn't ordered anything to eat yet.

George and I had narrowed down the candidates for Anaita's earthly avatar quite a bit, which meant it was more like studying actual people now and not just demographics. I had suggested several variables for George's search, including 1) apparently Persian or Persian-American—obviously, or the whole search was pointless, 2) wealthy (because why wouldn't she be?), 3) sporadic appearances (because I figured an important angel like Anaita wouldn't be able to hang out on Earth all that often), and 4) involved in local life but not *too* involved. Because of this last, I could eliminate at least four of the people George had given me, each of them with big, complicated families.

That still left me nearly a dozen to consider, but I took a flyer and crossed off the male candidates, just as an exercise. Certainly if Anaita didn't want to be found out it would have been smarter to pick a male persona, but I had a feeling she wasn't the type. I mean, she used to be a goddess, and unlike angels (at least as far as I knew angels), goddesses were proud of being female. And she was the goddess of fertility, right? Wasn't that what Gustibus had said?

Eliminating men quickly narrowed the field down to three. They were all interesting, but as I sat there staring I kept coming back to one particular name.

I was just about to email George again, to ask him to get me more information about that particular woman (as soon as he could get free from his roundworm treatments) when the door of the coffee shop went *ding!* and Clarence walked in. With Garcia Windhover.

G-Man saw me and trotted to my table, struggling as always to keep his pants from falling down. I don't want to sound like a cranky old guy, but come on—even rappers have to run for their lives sometimes, don't they? How do they do that with their pants around their ankles like a spanked toddler? Not that G-Man was a rapper or anything else but a white suburban kid from a nice, slightly hippie-ish family who had taken his interest in African-American culture way beyond the bounds of good taste. Actually, his outfit wasn't that bad this time, except for the bandana knotted in the front and, banging against his skinny chest, a ridiculous gold medallion that I could swear he'd stolen out of some ninety-year-old lady's jewelry box.

"A'ight, Bobby!" he said and tried to fist-bump me. I refused to produce my fist. I know, petty of me, but come on. "Don't worry, I'ma let you two talk, but I just had to come in and show you my new ink." He stuck out his arm, then turned it over to display a patch of baloney-colored skin that had presumably been nude until recently. Now it glowed with new black—the words "Mission From God" in complicated Gothic letters. " 'Cause you told me that time that you were the Lord's avenging angel, and that's cool, and since you're my boy . . ."

I took a breath. If G-Man was really just dropping off Clarence, it would be easier and safer for everyone if I kept the conversation brief and light, so instead of telling him what an idiot he was, I just nodded and said, "Yeah, bro. Nice ink." Yes, I said it. And if I hadn't already been to Hell, I'd say that was where I'm going someday for lying. But when I go back to Hell, it will be for dozens of much worse crimes and probably sooner than I want.

I gave Clarence a look that was meant to imply all the ways I would have liked to hurt him if I had the freedom to do so, which I didn't. "So. You caught a ride with G-Man. I thought you had a car of your own?"

"It wouldn't start," the boy angel said with a distinct tone of sulk. "And you said twenty minutes, Bobby."

"Know you two have to get on with your top-secret biznizzle," G-Man said loudly, causing one or two of the poor bastards already eating there to turn and look. "So I'll just go cruise around. When should I come pick you up, Harrisonio?"

While they worked out details, I just sat there with one eyebrow so far up it was almost painful. When he'd finally gone, Clarence turned back to me with a defiant look already on his face.

"Harrisonio?" I said. His earthly name was Harrison Ely, but nobody ever used it. At least nobody who was even halfway cool.

"At least somebody *almost* calls me by my real name."

"I never realized you were a gondolier. Hey, I'll call you Harrisonio too."

"Please don't." He picked up the menu. "What's up?"

"Whatever you do, don't get the corned beef here. It's made from people—ugly, dry people. Other than that, you're on your own. I'll tell you the details after you've ordered."

When we had summoned a harried-looking guy in an apron and told him what we wanted, I said to Clarence, "Now, do me a big favor and run down everything that happened before you met me and Sam."

"What do you mean? Like before I *died*? I don't know that. Neither do you."

"No, dumbass. I'm talking about your angelic life."

"Why?"

"Just humor me." I'd coaxed what I believed were honest answers out of the Amazons by pointing a gun at them, but that didn't seem appropriate here. For one thing: coffee shop, broad daylight. Also, if Clarence was still a stooge for our bosses, he'd just get rebodied if I plugged him, so it wasn't much of a threat—especially since he hadn't already died a couple of times like some of us had, so he didn't know yet how painful it could be.

The kid sipped his iced tea and told me how he'd woken up in Heaven, a story that was pretty much like mine until he was sent off to work in Records, which—as Clarence told it—had been a job of serene, fulfilling boredom. Fulfilling for him, boredom for anyone with half an ounce of interest in reality, including me. But I wasn't judging, just listening.

"Then, after I'd been there a while, my boss told me somebody wanted to talk to me. I went to this place and met this angel I didn't know, but he was really shiny, you know? Really bright. I could tell he was somebody important."

"Who was he?"

"I didn't recognize him."

"And this was still in Heaven?"

He shrugged. "As far as I know."

We paused when the food came. I was still feeling a bit unmanned by resuming my relationship with hard liquor the other night, so I mainly stuck to carbs—waffles and hash browns, with some fruit just to make me feel virtuous. I watched Clarence eat some of his blueberry pancakes before prodding him to continue.

"Anyway, so this shiny angel said that Heaven had something very important for me to do, something I was going to do that would make the Highest proud of me. It didn't really sound like I had any choice, so I said yes. Next thing I know, I'm on Earth."

"Really? You sure?"

"About the Earth part? I think so. It was like a warehouse or something, but it wasn't anything like any part of Heaven I'd ever seen. And it smelled. Things I'd never smelled in Heaven. Sweat. Machine oil. And the sounds were different, too." He stopped with a fork in front of his mouth. "Now that I'm talking about it, I kind of . . . thought differently after I got there, too. Clearer about some things, less clear about others. And I wasn't as happy as I'd been."

That did sound like he'd been tossed out of Heaven's nest. "Okay. Then what happened?"

"I more or less got trained. In some very basic stuff. How to use the needle gun they gave me, and a few other things. And the phones, especially the tracking software. There were about ten other angels there, too, learning stuff like I was. We sparred sometimes." He shook his head. "I wasn't very good at that."

"Hang on. You were being trained on Earth with a bunch of other angels? Trained with guns? And this *wasn't* Camp Zion, the big camp in the middle of the desert?" I'd been trained at Zion, along with every other angel that has ever been in a Counterstrike unit. If someone was training angels in a different location to do Counterstrike work, that wasn't just news to me, it was worrying news. How big *was* the shit going on up there?

"I don't know where it was, Bobby. Just this place Samkiel sent me. But there wasn't a desert."

"Whoa, hang on, cowboy. Who's Samkiel?"

"The shiny angel who sent me there in the first place—the important one. I heard one of the other angels mention his name once, and people weren't using names around that place much, so I remembered."

"Okay, Samkiel." I didn't know the name, but I filed it away for later. "That's something. Then what happened?"

He looked embarrassed. "I'm not exactly sure. To be honest, for a long time I hardly even remembered any of this, but once I started hanging out with you and Sam it started to come back a little." He looked up at me. "Hey, where is Sam? How come he never comes out with us anymore?"

I sat back and drank my coffee, thinking. I couldn't find any holes in Clarence's story, not that it proved anything. The people we worked for, if you can call them that, are much more powerful than we are. Since they were capable of wiping our memories, they might even be able to implant cover stories right into an angel's brain. At least I was going to assume that, until I found out otherwise. Still, I didn't have much choice but to believe him. I was running out of potential allies. "Sam and I had a bit of a disagreement. That's why I need to be able to trust you—and why we're starting with History 101."

"Trust me? Didn't I do that feather thing with the guy from Hell with you? Totally against every rule." He stopped scowling. "What do you mean, disagreement?"

"All right, argument. To put it more clearly, Sam said I was a stupid, paranoid dick. I'll tell you all the fun details some other time. I don't think he's given up on me, but I also can't count on him right this moment. So I need you, kid."

"For what?"

"I don't know yet. But shit is getting serious. From now on, don't talk to anyone in Heaven you don't need to, and don't talk about me to anyone—including Sam."

"Really?" He looked very worried by this.

"No, Clarence, I'm just joking with you. We're going to meet him at Chuck E. Cheese later on and play skee-ball. Yes, Sam. Until I know where he stands on Kephas, I have to play it very, very safe."

Well, Clarence wouldn't be satisfied until I told him the important facts about Kephas, that it was probably Important Angel Anaita who wanted my soul jerked out and fed to demon-alligators—although even if I was right that she was behind it all, I still had no idea why I'd pissed her off so badly in the first place. Yes, I had wound up with her feather, but I hadn't stolen it, and I hadn't wanted it. She didn't have any need to go after me at first. Of course, after the whole thing went down with Eligor and Caz I probably knew too much to be left alone.

"Oh, Clarence," I said, "one more thing. We're friends now, in a weird sort of way. But if you're not what you keep telling me you are— if you're still working for our bosses somehow and you rat out me or Sam, I swear on the Highest I will make you wish you'd never met me."

He was startled at the change in my tone and showed me hurt-puppy eyes. "That wouldn't be anything particularly new, Bobby."

"That's because I'm difficult. Because I'm rude. But if I have to come after you, you'll have entirely different reasons. *Serious* reasons."

"Thanks for the good faith." He scowled. "You give angels a bad name."

"Not my fault. I'm just as the Good Lord made me." Yeah, like I should automatically trust somebody who had started out as a fink for management.

I wasn't feeling particularly enthused about seeing G-Man again, so I left Clarence still shaking his head in dismay and I started home. While I still had bars on my phone, I pulled into a parking lot and called Alice at the office to tell her I needed a longer, indefinite leave of absence. Alice informed me in her cheerful way that there wasn't a snowball's chance in the Devil's backyard that would happen, so I asked her to address the request straight to Archangel Temuel. I hoped the Mule would back me up, or at least delay the request long enough to give me some time before it was turned down. Too many things were happening at once now, and I couldn't afford to be called to any surprise job reviews up at the Big Shiny.

While I was sitting at the curb I went back over Fatback's latest information-dump about prominent local Persian-American women. The more I looked, the more I liked my candidate; she was wealthy, had no immediate relatives I could find, and seemed very, very private. I called George's number and got the answering machine.

"Hey, hope the worm treatment is going great, and congratulations on that. Skip all the other people and just get me everything you can find—I mean *everything*—on this woman named Donya Sepanta. Fast, too, if you can tear yourself away from the mud saunas. Please."

Back at Caz's apartment, the Amazons had clearly been having a dress-up party. Oxana greeted me wearing a yellow Dolly Parton wig and a miniskirt that would have looked immodest on a '60s stewardess. Halyna sported a sleeveless red leather pantsuit and an Afro wig, although with those muscles she looked more like Ike than Tina. They were both still wearing their combat boots and various spiked leather armbands and neck straps, though; the combination was somewhat unsettling.

"Luckily for you two I already have enough money, or I'd be pimping you out to the small but select militant-Nancy-Sinatra-bondage-dyke market," I said. "No, you both look great, but I think we'll tone it down just a touch when we go into action."

"Not too much," said Halyna, primping her wig. "This is most fun we have in America."

"Our great nation has that effect on tourists," I said. "You're not the first and you won't be the last."

As entertaining as it was watching two young women enjoy themselves getting in and out of clothes, it only made me wish Caz were there. I locked myself in the bathroom for a while so I could concentrate on my work. After all, Heaven wasn't going to overthrow itself.

sixteen
letting it bleed

ONE OF those northern weather fronts had dropped down on us from somewhere in the neighborhood of Alaska, so as I drove across town I kept the defroster on and the windshield wipers at full speed. It was a cold rain, and I would much rather have been sitting in a warm apartment that still smelled like Caz (although with the Amazons each taking two steamy showers a day, the scent was almost gone). The Tierra Green Apartments had the oldest, most pathetic water heater outside the Third World, and its pilot light went out at least a couple of times a week. The women hadn't had regular hot water in months, and they were taking full advantage of it now.

I was listening to *Let It Bleed* by the Rolling Stones, a nearly perfect album both for rainy days and for considering the end of the world as we know it. Not that I was really planning to overthrow all of Heaven, just part of it—one certain, very powerful part of it, to be precise—but even so, "You Can't Always Get What You Want" and "Love In Vain" seemed disturbingly appropriate.

I parked out on Parade along the waterfront, still hoping to keep my recently painted car hidden from prying eyes, and checked for people following me as I took a roundabout walk to the Compasses. My fellow heavenly advocate Kool Filter was huddled in the doorway of the Alhambra Building, trying to stay dry under the awning, but since the rain was blowing sideways he wasn't doing very well.

"A silent protest against the unfairness of the city's smoking laws," I said as I walked up.

Kool offered me a fist. We bumped. "Silent, hell. I've been bitching about it for years. But it doesn't make much difference when nobody's listening."

"Our true condition in this world writ small."

He gave me a look. "What's that shit mean?"

"You know. We all work for shadowy forces, follow rules we don't understand, and when we complain, nothing happens."

"I don't know what happens when *you* complain, man," he said, grinding out his most recent cigarette in a puddle. "But I know when I do it, I get my ass kicked by the Mule."

I liked Kool. He was a good guy, a straight shooter—my idea of an angel. "Did you ever think that maybe it's all bullshit?" I asked.

"Yeah. And it is." He paused and eyed me again. "Hang on, what are you saying, exactly?"

"That maybe the folks we work for aren't as perfect as they seem. That maybe some of them are corrupt. That some of the things we're doing aren't just to help people or to bring glory to the Highest."

Kool laughed. "Shit, boy, what's got into you? Our bosses aren't perfect? Some of what we do is bullshit, and the rest is dubious?" He lit another cigarette. "I've got only one thing to say to that: so what else is new?" He let out a cloud of smoke. "But it pays the rent." He smiled. "In a metaphorical sorta way, anyhow."

I left him there, huddled in the doorway, trying to keep the rain off his nice clothes. The thing is, Kool was probably right. Maybe all my co-workers, every angel in every city, had figured this all out already. Maybe I was just refusing to go along with the way things were. Caz had called me a romantic several times, and it hadn't sounded like a compliment.

The Compasses was about what you'd expect on a Wednesday afternoon—some regulars and a couple of out-of-towners passing through. Pretty much every angel in the Bay Area knew where the good bars were, the safe bars where you could take off your halo and let your hair down, so to speak. I saw Jimmy the Table and several other familiar faces sitting at one table, and Monica at another with Teddy Nebraska. Monica waved. I hadn't had much chance to talk to her lately, but Monica Naber is another one who falls into the category of "good people"—even if, like me and most of my friends, she's not really a people.

I let Young Elvis corner me for a minute and tell me about what he'd done lately to his '72 Camaro, a bunch of upgrades which sounded flashy, expensive, and pointless—just the way I like it. But having so recently put my beloved AMC Matador Machine on the block, I wasn't really in the mood. I begged off with the excuse I needed a beer, which had the advantage of being true, then made my way up to the bar. Kacey the relief bartender was on duty while Chico was in the back doing inventory, so after she gave me a beer I headed to the stockroom.

The room back there must have been part of the original Masonic lodge, at least judging by the early twentieth-century floral wallpaper that still hung in strips where the wall was visible. Now most of it was covered by shelving racks, and although one side was taken up with freezers full of bar food, the rest of it was stacked with bottles. It was actually pretty fascinating, all the different bottles that booze came in, different shapes, different colored glass, with the one common factor that enough of what was inside would get you blotto. In previous days I would have happily pulled down a couple of the more esoteric ones for a test drive, but I was here on business. My own business, but business nonetheless.

I didn't see any immediate sign of Chico, so I called his name. He stood up, wearing an apron with a bunch of pockets, looking like the sweetest Suzy Homemaker in maximum security prison. He glared as if he wasn't thrilled to see me. I sometimes wondered if Chico and Alice from the office were secretly married, or at least long-separated siblings.

"Hey, Dollar. What you want?"

"Just a few minutes of your charming personality, which will give me the courage to make it through another gray day."

"Hey, guess what. Fuck you."

I love Chico. He's the nicest angel I've ever met who doesn't like anything or anybody. Except customers, and that's only for their money. Other than that, he really hates them. Since he can bend an iron pipe in his bare hands and is a pretty fair shot, too, I can't help wondering sometimes what very peculiar branch of Heaven spawned our bartender. Maybe that was the secret—maybe he and Alice had both come out of the same Counterstrike unit. "Right back at you, big boy. Actually, I need a favor."

"Needing ain't getting."

"You know those silver salts you use in your shotgun?"

He looked at me as though I was standing on his foot and hadn't figured it out yet. "Yeah?"

"Where did you find them?"

He shrugged and turned back to his inventory. "Friend of a friend. You know."

"Do you think your friend could get me some?"

"It's just silver nitrate powder. You can buy that shit on the internet. How much do you need?"

"I don't know—fifty, hundred pounds?"

He laughed harshly. "Shit, dude, that's going to set you back twenty thousand bucks or something—it's fucking silver! You going big-game hunting in Hell?"

It would have been funnier if I hadn't just got back a few weeks earlier. "No, man. But I got an idea I want to try."

"Well, don't tell me about it. It's bad enough you brought that big demonic motherfucker here and tore up my bar, man. I don't want to lose my license because you're doing some crazy shit."

At least I knew where to start. Maybe Orban could get me some kind of Weapons of Mass Destruction Discount on the stuff. "Cool, man. Don't worry. I wasn't even here. Thanks for the advice."

"Hey, wait a second," he said as I reached the door. He slid a couple of bottles back into a shelf and stood up. "I almost forgot. I got something for you."

"Just for me? It's a bit early for Valentine's Day, Chico—it's not even Christmas—but I'm touched."

"You know why I like you, Dollar?" he said as he led me across the storage room and into the boxy little cubicle he uses as the Compasses' office.

"Why?"

"Trick question. I don't." He reached in and picked something off the desk, handed it to me. It was a sealed envelope with my name on it— my earthbound name. "Some guy in a suit left it for you. Asked when you'd be coming in next. I told him, if it was up to me, not for years."

I looked at the letter. I didn't know what it was, but I already didn't like it. "Are you really still pissed about that Sumerian monster wrecking the bar? It was Sam's idea to come here, y'know, not mine."

"Two assholes, one brain." Chico led me out of the cubicle. "Don't trust either of you."

Back in the bar, I finished my beer and decided I could allow myself one more. I had a quick catch-up with Jimmy the Table, who wanted me to come in for the next Friday night poker game, now being changed to Thursday nights (although it was still apparently going to be called the Friday Night Poker Game) but I begged off.

"We never see you anymore, Bobby," he said sadly. "Sam, either. You guys find some new place to hang out?"

"Don't know about Sam, but I prefer to drink at home with my stereo, my collection of great books, and the two oversexed Ukrainian girls who live with me."

"Kidder," he said. "Well, don't be a stranger."

"No more than usual." I leaned in and gave Monica a kiss on the cheek, thumped Teddy Nebraska on the shoulder in a comradely way (because I seemed to make him nervous, and I kind of enjoyed it) and then wandered out. I really wanted to open the letter, but I thought I should be a bit discreet. Half of what I was up to these days needed to be kept secret from Heaven, so the middle of the most popular angel bar in San Judas might not be the best place to read my mail.

The rain had slacked a bit, but I was still cold and wet when I reached my car. The good thing was, it was now a lot easier to see if I was being tailed through the nearly deserted streets. Still, I drove a circuitous route out of downtown just to be on the safe side, keeping my eye on my rearview mirror, but I didn't see anyone tailing me.

I stopped to pick up a few sandwiches at a deli I like. I didn't really know what Amazons ate, although so far the answer seemed to be "everything that isn't nailed down," so I just took my best shot. Then I headed back to Caz's place.

It occurred to me as I pulled into the secure garage that since I'd sent a message back to Caz, or tried to, I was hoping to hear from her again. The problem was, I'd moved since the nizzic found me, and the new place didn't have windows, so I'd have a hard time knowing when it found me again. Something else I'd have to think about.

To my absolute lack of astonishment, Halyna and Oxana were watching television when I got there, one of those horrible reality things where the host confronts people over paternity and infidelity. They seemed to be enjoying it, so I dumped several of the sandwiches onto a plate and slid it in front of them.

"When is something going to happen, Mr. Bobby Dollar?" Halyna asked, but I noticed she didn't take her eyes off the sleazy boyfriend who was shouting back at the studio audience, *"You don't know nothing 'bout it! You don't know nothing!"*

"This man crazy," said Oxana, amused as only the young can be to find out how stupid lots of people are.

"No, really. We want to help you," Halyna said. "When can we help you?"

"Sooner than you'd like, probably, so enjoy the time off." I took a pair of rubber gloves out from under the kitchen sink, then went to Caz's desk where the light was better. Most of the lamps in the main room were hidden behind gauzy draperies, so that the place looked more than a little like a bordello. I'd been a bit taken aback the first time I saw it, until I'd realized that Caz, however sophisticated she'd become over the course of several hundred years of afterlife, was still at heart a medieval girl. She had probably dreamed of living somewhere like this when she was young—some idea of Moorish luxury that would have been quite different from her cold home in Poland.

Once I had the gloves on I checked the envelope again, but it hadn't been mailed so there wasn't much information to be had, only my name—"Mr. Robert Dollar," which was actually kind of funny—written on the outside in felt pen.

The inside was different, if only because the paper was fancy business letterhead, embossed with a familiar symbol:

Dear Mr. Dollar,

it read, clearly printed from a computer document in so-very-1990s Helvetica 14.

It has come to my attention that a truly unfortunate error has been made by some of my employees invading your privacy. I assure you that I personally would never have allowed it, and that when I heard that matters had gone so far as a physical encounter between you and my overzealous subordinates, I disciplined those responsible.

We are not enemies, Mr. Dollar, and we should not be enemies. I hope I can prove that to you. In fact, we have many goals in common and my organization could be helpful to you in reaching yours. I would very much appreciate a chance to discuss this and other matters with you. Please come to my office on Friday at 15:00 and let me explain.

I apologize for the unusual way of communicating with you, but you seem to have changed your address, and I had no other way to reach you.

If for any reason you cannot make Friday's appointment, please call, and I will be happy to set a new one. It is important that we speak and important that we have no further misunderstandings.

Sincerely,
Baldur von Reinmann
Regional Director
Sonnenrad.org

There was even an address—378 Centennial Avenue, San Judas, CA 90460. Right in downtown, convenient to stores and large coliseums suitable for torchlight rallies.

I couldn't help it—I laughed as I read it. Physical encounter? Herr von Reinmann must have been referring to his hired strong-arm guy beating the (almost literal) holy shit out of me. But it had all been a misunderstanding, of course. We could work together, me and the Nazis. I would find them very helpful.

"Yeah," I said. "Just like Poland did."

I jotted down the address and time, but didn't bother hanging onto the letter, since other than humor value it wasn't going to give me anything else useful. I got the pastrami sandwich I'd bought for myself, reheated some of the morning's coffee, and sat down to eat. By the time I was cleaning crumbs off the table, I'd decided that the Black Sun creeps were too dangerous to be ignored, especially if they had supernatural monstrosities like the Nightmare Children at their disposal. I needed to understand better how they fit in to the whole Eligor-Anaita-feather-horn *mishegoss*. The quickest way to learn that would be simply to accept their invitation.

That night, I made a laundry list of the things I was going to need before visiting Baldur and the Blitzkrieg Boys. The Amazons had retired to bed to practice their horizontal calisthenics, so when I'd finished the list, I took a beer and went out into the courtyard of the apartment complex to stretch my legs. There were lights on in a few of the other apartment windows, but so far I hadn't seen any of the neighbors. That made sense, of course—Caz would have picked a spot for her *pied-a-terre* where she wouldn't have to come into contact with others very often. But since I now knew I'd had neo-Nazis practicing black magic above me for weeks in the old apartment, I wondered if I was being too casual about who might be sharing these new digs.

I stayed out for almost an hour. The storm had swept through, but the chilly air hadn't. It was pretty cold even for an angel, but I was determined to give a messenger from Caz a chance to find me, and the nizzic had seemed to make all its visits after dark. But my only company at this hour was a dog somewhere down the street, who barked loudly and hoarsely, over and over, until he gave up in strangled despair, only to start again a few minutes later, protesting the stupidity of a world where the humans got to sleep inside and be safe and comfortable while he was outside in the cold.

"I know that feel, bro," I told the dog, then finished my beer and went back inside.

seventeen

sshhhh

THURSDAY WAS library day for me. I intended to put in a good few hours, so I gave the Amazons a map of the places where I needed things picked up, then had them drop me off on Middlefield Street on the outskirts of downtown Jude. Halyna could drive all right, but I doubted she had a license, and based on the trip out, I sure as hell wouldn't have let her drive my late, lamented Matador. Both women were dressed a bit more soberly today, (at my direction, because the last thing I wanted was to have some of the more dangerous supplies picked up by people who looked like they belonged to an anarchist cell). In fact, the Amazons now looked like a couple of teachers, which was the way I wanted it. Harmless.

"Professional," I told them as I got out. "If you have any problems, just call me. But be professional!"

"You too much worrying," Oxana reassured me. "We will shoot nobody."

The Harper Library downtown had once been San Judas's first fire station, and still showed its historic roots in the high ceilings and the arches along the facade (which had allowed room for fully loaded hook and ladder trucks to drive out at speed) but a lot had changed in seventy or eighty years. If the brick walls and the Spanish tile roof still looked much the same, the insides were completely different from anything the older citizens would recognize. Twenty years or so before, about the time I first arrived in San Judas, the city had rebuilt the whole thing, gutting the inside, putting in more windows, and expanding outward to the back, including a large garden full of winding paths and benches. Like most libraries, it now had extensive multimedia resources, computers and video-watching rooms and all sorts of other fancy stuff meant to lure in Jude's jaded, internetted youth. To me, it always seemed a bit like trying to get people to eat their good old healthy lima beans by offering artisan burgers, too, but I'm not a library professional, so what do I know? In fact, I'd only been to the Harper Library at all recently because of business. The head librarian had died at her desk—probably as she would have chosen—and I had a very interesting time seeing her through her judgement. I'll tell you about that one someday.

Anyway, I had genuine work to do this time, so I settled in with one of the catalog computers and began seeing what I could find on Donya Sepanta. I checked on the other couple of names, too, just to be careful, though I was pretty sure that Sepanta was the one. I kept the reference folks busy bringing me old magazines that hadn't been digitized and lots of newspapers, in screen-ready form and the old-fashioned, crackly kind.

After half an hour I gave up on the other names and really focused on the Sepanta woman, doing my best to assemble a biography. Considering that she was a major player in the city, especially in the Persian-American community, and very much alive and living only a few miles away, it turned out to be pretty damned hard work.

Despite conflicting information, everyone seemed to think she'd been born in the early 1950s. I found '52, '53, and '55 listed in various who's-who lists and in those little automated bios that pop up on the screen, primarily as an excuse to rub more advertising against your forebrain. But they all agreed that she was born in Hamadan, which rang a few bells with me, and turned out to be a contemporary city of about half a million in the northwest of Iran. More interestingly, though, it was built on the ruins of Ecbatana, original capital of the ancient Medean Empire and one of the oldest cities in the world.

Her years in Iran were difficult to trace, again because stories conflicted or just left things out, but most of the capsule biographies agreed that her parents had been wealthy, that they'd spent a lot of their time in Europe and America, and that they left Iran for good after the 1979 revolution. Strangely, I couldn't find any other mention of those parents, or their names, or what happened to them. Well, "strangely" if they were real, because their daughter Donya began to leave a fairly large track in the public record starting in the middle of the 1980s, when she moved from Southern California to little old San Judas.

Since then she had been involved in numerous charity benefits for the creation of community parks and buildings, and was listed as a donor for nearly every single project of any significance to the Persian-American community. She had long supported the resistance to the rule of the Ayatollahs in contemporary Iran and had been listed as one of the backers for the Shah's son, but (according to one article in a Persian-language newspaper) had fallen out with Reza Pahlavi's camp over their unwillingness to criticize militant Islam itself.

So she didn't like the new religion. New to her, anyway, if she was indeed Anaita.

The more I studied, the more Ms. Sepanta seemed to fit. What made me feel almost certain was her unwillingness to be photographed. In picture after picture she was represented only by stand-ins, generally board members of the Sepanta Foundation, her main charity. But everyone who spoke about her personally seemed to mention her beauty and grace as well as her generosity. I'm not saying there's no such thing as shy philanthropists, but the personal touch helps a lot with fundraising, I'm told—the desire of the hoi polloi to mix with the important and the glamorous. So it felt at least slightly out of character for the life Donya Sepanta lived. Also, though the fact itself was not given much attention, there was no mention anywhere of her having a family of her own, only her long-gone, largely anonymous parents.

Almost certain I had cracked it, I started looking for anything that might tell me where to find her, but beyond near constant hometown boosterism in the local papers, which usually referred to her as "one of San Judas's leading citizens," I couldn't find much of anything. A few articles suggested she might live in the hills. One article mentioned the Los Altos district, another Woodside, without ever going so far as to say she actually lived there. And based on many mentions of her "frequent travel" and "worldwide circle of influential friends" she wasn't even at home very much.

I looked up and realized it was getting dark outside. I was just about to pack it in when I stumbled across something very, very interesting in one of the last pieces I'd requested—an old issue of *Sunset Magazine*, believe it or not. For those of you who've never lived in California, *Sunset* was originally a travel magazine for Southern Pacific Railroad, but it outlived that long ago and is still going strong. It's a travel, home, and cooking magazine that appeals particularly to the upscale and those who would like to live that way. If you want to know how to make a perfect crab cioppino for eight people, and how to serve it outdoors in your garden pergola on a summer evening while surrounded by the twinkling light of dozens of Mexican *luminaria*, well, *Sunset*'s your bet.

And there, to my astonishment, in the June 1988 issue, between articles on pattern-punched aluminum cabinets, tapas bars (still fairly new back then) and managing an extensive garden during drought (a frequent California worry) I found an article titled, "A Persian Oasis in the California Hills." And the oasis-garden in question belonged to—yes—none other than "Bay Area socialite and philanthropist Donya Sepanta." I leafed through the article eagerly, not so much admiring the images of the garden, its low walls and pools, cypresses and fruit trees, but looking for a picture of the elusive Donya. I found one, but it was only of her shoulder and hand as she held a pomegranate for the camera. She had a perfectly nice, prettily manicured hand, but that told me almost nothing. A quick read didn't add anything else useful—a lot of information about Persian-style gardens but nothing else about Ms. Sepanta except a few references to "her view from the rolling California hills" and "looking down on the golden Santa Clara Valley" which was what they used to call the area before it became known primarily for silicon-related reasons.

But just as I was going to give up and go meet the Amazons, one of the smaller pictures in the article caught my eye. It showed a group of square ornamental pools that had been built at the front of the house—its caption mentioned looking down on Santa Clara Valley—and right down in the corner of the picture, beyond most of the roads and greenery filling the space between the nearest pool and the distant bay, a little white finger poked up above the trees, like a shy person trying to summon a waiter. It was Hoover Tower, at the heart of the Stanford Campus. More importantly, it was a landmark with four sides, and thus an orientation to the compass. I emailed the image to myself in the largest format I could find, then went over to the train depot to meet my ride.

The women were in a boisterous mood.

"We get everything!" said Halyna. She was squinting, leaning so far forward as she drove that her nose was almost against the inside of the windshield. I guessed I should have asked her if she was supposed to wear corrective lenses before giving her my keys, but it was too late now. "Everything. No problem."

"No, one problem—Packages Plus guy," Oxana reported cheerfully. Her English was improving, but I still had to work to make out what she was saying sometimes. "He make face, don't want to give silver powder. 'Your name not on this!' he say. 'This say Robert Dollar. You not Robert Dollar!'" But Halya tell him, "Just because we not Americans don't mean we not *work* for American!"

"He's always careful," I said. "That's why I keep a mailbox there. I gave you a note—didn't you show it to him?"

"I told you," Halyna said to Oxana. "I say to her, 'Where is note, Bobby give us note,' but she tell me no you didn't."

"I forgot." Oxana shrugged and looked guilty. "Leave it in other clothes."

"It's okay," I said. "I see the stuff here so he must have given it to you."

"After while," Oxana said, then brightened. "Halyna said, give it or Mr. Dollar will angry, plus I pinch you in the nose."

"Punch!" said Halyna, indignant. "Word is 'punch.'"

I rolled my eyes. I was going to have to go in and mend fences at Packages Plus, I could see.

"And we buy this at store. But why you need sugar, Bobby?" Oxana passed me a family-sized bag of C and H granular. "You make some cake?"

"Ha ha," I said. "I'm going to do a little cooking, yes. I have an important meeting tomorrow, and I'd like to take some treats." I hadn't told them about my invitation to meet von Reinmann and his Black Sun buddies yet, so I outlined it in quick strokes.

Halyna was so upset she pulled the car over to the shoulder, right on the Woodside Expressway, which even in the middle of the afternoon, an hour before the commute really got going, was still a bad idea. Horns blasted as the drivers behind us had to press themselves all the way over to the driver's side of the lane to get by. "You don't do that! You don't go alone! They are killers!"

"Just get back on the road please," I said. "I know what I'm doing. People have been trying to kill me since you were in kindergarten. You may notice that I'm still here."

"But you don't know these men. The Black Sun—they are very, very bad. They have powers!"

"Hey, a lot of the folks who hate on me aren't even human," I said, but I didn't make a point of it. I was pretty sure the Amazons still didn't know I was anything other than another mortal dude, and if I was lucky, Ballsack von Ryebread and his little group didn't know either. I know it seems like my secret identity is secret to no one, but that's because most of the people I hang out with already know. The rest of the folks in San Judas who know me think I'm an ordinary guy who just gets into slightly extraordinary situations from time to time.

For some reason, the Amazons thought me cooking in my boxer shorts was the funniest thing they'd ever seen.

"Look, I'm not just doing this to give you a thrill, ladies. I'm working with some very nasty stuff here, and I only have so many decent pairs of pants."

"No, is good," said Oxana. "You have very nice leg."

"Legs," Halyna corrected her. "He has two."

"Maybe she only likes one of them," I suggested. "Hand me that little plastic jar over there, will you?"

While I was stirring, I asked the Amazons to put on some music. Oxana chose. After about ninety seconds of the ghastly Europop dance music had jolted my brain like badly-administered electroshock, I put down my spoon and changed it for something that worked a bit better with precision and potentially explosive chemicals, in this case Nina Simone's first album, *Little Girl Blue*.

"You are old!" said Oxana.

"No, is nice," Halyna said, listening. "She has a lot of . . . person in her voice."

"Absolutely right," I said. "You have that pair of shoes?"

"Why you want shoes?" Halyna said. "And so boring shoes?"

"Because I wouldn't do this to a pair I wanted to keep." I took a black oxford out of the box and examined the heel. Hard rubber—perfect. It had to take enough shock to let me walk in it, without being so resilient that it wouldn't do the job. I took a little fine-grain sandpaper and started scuffing up the polish just a bit. After all, anybody who knows anything about me would be suspicious if I showed up with shiny shoes or, Highest forbid, wearing a tie. Most places I hang out, a tie would get me shot as an impostor.

By the time I'd finished the rest of my preparations, "Central Park Blues" was tiptoeing through the speakers and the Amazons had given up and gone to bed. I finished the cleanup, set everything carefully aside to dry or harden or whatever, then made myself a real drink. Considering I hadn't set Caz's apartment on fire or lost any fingers with my chemistry experiments, I figured I'd earned it. I left the hood fan running on the range to clear any fumes, since the place had no windows, and went into the bathroom, where I locked the door, took off my watch, and practiced opening a Zipper, then timing the difference between how long it felt like in the no-Time bubble and how long it actually was. (No, that's not a euphemism for anything.) Because soon it was going to be in my best interests to be able to judge how much time was passing in the real world while I was Outside.

The rains had ended, so I walked out into the courtyard, clinking ice in my glass and trying not to think too much about the first night I'd been here with Caz, because that hurt too badly. I sometimes thought it would be better if one or both of us had died, because then at least there would have been an end of sorts. Instead we were stuck in this netherworld, for Caz, literally; for me, only figuratively. And although I knew that what I was doing now was my only chance to ever get her back, sometimes I felt like I couldn't wait any longer—that at some point I was going to start shouting and punching things and that would go on until someone tasered me and hauled me off to a secure ward in Atascadero. But that wouldn't do Caz any good at all.

Had she even received my message? Why hadn't she sent one back? Maybe freezing and torturing a nizzic wasn't the best way to continue communication—how was I supposed to know? Flying booger-demons don't come with instructions.

Something whirred overhead, and I looked up, heart racing, but it was only some night bird passing. No message there, at least not one I was waiting for.

Twenty minutes or so drifted by, but I was still alone, just me and the smell of wet concrete and a few ice cubes rattling in the bottom of an empty glass.

eighteen
make friends and incinerate people

I WAS LIMPING as I made my way along Centennial Avenue, but it was only a tactical limp.

I saw my Datsun reach the corner and turn, heading back toward Ravenswood, the new paint job quite convincingly ratty after the recent hard use. I'd let the Amazons drive me because I didn't want to risk setting off the incendiary in the heel of my shoe, but I was damned if I was going to risk getting them hurt on this little scouting expedition, which was exactly the kind of stupid, probably unnecessary thing I do best by myself.

Centennial had been a major thoroughfare back in the 1960s, but it had fallen on leaner times, and the big downtown rebuilding program of the mid-90s had just missed it by a couple of streets. It was wide but didn't look it because it was crammed with boxy, multistory buildings built at the beginning of the previous century. These days people drove through it too fast, and although it was still a neighborhood where people lived—almost all the upper floors of even the more successful businesses were apartments—the gloominess, wide streets, and fast traffic tended to keep even local pedestrians moving quickly. Not to mention the less pleasant elements of street life, which were to be found on Centennial in profusion, as some guy on public television might say. The intersection of Centennial and Industrial a few blocks down was one of the best places in Jude to find hookers and drugs at pretty much any hour of the day.

Here, a little west of Cendustrial, as some of the locals called it, things weren't quite so grim, but they hadn't exactly caught the wave of gentrification either. The downstairs businesses were mostly small taquerias, Asian food joints, dry cleaners, and nail salons—the kind of establishments you find in strip malls out in the suburbs.

Number 378 was a big, sandy-gray building of about the same vintage as the rest of the street, but a floor or so higher than its neighbors. It was also a bit more upscale than the rest of the block, with three entrances on the bottom floor, one for a doctor's office, one for an accounting business, and one with "Sonnenrad Communications" written in gold paint on the glass. I pushed that one open and went in. There was no one inside, just a kind of sad little waiting room with a table and some magazines. (Nothing particularly neo-Nazi, I feel honor-bound to report, but I guess you don't want to leave copies of Genocide Illustrated out for the UPS guy to see.) A laser-printed sign taped to the wall said the reception desk was one floor above, so I limped carefully up the stairs to a smaller room. The receptionist was about twenty-five and as blonde as one of the German schoolgirls out of Triumph of the Will. Her accent, though, was strictly San Judas.

"Can I help you?"

"I have an appointment. My name is Dollar."

She nodded, punched a button, announced me into her headset, then said "Someone will be right out," before turning back to whatever important work she was doing for the good of the race, which seemed to be reading Us Magazine.

After a few seconds one of the bastards I'd caught in my apartment, the dark-haired missionary I'd named "Timon," opened the inner door and beckoned me in. As I entered, Pumbaa, his blond, slightly stockier buddy, stepped in on the other side of me.

"Herr von Reinmann is waiting for you," said Timon, stiff as your first slow-dance chubby. "We're very sorry about the misunderstanding of the other day."

I wasn't going to waste a lot of energy on pretend courtesy. "Let's get on with this."

We went up another flight of stairs, then Timon knocked on a door about halfway down the hall before showing me in.

The room had clearly once been a very nice office, a lawyer's practice or even an old-fashioned medical consulting room, though the faded wallpaper was at odds with the modernist furniture. One big window crisscrossed with wrought iron bars took up a lot of the north-eastern side. Across the wide room from me, behind a big oak desk, sat a man of about thirty or so with pale skin and black hair. His hair was military-short, like that of my escorts, nearly shaved to the scalp, but unlike Timon and Pumbaa, he had a full, thick beard. He looked less like a stereotype neo-Nazi than I'd expected—more like Abe Lincoln in the middle of a lice epidemic. This was emphasized when he stood up, because he was also quite tall, nearly six and a half feet, with long arms and long hands.

"Mr. Dollar!" He had a slight but definite Scandinavian accent. "So kind of you to come. Again, many apologies for my colleagues' mistakes. The guilty have been disciplined, I promise you."

It didn't look to me like either of my two escorts were suffering too badly, but I only nodded. "And you must be Baldur von Reinmann."

He smiled, as if I had recognized him in public and asked for an autograph. "I am! Yes! And we have much to speak about. But first, please forgive me, my colleagues must . . ." he made a gesture of regret, "well, let us be honest. They must search you for weapons. I have many enemies, and you and I have not yet established our friendship."

I shrugged and let them pat me down. One of them found my FN automatic, withdrew it with careful fingers, and set it down on the desk. The other one found my sleeve knife, but missed the second blade, which was down my collar at the back. Ever the good sport, I told them, then passed it to yellow-haired Pumbaa.

Von Reinmann frowned. "Thomas, you were hasty in your search." He set the pistol and the two knives off to one side of his desk, well out of my reach. "Now search again."

This time they found the third knife, a very small one built into my belt buckle, more of a punch-blade, really, and eventually they even noticed the lead rod sewed into my sleeve. Instead of having them pick my jacket apart, I just took it off and tossed it to von Reinmann, who folded it neatly and put it on top of everything else.

Thomas aka Pumbaa brought me a chair and set it in front of the desk, then he and the brown-haired guy stood on either side of me while I sat down.

"Can I offer you something?" the boss asked.

"No, thanks," I said. "I just had lunch with my daughter before I came."

I watched the bearded man's response, but he only nodded, which made me very happy. I had invented a daughter not just to explain away the Amazons if someone saw them drop me off, but more to see if the Black Sun Faction knew I was an angel. No reaction meant *probably don't know.* Which would make things way more likely to work out in my favor.

Now I had to sit through about five minutes of Baldur von Bullshit explaining to me how his men had totally misunderstood his directions to make contact with me and had then taken even their foolish surveillance of me further still, into that (his words) "so regrettable physical conflict."

"You mean beating me until I was coughing blood?"

He waggled his hand at these sad but minor details. "As I have said, Mr. Dollar, we can only regret the error. But we have taken great pains to make certain such a thing does not happen again."

"Really? I may be wrong, but two of the guys are standing right here breathing down my neck, and neither one of them seems to have had his legs broken."

BvW smiled with real pleasure, and for the first time I was worried. I mean, he was *happy* I brought that up. I remembered what the Amazons had said—these people were dangerous. "Oh, but they were only along to help. It was the so-called professional we hired who botched this so badly."

Bald Thug, he meant. So they were going to fob it all off on him. What was the point? *He isn't around, too bad, he's escaped somewhere,* whatever they were going to say—why even bring it up? "Well, he seemed pretty certain his job was to restructure my face."

"Terrible, terrible. But don't worry. We have taken care of it." BvW opened the laptop on the desk in front of him, the biggest monitor you could get and still carry it onto a plane, then turned it around toward me. "Watch. You will see."

For a moment there was only a blur of light and shadow on the screen, then the image regularized itself, and I could see a man lying on his side on what seemed to be oily concrete, caught in a pool of light. No, not lying exactly, but sort of kneeling, with his hands apparently tied behind his back. Someone was holding his head down against the floor. I could see enough of the kneeling man's face to recognize Bald Thug, and my nose sent me a nostalgic twinge of pain. Bald Thug was talking, but the volume was off, and I couldn't hear a thing he was saying.

"Okay, yeah, there's your boy. What, did you spank him for me?"

"Watch."

A moment later the figure that had been holding down B-Thug's head leaned in so I could see the rest of him. It wasn't possible to say for sure because the new figure was wearing a ski mask, but it might have been von Reinmann himself. The ski-mask guy brought out a long, wide-bladed dagger and displayed it to the camera. I could tell by the shape what it was, and although I couldn't read the etching on the blade in the dim light where they had filmed, I already knew what it said: "Meine Ehre heißt Treue"—*my honor called loyalty*, roughly, which was inscribed on all the Nazi SS daggers of that kind. I almost made a remark about collecting the whole set or something, but then a couple of other dark figures leaned in to hold Bald Thug more firmly, and the one with the dagger began sawing at his neck.

It was horrible to watch, even more so because it wasn't fast. Even a strong man is going to need a little time to saw through a muscular man's neck with a dagger, however sharp, especially when that muscular man is struggling for his very life, thrashing and screaming—not that I could hear him, for which I was grateful. The last minutes were just unsanitary, nauseating butchery. When it was all over the camera shut off, so that the last view was of the headless neck and the blood-spattered torso.

Baldur von Reinmann closed the laptop and sat back, his face pleasant and self-satisfied. "The honor of our group is very important to us, Mr. Dollar, and we do not take our debts lightly. And in case you think we staged this like some American television show, I have a gift for you." He leaned down and lifted something from the floor behind his desk, then thumped it down on top of his blotter. It was what they call a DJ case, a cube-shaped box about a foot on each side with a lid that snapped shut and locked; DJs use them to lug their vinyl records around from gig to gig. "A gift for you, Mr. Dollar, to show our sincerity. Go ahead, look inside. You will know that the unfortunate attack on you has been repaid."

I've seen a lot in my day, so it wasn't like I was worried I was going to throw up or anything, but I definitely wasn't feeling quite as light-hearted as I had when I came in. I knew from Gustibus and the Amazons that these guys were killers, so that was no surprise, but the positive pleasure von Reinmann took in showing me the execution put him in the next class down: sadists and crazies.

Not much of a surprise, I thought, *These are the kind of people the Highest made Hell for in the first place.*

I did my best to look unmoved, but I didn't open the box, either, just left it sitting there like a little spaceship from the planet Decapitron that had landed in the middle of the desk. "Okay, if you're done with your little presentation, I need answers. You said we could work together. What is it that you think we have in common?"

He smiled an empty smile. "The Horn, Mr. Dollar. You know it as well as I do, so I will not insult your intelligence. The Horn of Abigor."

Bingo. At least we weren't going to waste any more time. "Abigor? You mean Eligor?"

He waved his hand again. "Abigor, Eligor, Eligos—these immortal beings have as many names as they have men who worship them or pray for their mercy. You have shown a rare ability to obtain artifacts others can only dream of. The Horn of Abigor would be of particular use to us. Whatever you are being paid, I have been authorized by our leader to pay you one hundred and fifty percent."

"Your leader? I thought you were the leader."

He smiled, but this time it was a little tighter. "No, no. The Black Sun is an old and august society, and although I have been lucky enough to make my way into the upper ranks of our faction, we all give our allegiance to the master—the Imperator, all praise him." Timon and Pumbaa repeated the words in a murmur, like a catechism.

"We are a far greater force than you can know, Mr. Dollar—a powerful movement, an army. We can offer you much besides our friendship, but our friendship alone is a very good thing to have."

"I'm sure." I said. "And what will you do with the horn if you get it?"

He shook his head, still smiling. "Come, we cannot answer all questions. Besides, it will be for our master to decide. But you need not worry. Only good will come of it. We are not some nihilistic sect, some anarchist cell intent on tearing down all civilization. We are *builders,* Mr. Dollar!"

"Yeah, I'm sure. But it didn't take long for the Soviet tanks to bring down all that Nazi architecture in Berlin, did it?"

For a moment I saw something not just angry, but insanely so, a glint in his green eyes. I braced myself to get hit, but he only sat back in his chair and wagged his finger at me like an annoyed schoolmaster. "You will not see me rise to such bait, Mr. Dollar. We have a certain connection to some of the older *Volkisch* movements, but Hitler was a fool and an amateur—and a racist!" He said it like I might be surprised to hear it. "He wasted far too much time worrying about the Jews when the real enemies were closer, far closer."

"And those real enemies are?"

"We have spent too much time on this already, Mr. Dollar." He stood, unfolding his long, lean frame from the chair. "Now, do we make our agreement to cooperate? It will mean better money for you, and in the long run it will mean much more. You will find yourself part of a very, very influential movement, and we will only gain power in the years ahead."

"And what if I say no? Because I'm kind of used to working alone."

"But that is precisely the problem," said BvW. "Because it leads to misunderstandings. Like this." He indicated the box on the desk. "No, I think you will say yes. After all, what else can you say?"

"So I say yes, and then I walk out?"

"More or less," he said. He reached down and pushed a button on his phone and a side door opened. Three more men entered, all similar in age and appearance to the two missionaries (as I still thought of them). All wore the kind of jackets that were good for concealed carry, and this time I was pretty sure they were packing more than just pepper spray. "Some of my associates will go with you, of course, to pick up anything you might need before you move in here with us. We have extensive dormitories in the upper rooms, and many rooms to choose from. Surely you will like that better than, pardon me, the ghetto where you have been living." So they apparently didn't know I'd moved out of Tierra Green, or where I'd moved to. I was happy to hear that.

With the three new guys in the room, the odds had just become dramatically worse if I'd planned to fight my way out—but I hadn't. Still, I decided it was time to get the party started, before any more neo-Nazis appeared, so I stood and moved a careful step closer to the desk. As I expected, von R. shifted so that he was still between me and my weapons. He wasn't just big, he was smart. I reminded myself not to let the master-race bullshit make me careless.

"Oh, one thing I wanted to ask you," I said, pausing in front of the desk. "Why Baldur von Reinmann?"

He seemed caught off balance. "What do you mean?"

"I mean, Baldur, the Norse god of light? Reinmann—'pure man'? Isn't that a bit like calling yourself Jesus von Superman? I mean, doesn't anybody in your organization just start laughing sometimes?"

His long pale face went very cold. "Ah. I was told you had an odd sense of humor."

"No, really. I've been doing some research." I turned to Timon, Pumbaa, and the new guys. "Do you fellas all know this? I mean, your boss here has had a shit-ton of names. First he was plain old Morten Egge, son of an Oslo dentist and big into *Star Wars*. Then he was something else for a while—Svein Hvitkriger or something, when he started hanging out with the black metal crazies. Hey, did you guys play in one of his bands? Anyway, what came next?" I turned to von Reinmann, who was getting paler by the second. "Oh, yeah, the black metal thing was going so well he changed his name to 'Uruk' and became a movement spokesman—death metal church-burners and cough-syrup drinkers just *love* those Tolkien names. And now he's Baldur von Reinmann, *uberleutnant* of the Black Sun Faction." I shook my head. "Opportunist—or just kind of teenage? 'Help me, I don't know who I am!' Are you going to be a hippie next and name yourself Barley or Sunflower or something?"

Von Reinmann was distinctly not amused. "Hurt him," he told his men.

"Yeah," I said. "You can try." I threw a mocking Nazi salute. "Sieg heil, baby!" And then I stamped my right heel on the floor as hard as I could.

If my trick didn't work, I was going to be in a world of trouble. Give me a gun, a few sharp objects, a good night's sleep, and a lot of cover, and with my angel advantages I might—just might—be able to take five or six guys, but I'm not promising anything. In the middle of my enemies' turf in an upper floor office, with nothing in my hands but sweat, I was more likely to wind up shot to ribbons. That was why I had stayed up late the previous night.

You may not know this, but you can make a pretty damn good ninja flash-bang that also smokes like a motherfucker with mostly house-hold stuff. I'd added a few touches of my own to make the smoke cloud grow bigger and faster—and no, I'm not going to tell you about how to do that—but you can put together something a bit less oomphy with just potassium nitrate, sugar, and the pebbly stuff out of those little snap blasters you find all over during Chinese New Year, the ones you throw down that explode with a little pop.

I'd also glued a small metal plate into the upper side of the hole I'd hollowed into the heel of my shoe, so if I miscalculated there'd be less chance I'd blow my own foot off. I'm an angel and it would probably grow back eventually, but that still wouldn't make it fun.

Anyway, I stomped down as hard as I could and the charge went off. Wow, did it go off. Because I had only covered the hole with some black putty, all the force went backward (it still felt like someone had shot me in the sole of the foot), directly at Timon and Pumbaa. The *BANG* was loud enough to stagger everybody in the room who wasn't expecting it, strong enough nearly to knock me off my pins, and the amount of smoke that billowed out was very satisfying. Within a second and a half, before anyone could do more than paw at their holsters, the cloud was head high and swirling all around me. Baldur von Rightwing screamed something, then people were lurching all around, trying to find your humble narrator.

Which is why I was glad they didn't know I was an angel. I dropped to my knees where the smoke was thickest, opened a Zipper in the air, and then crawled inside.

See, the great thing about Zippers is that the bubble into no-Time that they open can only be seen by angels and other similar types of beings. As far as the Black Sun boys were concerned, I'd just vanished.

On the other side of the Zipper, I crouched in clouds of motionless smoke that were as resistant to my touch as cotton candy, and I waited. It's never an exact thing, the slippage between Outside and real-world time, so I had to give it long enough to make sure Baldur and his men had gone looking for me. If I came back out too fast I'd find myself in the middle of several angry, ear-damaged Nazis with guns, and my life would become painfully ugly.

I couldn't hear or see what was going on outside my little bubble, so I counted until I was pretty sure I'd lasted three or four minutes, then I stepped back through the Zipper and let real time catch up with me.

To my great happiness, I'd managed it correctly. The room was empty except for the remaining traces of smoke. Behind the screen of iron bars the window was now open; chill November breeze was clearing the room. I grabbed my gun and other weapons off von Reinmann's desk, and when I noticed a flash drive sticking out of his laptop, I grabbed that too. Then I slipped out the door into the third floor hallway as discreetly as I could.

The Black Sun people had no idea what I'd done, so they had scattered through the building looking for me. I could hear a couple of them shouting from the fire escapes at either end of the corridor, which had been my first choice for a getaway, so that wasn't going to work. Instead, I hurried down the stairs to the second floor where the receptionist was still sitting at her desk, no doubt wondering why her co-workers were running all over the building shouting and waving guns.

I stopped in front of the desk. Her eyes went wide with fear even though I didn't point my gun at her. "Look," I said, "I don't know if you're one of these Kool-Aid drinkers, but if you're *not* a racist monster, I suggest you grab your purse and your coat and get the hell out of this building and never come back. There's a severed head on the desk upstairs. Police are going to be here soon and things are going to turn, well, difficult."

I didn't wait to see what she did, because I could hear the street-level door bang open below and footsteps mounting the stairs. I dashed into the stairwell and halfway down, then opened another Zipper, not to dodge them this time, but just to give myself a couple of seconds to think about how this could play out. Then I stepped out of it again and smacked the first guy coming up the stairs with the butt of my automatic, right between the eyes. He went down like a cow hit with a captive-bolt gun, and tangled his comrade so that the second guy's gun discharged right over my shoulder. I jumped over them both and hit the door running. Embarrassingly, I forgot about the steps outside and almost broke my leg, but when I got up I hadn't done anything worse than skin my knee and ruin my pants.

I was trying to decide which direction gave me the best chance of escape without a public firefight when the second guy from the stairs (who'd only fallen down) came crashing out the door after me. I think it was the brown-haired missionary Timon, still holding his gun and looking distinctly unhappy. By then, of course, I was running.

Pow! A shot flew past me and snapped off the brick facing, sending chips everywhere, including into the skin of my face. I turned to shoot back at him as I was running, trying to find an angle where I wasn't going to hit anyone on the street if I missed, and ran right into a fucking parking meter. It was like being whacked with God's three-iron. My gun flew out of my hand, and I went stumbling, falling, rolling into the street.

By the time I got myself sitting up, Timon knew he had me and had slowed to a walk, his gun leveled at me. I was calculating the ridiculously small odds that I could hit him with my one throwing-knife while lying on my back thirty feet away, when my pursuer suddenly stumbled and let out a shriek like a man getting a surprise, no-anesthetic appendectomy. He dropped onto the sidewalk and lay there screeching hoarsely, rolling from side to side, something long and thin sticking out of him like a misplaced chopstick.

A car screeched to a halt next to me. The door opened and before I knew it someone was trying to pull me in. I started to fight until I recognized Oxana. I shook her off, crawled back to retrieve my gun, then scrambled into the back seat. Before I even had the door closed, Halyna pushed down the accelerator and threw the boxy little car into a broad u-turn that had oncoming traffic honking and swerving. Timon was still wailing on the sidewalk when we turned the corner.

"I shoot him!" said Oxana proudly, waving a competition crossbow at me from her place in the passenger seat.

"You were supposed to stay away," I said, but mostly I was trying to catch my breath.

"He was try to shoot you, so I shoot him!" she said, ignoring me.

"Pretty good aim," I admitted. "Right in the knee. I guess he'll have to quit the Aryan University track team."

"Knee?" She sounded disappointed. "I was try to shoot him in testes."

"You know what?" I said. "You girls are fun. But scary." I leaned back in the seat, still sweating. "Before we reach the freeway, let's find a pay phone, if such a thing even exists any more. I need to call the cops and make an anonymous report about some really bad people on Centennial Avenue."

nineteen
karma comedian

THE WOMEN were still talking excitedly about arrowing people in the balls when we pulled into the garage at Caz's apartment.

"I wish my mother still alive," Oxana said suddenly.

"What?" I was examining the bottom of my shoe. The explosive packed in the heel had melted half the sole, which explained why the back of my foot felt sunburned. "Your mother?"

"Yes. She very church, very religion. I tell her I save angel, she is so proud!"

For about half a second it was silent in the car, like someone had loudly passed gas. "You two know I'm an angel?" I said at last.

"We know, of course," said Halyna as she turned off the engine. "You think we run away with some normal man to fight Anahita? She is much bigger, stronger angel even than you!"

I was a little hurt that I hadn't won them over with just my swagger and charm, but I had to admit it would save me the long, embarrassing lecture I had been planning about how when a Deity loves a planet very much, they get married and make little cherubs.

"Okay," is what I said instead. "Glad you're cool with it."

I don't know about you, but I'm always kind of wired after people have been shooting at me. As for the Amazons, they were pretty high on the whole adventure, so after we got back I let them take my car and go over to Junior's Catering to pick up some food while I did some strategic thinking.

The Junior Burger, which you can only get there, and only when Junior wants to make them, is one of the great inventions of modern cuisine. He puts the cheese and grilled onions and hot peppers between two patties, then crimps them into one big patty and slaps it on the fire. When it comes off, it's magic. I sometimes think that Junior props up the entire economy of the Ravenswood district. Certainly the place is always crowded, with a dozen people waiting outside just to get in and order, and about three-quarters of them are from the rich side of the freeway.

It was a reasonable evening, so I took a beer and went outside to the courtyard to think. I finally saw a neighbor, a young guy in a suit who kind of half-waved at me (like a man meeting a dog that may or may not be dangerous) before scurrying back into his apartment. The people who lived in this semi-expensive oasis in the middle of a poor neighborhood seemed to be the kind of folks who were making money but were never at home; singles who drove to Tahoe every weekend to go snowboarding or something. I wondered what they'd think if they knew an angel had sublet the demon-woman's apartment. I'd be willing to bet they wouldn't have cared as long as they didn't have to make small talk with me on their way from the garage to their sturdily bolted doors.

My cell rang, which startled me a little. The call failed, so I walked away from the apartment until I got a whole bar. It rang again, and I picked up but didn't say anything.

"Bobby?"

I was slightly relieved. "Clarence. How are things for our littlest angel?"

"What's going on with you?" he asked. "Everybody in the Compasses is saying you quit or something."

I laughed, despite myself. "As if. You know what the retirement plan for ex-angels is? Neither do I, because there's no such thing. I just asked for a little time off." But I wasn't thrilled with the idea my colleagues were already talking about it when I hadn't had an official reply from Heaven. "How did you hear about it?"

"Who hasn't?"

Alice. Why was it that you couldn't get the time of day out of our superiors without a feasibility study and an environmental impact report, but Alice could announce my business to everybody she talked to? "Nah, I didn't quit, I've just got stuff to do. In fact, I need to talk to you. Is your car working?"

"I have one I can use."

"Good. Meet me in the Crescendo Club parking lot. It's on the Camino Real between Santa Cruz and Valparaiso."

"You mean now?"

"No, I was thinking right after the Last goddamn Trump—you know, while everyone else is hurrying to final judgement. Yes, now."

"But I just got in!"

"Sorry, but I really need you to meet me there. Do not—repeat, *do not*—bring Wendell. And do not even *consider* calling Garcia G-Man Windhover. If something goes wrong with your ride, let me know, and I will come all the way up to Brittan Heights and get you, even though it's been a long fucking day where once again bad people tried to injure me, and I am exhausted and sore."

"I said I've got a car." The lad was sullen as a scolded teenager.

"Good." I remembered that the Amazons were still out at Junior's. "I just thought of something. Better make it about forty minutes."

I drove the Camino Real with a burger in one hand. Here's an important Bobby Dollar lesson for life: You cannot eat a good burger with one hand if you don't want stuff in your lap. Luckily I have had years of driving-while-eating experience: I know to use the wrapper as a picnic blanket so I don't show up to meet the recently dead with pickle chips and mustard splotches on my crotch.

Clarence was parking an obscenely large car when I got there, the kind of thing that looked like it should be towing water-skiers. I pulled up next to it.

"What the hell is that?" I asked. "Company ride?"

"Mine's in the shop. This belongs to my landlady."

"I never would have guessed. Come on, hop in."

"Why? I thought we were going to have a drink and talk?"

"No, I picked this place because it stays open late so your car won't get towed. We'll drink and talk, all right, just not here. Don't worry, your landlady's wheeled yacht will be fine. Nobody's going to steal it because nobody knows how to drive a Toledo Steam Carriage anymore."

He just gave me a look. The kid was learning. "Where are we going?" he asked as we sped back across town.

"I'm taking you to meet the rest of the team. But where we're going is a secret, and that really means *secret* this time. You don't tell Wendell or G-Man or your landlady, and especially you do not mention it to Alice, who would immediately broadcast it to the entirety of Heaven and Earth. Understood?"

"Why would I tell Alice?"

"I don't know, I'm just trying to make a point. Shit has gotten real serious now, and it's going to get seriouser soon."

" 'Seriouser'?"

"Fuck the shut up, kid. Listen. From now on, I am *at war*. To the extent that your existence is tragically but irrevocably linked with mine, so are you. Got it?"

He was silent for a while as we made our way down the Embarcadero, the height of the buildings going up and down like a bar graph depending on how wealthy the part of town. "You know," he said at last, "I really didn't appreciate that threat the other day."

I didn't really know what he was complaining about—I'd stuck a pistol in the Amazons' faces, but they weren't bitching. "Well, I'd say sorry, but I'm not. I am totally not kidding—I'm at war. Nazis were trying to shoot me today, and believe it or not, armed fascists are actually the least of my worries."

"But I'm already risking my career, Bobby. Actually, I'm risking my soul for you and Sam. Why do you keep treating me like I'm some stupid kid?"

Okay, I admit I felt a sting. "Look, I'm doing the best I can, but I'm not real trusting by nature. When I trust people, I usually get fucked over. And as for you, hell, I'm not even sure I *like* you yet."

"Thanks a lot." But he sounded almost as amused as angry. "I just thought maybe you didn't trust me because . . ."

"What, because you're gay?" Now I got angry. Good thing I'd finished my burger long ago or there would have been dill chips flying everywhere. "Shit, do you really think I care? I've been to Hell, kid! I could care less what you or anyone else does for love and companionship in this stinking universe. I do not care who you get sexy with. Got it? Do. Not. Care."

"Actually, I was going to say, *'because I tried to arrest Sam.'*" He laughed. "Wow, somebody kind of made a big old Freudian mess all over themselves, huh?"

"Shut up."

As you can see, I won the argument. Because my car, my rules.

After I introduced him to the Amazons, who were still wiping mayonnaise from their faces when we came in, and wearing the happy glow of a couple of world-class cheeseburger virgins who'd just had their cherries popped in a big way, Clarence walked around Caz's apartment, eyes wide. "This is crazy," he said. "I mean, the decor, it's . . ."

"Don't." I was a little sensitive about it.

"I didn't mean anything bad." He paused in front of the desk, where I had been working on Caz's laptop. "Is this safe? I mean, if you're trying to keep your location a secret."

"I'm not stupid, Junior. It's a proxy connection—several proxy connections, in fact. If Hell couldn't find Caz through this, Heaven won't be able to track us either."

(A quick aside: when I first moved the Amazons into the apartment, I looked through Caz's computer to make sure there wasn't anything on it that would compromise her safety if the Amazons saw it. Doing that felt creepy, but necessary. But the really weird thing was that, other than factory-installed apps, her computer had only about three or four things on it, all of them completely innocuous, like local restaurant reviews. Seriously, it was like examining your grandmother's computer, except with fewer cat pictures. Even with all the precautions she'd taken over the connection, I guess somebody like Caz, born a century before Leonardo Da Vinci, still didn't feel all that confident about technology.)

The laptop screen Clarence was staring at was full of Google Earth satellite photos. I had also covered about forty pieces of scratch paper with complicated (and probably useless) attempts to figure out the angle of the photo from Donya Sepanta's garden, and thus narrow down the location of her house for a close-up search. I started to explain all this to Junior, but the little upstart interrupted me. "I get why you think you've found Anaita's secret identity. But why don't you just find her address the normal way?"

"What normal way? Do you think that an important angel like Anaita—who's not supposed to be spending large amounts of time on Earth, plus is up to her holy neck in all kinds of weird intrigues, not least thwarting the entire plan of Heaven and Hell by creating an alternative destination for human souls—is going to have a listed number?"

He shook his head. "No, but if she's living an earthly life, even part time, she's probably not pruning her own shrubbery. She has parties, right? Some kind of social life? She must have caterers, a dressmaker, employees, gardening service, you know, stuff like that. You could spend weeks trying to figure it out with all this . . ." he grimaced and waved at the messy table, ". . . Boy Scout stuff. Do you always light a fire by rubbing sticks together, too? Are matches for pussies?"

"Don't get snippy, Sunny Jim."

"Look, just let me do it. I came from the Records Hall of Heaven, Bobby. I know something about finding information."

"Yeah, but you're not a very good liar. Sometimes you have to lie to people."

He directed me away from the desk and sat down. "Find something useful to do. Clean your gun or something. If I need someone who couldn't tell the whole truth if his life depended on it, I'll let you know."

Needless to say, with sexy Amazons running around half-naked in the next room and loudly making out for hours most nights, all my guns were already pretty damn clean, and every blade I owned had been sharpened and re-sharpened until they were all as thin as fingernail clippings. However, I had been trying to decide what to do once I actually knew where my suspect lived, so I figured I might as well get on with that part.

Monica picked up on the second ring. "Naber."

"It's Bobby."

There was a bit of a pause. There always is. The kind of history Monica and I have is just pleasant enough that I can always call her, but not so much that we don't usually start off with one of those awkward pauses. "Yes, hello, Bobby. How are you?"

"Been better. Been worse. Any chance I could buy you a cup of coffee?"

I swear I could hear her thinking. "What does that mean, exactly?" she said at last.

"Nothing weird, I promise. I really need to talk to you. In fact, I need a favor."

"Ah." She sounded more comfortable now. "When? I'm just on my way to a client out in the hills."

"I could meet you on your way back."

"Okay." She named a restaurant we'd been to before. "Give me an hour before you set out. Alice said it would be a quick one." The tone of her voice changed. "I think that means it's a kid."

"Sorry to hear it. Yeah, an hour. I really appreciate this. You're a sweetheart."

"Yeah, that's me—the sweetheart of the regiment."

Look, I know I'm not the most sensitive guy in the world, but when Monica came in I could tell it had been a bad one, so I just went to the bar and ordered her a drink, then let her get about half of it down before I said anything.

"Bad night?"

"You know. A nine-year-old girl. Beaten to death by her stepfather." She stirred her drink, then took another long swallow until the ice sounded dry. "I hate kids. I mean, I hate working with kids. In our job."

I could only nod. Kids are the hardest, not so much because they don't understand, unless they're really little, but because they ask so many questions, and you have to keep saying, "I can't tell you," or, if you're more honest, "I don't know."

"You want another drink?"

"No. I have to drive." She looked up. Her eyes were a bit red. "What can I do for you, Mr. Dollar?"

I wasn't quite ready to dive in. "I've been meaning to ask you, how are you and Teddy Nebraska doing? Is it serious?"

"I don't know. He's sweet, but he's so old-fashioned. I swear, he couldn't have been alive past the late eighteen-nineties."

"Is that why he's been acting so weird around me?"

She laughed, but it wasn't one of her good ones. "I think it has more to do with the fact that you scare him to death. He wants to make sure you're not angry with him for dating me."

"Really? Scared of me? Why? Does he think I'm jealous?"

"I told him you wouldn't be." A smile, shadowed with regret. "I kind of wish you would be, but I knew you wouldn't. Yeah, I think he's worried you might beat him up or something."

I sat back. "You're kidding. Me?"

"That's right, Dollar. I know you're a useless softie, and you know it, but everyone else down at the Compasses thinks you're kind of a bad-ass. Fighting demons and monsters, mysterious absences—you're the cool kid on the playground."

It was so different than the way I saw myself—hapless pawn of fate, barely able to keep it together for nine or ten minutes at a stretch—that I laughed loud enough for the drunks in the next booth to glare at me. "You're joking."

"I don't have the energy." She put the glass down and sighed. "So what do you want, Bobby?"

I told Monica, without explaining who I thought the target really was, of course, that I needed to get to Donya Sepanta, close up and personal.

"Why don't you just do what you ordinarily do? Smash through the front door and keep going until someone tries to kill you?"

I bowed my head. "I'm trying to improve my karma, sweetie. From now on I'm going to do it the peaceful way first. Then when I fuck that up, I go back with guns blazing." I was stopped by her look of alarm. "I'm kidding. There will be no guns. I just need to get in and meet this woman face-to-face."

"She must be very good looking. But I thought you had a new girl-friend."

A moment of constriction around the heart and lungs. Who'd been talking? "Where did you hear that?"

"Gossip doesn't come like email, with To and From in the header. I don't know. Everybody talks about it. Some mysterious woman no one's ever seen." She smiled, and it was a little better this time. "Honestly, Bobby, I don't mind. We were never serious about each other, were we?"

I smelled another trap. "I always cared about you, Monica. I still do."

"And that calls for another drink, I believe." She waved until she caught the harried waitress's attention. "How about you?"

"Yeah, why not?"

"So, then—your new girlfriend?"

"It's complicated. And she's out of town. For a while."

"So you're scouting up new talent?"

"If I swear I'm not, you won't believe me. Think what you want. But I do need to meet this Sepanta woman. Help me?"

"I'm not trying to be mean, honest. And if you're serious about this new one who you never talk about, I wish you the best. Now, what can I do about Donya Sepanta?"

I was still inventing the plan, so I briefed her as best I could, doing my best not to harp too much on the need for secrecy, although I was scared to death my pursuit of Donya Sepanta would also become news around the Compasses. If people found out I was after Anaita it could have even worse repercussions than people knowing about Caz. Although now that I thought about it, the downside of both would be immediate ejection of my immortal soul from Heaven and its prompt conveyance to the lower depths, so it was kind of a pick-'em.

Monica agreed to help, pending the rest of the information on Donya Sepanta, which I promised I'd get to her as soon as I had it. "She is beautiful, or at least that's what I've heard. You sure you're not aiming a bit high?"

"It's nothing to do with sex, Monica. I swear on the Highest."

"Bobby, everything you do is something to do with sex. I just don't have the strength to dig deep enough to find out. Let me know when you need me. I'll look up some of my old contacts."

"Bless you. I mean that."

"Yeah. Give an old trooper a kiss on the cheek, and we'll say goodnight. I have to go home. Some of us are still working for a living."

Which sounded like she knew about my leave of absence, too. Did everybody know more about my life than I did? Probably.

We hugged goodbye in the parking lot, and I tried not to think much about how warm and alive Monica felt, or the absence of Caz, which was all I had instead.

When I got home, such as home currently was, I found Clarence dancing with the Amazons in the middle of the living room to Junior Walker and the All-Stars' "Shotgun." I didn't even know Caz had that song in her collection. How did a fifteenth-century Polish countess know about Junior Walker?

"Sorry to interrupt," I said loudly over the music, "but I've had a long day, what with people trying to murder me and all, and I still need to get Clarence back to his car."

"Join us!" cried Oxana. "We are having a celebrate!"

"Yes, we are getting on our groove," said Halyna.

"Because I found the address, Bobby," Clarence announced without ever stopping his science-grad-student Watusi. Before that moment I would have guessed that all gay guys could dance. "Number One Hill-top Way," he shouted. "The place is huge! There's a satellite picture on the laptop!"

I wandered to the desk to look at it. If Casa Sepanta had been built a few hundred years earlier, it would have been a castle. Outside the very large house and numerous outbuildings were walls, a guard booth, the whole nine yards. And there, nestled beneath a bunch of trees, was the outline of the pools from the *Sunset* article. Junior had come through. Phase Two could begin.

So why did I feel like I'd swallowed a large, cold stone?

twenty
lioness

IT WAS a beautiful late fall morning in Northern California, the trees still bright with the previous night's rains, the sky frothy with clouds, and shafts of sunshine striking down like God's own search-lights. It would have been a perfect day to drive in the hills, if that had been all we were doing. But it wasn't.

I didn't have any music going in the car because I was tight and worried. Also, every time I put anything on the Amazons begged me to play Lady Gaga instead, and I just wasn't up for that discussion. They had caught a bit of my mood, perhaps because I'd lectured them for about half an hour before we left Caz's place. Monica had come through, I had an appointment, and the only thing that would stop me from keeping it would be if I had to pull over along the way and throw up repeatedly.

I know, you're wondering why a guy who's been in Hell would be sweating something this simple. I can't really explain, but I think it has to do with the literal fear of the Highest every angel has. I mean, this wasn't just something I normally wouldn't do, this flew directly in the face of everything Heaven had taught me. You don't question your superiors. You certainly don't go to their houses (if I was right about that, which still remained to be seen) and more or less dare them to do something about it. But if I was truly going to commit myself to angelic treason, I needed to see for myself that I had the right suspect. I can't explain it any better than that.

"When we get there, Halyna, you're going to stay with the car."

"That is not fair." She looked at Oxana with resentment. "Why is she pretending the photographer?"

"Because she can't drive. And despite all my careful planning, it's my experience that a good percentage of my work ends in screaming, shots fired, and things catching on fire. If that happens here, I'd prefer not to be hunting for my car keys as I run."

Just at that moment I turned onto Hilltop Drive and continued up at a steeper angle.

"And you, Oxana. You remember what I told you?"

"Yes. Walk in house. Don't go far. Take pictures." She lifted her digital camera. "I know."

"And 'don't go too far' means stay near me, no more than one room away. Go along with anything I say. Smile and nod. If anyone asks you a question that you don't want to answer, forget your English and speak Ukrainian—"

I suddenly stopped talking, because we had rounded another bend, and now I could see the house. It wasn't just on the hilltop, it *was* the hilltop, surrounded by so many acres that you could have dropped the entirety of downtown San Judas on it and still had room for most of Spanishtown as well. It was really quite beautiful, a combination of Moorish and California Spanish architecture from what I could see, but we were still too far back to make out most of the details.

We soon reached the outer fences, impressively nasty things with iron spikes, and the first guardhouse. Two serious-looking private security guys sat inside, and I was pretty sure they were armed. The gate, fortunately, looked like something we could probably ram our way through on the way out if we had to, especially since I'd left my puny little Datsun behind and rented a fairly hefty Chrysler sedan for the day in enemy territory.

"My name is Richard Bell," I told the unsmiling fellow in the booth. "I'm expected."

He looked at a screen I couldn't see, then the two halves of the gate slid apart with only the softest *thrum* of machinery. "Follow the main road all the way to the top," he said. He handed me a ticket for my dashboard and three visitor passes, all laminated and almost certainly electronic. "The guard there will tell you where to go."

More guards. I was very glad I hadn't decided to do my usual and just climbed over the fence to see what happened. I was fretfully aware I had more than my own life in my hands this time.

"Just remember," I said to the women as we followed a long curving driveway lined with palm trees, "this is deadly serious."

"We know," said Halyna. "You tell us many times."

"Yeah, but it's my job to get you out of here safe, and I'd like to do my job right."

Halyna smiled. It wasn't nervy or innocent or anything except an acknowledgment of a difficult choice made. "Do not worry too much for us, Bobby. We have had good training." She was game, that one.

The second guard booth was coming into view, this one next to an even larger ironwork gate set in a no-shit stone wall that looked like it could hold off an artillery barrage. What did Anaita, if it really was her, need with this much security? Maybe this was her idea of normal. If Gustibus was right, she had been a goddess once. Maybe once you've been one of those, it's hard to live down to mortal standards, even if you're trying to pass for human.

Then again, I thought as we were processed by the second set of guards, *maybe I'm completely wrong. Maybe this is just some extremely rich Persian-American lady who does a lot of work for charity and lives in a fabulous mansion.*

The inner gate guards had shotguns in the booth, and who knew what else that I couldn't see. I really, really hoped we weren't going to have to crash that gate under fire.

The gate opened, and we rolled into a huge semicircular driveway that looped past the facade of the main house, which had to be thirty thousand square feet if it was an inch, a tasteful combination of European and Middle Eastern themes.

I parked, then left Halyna with the car keys, telling her to text me if she saw anything that seemed weird or dangerous. She agreed, but from the sad look she gave me I might have been asking one child to wait while I took the other in for ice cream and candy. These women were tough, yes, but they were still innocents in some ways, certainly in the ways of Heaven versus Hell. If I hadn't needed warm bodies, if I had still had Sam, things would have been different. But the first rule of Bobby Dollar Club is, "Things are just what they are. Stop bitching." (The second rule is, "Never ask 'How could things get any worse?' Because they will.")

We were met at the front door by either a butler or a personal secretary. It was hard to tell because he wore a long robe and introduced himself only as Arash. He looked me over with a professional eye. "And you are Mr. Bell, from *Vanity Fair* magazine? Ms. Sepanta has been looking forward to this meeting."

"Thanks. This is my assistant. I hope Ms. Roth explained on the phone that this is just a pre-interview. We're going to get a feeling for the place, and then we can set a date for the photographers and do the rest of the interview in email or on the phone."

Yes, *Vanity Fair*. Don't even ask about all the favors Monica had to call in to make this lie work for me. You can get people to give interviews who'd never let you across their doorstep otherwise, especially if it's for a big-name publication.

"Just so." Arash made a funny little bow, then led us down a hallway and across a courtyard where a tiled fountain blipped and splashed, to a high-ceilinged reception room chock-a-block with (I had no doubt) precious Middle Eastern antiques and some of the most beautiful carpets I'd ever seen, in or out of a museum.

"Please wait while I tell her you're here." He slipped through a tall door into the next room.

I looked at Oxana, whose wide eyes suggested she'd never been inside any private building this big in her life. "Pictures?" I whispered. "Remember, anything written down or any photos that look contemporary."

She turned to me, confused. "Con-temp . . . ?"

"New. Any pictures that look new."

Arash emerged and graced us with another bow. "Ms. Sepanta will see you."

"Wander around a bit," I told Oxana loud enough for him to hear. "I'm sure Mr. Arash will be happy to show you a few likely locations for the shoot."

Mr. Arash didn't look all that happy, to be honest, but he nodded and gave me a tight smile. "Of course."

He showed me through a door and into a greenhouse. That's what it seemed like at first, anyway, even though the roof wasn't glass. An amazing number of plants turned it green on all sides—plants in pots along the walls, in smaller pots on various surfaces, and even in hanging baskets. Several of them had their own individual misters attached, which made the orchids and other blossoms sway like the heads of colorful snakes. The room was so thick with moisture that I felt like I'd suddenly developed a head cold.

The second thing I saw was Donya Sepanta, rising from a teak desk at the far end of the room. Two thoughts struck me simultaneously.

The first was, *"I'm in love."*

The second was, *"It's her."*

Monica had been right—she was beautiful, with long black hair braided into several intricate loops, and yet with most of it still loose and flowing over her shoulders. She was tall, with skin the color of flawless old ivory, and the most perfect bone structure I'd ever seen on a mortal body. She might have been thirty or she might have been fifty, but it didn't matter. Any room she walked into, she would have been the only woman anyone saw.

Luckily for me, I recognized that the immense urge I suddenly felt to throw myself at her feet and apologize for ever having thought her guilty of a single bad deed was not only a very bad idea, it was not even real. No, it was glamour of the oldest, most magical sort, the kind that caused mortal men to dance away their lives in a fairy mound, or return every year of their lives to a hilltop where they'd once seen beauty running naked on Midsummer's Eve, until they finally died miserable and unfulfilled old men.

"Ms. Sepanta," I said, somehow mustering enough saliva to speak without croaking. "So nice of you to see me. My editors are going to be thrilled."

"Come in, Mr. Bell." The voice was a stunning, throaty alto, but I thought I could also hear the childlike tones of Anaita, the angelic ephor, lurking inside it, like tiny pearls wrapped in black velvet.

As she walked toward me I saw her eyes widen just a small, almost unnoticeable fraction; she quickly covered it with a smile so white and perfect I had to fight the urge to fall to my knees all over again. Either she'd just decided I was one sexy dude or she'd pierced my cover already, from all the way across the room. "I've been waiting for you." She took my hand in her warm, dry one—and how did she stay dry in a room that felt like a sauna? She looked me in the eyes long enough to make my hand sweat even more, then let it go. "Will you have something to drink?"

I said yes, hoping that Oxana might be left alone somewhere while

Arash the high priest or whoever he was went to fetch it, but Donya Sepanta only returned to her desk and pushed a button on her phone and asked someone to bring in some refreshments.

"You have an amazing house," I said. My heart was beating so hard I was surprised it wasn't rattling the windows. It was really her sitting there, the one who'd tried to erase me from existence. We were finally, actually face-to-face. "Just beautiful."

"Thank you." She paused as a maid dressed in a tunic over loose pants tiptoed in with a platter and set out ice water and lemonade on a small table near the window, then put down a plate of fruit and went out as silently as she'd come in. "Let's sit here where we can see the garden. It is my greatest joy." Her voice was like honey. I'm not talking about the cliché, I'm talking about how hearing her talk really felt like something sweet and golden and warm and sticky was being poured over me.

Goddess of Fertility indeed. Just being in the same room with her made me want to fertilize everything in sight. I took a few pieces of melon and a half a pomegranate onto a plate to give me something to fiddle with, then forced myself to concentrate, when all I really wanted to do was lie down and listen to her.

Despite her enormous beauty and supreme self-confidence, I thought I could sense a bit of tension in my hostess. She knew who I was, I felt sure, or at least *what* I was. Which was no more than I had expected would happen, although I had hoped the suspense might last a little longer.

"So, here we are," she said, and laughed. Her laugh was predictably melodious. "You must have lots of questions you want to ask me. Please, feel free."

Don't be stupid, Bobby, I told myself. *She's playing it straight—you have to, too.* But I couldn't help feeling that maybe what Anaita was playing was me. "Oh, we have lots of questions about your fascinating life and your even more fascinating work, Ms. Sepanta," I said. "Everybody I've met here in San Judas talks about all the things you've done for the city—but we'll do most of this in the interview, of course. I just like to . . . get a feel for people. See them on their home turf."

"Well, you are a most thorough young man!" She laughed again. She might be a little tense, but I was feeling more and more like I was the one sitting in a cage with a very large, very beautiful lioness who could swallow me whole without crimping a whisker. "I admire that. And are you . . . getting a feeling?"

"I'm a bit overwhelmed, to tell the truth. This is all so impressive."

She gave a careless flip of her perfectly manicured hand. "I need a place where I can get away from the stress. The modern world is a very tiring place, I think. How about you, Mr. Bell? Do you find the modern world a bit much at times?"

"I guess. But it's the only world I've got."

"Ah." She sat back with her glass of water, toyed with the lemon peel floating in the glass. "Myself, I long for the old days. You know this is not my native home, yes?"

"I've heard that."

"Then you can imagine how much more important it is for me to feel safe here, in this new home of mine. That is why I have so much security. I'm sure you must have noticed the guards."

"Yes. Yes, I did."

"I do not wish to be . . . paranoid." She smiled again. "But a woman in my position—well, there are people against whom I must protect myself. Bad people. Both from my old country and from this new land, where privacy is so hard to acquire. Satellites, computer hackers, so many people and magical devices which can pierce secrets, destroy privacy, ruin lives."

That was clearly a message, but I wasn't sure how to read it. Still, I was ahead of the game at this point simply because she hadn't called in the guards to rip my head off—or worse, called Heaven to let them know she had a rogue angel in her conservatory. "Is that a worry for you, Ms. Sepanta? People from your past trying to hurt you?"

"Oh, I have made it sound too dramatic. No, most of the reason I desire privacy is because I wish to avoid the kind of people who prey upon the rich and the successful. Kidnappers. Blackmailers."

Ah. I was beginning to get it. I deliberately went another direction. "Kidnappers, yes, of course. Do you have family, Ms. Sepanta?"

Her lip curled, and the fear came back into my chest. "I do not wish to talk about such private things, Mr. Bell, to you or your magazine." Her expression softened. "I'm sure you can understand. And we have lots of other things to discuss." She poured herself a little more water, and when she spoke it was very deliberate. "Now, tell me exactly what you need from me."

Anaita thought I was blackmailing her. She thought I was here to let her know I was aware of her earthly life, and maybe even to suggest there were other, more deadly secrets I knew, in hopes that she would pay me off. Or maybe just in hopes that she'd leave me alone. I didn't know whether I wanted her to go on thinking that or not, so I proceeded very carefully.

"All I want from you, Ms. Sepanta, are a few answers. I know your time is precious, and that you have other places you need to be and other people to answer to besides a humble journalist like myself. I'd just like to know a few things about what makes you who you are."

"Is that really what you want?" She leaned back a little and looked at me with a calculation I hadn't seen so far. I was stupid if I believed I could outthink her, I realized. This was a being that had been around forever, or as good as, and had survived the loss of her worshippers and her country, only to set herself up all over again as a major player in Heaven. She was a survivor, and they were the toughest kind of enemy to deal with, because they played the long game and didn't jump to ordinary bait. Why should she blast me to cinders now? She had as much time as she needed, and I had nothing but stubbornness and the occasional streak of dumb luck. Those streaks never lasted very long, either.

"I'm just curious," I said. "You've gone to so much trouble to create an entire world for yourself—a beautiful world." I looked around as though I was talking about the huge house and the vast grounds, but we both knew I wasn't. "A beautiful world that isn't your old world, but isn't part of your new one, either. A kind of between-place, I guess you'd say." I let that hang for a moment. "Why? I mean, forgive me for being blunt, but you must have invested a great deal in this project. Is it so important to you to have something that is not of either world?"

Her smile, when it came, was slow and extremely sexy. If I wasn't an angel, or at least if all the non-meat parts of me weren't angelic, I would have instantly had a hard-on or a heart attack or both.

"You are a *very* interesting man, Mr. Bell. Are those the kinds of questions you intend to ask in your interview? Nothing more mundane and practical? Others always want to know, how much do you have, what do you own—material things. But you want answers to difficult questions."

"That's my nature, Ms. Sepanta. I've always been more interested in the why than the how much."

"Well, then," she said, and rose from her chair with a movement so sudden and yet so graceful that it was like watching a great bird take wing, "you must think of all such questions that you can, Richard Bell, to prepare yourself for the next stage of our interaction. May I call you Richard? Because we will have our interview. I can tell already that it is fated for us to meet again." She pushed a button on her desk. "I'm sorry to cut this short, but I have an important phone call coming."

"Of course," I said, caught by surprise but quite ready to get out while the getting was good. "I wouldn't want to keep you."

"But do prepare yourself." The door opened and Arash stepped in, clearly waiting for me. "Because I promise you, next time you will have your answers," she said. "All of them. And some of them will surprise even a man like yourself." She nodded to Arash. "You may show our guest out."

I grabbed Oxana from the reception room and tried to walk like something other than a guy who had almost pissed himself in terror because a beautiful woman had told him they were going to meet again. When we got to the car, I threw myself into the back seat and concentrated on breathing again. It felt like I hadn't really done it for a while.

"Drive," I said. "Just drive."

Halyna shrugged and put the car in gear, and we crept around the long driveway. Oxana started chattering to her friend about the inside of the house, then turned to me. "Lots of pictures, Bobby. I took them just like you said."

We rolled through the first gate. Beyond the green hills I could see the bay, far, far below and far away—an entire world away.

"Did you hear, Bobby?" Oxana said. "I make lots of pictures."

"Don't talk for a while," I said. "Please. And Halyna, take it slow on the curves, will you? I don't feel all that great."

twenty-one

car problems

IT WAS barely past noon when we got back to Caz's apartment, but I
went and lay down on the couch, pulled a pillow over my head to
kill the noise of the Amazons' watching Judge Judy, then fell into a
deep, unpleasant sleep. I was exhausted in mind and body—just being
in Anaita's presence had been like a couple of hours under fire in combat, plus the idea of what I'd done was just beginning to settle in.

I dreamed of Caz, but this time I was on a high hilltop looking
down, like the view of San Jude I'd had from Donya Sepanta's house.
Terrible things being done to the woman I loved were happening far
away, which didn't make them any less horrible, it just made me more
helpless. I woke up sweating, got myself a real drink, and went out into
the courtyard to mull it all over.

Whatever heat the late November sun had brought to San Judas was
already starting to fade by mid-afternoon, but cold doesn't bother me
as much as it does ordinary people, and I needed to breathe something
other than air-conditioning, especially ours, which was getting a bit
strained. Halyna was a smoker, and she had discovered a couple of
cartons that Caz had left behind in one of the closets. I tried to get her
to go outside when possible, but as an ex-smoker myself I didn't have
the heart to send her into cold rain or fifty-mile-an-hour winds, so the
apartment was beginning to smell a bit.

As I sat thinking, I realized my heart still felt like it was beating
faster than normal. Confronting Anaita had really rattled me, because

now I'd taken a decisive step that couldn't be undone. Once she realized there was no blackmail, it was going to be war. I had basically told her, *You want to get me, I want to get you. Gloves off. Let's settle this thing like grown-ups.* But the difference in power between us made it a bit nearer to a six-year-old kicking a Sumo wrestler in the knee. A Sumo with a bad hangover and anger issues.

Honest, I really don't do these things simply because I'm an impatient fool. I mean, that contributes, but my old boss Leo taught me better than that in my Counterstrike days. There often comes a point when all the clever plans aren't enough to get you what you need, so you have to shake the trees instead and see what falls on you. Sometimes it's a coconut and instead of starving, you get to eat. Other times it's a leopard, and . . . well, at least then you know where the leopards are. They're all over your ass.

And I *had* learned things today, some of them pretty damned important. For one, I now knew that I was right: Anaita was the one behind the Third Way, and so she was also almost certainly guilty of sending Smyler after me, as well as transferring poor Walter to Hell. How did I know that? Well, I can promise you that if there hadn't been something fishy going on, the Angel of Moisture wouldn't have spent half an hour exchanging coded doubletalk and subtle but unmistakable threats. If she had been innocent, the moment she'd recognized me she would have said, "You're Doloriel. What are you doing here, bothering me during my free time?" But she didn't, and in fact she'd made more than one reference to blackmail. Angels, especially the old ones, don't just say things by accident. By not immediately calling me out, she had as much as admitted she had something to hide.

The next thought hit me hard, although it was the reason I was sitting in a pretty apartment garden right then instead of being dragged through the streets of Heaven in disgrace. Not only was Anaita admitting she had something to hide, she was afraid of me. Me, the angelic equivalent of the guy who mopped her floors. She didn't know what I knew or who I'd talked to, didn't know what kind of allies I had, who might be backing my play. In fact, the boldness (yes, some might call it idiocy) of my walking right into her home had worried her badly. Because why would any sane angel dare to anger one of the Powers and Principalities right in her own house?

Just because *me,* was the real reason, of course. And Anaita knew me and my history at least well enough to guess that might be the case. But she couldn't be certain, which was probably all that was keeping me alive and relatively comfortable in my fleshly shell.

Was there some way I could bring in bigger artillery on my side? I couldn't believe all four of the other ephors were in on this with her, Karael and Terentia and the rest. But I didn't know the territory well enough, didn't know what was going on among my superiors—heck, I didn't know if I could trust my own archangel, Temuel, even though he'd helped me several times. I wondered if another talk with Karl Gustibus might be useful.

As I sat and watched birds hopping across the cement paving stones looking for seeds, performing their due diligence before winter came for real and fucked everything up for them, I felt a surge of resolve. The only good alternatives for me required me to neutralize Anaita some-how, once and for all, so there was no point in letting the scary magni-tude of what I'd gotten into affect me too badly. I had been heading in this direction for most of a year. Yes, I'd shut a door behind me today, but I had already been long past the point when I could have turned around and gone back.

One good thing that had come out of the trip to Donya Sepanta's sprawling estate was that I'd seen the Amazons in action, at least the low-level kind, and they were good soldiers. No nonsense, no second-guessing, and they had both done what they were supposed to. That was important, because now that I had officially put Anaita on notice, I could feel trouble coming like a sailor feels a storm.

I had some errands to run, and Oxana was trying to get her new pictures downloaded onto Caz's computer, so I invited Halyna to drive downtown with me.

"Where do we go?" she asked as we headed north on Middlefield, past shops and chic restaurants and a few crazy-expensive houses now subdivided into merely expensive apartments.

"To get some new phones."

"But you have a really good phone!"

"Yes, and it's been tapped by so many different people they have to take a number and wait in line to eavesdrop. I'm not going to war with compromised communications." She looked at me, confused. "I don't trust my phone anymore," I explained. "My bosses gave it to me. I don't trust them, either."

"But is your boss not God?" Halyna asked, intrigued.

"Supposed to be, but there's quite a few levels of middle management between me and the perfection that is the Highest." I shrugged. "Who's your boss? Back home, I mean. In Amazon Land."

She scowled, but not too seriously. "It is not called that."

"But seriously, who runs the place? You said it was some politician."

"She once was a politician. Now, she is only the leader of Scythians. Valentyna Voitenko is her name. A very strong, smart woman."

"I'll bet. What about you, Halyna? How did you get involved with the Scythians?"

Now it was the redhead's turn to shrug. "It's not interesting, very much."

"Tell me anyway, if you don't mind. It's still a ways to Cubby's place."

"What is Cubby's Place?"

"It's a who, not a what. Cubby Spinks is the lady I get my phones from—her and her husband. You'll meet them. But I'd still like to hear how you wound up in a mountain camp training to kill Persian goddesses."

She made a face. "Much more than that. Scythia—it is a way of life, you understand? Like a religion, but a religion of women. Not a God-religion. It is about living the right way, the way that women were once living in the old days."

I nodded. "And how did you find out about it? Was your family involved?"

Halyna snorted. "Them? They are useless. I get nothing from them, just watching television, and they tell me not to make trouble." She was struggling with her English a little, as if returned to a younger state. "New government comes in, everything is money, money, money. My family just wants some of the money." She paused, choosing her words. "Me, I am just . . . ordinary girl. No politics, nothing like that. I have girlfriends, even one or two boyfriends. I drink, I fuck. I smoke hashish. But then I run away one day, and the Scythians, my sisters, take me in. They teach me. Valentyna shows me what life it really means. Valentyna gives me understanding, gives me reasons." She waved a dismissive hand. "Where is my father now? I don't know. Where is my mother? I don't care. I have my family now. I have a family."

"And Oxana?"

"She is family, too. She is like my favorite sister."

It didn't sound like that late at night, but I wasn't going to quibble over definitions. We were skating around the edge of downtown, headed toward the apartment towers along the edge of the bay. Not every waterfront building in San Judas is a showpiece, and we were going to one of the non-showpiece type.

I hadn't seen any sign we were being followed, so when we got there I parked in front of the building. We went up to the sixth floor on the world's slowest elevator, then I knocked at number 68.

Cubby Spinks opened the door. She's about sixty years old and absolutely round, with hair in a military crew cut and a tan like walnut furniture oil. The tan comes from sunning on the balcony all day during the summer, listening to baseball games, although by this time of year she had faded to a dull teak color. She was wearing her usual outfit, Bermuda shorts and a wife-beater T-shirt. "Bobby D!" she said. "Come on in!" She looked at Halyna and raised an eyebrow. "Wow," she said in an extremely loud mock-whisper, "so you're dating high-schoolers now. You told me that Parmenter kid was just business."

Halyna looked at her, unsure of whether or not she was being made fun of. "Ignore Cubby," I told her. "God ran out of senses of humor, so He gave her something else."

Cubby's husband Gershon appeared, dressed pretty much the same as his wife, except for the addition of an apron, and made his way gracefully through the piles of electronics boxes stacked all over the living room—no easy task, because he was even rounder than Cubby. "Hey, Bobby." He extended a hand encased in a padded potholder. I shook it. "I'm just doing some satay under the grill. You and your friend want to stay?"

"Can't, sorry, Gersh. This is Halyna. We need some new phones. Five or six, I'd say, just in case some get lost."

We spent the next fifteen minutes or so waiting while Cubby and Gersh trolled through various crates. At last Cubby found what they'd been looking for. "Brand new," she said, handing me the box. "Cheap, because all the instructions are in Serbo-Croatian. They fell off a truck in Belgrade, if you know what I mean. They're totally clean, though."

We haggled over price for a while, in a friendly way, which lasted long enough for the first of Gersh's satay skewers to come out of the oven, the chicken just right, juicy and smelling divine. We had a couple, thanked the Spinkses, and then headed back downstairs.

"They are nice," said Halyna. "Remind me of Ukrainians."

"I'll tell them you said so. I've known them awhile. They're good people, that's for sure. Cubby used to be in the Navy. I think Gersh was some kind of drug dealer back in the sixties."

Halyna nodded. She wasn't the judging type. I liked that.

We had almost reached the expressway when she said, "Oh, I know where this is! The apartment is near. Can you stop there? I want to get something."

"Our old apartment building? Tierra Green? I don't think that's a good idea."

"It is important. That is the truth, Bobby. Please stop, just for one minute."

That's when I made my one, really bad mistake. I was immersed in planning mode, thinking out who should get the phones, where we would go if Caz's place was compromised, and how I was going to deal with a summons from Heaven if I got one. In other words, I was distracted. "I guess," I said. "But it has to be fast, and I'm not parking anywhere near the place."

We stopped two blocks away on Hilton Drive, and I let Halyna out. I stayed with the car, sat low in the seat, and kept my eyes open. Although it was near the end of the working day and lots of people were on the sidewalks and streets, I didn't see anything that worried me. But when Halyna hadn't come back in fifteen minutes, I began to feel differently.

I left the car locked, with the new phones under the seat, and walked a casual route through the deepening twilight, back toward my old apartment building. I watched the place for several minutes, but although a few people went in and came out, I didn't see anything that looked like serious trouble. Even so, I was holding my gun in my coat pocket and was just about to head in when Halyna appeared. She kept looking from side to side as she walked, a worried expression on her face, but she didn't look hurt. I waited until she was out of sight of the building before I crossed the street to join her.

"Bobby!" she said when she saw me. "I saw one. I saw one man."

"Hold on," I said. "Not so loud. What man?"

"A man I saw before. Black Sun, the one with yellow hair. He was in the back of the apartment, I mean downstairs. I saw him from the window!" She looked far more worried than I would have expected from a woman who could probably turn most grown men into hamburger in any fair fight.

"Shit." I was angry with myself, so worked up about Anaita that I had all but forgotten my neo-Nazi friends. I'd made it clear I wasn't going to help them, and had probably fucked up their local operation pretty good by calling the police, but even if they just wanted to punish me for that, why were they hanging around an apartment I hadn't visited for a long time? "We shouldn't have come here, damn it. What did you have to get that was so important?"

She held up a rumpled brown paper bag, folded into a package the size of a hardcover book. "Letters from my sister." She looked sad but defiant. "I could not leave these. She is the only one from my home I still care about!"

"Yeah. Well." I didn't really know what to say. I was angrier with myself than with her. "Just hop in and let's get out of here."

As we pulled out, I saw something skitter along the sidewalk near the car and disappear into the bushes. It might have been a squirrel or a cat, but I was pretty sure it wasn't either of those things. I cursed, but I decided not to tell Halyna. Instead, I concentrated on making sure we weren't followed.

It was getting dark and the commute was in full flow, so it took about twenty minutes to escape downtown Jude. I wasn't going near the freeway at that time of day, so I took the bumper-to-bumper route along the Woodside Expressway until I could turn onto Middlefield. South of the expressway there's a long belt of industrial buildings before you reach the edges of the Atherton district, and I thought we'd be able to get home faster that way. In most circumstances, I'd have been right.

The sky to the west had been red when we were on the expressway, but the sun had just dropped behind the hills, and in front of us the horizon had cooled to such a dark blue it was nearly black. The streetlights were on, but the sidewalks and buildings seemed largely deserted.

"It is too dark," Halyna said abruptly.

"This part of town shuts down after five," I said, but the Amazon had twisted in her seat and was staring into the back of the car.

"Bobby," she said, "something is on the window."

I slowed down and looked over my shoulder to see what she was talking about. It took a moment before I realized that the back passenger window on her side had gone black. Totally black, although I could see lights all around us through the other windows.

The wheel of the car bumped up a curb, and I had to look at where I was going, just in time to avoid ramming a soap-scribbled showroom window. I got back onto the road, narrowly avoiding a fire hydrant.

"Something is coming through the window," she said, her voice shaky. "Like black snakes . . . !"

I looked back in time to see something squeezing through the top of the window, something dark and faintly shiny that had made itself almost as flat as paper to slide through the crack between window and doorframe. An instant later, the questing tendrils became a streaming, rubbery sheet, ribboning into the back seat like someone was pumping in liquid latex.

A tentacle of the dark, rubbery stuff whipped out and grabbed my neck. Another flopped over my eyes. Halyna screamed in surprise and kept screaming. I probably would have too, except the blob around my neck was now blocking my mouth as well. Whatever had crawled into the car seemed to have no shape, no bones or limbs, but I felt something sharp biting at my arm. And I couldn't see. Did I mention that? Not good when you're driving.

Still mostly blinded by the thing wrapped around my head, I jerked the wheel to the right and jammed my foot down against the accelerator. The Datsun leaped ahead and hit the curb again, this time so hard that I could hear the tire blow out. Then something like a giant fist rocked the entire car. The Datsun was way too old to have airbags, but the jelly-like substance that was currently smothering me kept me from going through the windshield.

The collision with whatever we'd hit had stunned the rubbery thing just enough for me to get my arm up and yank the slippery tendril loose from my eyes. The windshield was spiderwebbed with cracks but still intact. We had smashed into the side of a building; chunks of plaster and brick were piled on the ruined hood. Halyna was still screaming, but she was also struggling with the strands that had grabbed her.

I still didn't have the slightest idea what we were fighting. It was ridiculously slick, shapeless, and definitely stronger than a human—that is, if it was just one thing. I grabbed at the tentacle or pseudopod or whatever the long, sticky thing was that had snared Halyna, and pulled hard, trying to get her free. Meanwhile, the thing began exerting itself to drag me into the back seat, where the dark, shapeless bulk of it still lay.

I was almost standing on the driver's seat now: it felt like fighting a giant octopus, something immensely strong and slick, but with no actual shape I could make out. Luckily, my struggle distracted its attention enough that Halyna finally got the passenger door open and fell out onto the pavement. After a moment, she kicked her legs free and rolled a couple of yards away.

"Run!" I yelled just before the thing slapped another slithery arm over my face, but I didn't have time to see whether Halyna had escaped because now something was also trying to eat its way into my chest. Using my legs as well as my arms, I finally managed to wrench the pseudopod loose from my face.

By this point I was nearly upside down in the driver's seat. My unwanted passenger started to flow over me, and that didn't seem like a good or healthy thing. I yanked a hand free, reached down to the floor, and grabbed the first item I could find, the bag of phones, then used it to bash the nearest rubbery arm as hard as I could. It knocked the blob-creature back a little, but didn't discourage it much. The problem was that I was stuck half under the steering wheel, with no room to maneuver. I pushed myself around and toward the passenger seat until I could finally draw my gun. I fired straight into the thing, silver slugs, four or five as fast as I could pull the trigger. The noise was ear-splitting in the enclosed space but the shots did absolutely fuck-all, making several holes in the jelly-beast that quickly closed right up again, and some in the roof of my Datsun that didn't.

I knew I had to get out of the car or I was dead. I didn't know what this boneless monstrosity would do to me—the word "absorbed" flitted briefly through my imagination—but I knew it wouldn't be good, so I dropped the gun and reached into the glove compartment, hoping to find something sharp to cut myself out of its grip. I was lying across both seats, gear shift poking my back and open passenger door only a foot away from my head, but the thing had wrapped itself around my legs, hugging like a python, while the rest of it tried to ooze over the seat and smother me, like two hundred pounds of lust-crazed gelatin.

I couldn't find anything useful in the glove compartment, and every second of fighting one-handed brought me closer to destruction. Maps, a garage-door opener, all kinds of crap came tumbling out, me trying to figure out what they were by distracted touch. Pens, a road flare—a road flare! I tried to pull it toward me, wondering if fire might succeed where bullets failed, but the blob slapped at my head and arm with one of those flapping jelly tentacles and the flare flew out the open passenger door.

Now it was most of the way over the seat, its flabby bulk pressed against the dome light cover, and the only thing holding it away was my kicking legs. I reached out and found the bag of cell phones again. I started to beat the creature as hard as I could with it, over and over, but it was like punching the world's biggest, nastiest gummy bear. Then it finally got between the driver's seat and the ceiling and poured slowly down on top of me, the weight pushing my knees back against my chest. Then I saw the great, blunt knob of the nearest jelly arm begin to change.

It *hardened*, at least that's how it looked—like ice forming on a windshield. The dark, rubbery material turned paler, almost white, then split. The pale bits were getting longer, sharper, a Moray eel's mouthful of ragged fangs. *I'm so fucked*, was all I could think. Because this thing was growing teeth on the end of its arm.

I had just a half a second or so to prepare for getting my face bitten off, when something incredibly bright white and red shoved in from the passenger door. The limb with the new teeth jerked away from the glare, pseudo-mouth gaping. It even hissed. I think it did, anyway, though it might have been the flare that Halyna was holding.

The jelly monster retreated halfway into the back seat as the flare came near, flattening itself into a shape somewhere between a sunflower and a buzzsaw. I scrambled toward the passenger door. My automatic was lost somewhere under the seat, but I grabbed the bag of phones before I tumbled out onto the sidewalk, then kicked the door shut behind me.

We had crashed the car into the side of a big white building that said "Carquinez Auto Repair" in block letters along the top, but I didn't think a mechanic was going to do us any good. The thing in the car was going crazy, thumping the windows until they were all cracked, making the small vehicle shake like a pudding in an earthquake. Halyna did her best to help me up. Her face was covered with bloody scratches. I grabbed the flare out of her hand.

Crash! A big, purple-black arm knocked a hole in the back seat window. The thing was already starting to ooze out the opening when I tugged open the gas tank cover. Thank God this car was old enough that the cover didn't lock. I shoved the flare in, grabbed Halyna by the arm, and ran.

A white-yellow jet of flame jumped out of the gas tank, then a second later an immense *whump* of an explosion knocked us staggering. Pieces of metal and plastic began to rain down around us. When I turned, the Datsun was engulfed in flames, the new black paint bubbling, so that, for a moment, I could see bits of the old green paint beneath, then a second later those bits turned black too. Inside the car, the jelly monster thrashed in the flames for long moments before sinking down out of sight. I had a second or two to breathe, then a dark arm, flat as a ribbon, pushed its way out through the tiny space between door and doorframe, like something shat out of the Devil's own Play-Doh Fun Factory.

Whoompf! Another explosion sent flames even higher, and the flattened, reaching arm straightened and then began to shrivel. A bit of the end dropped off and fell on the pavement where it lay, twitching. People were running toward us now from several directions, so I hurried forward and held the flare against the fallen piece of awfulness until it turned to greasy char.

"Fuck," I said. "Fuck, fuck, fuck! My car!"

"Your car *is* fuck," said Halyna sadly. She wiped a sweaty ringlet of red hair out of her eyes. Her face was ghost-pale. "Totally fuck. Now how do we get home?"

I could hear sirens in the distance, coming closer. The pyre of ashy black smoke had risen far above the building, and the flames reached almost as high. People could probably see my burning ride from every tall building in downtown Jude.

twenty-two
fortune's favorite

B Y THE time I'd finished dealing with the police and we got a cab home (or at least close enough to walk home, since cab companies keep records of where they drop you off) I was in about as shitty a mood as you'd expect. It wasn't the loss of my car so much—well, yes, it was, because cars are expensive, and I was going to run out of money at this rate long before I'd planned—as the feeling that I'd dropped the ball.

While Oxana rushed off to find first aid for Halyna's scrapes and cuts and bruises, I sat down and examined my own injuries in good light for the first time. Nothing too severe, but a number of weird bite-shaped traumas on my arms and legs.

"Okay," I said. "Can anybody tell me what that was?"

Halyna and I had tried to discuss it while the police were there, but all she'd been able to whisper to me was that it was a "bug," which made no sense, unless they were raising bugs in nuclear reactors these days.

"Black Sun gets them," said Oxana on her way past with a bottle of hydrogen peroxide. "Bird bug."

"There is no such thing as a bird bug."

"Not bird. *Bear* bug." Halyna separated herself from Oxana's minis-trations. "That is the name. I have heard it. Bear bug."

I stared at her for a long moment, then it clicked. "Bugbear. Not bear bug—bugbear. I've heard of those, too. But they're not easy to summon."

"Black Sun is very bad," Halyna said. "We told you. Told you. They have things like this they can call."

I groaned. "Great. So not only do I have an angry goddess after me, the Black Sun Faction is now trying to kill me with vicious pudding monsters." But it did seem strange. I'd never seen one of the four-limbed Nightmare Children before or even heard of them, but I knew a little about bugbears, and they were no small potatoes in the Monsters of Ancient Darkness category. How could a bunch of idiots like Baldur von Ridiculous and his merry band of racists call on something like that? And if they thought I had Eligor's horn stashed somewhere, or just knew how to find it, why were they sending monsters to kill me instead of just following me?

I set my gun down, then opened the bag of cellphones, which rattled ominously. But when I set them out on the table I discovered to my immense joy that nothing worse had happened than the backs had popped off a couple of them. My coat, though, smelled like burnt oil and burnt bugbear (which was much worse). I wanted that stench gone, which meant I'd have to hang it in the garage until I could get it to the dry cleaners, so I started emptying the pockets. As I did, my fingers found something in the bottom of one of them.

"Well, shit," I said, holding it up. "No wonder."

The Amazons crowded in. "Is flash drive," said Oxana.

"What's more relevant is that this thumb drive came out of the Black Sun guy's laptop," I said. "I grabbed it when I was bailing out the other day. What with all the other stuff, I just forgot. I wonder what's on it that made them send a bugbear after me? I must have really pissed them off. And where did they find the power or the skill to manage something like that in the first place?"

I stuck it into Caz's computer, but the thing was encrypted up the yin-yang. We tried a bunch of predictable passwords, things like "Sonnenrad," "Aryan," "Fatherland," but without luck. It occurred to me they might not be as stupid as people in the movies and the password might be "4Dkah2%9ja3mv5" or something. I opened myself a beer and thought about it for a moment, then went outside and walked until I had some bars on my phone.

"Clarence," I said when he picked up. "I need you again. I've got a thumb drive from that bunch of neo-Nazis I keep having problems with. It's related to the other thing. I need someone to get into it, but it's got all this encryption shit I can't deal with."

He was silent for a long moment. "First of all, Bobby, I want you to start calling me 'Harrison.' It's my Earth name and, as I keep telling you, I don't like being called Clarence."

"Okay, okay. Blackmailer. I'm sorry, *Harrison*, but I need your help. Can you come over?"

I could hear how pleased he was, and it made me want to put a wastebasket over his head and bang on it until he was less happy. "Thank you, Bobby. Now, as far as your thumb drive goes, I'm not really very good with that stuff."

"Oh, shit, come on! You found that address ten times faster than I could have!"

"That's different. That was just a records search. You want someone to break encryption." He paused. "You know, that's actually something Wendell used to do."

"Wendell? As in your boyfriend?"

"He's not really my boyfriend, Bobby. We're seeing each other, but we're not ready to make that kind of—"

"Don't. Just . . . don't. Tell me this—how did you meet him? Did he come up to you in a low tavern of some kind and say, 'Hey, you're really cute. I hear you work with Bobby Dollar—let's hang out, you and me.' Or anything similar?"

"No." He was insulted. "If you have to know, I met him at a club, but *I* went up to *him* and asked him to dance."

"If your relationship survived the dance floor, he's either desperate or blind. Does he take a dog with you everywhere you go, even into restaurants?"

"You're not funny, Bobby. And you're the one who wants the favor, remember?"

I was getting desperate. Things were mounting up fast, and the number of questions still far outweighed the answers, especially adding the Black Sun Faction back into the problem. And on top of everything else, I no longer had a car. "Okay. I'll give him a chance, but don't bring him here. There's a coffee shop on University Avenue, just on the Palo Alto side of the freeway. Can you find it? Bring Wendell, and we'll talk. I have to walk, so make it twenty minutes, minimum."

"Why are you walking?"

"Why are you talking? Twenty minutes. Wear a white carnation. The code phrase is: *Gay Mafia Strong-arms Angel in Need.*" I hung up before he could gloat.

Despite having to limp there on foot, I beat the pair by a few minutes, which gave me time to down the first cup of coffee I would need to make it through the evening. I don't know how you'd feel, but having a very powerful angel laugh knowingly at me in the morning, then a squishy gelatinous mass with teeth try to kill me in the afternoon made for a wearying combination. What I really wanted to do was take a nap, because I was beginning to think that sleep might be a scarce commodity in the days ahead.

What can I say? The Highest knew what He was doing when He invented caffeine. Seriously, hats off to the Big Guy.

Wendell was just as fair-haired and handsome in person as he had been from my apartment window, with a mustache so neatly trimmed it almost didn't look real. Even more depressing, he was a nice guy. Which didn't prove he was trustworthy, of course. We shook hands. His grip was pretty impressive.

"I've heard a lot about you, Bobby," he said.

"I have alibis for everything except the misdemeanors. I don't worry about those."

He laughed, which just pissed me off. I hate it when people I don't want to like think I'm funny. I'm pretty much a cat that way. Scratch my stomach, and I'll purr at you, but I'll want to gut you with my claws even more than if you'd ignored me.

"No, really," he said. "And not just from Harrison."

I must have looked skeptical, because Clarence broke in. "Wendell used to be in Counterstrike!"

Now skepticism became something a little deeper. "You're joking."

"CU *Nephelai*," Wendell said. "The Clouds. You were *Lyrae*. People still talk about you."

The Clouds were one of the support groups for the frontline Counterstrike units like mine. We often took one of them with us to run special commo or mess with various kinds of machines. Somebody like that would be a goldmine for the kinds of things I might have to do in the days ahead—which meant it all seemed a little too perfect. Or was that just my paranoia engine running hot? Two different kinds of near-death experiences in one day can do that to a guy.

I quizzed him a bit, but everything Wendell said made sense. He knew the right people, the right things, even remembered the busted soda machine at Camp Zion that people called Saint Peter because it turned you away just when you thought you'd reached the Promised Land. That didn't prove anything, of course. If I needed to, I could put together a spurious background in a day that would convince you I was a Secret Service agent or a children's television host. Besides, I wasn't worried that he'd been working in a CU; I was worried that he might still be working for our bosses, and I might be his current assignment.

"I don't know if Clar . . . Harrison has explained to you, but simply hanging out with me is probably a capital offense these days. And what I'd be asking you to do is a lot worse than that. I don't like other people getting in trouble because of my problems."

Wendell gave me that sensible, clear-eyed look I was already beginning to resent. "Harrison told me a lot. Enough to know that I think you're trying to do the right thing."

I shook my head. "Easy to say now. Harder to say when our bosses toss you in the dumbwaiter and drop you into the burning basement for keeps. This is serious shit I'm in, and none of it is fun. Why should I trust a novice?" Why should I trust *anyone* was the real question, but I didn't have much choice, I simply couldn't do this without allies.

Wendell nodded. "I first figured out I was gay when I was at Zion," he said. He looked at Clarence and smiled. "I kind of freaked out. I went to my loke . . . I mean my NCO."

I almost smiled myself. "Don't worry. I know what a CU loke is."

"Right. Of course. Anyway, I went to see him, and I told him. I was fresh out of Heaven and I figured something had gone wrong with me. I didn't know if I had been given a homosexual body or I'd messed up the new body with a homosexual soul, but obviously I wasn't doing things right. He said, and I'm pretty much quoting him, 'Son, soldiers have been humping soldiers a long, long time. Hell, those ancient Greeks went into battle without any pants on, ring-a-dings swingin' in the breeze! And any army grunt will tell you that most navies are as queer as dinner theater. Now me, I don't care if you like ladies or gentlemen. Just remember, No means No. Be respectful of your fellow soldiers, because you all have to protect each other out there, and that means you gotta trust each other.' That's all he said."

"Nice story," I said after a moment. "But I'm not sure . . ."

"Hang on. Three months later, our loke refused to participate in an operation because there were hostages. Children. A demon had got into a guy, and he'd gone into a preschool with a machete and was threatening to start throwing bodies out. Raguel—that was my NCO— said let the regular mortal police handle it, because right now it was just ordinary crazy, but if we stepped in it might escalate into a Heaven-Hell thing. He thought the kids had a better chance if we let the cops handle it."

"But you know the rules," I said, as seriously as if I agreed with all of them myself. "You can't choose which orders from Upstairs to obey. Our job is to protect souls, and as far as Heaven's concerned, that was the important part. You don't let a demon go once it's broken cover on Earth."

"Yeah, but I've been an advocate too, just like you, Bobby. I deal with souls, including a lot more children than I like. None of us wanted any dead kids, no matter how much confetti they were going to throw at them when they showed up in Heaven. But my loke got cashiered for that. I never saw him again. When I found out, I decided that what Heaven wanted wasn't always right, and I've never seen anything since that convinced me otherwise. Scared the shit out of me at the time, but I don't get surprised much anymore."

Clarence reached over and squeezed his hand.

I honestly didn't know what to do, whether to trust this guy or not. If Sam had answered the two or three messages I'd left him in an attempt to reconnect, I could have asked his opinion. Sam's advice is almost always good—not that I follow it most of the time, but it's nice to know why I'm about to fuck up. Without him, I was on my own. Of course, I wasn't completely sure of Sam, either. Did it really even matter whether Wendell was on the up and up? If our bosses wanted to bust me, they already had enough evidence to bag me, wrap me, and send me straight to Hades. And if Wendell was working for Anaita, instead—well, that was different, but it might still be better to have him on the inside where I could keep an eye on him. This was assuming that if he was crooked, Clarence didn't know. But maybe Clarence was in on it, too.

I swear, this is the kind of stuff I think about all the time. Because I have to. No wonder people say I don't play well with the other kids.

"Fortune favors the brave," had become my official motto lately. I was hoping the full version was something like, "Fortune favors the brave, the stupid, and the hopeless-but-at-least-entertaining," because "brave" isn't my best trick. But if I was going for broke (and that was pretty definitely what I was doing) there was no point holding back at the last moment. I mean, you can say, *"Okay, I'll run out in front of the motorcade and shoot the Pope, but only in the arm."* They're still going to be picking Swiss Guard machine-gun bullets out of your corpse afterward.

"Give me a ride back to my place," I told Clarence. "Wendell might as well meet the rest of the gang."

So that was me—signed up and in for the long haul. Sergeant Dollar and His Howling LGBT Commandos against Heaven itself.

After Clarence had shown Wendell around and they'd both had a chance to catch their breath about the decor, I let Wendell have Caz's computer to see if he could crack the Black Sun's drive encryption. Meanwhile, I filled Clarence in on my last few hours. He was suitably agog.

"Anaita?" He said it almost in a whisper. "You're joking. You went to *her house?*"

"Hey, I just brought my second crooked angel to our safehouse, Junior. I live dangerously."

"Harrison, remember? And are you calling Wendell crooked? Hang on, are you calling *me* crooked?"

"One way or another, babe. You two are now officially either cheating Heaven or cheating me. Take your pick. Now help me examine these pictures from Anaita's stately pleasure dome."

It was slow going because we had to do it all on Oxana's phone. She'd taken a couple of hundred pictures, and although the first dozen or so seemed to be pieces of expensive furniture, and Oxana herself could only explain that she'd thought they were interesting, we quickly got to Anaita's visitors' waiting room—not the place I'd been, but something a bit more official in another part of the house. The room was large and tasteful, but the walls were covered in photos, and Oxana, bless her shuriken-loving little heart, had taken close-ups of almost all of them. Unfortunately, the photographs seemed, if not use-less, at least not immediately helpful. Most of them were staged public-ity shots from various dinners and awards ceremonies or even less formal public situations, rich people's parties and things like that. The number of faces I didn't recognize outnumbered those I did, despite the fact that Anaita/Donya clearly knew a buttload of important and even famous people. She had a picture of herself with Jon Bon Jovi, for God's sake. I mean, isn't that about the weirdest thing you've ever heard? A goddess turned angel thousands of years old at the mini-mum, and she puts up a picture of herself with Bon Jovi? I supposed it was all part of her desire to create a human persona. Yes, I guess if you were a rich Iranian exile, you might well display pictures of yourself with rock stars and Ronald Reagan.

"What exactly are we looking for?" Clarence asked after a while.

"I don't think she would keep the horn at her house," I explained. "It just doesn't make sense. The one place everyone would look."

"But you said she had a private army of guards."

"She does, but think about it. Who's she hiding this from?"

"Everybody." Clarence frowned. "I mean, everybody in Heaven."

"Yeah, of course, which is why she wouldn't keep it in Heaven. But who does she really need to keep it from?" He was still thinking. "Come on, Junior—who did it belong to in the first place?" I looked over at Wendell, but he was at least pretending not to be listening too closely.

Clarence nodded. "Eligor, of course."

"Yep. And if there's anyone who could get around guards—or *under* them, or even *through* them if he wanted, it's Eligor. Hell, those fucking Black Sun chumps got a bugbear into my car with the windows closed! How hard could it be for one of the most powerful demons in Hell to get access to Anaita's place? At the very least, she'd have to be con-stantly on guard. Some vacation from the stresses of Heaven that would make! And I got the distinct impression she likes pretending to be a mortal and lady of the manor."

"So what are you looking for?"

"No, it's what *you're* looking for, Sunny Jim. Remember, you're in this with me, right up to your collar buttons. I need you to figure out where all these pictures were taken, when, and who was there."

"And what are you going to be doing, Bobby? Strapping on your pearl-handled six-shooters and calling out the Black Sun Brotherhood? High noon in the middle of Centennial Avenue?"

I kind of liked the idea, actually, but I shook my head. "No, I'll deal with them later. I'm going to be making a systematic check on all of Donya Sepanta's holdings. Because if she's got another property, and she's probably got more than a few, then that's where I'm going to start looking for Mr. Eligor's lost noggin-topper." I thought I might get a little help out of Gustibus on that, since the private lives of Heaven's biggest stars was his vocation, but I didn't want to announce that to everybody here, which would only make them think I wasn't going to be working as hard as they were.

"Mr. Dollar?"

I never really have got used to being called "Mister." If I knew my father, I'd probably be one of those guys who says, "No, Mr. Dollar's my dad." But of course, I don't. "Yeah, Wendell?"

"I got it open—the neo-Nazi group's files. It wasn't that difficult, honestly, I mean, these guys aren't pros or anything."

"Hallelujah." I picked up my beer and went over, Clarence following. The Amazons were still looking through the pictures on Oxana's phone, oohing and aahing over the security arrangements as much as the expensive furnishings.

"I actually unlocked the drive a few minutes ago," Wendell said, "but right away I saw this video file labeled *Die Beschwörung* that had its own encryption, and I just got that open. I really think you want to see this."

"Why? Oh, please, it's not Uruk the Aryan Beast doing the Pants-Off Dance-Off, is it?"

"I wish," said Wendell. Even based on our short acquaintance, he seemed strangely grim. "Just look." He clicked. The video started.

It was a dark room, that was all I could see at first. I was prepared for it to be another cult-murder, or maybe even the one I'd already seen. But something else was going on. "Oh, my sweet Lord," I said as I began to understand. "These Black Sun people really *are* nuts."

The Amazons and Clarence crowded in behind me to look over Wendell's shoulder. "What do they do?" asked Halyna.

"Well, I might be mistaken," I said as I watched the tiny, poorly-lit figures setting out their implements and readying their books. "But I'm pretty darn sure those crazy Nazi kids are trying to open a doorway to Hell."

The last thing they placed on the floor of the dark room—it looked like the same warehouse floor where Bald Thug had met his untimely but probably richly deserved end—was not much bigger than a corgi dog. It wasn't a dog, though, it was a human baby. We could hear its thin cries, the hoarse, hitching sobs of a child who'd been crying a long time.

"I cannot watch," said Halyna and turned away.

I wish I'd done the same, but instead, I watched it all. One of the robed figures lit a fire in a trash can lid. None of us made a comment now, except for sharp intakes of breath when the knife came out, and helpless noises of disgust and horror when one of the masked men slit the child's throat and drizzled the dying infant's blood into the flames.

I wanted to kill the Nazi bastards *so bad* now, I wished I'd gone into their place with C4 strapped to my chest and taken the whole floor out in a blast of cleansing fire, even if it meant I went with them. But I hadn't. I'd played with them like they were just punks. I hadn't thought them worth my attention beyond that. My bad.

So I kept watching their miserable, badly shot little video.

It only got worse after that.

twenty-three
shadow swimming in light

IT WAS so bizarre, watching it happen in that tiny little window on a laptop computer screen. It almost felt if we were spying, as if this were happening right now and we were kids staring through a keyhole, trying to find out what grown-ups really do.

"Is horrible," said Oxana. The child had stopped moving, and was tossed to one side like an empty bag.

"Who are these people?" Wendell asked.

"Neofascist crazies," I said, "but they clearly have bigger ambitions than just making the trains run on time. They've been spying on me for weeks. They think I know where Eligor's horn is hidden."

"Is this really *the* Eligor we're talking about?" Wendell asked. "Grand Duke of Hell?"

"You know him?" Clarence was surprised. I guess he thought only crazy angels like me dabbled in this kind of stuff.

"I know about him, just like any American GI used to know who Himmler or Goering were. He's one of the worst there is." Wendell looked at me. "What do they want his horn for?"

"No idea," I said. "I suppose they could be working for Eligor, but I can't imagine him hiring a bunch of clowns like that. He's too smart."

"And do you have this horn of his, or know where it is?" Wendell watched me, daring me to explain what an angel might be doing with such a thing.

"No. But I want it for reasons of my own. Good reasons," I told him, stung by his doubtful look.

Clarence leaned over to Wendell and said, in a loud, theatrical whisper, "*Girl problems.*"

"It's nowhere near that simple, damn it! But I promise you that it's connected to everything else going on here, that my reasons are honorable, and I want these murdering fascist fucks *not* to have it almost as much as I want to have it myself."

"What happening now?" asked Oxana, who had barely been listening to us. "Is all dark."

I turned back to the laptop. The little rectangular window had indeed gone black, as though Uruk's little snuff film had ended. But it only stayed that way for a moment. Then something began to grow in the darkness.

At first it was only a bloom of yellow light, pulsing slowly on the floor around the smoky fire. *Blood smoke,* I reminded myself. *Blood of an innocent.* But then it began to rise, more like fog than light, and as it gradually grew into a column of shifting, sickly yellow, I could see that something crouched at the center of it, where the fire had been. That something was barely touched by the surrounding glow, its shape distorted and wavering as if this were being filmed beneath the ocean, or on another planet where the pressure was a thousand times greater than here. The light rose in a circular yellow smear until it became a single, unbroken column, a pillar of poisonous-looking vapors.

The thing that crouched inside the light was huge, and blanketed in shadow. I could see no obvious shape to it except that at the top of the mound of darkness two narrow slits blinked, gleamed. Eyes. Then the mouth sagged open. "Who summons me?" it said, in a voice like a cement mixer full of stones and offal.

I knew that voice.

Halyna had come back, drawn by our shocked faces as much as by the terrible, rumbling voice.

"So it's you, you fat bastard," I said.

Baldur von R. now came back into frame, kneeling beside the column of light, dwarfed by the thing he had conjured. "Sitri, great prince! You who are called Bitru, Master of Secrets! We summon thee! We bind thee! While you remain in our circle you will do no man harm!"

"Excuse me while I swear," I said to Wendell and Clarence. "Fuck me sideways! I can't believe even the Black Sun are stupid enough to make deals with Sitri. He's as bad as they get."

The figure in the column of light suddenly shifted, stretching in some places, shrinking in others, still a shadow-puppet but a little easier to see. It had the shape of a man, now, but with great hawklike wings and the face of some kind of cat.

"And what do you wish of me?" The deep voice sounded amused.

"Your help to throw down the mongrels and unbelievers! Your help to bring an age of purity back to the Earth, an age of power for those who truly deserve it!" I could hear the hitch in von Reinmann's voice—he was terrified by his own success. I might have hated his slimy guts, but I didn't blame him for being shocked. Performing a demonic invocation and having Sitri show up is like setting a mousetrap and finding you've caught a grizzly bear.

"And in return, will you perform a certain task for me?" The voice stayed the same, but the silhouette in the oceanic currents of light and wavering shadow stretched into something else—a tree with human fingers, but still with eyes of fire. Before von Reinmann could respond it shifted again, becoming the shadow of a crude, crooked chair.

The neo-Nazi leader was mesmerized by the changing shapes. "Of course, Master," he quavered. "Of course, great Sitri! We will do anything you ask. You honor us with your trust."

Sitri became a pillar of standing stone. "I honor you with my *restraint*," the grating voice said. "One word from me and your souls would be strung like ribbons on the doors to outer darkness. Remember that." This time the shift was more convulsive, and when it ended the shadow was swimming in the pillar of light, a thing of tentacles and beaks and trailing strands, part squid, part jellyfish. "You will find that which I desire, and you will bring it to me. To aid you in this, I will give you power over three servants, the Nightmare Children, the Boneless Ones, and most fearsome of all—"

The shape stopped speaking. For a long moment, nothing moved in the yellow light except a few strands tugged by some impossible current. Then the figure shifted again, suddenly and violently, stretching into a shape that seemed too long, too many-jointed and angular to fit into the slender column. It might have been a man made of broomsticks; it might have been a scarecrow built of long, thin bones.

"What is that?" it asked, and the harsh voice took on a colder, even more threatening sound. "What does that creature do?"

Von Reinmann looked over in the direction of the camera. "He . . . records this historic meeting, great Prince Sitri! For the glory of the Black Sun!"

"No." A moment later a great blackness leaped out of the light, straight toward the camera. Every single one of us flinched. Halyna, who had been leaning on my shoulder, damn near got knocked on her ass. The monitor went black. The video was over.

For a long moment we all stared from the blank screen to each other. Then Clarence said, "I think I might have to be sick," and staggered off toward the bathroom.

"And this is who you're up against?" Wendell had lost much of his healthy color. He looked like I felt.

"Every fucking day. But not just him." I turned to check on Halyna, but she and Oxana had retreated to the couch across the room and were whispering anxiously. "In fact, to be completely aboveboard, I don't think Prince Sitri gives a damn about me at all. It's Grand Duke Eligor he wants to damage. They hate each other. If that horn goes public, Eligor is in serious trouble with the rest of the nobles of Hell, so Sitri wants to find it."

"But why?" Wendell closed the black video window. "What's the struggle over the horn all about? Why is it even in circulation?"

"You'd better get yourself some coffee," I said. "Even Harrison doesn't know all of this. And when you know the whole truth, you may want to re-think getting involved. Like I said, these are some serious bad folks."

"I don't care if it's the Adversary himself," Wendell said. "They have to be stopped."

"The Black Sun? Yeah, I'd be happy to take them out if the chance arises. But they're not what matters here."

Because though I could never make anyone else understand it, the only thing that truly mattered was getting Caz back. Demonic rivalries, Nazi child-murderers, angelic vendettas, none of it meant anything if I couldn't save her.

"I feel it too," she'd admitted to me. *"I have since the first."* That was what mattered.

*   *   *

Once I'd laid it all out for them, Wendell and Clarence seemed so over-whelmed that I sent them home, sending two of the new untraceable phones with them. They looked like they'd been in a firefight, which wasn't that surprising. I mean, it's one thing to find out that things are different behind the scenes than you thought they were, another to find out that not only are things different, but that the truth is batshit crazy. We all, angels included, spend most of our time acting like reality is pretty safe, that the world is more or less familiar, and most difficulties can be dealt with simply by determination, hard work, and (if we're sentimentalists) good intentions. But it just isn't so, and sometimes it's painful to be reminded.

The Amazons retreated to the bedroom after the angels left. When I heard the noises begin I thought they were taking comfort in each other's bodies, but after a little while I realized that, while that was true, it wasn't in the way I thought: They were sparring. At some point they must have changed to bladed weapons, because the *tank, tank, tank* noise of steel on steel filled the apartment. Our neighbors had no idea how lucky they were that Caz had insisted on thick concrete walls.

It was nearing midnight, and I was exhausted after one of the lon-gest days I'd ever had outside of Hell, but I still had a few things to do. I didn't want to wait for Fatback to be human-brained, but I did want to get him going on some of the new information I wanted, now that I'd confirmed that Donya Sepanta was Anaita. I especially wanted to know more about bugbears, or at least more about how to kill them. Also, I now had the ominous words of Prince Sitri to consider. "*I will give you three servants,*" he'd told the Black Sun crew. I already knew the Nightmare Children better than I'd like, but the bugbears, or as he'd called them, the Boneless Ones, were a lot more powerful than the swastikids. I didn't even want to guess at what the third servant might be, but it was likely to be another escalation and I wanted to be pre-pared.

To my pleasant surprise, old Javier answered the phone at Fatback's house. George was back in town, he told me, and was feeling much better for his stay in the valley. Yes, he'd let me ring through to voice-mail, although if I just called back in half an hour, he said, I could talk to the boss in person.

I was simply too tired. I left a message for George, then, on an impulse, called Gustibus. One of the Russian nuns picked up the phone and informed me Gustibus had retired, which I hoped meant only that he'd gone to bed for the night. I asked her to have him contact me and gave her the number off one of the new phones.

I could scarcely keep my eyes open at this point, but I also felt a kind of jerky, wired restlessness that made me want to drink. That's one of the things about booze that keeps bringing me back, like a man who can't give up a woman who keeps breaking his heart: It shut my brain up sometimes when nothing else would. It sucked the jangle out of my nerves enough to let me sleep on some bad nights when sleep was the only thing that might help me.

That's not an excuse, or rather it *is* an excuse. Yes, I drink more than I should, and if I didn't have a very fit angel's body which could heal a deep wound in twenty-four hours or less, I'm sure my liver would be in a jar somewhere in a medical museum, next to Rasputin's famous kielbasa and Einstein's deli-sliced brain.

I had just stretched out on the couch, hoping to watch some sports news or something that would shut off the parts of my brain the vodka hadn't reached. Halyna came padding out of the bedroom in her socks, pulled on a hoodie, and went outside to smoke a cigarette. I had just decided that college football must be the second most over-discussed sport in the world—after golf, of course, which has no serious competitors—when Halyna came back through the door with a very weird look on her face.

"Do you know bats?" she asked.

It took me a moment to shift gears, but the baseball season was long over. "Bats? Like flying rodents?"

"Yes. Bats. Do you know them?"

"I know a little bit about them. Why? Did you see one outside?" I thought maybe she'd found an injured or sick one and was about to warn her about rabies, but the expression on her face was weirder than that. "What's going on?"

"There is . . . bat on the fence. I think. And it is talking."

For a full two seconds I literally couldn't figure out what she was saying, what bizarre wrong-turn in her mental Ukrainian-English dictionary had taken her so far down the road to impossibility—then I suddenly realized what was going on. I leaped up and rushed to the door, pushing past her in my hurry. She followed me out into the apartment courtyard.

"There," she said, nervously quiet. "On fence."

Something was indeed hanging on the fence, and it did look quite a bit like a bat, except that one wing was much larger than the other, and the body itself looked more like some kind of slug, except with a lot of furry legs. As I approached, the little beast turned its head all the way around on its shoulders, so that it faced me even with its back toward me. It looked a bit like one of those tree-climbing, branch-tapping critters, a potto or a loris or something, if pottos and lorises were made of mucus and had one really large eye in the middle of their faces.

"*You are the most stubborn, frustrating, self-absorbed man I have ever met,*" the thing on the fence said in a voice that, despite the distortions of demon-throat and -mouth, was unmistakably Caz's. "*And remember, I've spent centuries in Hell, so I've met some pretty irritating men. And did I mention your insanely swollen idea of your own capabilities?*"

"I'll take this," I told Halyna. "It's for me. Long-distance."

interlude: via snotgoblin

Y OU ARE the most stubborn, frustrating, self-absorbed man I have ever
met. And remember, I've spent centuries in Hell, so I've met some pretty
irritating men. And did I mention your insanely swollen idea of your own
capabilities?

For one thing, you are very, very hard on nizzics. The one you re-
programmed, to use your modern word, is ruined. It sits on top of the candle
flame all day, shivering and moaning. If you feel the need to reply, and I'm
sure you will—because when have you ever kept your mouth shut, even when
you needed to?—you can just burn a little white camphor under this one's
nose, and it will be ready for a new message. Please don't do what you did to
the last one. You have no idea how hard it is for me to get hold of these and get
them to you.

Now here's the important part: You CAN'T get me out of here, Bobby.
Don't even think about it. You had every piece of luck imaginable last time,
but you still barely made it back to the world. Eligor wanted something out of
you, so you survived. That won't happen twice. I'm serious. Don't do anything. Let it go. We would never work out, anyway. In real life, you'd leave
me, or I'd throw you out before a year had passed. We're too different, and I'm
not just talking about the Heaven and Hell difference.

Take care of yourself, you stubborn, terrible, wonderful man.

Later, sent back in reply:

<Are you even paying attention, you squishy little crooked-wing bastard? Then sit up straight, sniff your camphor, and look like you're listening or you'll get the box like the last guy did.>

Okay, it's about two hours since I got your message, Caz. Do you have any idea how hard it is to find white camphor after midnight, even in Jude? I finally found an Indian grocery store that's open twenty-four hours.

What do you mean, we couldn't be together? Do you think I really like being who I am and living the way I live? I went to Hell for you, don't you think I could learn to wash dishes and keep my mouth shut while you watched stupid reality television shows that you liked and I hated? I don't claim to be perfect. There's probably a sliver of room for improvement.

In fact, my number one goal these days is to try living like any old suburban working stiff. I'm not joking, Caz, I'm really not. I'd give my wings and halo—okay, I don't have either of those, but you know what I mean—to be able to lie in bed with you all day, to make love and read the Sunday papers (if people still print actual newspapers). My bosses could tell me, "Thousands of souls aren't going to get to Heaven if you leave your job," and I'd say, "Yeah, sorry to hear it. Just send my severance package to my home address. I'll be in bed for at least the next month."

Seriously, don't you think you'd be willing to give that a try? You and me, a boring ordinary couple? Walk into a party together and not worry some ancient Old World demon is going to jump out of the guacamole and try to kill us? Go on vacation without worrying that the apocalypse will start as soon as we're away from our desks? I could happily spend years kissing up one side of your body and down the other. I'm not exaggerating. I dream of you all the time. I would love to lick, bite, and suck on every inch of your chilly skin. You are like a giant coconut Popsicle, pale and cold and sweet. Oh, but warm inside. So warm.

Don't you dare give up on me, woman. Don't you dare give up on us.

twenty-four
werepig worries

I DON'T WANT to seem like the kind of guy who's always complaining (even though I am) but when I first started out in the angel business I really thought there would be more harping, clouds, and streets paved with gold, rather than Dear John messages from my girlfriend in Hell and six a.m. calls from worried werepigs.

Actually, it was more like five-twenty when my phone rang, and I could ratchet my eyes open just wide enough to recognize the number for Fatback Central.

"George," I said, "welcome back." I think I made those sounds, anyway. I'm not a morning person even on my good days.

"Bobby, I've been hacked. I mean robbed. I think someone was in my house."

"What are you talking about?"

"We just got back yesterday. Javier's grandson was in charge while we were gone, but he went out one night even though we told him not to. Somebody's been into all my stuff."

"Slow down. What stuff?"

"My computers, my voice mail—all that stuff from you, Bobby."

"Shit, you're kidding. All our communications, emails, everything?" This was disaster on a huge scale. I'd been doing business with George for years, and only about half of it was legitimate, by Heaven's standards. Also, most of the illegitimate stuff had happened in the last year.

"No, no, not everything. It's okay—I'm not an idiot, Bobby. I took my drives with me. But everything that came in while I was out of town, because all the emails were copied to my home system. All your voice messages, too. It was meant to make sure I wouldn't lose anything. I'm sorry." He went quiet for a moment. "I think I've checked it all. I can't be positive, but I don't think they got anything that would let them hack into my main records."

Even if it was only the last couple of weeks' worth of stuff taken, it was still fairly catastrophic, because Donya Sepanta's name and a ton of research about her had all been there, not to mention research into the Black Sun Faction and some other things. Was Anaita behind this burglary? I almost hoped she was, because there was no way she could use it against me, not without opening herself to some very painful questions from the other ephors and heavenly authorities in general. It was more likely, though, that the neo-Nazi boys were trying to find out what I knew about the horn. "What happened?"

He told me Javier had already located tire tracks, probably from a Jeep or Land Rover, which led right onto the property from a disused fire road. It sounded like the bad guys had pretty much waited until the coast was clear—in this case, until grandson Steven snuck off with some friends to go see some 90s hip-hop group at the Catalyst in Santa Cruz, leaving the house and barn unguarded. Then the bad guys had swept down for their little smash-and-grab, or in this case, smash-and-hack. "Did they take anything else? Money or valuables, or anything unusual?"

"Nothing. Just information, and most of it from you."

"Did you call the police?"

He laughed in a not-happy way. "When should I have them drop by? When I'm a giant pig? Or during regular working hours, when I have a human body and the brain of a giant pig? My family doesn't call the police for anything."

George was beginning to feel the approach of the dawn, so I told him I'd get up to see him when I could—not that I thought there was anything I'd find there, but just because I felt bad about it. It wasn't George's fault he'd been haunted and now home-invaded, it was mine. He was kind enough not to point that out, but I felt I owed him a visit.

"I don't have a car right now, though, so it might take me a few days."

"What happened to your ride, Bobby?"

Under the circumstances, I didn't think it would make him feel any better to know that the same people who'd been in his house had slipped a giant murder-slug into my car, so I just told him it was in the shop.

One thing I never figured on in this angel business was how much I'd have to lie. It's a very lucky thing I'm good at it.

I did my best to get back to sleep after George and I hung up, but I probably managed only an hour's actual unconsciousness before nine o'clock rolled around, which was when the Amazons woke me up with breakfast. They'd walked to the nearest fast-food place and brought me back a slice of pure madness called a Breakfast Taco, accompanied by a bag of soggy Good Mornin' Taters. I actually ate this meal, and then did my best to pretend I didn't want to run to the bathroom and immediately recycle it. The women meant well, but they hadn't yet learned that the incredible bounty of America also spawned horrors Man was not meant to experience, especially in the early hours of the day.

I hadn't noticed anything immediately noteworthy in Oxana's pictures from Anaita's house, so I had the Amazons send them to Clarence for further study. Then, once the Breakfast Taco had passed the make-or-break point in the digestive process, and I knew I could leave the house safely, I set out for Orban's semi-legitimate gun shop and vehicle emporium. I wandered far enough from the apartment to be out of the blocked zone, called a cab to meet me out on University Avenue in twenty minutes, then started walking.

I had to go to Orban because the number one problem at this moment—number one out of about four hundred or so—was my lack of car. See, I can't do rentals anymore under my own name because, well, because I tend to break them. Not on purpose, it's just that stuff keeps happening to me. You may have noticed. Strangely and unfairly, the rental companies keep track of things like that. I'd had to use a fake ID to get the Chrysler we drove to Anaita's house, and I didn't want use those too often.

Also, I'm always a tiny bit more cautious with a car I haven't paid for, and even a half-second hesitation might be a problem. I once rammed a six-legged something-or-other with a car that belonged to one of the other guys in the Harps, back in the Counterstrike Days. I saved both our lives, but he still made me pay for all the bodywork. So I was going to have to go back to Orban to get another vehicle, but I was worried. I'd planned out what to do with the cash I'd made from selling my Matador, and although I still had a lot of the money, I already knew I'd have to give a lot of it back to Orban for things that went bang and things that went boom; I couldn't really afford another big chunk of it for something that went vroom-vroom. But what choice did I have? You can't fight neo-Nazis and powerful angels using only the SJTD bus system.

It's true. I swear I'm not just being picky.

Anyway, by the time I hiked out to University the cab was already waiting. The driver was a slightly schlubby-looking guy with glasses and a beard, the kind you can usually find in almost any bar explaining why everyone else is wrong about everything except him, but as long as he didn't expect me to talk libertarian politics, I didn't care. I spent the first part of the ride trying to read the instruction pamphlet for my new phone. The only problem was that it was in Serbo-Croatian, and mine is a little rusty.

"Nice day, huh?" the driver said. Since it was raining lightly, and gray and cold, I wasn't quite sure what he meant, but I nodded. "I mean, it could be worse," he added. "Am I right?"

I didn't know about him, but the only way I could imagine things being much worse at the moment was if this guy had a bugbear in his trunk, too, but I just nodded again. "I guess."

"Me, I always try to remember that it could be worse. You know, like I could be in Hell or something."

I stiffened and snuck a look at his face in the mirror, but he was chewing on a toothpick watching the traffic go past at the intersection where we'd stopped at a red light. "You worry about that much?" I asked.

"Not too much. But it's good to remember. I mean, some people don't know when they've got it good. Know what I mean? We never know what's going to happen. And we never know until it's all over who our real friends are. Or our real enemies."

Now I was feeling distinctly uncomfortable, although it was far from the weirdest conversation I've ever had with a cabbie. Still, I shifted a little bit so I could reach my gun easily. The Belgian FN had gone in the car fire, but I still had my good old Smith & Wesson revolver, my sofa gun, now back on the starting team. It was a bit depressing, actually. I couldn't remember the last time I had gone anywhere unarmed.

We slid onto the Bayshore and headed north toward the Salt Piers and Orban's place. I had almost stopped worrying about the driver when he suddenly said, "You sure this is where you wanna go?"

"Yeah. Why?"

"Oh, I don't know. It's just the kind of place . . . well, people probably know you there, know you go there, I mean. So some other people might be watching."

I carefully set the muzzle of my .38 against his neck so he could feel it against his bare skin. "I don't like you much, pal. I think you're going to pull off at the next exit. Right?"

He wasn't very upset, or at least he didn't seem that way. Maybe I wasn't the first passenger to have this reaction. He carefully moved into the right lane and we exited on Marsh Road, heading out toward the edge of the Baylands Preserve. Before we left civilization behind entirely, I had him pull over in front of what was probably an abandoned cement plant, a great pale cube set behind razor wire. On this ugly gray day it looked like the kind of place that might house a concentration camp instead. When the driver stopped the car, he remained very still. Smart.

"I'd prefer not to shoot you," I said. "Because I'm just that kind of dude—agreeable, friendly, interested in others. However, if you don't explain this weird shit you're talking to me, I may just have to shoot you a few times anyway, working my way up from the expendables to the oh-god-not-those. Are we clear?"

"Perfectly," he said. "I guess I'm getting better."

"What the fuck, if I may be so bold, are you talking about? Because you're not about to get better, you're about to be very unwell. This thing is jammed full of thirty-eight caliber semiwadcutters, and if I shoot you in the neck they'll probably pop your head right off like a grape off a stem."

"I've always admired how well you do this," he said. "You must practice."

"Talk! And not bullshit!"

"You really don't recognize me?" He sounded thrilled, and all of a sudden I realized what was going on.

"Temuel?"

"I probably should have talked about sports—isn't that what these kind of people do? But I don't really know anything, and I would have got it wrong."

"What the hell are you doing, Archangel? If you don't mind me asking? Because you just freaked me right the fuck out, and I was about to pistol whip you."

"See? I love that. It sounds so authentic! How do you whip with a pistol?"

I fell back in the seat. I know, I still couldn't be one hundred percent sure it was Temuel and not some especially tricky, well-informed demon, but seriously, who else would be such a dweeb? "Why are you here, Archangel?"

"I thought it was time we had a talk. Some very worrisome things are going on, and—"

"Hang on. Why are *you* driving the cab I ordered? How did that happen?"

"Please, Bobby, give me a little credit. Do you really think an archangel can't get his hands on a cab when he wants one?"

"Don't bullshit me, please. How did you know I called for a cab?"

No answer. His eyes caught mine in the mirror for a second, then he looked away. I could swear I saw something that looked like shame.

"You told me you took *all* the tracking software and surveillance doo-hickeys out of my phone." I don't know why I was angry. What had I expected? "You gave it back to me, and said it was clean. You told me you took that shit out!" I'd only figured out that particular bit of management treachery after Clarence had shown up at Shoreline Park when there was no way he could have known Sam and I were there.

"I did." Temuel seemed agitated. "I swear by the Highest that I told you the truth. I took out or disabled all those things in your phone."

"Yeah, well, that's bullshit," I began, then realized that he might actually be telling the truth. Because I wasn't using that phone anymore. What was in my pocket was my new, clean Serbo-Croatian Cubby Phone. "Hang on—how *did* you know?"

"I can't tell you. You'll have to trust me."

"I beg your pardon? Is this the comedy portion of the evening's entertainment? Damn you, just tell me what's going on!"

"Please don't talk to me like that."

For just a moment, I heard something in his voice I hadn't heard before, a steeliness, perhaps even a cold, hard anger under the mild words. It reminded me that whatever else he was, Temuel was an archangel of the Lord God, and I had been talking to him like he was a street punk. "Look, I'm sorry. I'm under some stress. And I'm up to here with secrets."

When he spoke again, Temuel sounded like his ordinary self. "I promise, Bobby, that I'm only trying to keep you safe. I want to know where you are in case I have to help you. Like now."

"You may be a very good angel," I said, grumpy again but taking things down a few notches, "but you are a terrible-ass liar, Archangel. I'd bet that 'keeping me safe' also has something to do with keeping yourself out of trouble as well."

Another embarrassed look, like someone in a sitcom caught stealing ice cream from the fridge. He'd have been adorable if my soul and sanity weren't in jeopardy. "Of course. I'm letting you run on a long leash, so I need some idea where you're running."

I filed this away for later. Was he telling me he knew about my visit to Anaita? How was he keeping track of me? I was ready to swear no one had been tailing me or spying on the apartment. But if he wasn't going to tell me, he wasn't going to tell me. You don't force an archangel to do anything. Unless you're a higher angel.

I realized I was still holding my gun on him and slipped it discreetly back into my coat pocket. "Just tell me what you're doing here now. What's going on? Why another surprise meeting?"

"It's your request for a leave of absence, actually—I warned you, remember? I held onto it as long as I could, but people notice when you're not doing your job, Bobby. You're a bit infamous. Now the Ephorate is unhappy again, and they're talking about bringing you back in for disciplinary action."

"Which means?"

"Probably nothing good."

"When you say the Ephorate, who do you mean, exactly? All of them?"

He looked troubled. "It's very hard to explain all the ins and outs, but Chamuel, Anaita, and Raziel are the most disturbed. Terentia and Karael have, well, not defended you, but suggested that more information is needed. Karael even said that he thought you might have been more seriously affected by the disappearance of Edwin Walker's soul and all the trouble that came afterward than anyone realized."

"Karael defended me? Well, bless him."

"He's loyal to his soldiers, and you used to be a soldier. That's mostly what's kept you out of trouble so far."

"As well as some string-pulling behind the scenes by you?"

He shrugged, but he still looked unhappy. "I do what I can, but I have no real power. Not compared to Terentia and the rest."

The problem was, I didn't know where Temuel himself actually stood, especially with Anaita, so I couldn't question him about the things I most needed to know. You just can't make too many assumptions where my bosses are concerned. I mean, from what my old top-kicker Leo and others like Gustibus had told me, there were grudges and vendettas being acted out in Heaven based on petty slights that took place while humans were still drawing bison on cave walls.

"So what do you suggest I do?"

"If I were you, I'd ask to be interviewed by our superiors about your reasons for taking leave. Make them more comfortable with what you're doing, why you're not doing your job. At the very least it might buy you a little more time."

"Time for what?"

Now it was his turn to give me a hard look. "I don't know. And to be honest, Bobby, I don't want to know."

That hung in the air for a good long time—several seconds at least. "Why are you helping me in the first place, Archangel?" I said at last.

"Anything I say will sound like . . . bullshit," he said. I think it was the first time I'd ever heard him swear. "But I care about you. I even admire you, except when you're being a complete idiot. And I think there are things that need to be discovered, unhealthy secrets that should not remain secret. If you can do that, then Heaven will be a better place."

"But how can Heaven be a better place?" I said, only half-sarcastic. "It's already perfect."

"We all wish that were true," Temuel said. "But some of us know it's not."

He'd brought the conversation to a halt again. I couldn't think of anything else I could ask him without revealing my particular problem with Anaita. "I appreciate it, I guess. But next time, could you just, I don't know, tone down the who-am-I-this-time games? It's nerve-wracking."

"I'm sorry. Perhaps I get a bit carried away. But I confess, I do enjoy it." He was being cute and twinkly again, which made me mistrustful. God, it sucks to be me.

"Yeah, that's pretty obvious. Can you drop me at the Salt Piers, or do you have to get this thing back to the real cab company? I need to do something about my car situation."

"Ah," he said, "I almost forgot! Get out, please."

I did, and stood stretching my legs. Temuel came out of the front seat, dangling the keys in his hand. The keychain fob was a little enamel angel on cheap silver. "You kind of overdo it a bit, you know?" I told him. "That's my main suggestion—just dial it back a little."

He looked guiltily at the keys, then handed them to me. "Take it."

"What do I want with an angel keychain?"

"No, the cab. It's yours. You need a car, right?"

I couldn't help it. I stared at him with my mouth half-open. "You're giving me the *cab*?"

"Yes. Don't worry—I didn't steal it. Not from a cab company, any-way." He put his finger beside his nose. I'd never seen anyone do that outside of an old movie. "Just don't mention it to anyone in accounting upstairs, all right? Mum's the word!"

"But what am I supposed to do with a freaking taxi?"

"Drive it. I'm told people don't pay much attention to taxicabs. It should be good for your . . . for all the things you're doing."

I could only shake my head. While I was still shaking it, he started off down the road on foot, headed toward the bay. "Where are you go-ing?"

"Back home," he said. "But I thought I'd have a walk first. It's nice to get out of the office."

I watched the archangel until he was only a small shape outlined against the switch grass and rushes, just another schlubby guy out communing with nature. Then I got in my taxicab and headed home again.

Fucking thing didn't even have a CD player, and it drove like a truck, but I guess it was better than walking.

twenty-five
the smart set

WHEN I got back to the apartment, everybody hurried out to the garage to see (and make fun of) my new ride.

"That is so cool!" shouted Halyna. Oxana was laughing. "You are very funny, Bobby!"

"What are you supposed to be now?" Clarence asked me. "The Beatles?"

"Listen, you young whippersnapper, *that* Yellow was a Submarine. What you mean is, 'Who are you supposed to be, Joni Mitchell?' because her old man was taken away by a Big Yellow Taxi. Your grasp of culture is appalling, Junior."

"Every time you open your mouth," Clarence said, "you just seem older and weirder."

Inside, the Amazons returned to lazy alternations of sparring and making dinner. (I'd told them I was tired of doing all the food prep.) I didn't like what I was hearing of their meal plans, something about barley soup, so I sat down with Clarence. He'd brought his own computer and was scrolling through the images Oxana had taken at Schloss Sepanta.

"I've labeled as many of these as I can, Bobby. I never wanted to know this much about rich San Judaeans." He paused on one. "See, that's the governor. Do you think he's in on this, too?"

I gave the kid a look to make sure he was kidding. "I'm not worried about politicians, although you'd be surprised how many have connections with both sides."

"Well, that's too bad, because there's a ton of them here. Look, there's the mayor of San Judas. And a here's a bunch of congresspeople at this event, whatever it was. But most of the people in the pictures aren't that well-known, or at least not that easy to identify. It's going to take forever to put names on all of them."

"You can skip most of the really famous ones, because why would Anaita hand the horn to one of them? She wouldn't trust any mere mortal to keep it from the Grand Duke of Hell, least of all a politician." I frowned at the images of Donya Sepanta going past; formal, ceremonial ones mostly. She, or Anaita rather, was still beautiful in the pictures, but not in the astounding way she'd been at our meeting, more like her own slightly more ordinary-looking sister. The angelic glamour didn't come through in any of the photographs. In fact, she might have just trotted it out for yours truly. "All I really want to know is where that damned horn is. I'm just hoping . . ." Something occurred to me. "Hey, aren't you on call? This place blocks cellphones. They could be calling you and calling you and you wouldn't—"

Clarence rolled his eyes. "Yes, Bobby, I know. You told me. That's why I go out into the yard every little while to check." He flicked to the next image.

"Hold on, go back. No, that one. I saw something. What is this?" The photo was Donya Sepanta and another woman standing with two men.

"Some charity thing, that's all I know, and I only know it because she's wearing the same dress in another picture where she's giving someone a giant fake check. And Ms. Sepanta, whatever she really is, never wears the same dress twice. Why? Do you know those people?"

"No." The men were both Silicon Valley executive-types, badly shaven and slightly long-haired in an "I'm not really an evil plutocrat" kind of way, and the unknown woman was the female version of that, which meant she dressed a little better than the men (because she had to). The four of them were standing with champagne glasses in the kind of awkward group photo you get when you interrupt people having a conversation and ask them all to smile. But it wasn't Anaita or the main figures that had caught my attention, but something in the crowd of a couple of dozen people, out of focus but visible behind them—something that I couldn't see now. "Can you make it clearer?"

"No. I can make it bigger, but this is a picture that Oxana took with her phone of a photograph behind glass in less than ideal lighting. The best government photo labs in the world might make it better, but I can't." He frowned. "Believe it or not, Bobby, sometimes even angels can't do miracles."

"You're not telling me anything I don't already know, Junior."

"I thought you were going to call me by my name."

"No, I said I'd call you Harrison instead of Clarence, Clarence—I mean, Harrison. I never said I wouldn't call you kid, or Junior, or Mr. Smarty-Pants."

"The irony is that the one who acts like an eight-year-old is calling me 'kid.'"

"No, the irony is that you, the one who dresses like a sixty-year-old, aren't grateful for it. Get a better copy."

He stared at me. "I just explained . . ."

"Get a better copy. If this wasn't taken by Sepanta's own personal photographer or something, then maybe it was on some website or in some magazine. Come on, you're Captain Records Hall, right? So find a better copy. I'm going back to looking up her other properties." I patted him on the shoulder. "Remember, God loves you."

I couldn't quite hear his reply as I walked away, but I don't think he said the same thing back to me.

The Amazons' barley soup smelled a lot better than I thought it would, especially once they started to put in the mushrooms and onions and little bits of bacon. In fact, I was beginning to look forward to dinner when Clarence stepped out to check his messages. He was out there for quite a while, and when he came back he said, "No rest for the weary. I've got a client over in Friendly Acres. But I think I found a better version of the picture."

I looked at the screen. "It's not the same picture."

"No, but it's the same event and the same people from a slightly different angle." He slapped at my fingers as I tried to enlarge it. "If you're going to look at my computer while I'm gone, *don't ruin anything.* Old people get really cranky with technology sometimes, and they break things."

"Cute. Hurry back." But I was already examining the new image. It had been taken at a very similar angle, but whatever had caught my attention in the first one didn't even raise a flicker now. I scrolled back through Clarence's recent history and found the rest of those pictures on a photographer's web page under the heading, "Charity event, San Judas, 6/17/03." It named the other high-rollers posing with Anaita, but I didn't care about the main figures. It was something in the background that had snagged me in the first place.

I went back to the first picture and stared at it, then got up and looked at it again from a few feet away, then from so closely that my nose almost touched the screen. Back to the far wall before moving in slowly. Sideways. Upside down. Then I printed out a copy and walked around with that in my hand for a while, turning it and turning it, letting my eye drift over the blur of shadows and faces and shapes in the background until they became almost meaningless, looking for the pattern that had first caught me. And then suddenly, for no reason I could name, I saw it again. It was a shoulder and the back of a head, a man in the crowd who had turned away just as the photo was taken. Whoever it was, I still didn't recognize him, but now I knew what I was looking for. Something about the guy made my Dollar Sense tingle.

Clarence showed up just as the Amazons were serving soup. I had cracked a bottle of Caz's best wine, a really old-looking Burgundy (that's good, right? Because I might have told you, I'm more of a vodka man myself) and I was pouring it.

"Smells good," he said. "May I have some? Wine, too? I've just had the most horrible, nasty old woman to deal with. Even worse, I got her off with only a century of Purgatory. I would have sent her to Hell, personally."

"Don't joke 'til you've been there," I said. "But I have something that may make you feel a bit better. We have a lead."

I handed him a glass, then led him over to his computer. "See that guy? Right there? He was in the back of the crowd. I finally found one of your other pictures where you can see his face."

Clarence shook his head. "Not the most pleasant-looking person I've ever seen, but I don't know him."

"You wouldn't, but Sam and I would, because the last time I saw him he was about to have Sam blown to bits and me dragged to Hell."

"But that's not Eligor . . . what's his Earth name? Kenneth Vald? That's not Vald."

"No, but it's Vald's ex-security chief, an ugly piece of work named Howlingfell, who I'm pleased to say wound up being swallowed by that monster you met later, at the old sea baths at Shoreline Park. You remember the *ghallu*, right? You remember how it . . . kicked you?"

He gave me a really unpleasant look. "Not exactly. I remember how you coldcocked me with a gun and told me the monster did it."

"I was improvising. Look, you want an apology, I'm sorry. You were trying to arrest Sam."

He didn't look happy, but he turned back to the screen. "But what's so interesting about this Howlingfell guy? I mean, he'd go everywhere that Eligor would go, right? That's what security guys do."

"Right. And I'm trying to find anything that might link Anaita with Eligor, so that's point of interest number one. But you haven't heard the rest." I took a swig of my Burgundy. I'm not sure I'll ever be a serious wine drinker, but I have to say, right then, that shit tasted *good*. "See, I tracked down the fundraiser, too. Yes, your old Grampa Bobby's got some gosh-durned computer skills. The party was held at the Elizabeth Atell Stanford Museum of the Arts, that big old thing out on the campus. They were celebrating breaking ground on a new wing for the museum. And Donya Sepanta was one of the main fundraisers."

Clarence was perking up. "And Eligor was there?"

"No. I've found a bunch of articles, society page stuff, some PR crap in the magazines that cater to rich dicks who love to hear about their own good works, things like that. And Kenneth Vald wasn't there. Or at least, nobody made any mention of one of the most newsworthy billionaires in the world—and certainly in San Judas—being at the museum gala."

"But then what's the big deal?"

"Because, Junior, why would Howlingfell show up if it had nothing to do with Eligor? He was either there because Eligor *was* there, or he was there because he was casing the place for a proposed meeting. Either way, it's the first real lead we've had. Now we need to research this museum, especially the new wing. We need to get deep, deep into it and find out everything we can. In fact, *you're* going to do just that. You can have dinner first, though."

"What do you mean me? What are you going to do?"

"Have another glass of wine. And think about what I'm going to need to break in there."

"Break in?" Clarence almost dropped his glass. "Why on earth do you want to do that?"

"I like to get the feel of a place, and that includes smelling and listening and poking my nose where it doesn't belong. And let's not forget, our friend Ms. Sepanta was celebrating having plunged ten million dollars, reportedly half her own money and the rest from her personal fundraising, into a new Asian wing for the museum where she and Eligor were probably going to have their meeting. So she's invested a lot in that place, and I want to know why."

"But why break in? You said we're going to research—"

"Yes, research first, and maybe it will turn out to be a blind alley. But in case it isn't, I'm going to be ready to get in there and have a look around. Because that's the way I roll."

Clarence gave me another disapproving look. "That's how you *roll?* Like a teenage meth addict looking for stuff he can fence for drugs?"

I poured myself some more red vino and sat down in front of my soup bowl. The steam was very pleasantly scented. "It smells lovely."

Halyna and Oxana were already finishing their first bowls, so I hurried to catch up. Clarence finally sat.

"But, Bobby, when you do things like that, crazy, bad stuff happens. And it almost always goes wrong. Remember you and Five Page Mill?"

"Yeah, crazy, bad stuff happens. And that's exactly why I do things like that. Because it's when things get out of control that other people's plans collapse."

"Including your own."

"Including my own, sometimes. But I'm used to living that way. The others aren't. And it's been a long time since Anaita's had anyone stand up to her."

"That's because the rest are all dead," said Clarence.

"Or raped," said Halyna.

"Or make into slaves," said Oxana.

"My, you're a cheery bunch. Shut up so I can celebrate." And I did, damn it.

twenty-six
kids today

DON'T GET the idea that I only ever scream "Geronimo!" and leap into dangerous situations. Sometimes you're not hearing the rest because I'm skipping over the boring parts. The next week was one of those boring parts.

As November clicked over into December, the Amazons and I spent a lot of time staking out the museum and checking out Anaita's other holdings. I discovered pretty quickly that Donya Sepanta had a lot of properties, but the only one in the Bay Area was the estate we'd already seen. I still believed she wouldn't hide anything important there, in part because it was so obvious, but also because it would have been pretty easy for Eligor to infiltrate her household staff, who were all human. But that still didn't mean the museum was anything more than somewhere that Anaita once met Eligor.

Our preliminary surveillance of the Elizabeth Atell Stanford Museum of the Arts, or as much of it as we were able to do from a taxi (which, fortunately, are as common on big college campuses as empty beer kegs) showed us that not only had Anaita helped raise a lot of money for the place, she actually dropped by there every few days, and usually stayed at least a couple of hours. I decided I needed to know more, so I called up a friend.

"You want to do some work for me, Edie? I'll pay your usual rate."

"I guess," she said. I could hear the television in the background.

"But I have finals right now, Mr. Dollar. What do you want me to do?"

"Nothing too difficult. Just visit a museum."

"Oooh, I love museums. Well, most of the time. Sometimes," she lowered her voice. "Sometimes I get a bad one, you know?"

"Bad?"

"You know—not so much the museum itself, but something in it. Something that's got a totes ugly vibe. It's even worse if I touch it."

I assured her that I didn't want her touching anything this time, and we picked a time after school to meet up, on a day when Mr. and Mrs. Parmenter wouldn't freak out if their daughter came home a bit later than usual.

"Okay. I'll tell them I'm studying with Molly."

As you may have guessed, one of the reasons I was working at this so hard was because it kept me from thinking too much about Caz. Because it was really hard to stop thinking about her. From the very first moment the Countess of Cold Hands and I were together alone, something special had been going on between us, something stronger than sex and more binding than compatibility. We completed each other, somehow. We hadn't really realized it before then, but we were both unfinished, like a puzzle with its sad little, bumpy, jigsawed edges exposed. And then we came together. Then we were whole. And then Life, the Universe, and especially Eligor, Grand Duke of Hell, ripped us apart.

I'd never get used to it. It had been an amputation. It was conceivable that someday I might learn to live with the loss, but I sure wouldn't ever be normal again without her.

For a guy who had gone through his angelic life wondering why he didn't fit, why he didn't take things calmly the way other angels did— like my buddy Kool Filter, shaking his head at the craziness of his life but accepting it—that had been huge. It still was huge. I needed her. Now I knew that she needed me, too. Everything else, including the impossibility of it all, was just detail.

I read up on the Elizabeth Atell Stanford Museum of the Arts. It was named for the second wife of university founder and all-around rich important guy, Leland Stanford. The university itself had taken a rather dark turn in architecture and landscaping after Stanford's son and first wife had died, and there had been no shortage of people even in the early part of the Twentieth Century who thought that the Gothic look of the school had been inspired by Elizabeth Atell, who began keeping company with Stanford after he'd spent almost ten years as a widower. The second Mrs. Stanford was quite a bit younger than her new husband, a woman of many interests, including spiritualism and the occult, which were both pretty common and socially acceptable in those days. Not only did Leland's second wife have a lot to do with the design and building of the museum, but she was rumored to have used the place at night for seances with her like-minded friends. One source even claimed she had meant the whole place to be a monument to Spiritualism, but I never saw anything to confirm that.

Whatever its original inspiration, though, the Museum of the Arts had been thoroughly revamped a few times, like in the nineteen-thirties and the early seventies, but only once since Yours Truly appeared on the scene in San Judas. That refurbishment of ten years or so back, which included the new wing so important to Donya Sepanta, had added an entire section on Western Asia to the Asian Arts display, including a huge Persian exhibit. I'd been to the place once or twice myself, before all this Anaita stuff came along, but had never noticed anything unusual about any of it, although the sculpture garden was famously odd—full of grotesque stuff Elizabeth A. Stanford brought back from Europe in the twenties, a modern-day magnet for goth tourists and other seekers of the weird.

I had been waiting in my cab in a parking lot on Bloch Drive for almost two hours, scribbling notes to myself and reading when I got bored. (It was a Jim Thompson book, in case you wondered.) I waited so long that I began to get worried visions of the Amazons and little Edie Parmenter being interrogated in some kind of sub-museum dungeon. I was about two minutes away from crashing into the museum like the U.S. Cavalry when I saw them trotting toward me along Campus Drive. They piled into the cab. Edie was the last and she looked a little pale.

"Are you okay?" I asked her.

"Just drive, Mr. Dollar."

Halyna opened her bag and spilled a bunch of maps and other tourist information onto the front seat beside me. "The guards don't like us.

They always watch us. We had to stay so long because then they think we are serious about being there."

"Yeah, but did you find anything?"

"There's something in there, Mr. Dollar," said Edie from the back seat. "Something super strong! It kind of made me feel sick." She made a face. "I can still almost *taste* it!"

"Taste it? What are you talking about? Did you guys spend the whole day in the food court?"

"There was food court?" asked Oxana.

"No, that's just how it feels when I get near something powerful." Edie rolled down the window, although it was getting dark outside and pretty cold. "Like . . . I don't know, have you ever licked a battery?"

"I'm not allowed to discuss that with a minor," I said. "Court order. Now, this powerful thing, Edie, did you see it?" I waited, engine idling, until the bored guard at Teller Gate finally decided to wave us through. "Is it in a case or something?" I was getting excited—maybe I wouldn't have to arrange anything more complicated to recover Eligor's horn than a smash-and-grab raid.

" 'Fraid I can't say, Mr. Dollar. I didn't actually see anything. But I can tell you, there's something down at the end of the Asia wing, and the energy is so *scary*. I don't think I've ever felt anything that strong. I still feel like I kind of have a fever."

On the way back to Edie's place, north of downtown, she and the Amazons told me how they'd wandered around for a long time on the main floor, drawing pictures and making notes of various exhibits. When one of the guards had stopped to make conversation, they'd told him they were doing it for their college art history course.

"But it was in the Asia part on the third floor that I really started to notice something," Edie said. "What is it, exactly, Mr. Dollar? I've never felt anything like that before."

No, you probably haven't, I thought. Even a sensitive as talented and in demand as our Edie wouldn't have run across many authentic grand-ducal devil horns. "Better you don't know. What did it feel like?"

"I'm not sure. Just . . . strong. The farther we went in that part of the museum, the stronger it got. I even asked Halyna and Oxana if they felt anything. I thought maybe somebody was, I don't know, drilling the street outside or something. It made my teeth hurt."

"And that's all you could tell? Just that it was strong?"

"It got a lot stronger in the West Asia part, down at the end. That's where it was so bad I couldn't even stay there for long, but I couldn't locate a source. I mean, there wasn't anything that *made* the feeling, it was, like, all around."

Which probably meant that, unfortunately but unsurprisingly, the horn was hidden somewhere, maybe in one of the back rooms.

When we dropped Edie off, I slipped her an extra fifty as hazard pay. Bad enough exploiting a kid's supernatural gifts without compounding the sin by underpaying her.

So, the museum. Donya Sepanta, aka Anaita, Angel of Moisture, was a regular visitor. She'd apparently met Eligor there when they were beginning their partnership—the partnership that led to all the crazy, dangerous stuff that had been happening to me in the last year. That partnership had resulted in the exchange—her feather for his horn. And now Edie Parmenter had told me that something extremely potent was hidden in the Asia Wing that Anaita had helped build. That meant the boring part was over. Now it was time to start thinking about how to rob a powerful angel of something she very much did not want to lose.

The thing was, though, after taking days to lay the groundwork properly, I really couldn't afford to wait much longer, and my hurry didn't have anything to do with the Christmas shopping season that had descended upon us, or the red, black, and green Kwanzaa banners hanging over the main streets of the Ravenswood district near Caz's place. I'd started the snowball rolling and now it had a momentum of its own. I didn't know how much longer I could stall my bosses with my "leave of absence", and I had already alerted Anaita that I was onto her. Not to mention that the Black Sun Faction, if they'd been the ones who burglarized George (as I was pretty sure they were) knew that I was interested in Donya Sepanta and her doings and holdings. So it was now only a matter of time until one of these houses of cards I'd built caught an unexpected gust and collapsed.

I initiated Phase Two the day after the museum visit.

The Amazons had brought back Junior Burgers and onion rings, two things they had both developed a passion for, so I let them finish their lunch before announcing, "Okay, folks. We're going out shopping again."

"Frozen pizza," said Halyna. "Here in America the frozen pizza is good. In Ukraine, only frozen, not really pizza."

"I'm a little worried about you two and your dedication to the Scythian cause," I said. "You seem to be spending a lot more time trying new kinds of junk food than recruiting little American Amazons."

"We not recruit," said Oxana seriously. "Only take who come to *us*."

"And it is a long walk to our camp in the mountains," said Halyna, chomping on an onion ring. "Most turn back. That way we know they are not true Scythians."

I wasn't sure I'd want to hike through the cold, snowy Carpathians with only a vague hope that there would be friendly folk waiting for me in the woods somewhere, but I wasn't going to argue with them. "Anyway—no, we are not buying more frozen pizza already. It's not my fault you bought those horrible yuppie ones you don't want to eat now. There are many things that do not belong on pizza, and Kung Pao chicken, squid, and tandoori lamb are three of them. No, don't argue. Today we're shopping for weapons."

This proved to be even more popular than buying pizzas. Since we were going to Orban's I didn't even bother to suggest the Amazons change clothes. In fact, I was interested to see what the bearded militia-types who worked there would make of my young Ukrainian friends and their lesbian-anarcho-feminist punkitude. After I'd loaded the stuff I wanted to take with me into the trunk, the women piled into the back seat of the taxi. I sat in the front. For the fortieth or fiftieth time, I refused to play Lady Gaga—I'd finally found a jazz station I could get on the cab's ancient radio—so they sang "Poker Face" the whole way, loud enough to drown out Oscar Peterson and the rest completely.

Because Amazons are assholes.

Surprise number one: The women and Orban's gunsmiths *loved* each other. I mean, you would have thought I had brought in a basket of puppies. It helped that the Amazons loved guns, of course, and immediately let themselves be lured off to the firing range to try various small and large arms.

Surprise number two came when Orban, who was standing next to me watching them all trot off like a bunch of Oxford students and their dates going punting, suddenly said, "I am worried about you, Bobby."

After "I love you, Bobby, and I want to make romantic sex with you," this was one of the things I least expected to hear from Orban. His normal conversation is so gruff you could use it to clean bathroom tiles, and the only time I ever remember him saying anything else about my health and safety was the time he'd loaned me a machine-pistol and reminded me not to accidentally shoot my dick off with it.

"If you're concerned about me being screwed to death or something, relax. Those two ladies and I have a strictly platonic friendship based around blowing the shit out of some people we both don't like."

"No, not them. Them I like okay. They seem too smart to have sex with you unless they are sleeping or drunk. I am worried because I hear things. Sometimes. About the place you work."

This was interesting, because although I always assumed Orban knew everything about everything, he only gave out information in tiny, constipated episodes that lasted a few seconds and then were usually denied afterward. I was careful not to scare him off. "And . . . ?"

He inclined his head. "Come on. We talk in my office."

Orban's office was a room largely decorated with firing buckets full of sand to shoot into, but he also had a desk, a safe, and an old-time adding machine. He poured himself a glass of wine and offered me one. I wasn't certain I actually wanted any, but I didn't want to break the mood. I took a sip and said, "So?"

"So I hear things, like I say. And I hear a lot of things about how bad you are."

I was puzzled. "Bad?"

"Yes, bad. Like, 'That Bobby Dollar, always in trouble. I hear he is mixed up in something bad.'"

"Who told you that?"

He shook his head. "I will not tell you. It is not important. It is not someone who knows you, only someone who knows about you a little bit. But he is not the only one. I hear from another one, 'Bobby stole something important, and now bad guys are after him and Heaven is angry.'"

"Well, both those things are partially true, but leaving out the stealing part you could have said that about me for most of my career." I laughed, but it didn't convince Orban. "Come on, people who get things done get talked about, Orban. People talk about you, too."

"Because I let them. Because I have no use for secrecy. Anybody wants Orban, here Orban is." He stroked his shrublike beard for a moment, probably thinking about what interestingly painful things he would do to anyone who showed up "wanting Orban." He took a drink, long enough to finish the glass. "But you, I think, you don't want everyone to know your business. And people who truly know your business, they aren't talking. But others are."

I nodded my head, although I wasn't sure where he was going. "And that means . . . ?"

"That means someone talks bad about you on purpose. Someone is trying to take you down, Bobby. Maybe they even make up a story so nobody is surprised when something happens to you."

I already knew it was happening, because just about everyone else in Creation, including an albino fox-fairy who haunted downtown, my boss Temuel, and every single angel I could call a friend, had made it clear to me already. But for some reason hearing it from Orban, the most stolid, stoic guy I knew, gave me a real chill. If it was Anaita, she wasn't in a hurry. She wasn't just going to reach out and swat me, she was going to make sure everyone knew that I was a dangerous pest first. Then, not only wouldn't anyone ask questions when she finally did it, they'd probably give her a medal for erasing me.

"I appreciate it. I really do. But I'm kind of on the road now, full speed ahead. I can't turn back."

"Then be very careful."

I wasn't used to Bleeding-Heart Orban. It made me nervous. So I changed the subject. "Did you sell my car?"

"Found a buyer, yes. A very nice fellow, a collector in Seattle. He will take good care of it."

Like I cared. *"The Arab sheik we sold your daughter to is a very nice fellow"*—yeah, that would make you feel great. But me losing the Matador wasn't Orban's fault. "Thanks," I said. "And now some other business. Can you figure out a way to make a pressurized spray of silver nitrate?"

He looked at me like I'd just started shouting monkey noises. "A what of what?"

I explained. He frowned. That made me feel better—it was a much more familiar look for him. "I don't know until I try. Research and development cost extra, you know. I should have just kept all the money I gave you."

"Yeah, you'll probably get most of it back by the time I'm done." Still, I had a plan (well, I was planning to have one, which was practically the same) and I was ready to start outfitting myself and the others to make it happen. That was what was important. Yes, I had lots to worry about, but I had work to do. "But that's life, right? You can't be rich and happy, too."

Orban snorted. "That is a lie. I have been both."

"Yeah, well, you're Hungarian."

While he was searching for a hidden insult, I led him back out to find the women so we could decide what kinds of guns they were going to need. They were whooping it up with Orban's engineers, getting the full guided tour of the mayhem factory, and they were loving it.

"Bobby!" said Halyna. "They have a tank! It is Russian. We should get it!"

"That is good fun," Oxana agreed. "Then we smash right into that—"

I cut her off before she started talking about blowing up the Elizabeth Atell Stanford Museum. I trusted Orban with my life, but I didn't know his workers that well. In fact, some of them looked like the kind of guys who might have a sneaking fondness for the Black Sun's way of looking at the world. I know, I'm a bigot, but tattoos that say, "White Power" encourage jumping to conclusions.

"We'll need to be a little more discreet than that," I said. "But I think we can spring for at least one flamethrower. How's that?"

"You are serious?" said Halyna. "Hah! That is for me!"

"You have to share." Oxana sounded like the kid who'd just received a toothbrush in her Halloween treat bag. "What do I get?"

"Guns," I said. "And probably some kind of pressurized silver nitrate sprayer, too."

"Does it make burning?"

"Sadly, no," I said, then leaned close to whisper in her ear. "But it will make those nasty-ass Nightmare Children bubble like salted slugs."

"Okay, I guess," Oxana said with a tragic look. Beside her, Halyna was making *whoooosh* noises, pretending to torch the engineers as they wandered back to their workbenches. "I guess I can do."

Kids today—am I right? You can never give them enough.

twenty-seven
another death threat

I KNOCKED ON the door and one of them said "Come in." So I went in.

Both of the Amazons were in Caz's expansive tub. Naked. Slick and wet and covered in suds, tattoos gleaming. There was water all over the tiles. Halyna had made little pasties for herself out of soap bubbles that bobbed up and down as she rubbed shampoo into her red hair. Oxana hadn't bothered, but she had a dollop of soap froth on top of her wet head like she was a cappuccino. Lots of lean, muscular, young body, two women's worth, dripping and soapy. I saw all that in about two seconds, then I jumped back and slammed the door.

"Jesus Henry Christ!" I said. "What are you doing? Do you want to kill me?"

"What is wrong, Bobby?" Halyna called from the other side of the door.

"What's wrong? You two are nude. I am fucking celibate and not liking it at all. You are either monsters or dumb-asses or both."

I could hear them both giggling. I never knew Ukrainian dykes could make that noise—like evil Campfire Girls. "But you are angel, Bobby!" called Oxana. "That means you are like doctor."

"No. No, it doesn't mean that at all. And do you get naked and lathered up to go to a medical appointment? I hope not. Seriously, don't do that shit to me."

"Sorry, Bobby." But they didn't sound sorry at all. I hate it when people take advantage of my kind nature, because I never fucking wanted to have a kind nature in the first place. "I was going to tell you the boys are here. Come on out so we can get to work." I paused, realizing I'd left them a loophole. "Come on out *with clothes on that cover all the important bits*. Clarence and Wendell may not care, but I'm wired differently than they are."

"That's true," said Clarence from the other room. "You're wired to be an asshole. My name is Harrison, remember?"

I went back to the living room and sat down heavily. "Look, I promised I'd try. I make mistakes sometimes. Do me a favor and don't correct me every time, okay?" I started laying out the maps, waiting for the women to make their appearance. "How are you two, by the way? Everything okay with work? Not too many questions?"

"Most of the others don't even know we're a couple," said Wendell, smiling at the kid. "We've been kind of keeping it on the down low, because of this."

"That's not really what I was asking." I made a few marks on the museum map. "Maybe Wendell's really keeping quiet because he's ashamed of you, *Harrison*. After all, nobody likes a nag."

"Trying to get you to behave with normal human decency is not the same as nagging, *Bobby*." He rolled his eyes. "As angels go, you're a complete pig."

"Yeah, which is why I just shut the door on a couple of naked women in my tub without standing there long enough to read all their tattoos."

"You couldn't anyway. The words are all Ukrainian."

"Hmmm. Wonder if they have a word in that language for 'vicious, premeditated exhibitionism.'"

"The only people who needs medication is you, Bobby," said Halyna, her hair up in a towel-turban, the rest of her clothed in a t-shirt and shorts. Things were swinging and bumping in there as she moved, but at least I didn't have to see them live and in person.

"Not medicate, medi*tate*. Shit, they run around naked, have loud sex in the next room, and then I still have to explain all the funny things I say. I've had better roommates in prison."

"Probably you got more of the fucking there, too," said Oxana, appearing in her bathrobe.

"Shit, and they tell jokes as well," I said. "I assume that's what those are. I'm sure they'd be rip-snorters on the Siberian gulag circuit. Come on, sit down. We've got a lot to talk about."

"I don't want to stay outside if Harrison's going in," said Wendell. "I have experience in this kind of thing. He doesn't."

"I can take care of myself," said Clarence, sounding like he was nine years old. But it reminded me that these were real people, and unlike the Harps or Wendell's Clouds, I couldn't promise them I'd get them into new bodies if anything went wrong.

"That's not the point," I said. "Don't worry, I promise I'll keep an eye on Harrison."

"Hey!" he said. "I'm not a child."

"*But*," I continued, "he's already sort of compromised. I mean, our bosses know he chose to stay an advocate after being their spy, and that he's been hanging out with me. But nobody knows you're with us, Wendell."

"So?"

"So if things go wrong, we need someone on the outside to make sure they don't just disappear us."

"You think it go wrong?" asked Oxana.

"I don't know, but let's face it, it certainly could. We're going into enemy territory. At the very least, even if there's nothing there at all, we're breaking into a very prestigious museum. I don't know about you, but I sure don't want to shoot my way out and kill any innocent humans, so it may come down to us surrendering. That's why we need you to stay out of the worst of it, Wendell. Besides, you'll have plenty to do on the outside. Can you do that trick with the cameras you mentioned?"

"What, looping the footage? Yeah, but it's not foolproof. The clocks won't move, if any of them are visible on the video feeds. Plus I'd really like to know how many guards there are."

I consulted my notes. "Two in the Asian wing, from what I can tell. Four more and a supervisor in the other building, where they keep the video monitors. But I'm going to need you to watch the feeds and let us know where they are, so you have to stay on top of it."

Wendell waved at this. Handled.

"But why all the weapons, Bobby?" Clarence asked. "If you don't want to shoot anyone, you're sure packing a lot of firepower."

"I didn't say I didn't want to shoot anyone, I said I didn't want to shoot any innocent humans. As far as we know, this may be Anaita's second most important spot to protect in all of San Judas—maybe the most important, if the horn's really there. I literally have no idea what we might find, especially if she's got some kind of secret room. There are things that can sleep for years and only wake up when a stranger approaches. I know, because some of them have tried to eat me in the past."

"Yeah, we know, we know," said Clarence. "Bobby Dollar, deadly stud, no stranger to danger, a lethal combination of Sam Spade and Eddie Murphy . . ."

"I think that's Audie Murphy," said Wendell quietly. At least one of them watched the right movies.

"Whatever. But you can overthink this stuff, Bobby."

"No, you can't, Junior—not if you enjoy being alive. That's why we're going to go over it again."

The Amazons were playing tic-tac-toe on one of my maps. Clarence groaned. "We've been through it all three times!"

"And we've got time for once more before I have to leave." I gave them a stern look. "Daddy has a meeting in forty minutes at the Crown Roast."

Clarence gave me the eyebrow. "The Crown Roast? Doesn't seem like your kind of place, Bobby. Meeting an informant?"

I was going to lie, but I was asking them to risk their safety and even their lives, after all. "Sort of. Not really. I'm having dinner with Monica Naber, to thank her for setting up that *Vanity Fair* thing. She said to pick someplace that didn't serve raw fish eggs or noodles made from radish whiskers—I'm quoting—so I decided we'd go to the kind of place she likes. Surf and turf. Endless Sangria pitchers." I shook my head. "Just another sacrifice your fearless leader is making for the greater good. I'll bring you back some jalapeño cream cheese poppers or something."

"Ooh, does that mean you will be doing some sex tonight, too?" asked Halyna.

"Maybe then not so grumping." That was Oxana.

"Bite your tongues. I mean, really, don't even say that. This is going to be complicated enough without any of that crap. And remember, we go in forty-eight hours. Get everything ready and get your cover stories straight. You all know what to do, right? But just in case, I'm going to tell you one more time."

By the time Monica had brought me up to date, we had almost finished our meal. I had prime rib, a baked potato, the whole schmear. Being female, Monica had a tiny little steak you couldn't put on a hamster's black eye, and a huge salad. If you'd dumped that salad on the same hamster, the little bastard could have lived in it for weeks.

We drank sangria. We gossiped a little. Apparently Young Elvis had a new girlfriend, a mortal. "She's exactly what you'd expect," said Monica. "False eyelashes, ratted hair. If she was wearing a poodle skirt, you'd be positive she was waiting for poor Buddy Holly to come home from his tour. But he never will."

I smiled. "If she goes for Young E., she'd be more the Big Bopper's type."

It was good to see Monica. For one thing, she understood the same things I did. For another, she didn't have a Ukrainian accent. "How about our friend Sweetheart?"

"The same. A succession of broken hearts, usually his, occasionally some poor boy's that Sweetheart loved and lost the next day. But it's all a part of the parade of fabulousness. I swear, Bobby, I've never known him to be actually sad about anything. Even when he's upset about some tragic romance, it's like hearing the plot of a really good sitcom."

"And the rest of the gang?"

"You know. Same old, same old. Walter's getting back to his old self. He told me to pass along his greetings. And how are things for *you?*"

Caught by surprise, I handled it with my usual flair. "Huh?"

"You, Bobby. You ask about everyone else—you even asked how Teddy and I are doing—but you don't say anything about yourself. What's going on?"

"You never did finish telling me about you and Teddy, now that you mention it. You two getting on all right?"

She gave me a look—she knew I was changing the subject again—but gave in with dignity. "We're okay. I wanted something different than you. I got it. He's dependable, kind, always returns phone calls. He opens doors for me."

"I used to open doors for you!"

"Only because you had that stupid little car where the doors wouldn't stay open by themselves and kept shutting on my head when I tried to get out."

"Oh, yeah, that ragtop Buick. I miss that car. You could feel every bump—like riding a giant, high-powered skateboard."

"My tailbone is still bruised."

"I had to sell my Matador, you know."

"Was that the one with the checkerboard upholstery?"

"Yep."

"I'd like to say 'too bad,' but honestly, it was like being in a clown car. No, like a booth in an imitation fifties diner."

"Yeah, pile it on, now that my poor Matador Machine isn't here to defend itself."

"You're still avoiding the subject, Bobby."

"What subject?"

"The subject of what's going on with you. And something is definitely going on."

I had a little tingle up the back of my neck. "Why do you say that?"

She laughed. Sourly. "Oh, come on. You take me out to dinner? When was the last time you took me out to dinner, even when we were sleeping together?"

"I'll have to go through my canceled checks."

"For the early two-thousands. Seriously, you take me out to dinner, you ask politely about all the old friends you never bother to come see, even though they hang out in the exact same bar as always—hell, most of them are in the exact same *booths*." She frowned. "I know you, Bobby. You can't wake up with a guy for three years, admittedly off and on, without learning a little something about him. You're worried. No, you're scared shitless about something. You've got a new girlfriend, but I never hear anything about her from anyone, and it's not because they're protecting me. Nobody knows, and you never talk about her either. And the only time I hear from you is when you want help to sneak into some rich lady's house. What? Did you get your new woman knocked up? Were you planning to steal some Persian art treasures to pay for her to get it dealt with?" Suddenly her face changed. "I'm sorry, that was terrible. I didn't mean it to sound so mean. But what's going on with you? I thought we'd agreed to stay friends."

"We *are* friends. Look at us, sitting here all friendly. Me eating your leftover croutons."

"I've seen nearly every cute trick you have, Dollar, and heard every excuse you make. I'm not that easy to distract. If I am your friend, talk to me."

And I would have. At that moment, I was dying to talk to someone. It was why I'd insisted on taking her out to dinner. Monica was the one person I could talk to who would both understand and sympathize. It wasn't even the Caz thing, not anymore. But I couldn't do it. I couldn't tell Monica something that she would have to keep secret, especially if everything went badly sideways at the museum. At the moment, the *Vanity Fair* ploy was her only involvement, and she didn't know what she'd done or why. How could I change that and make her part of this, just to have a shoulder to cry on, just to have someone who would pat me on the back and tell me everything would be all right? Shit, even I'm not that selfish.

No, this whole thing had been a bad idea, and the fact that it felt so good to see Monica again, and to be reminded how much fun she could be to hang out with, only made it worse. "I can't," I said at last. "You have to believe me. It's not that I don't trust you, it's that I don't want you involved."

"Really? This isn't one of your *it's-not-you-it's-me* speeches, is it?" She stared across the table, really stared, like she could see right into me. I used to think she could, sometimes, but most of the time I knew better. I mean, what woman would hang out with me if she really could see the inner Bobby? "Oh, shit," she said.

"What?"

"Now I'm scared. I think you're telling the truth. What are you into, Dollar? Tell me. Please, talk to me."

"Nothing I can't handle." And that was my biggest lie of the week, no doubt. "Honestly, don't let it worry you. I'm just being cautious." I handed the check back to the waiter, along with enough cash to cover the meal and the tip. "Keep it," I told him. "You want a drink for the road, Naber?"

She was still looking at me like you'd look at a senile grandfather who had just announced he was going on a long trip. "I shouldn't. I'm supposed to stop at the Compasses to meet Teddy, and I'll probably have another glass there. Assuming I don't get a call. Are you really on leave of absence?"

"Temporarily. Just 'til I get some stuff sorted out."

I walked her to her car. She stopped, turned, and put her arms around me before I was ready for it, and got in a good squeeze before I could stiffen up and lean back a little. She felt very good, and without thinking I let my hands drop to her hips. They're very nice hips.

"You'll call me soon, right?" she said. "Let me know you're okay?"

"Sure." Usually I had no problem saying things like this to women without meaning it, even women I really liked, like Monica. "I'll be fine. Everything will be fine." I paused. I should have let go then, but I didn't. "And thanks for everything. You're a wonderful person, Monica. Heaven's finest."

Her grip on my waist tightened. "You're scaring me again. Unless you're making a pass."

"No. No pass." I leaned and kissed her, gently and carefully, on the lips. Nothing romantic, not at first, but for a second we didn't break apart either, and then it started to seem like something else was happening. I was lonely, I was scared, and she felt so good—not just familiar, but right, someone I knew and trusted. Someone I wanted to hold onto. Someone I definitely, at least for those few seconds, didn't want to let go of. My hand started to slide up her back, and then I remembered why I was in all this trouble in the first place: Caz. Small, fierce, shiny-bright as a Fourth of July sparkler, and right now under house arrest in Hell. A prisoner forever, unless I did something impossible. And I had to try.

I let go and took a step back. "I'll always care about you, Monica," I said. "No matter what." I turned and walked toward my car.

"Oh, my God," I heard her say loudly from behind me, perhaps in part to wake herself up from what had just almost happened. "You got rid of the plaid-seats clown car and bought a *taxi?*"

"Not everyone can pull it off," I said, still not looking back.

If she had said any number of things, I might have turned around. Luckily for both of us, she didn't. "*Nobody* can pull that off, Dollar."

I gave her my best casual wave. "Oh, ye of little faith. Just wait 'til you hear this baby roar. I've got seven or eight horses under the hood, minimum."

"Take care of yourself, Bobby," she called as I opened the door and got in. "Seriously. That's not a joke. If you do something stupid and get yourself killed, I'll . . . I'll murder you."

It was the nicest death threat I'd received in a long while.

twenty-eight
what happens in oceania

"**O**KAY," I said into my walkie. "My turn. The rest of you, stay here and try to look grotesque."

It wasn't an insult or even a joke, really. We were in the sculpture garden behind the E. A. Stanford museum and, as everyone who's ever been there knows, the place is full of really, really bizarre statues.

I found my first handhold and started up the wall. There was lots of ivy, mostly shriveled and leafless this time of the year, and I've learned from hard experience not to trust the stuff except in an emergency—you know, like when you've had to leap out a window unexpectedly. Instead I was going the slow, steady way, and the brick facade was a big help.

The museum is in the former Stanford family residence, deep inside the campus walls, and is what the British like to refer to fondly as a "pile." The Brits should know, because the original version was still in England somewhere, named after some duke. You could look it up. Anyway, like the manor house it had been copied from, the museum was a monstrous assembly of reddish brick, with crenellated towers and the whole bit. The part we needed to get into was the new wing, which would have been the stables or something in the original, but here was a long two-story building with a glass roof. However, because the new wing had been built less than twenty years ago, it was going to be easier to make rooftop entry from the old building. That was why I was climbing up those bricks, carefully picking out toe-holds and fin-ger-holds, almost exactly like someone who knew what he was doing.

I had a difficult moment when a rain gutter started wobbling under my feet, but I managed to get my belly up over the edge before anything noisy happened, then I just lay for a moment, breathing. I pulled the rope ladder out of my backpack, anchored it, and let it unroll with what I hoped wasn't too loud a clatter down to my team waiting below. I didn't wait for them. Once my legs stopped trembling, I inched along the top of the wing very carefully, because I was crawling over glass panes, until I reached the roof of the main building. Then I got up and moved (okay, scurried) from chimney pot to chimney pot 'til I reached the service door. The door was modern, and had a massive dead bolt, which would have been hard to get through without sounding like someone was holding military exercises on the roof, but it also had a card reader.

"Duster, this is Cash," I said quietly into my com. "I'm here at Door One. Do you have a handle on the alarm system?"

"Yes. The guard's just left Oceania, headed downstairs. Do you have the card?" Wendell was sitting in Clarence's awful Plymouth out in the parking lot adjacent to the main campus auditorium, a couple of hundred yards away from us through the trees. A controversial East Coast academic was giving a talk tonight; lots of people were on campus and in the parking lots, which made better cover. The Stanford campus police don't like people hanging around for no good reason.

I pulled the smart card out of my pocket. "I'm using it now."

We were lucky that museums, even nice ones, don't have quite the same attention to security detail as, say, financial institutions or government labs. Not that the Stanford Museum of the Arts was particularly vulnerable, just that it was a lot easier to steal data from museum employees than NASA scientists. Thus, the card, which had been duped using a real museum curator's information. Not only would it open any door locks that used cards, it would leave a false and somewhat confusing trail, because the real curator was on duty tonight, helping to set up a big new exhibit in the North American Hall in the main building, not too far below where I stood now. I slid the card. The light went on, the door popped open. "Perfect," I said. "I'm in."

I had to admit that if I'd had any doubts about Wendell's credentials and background, they were gone. He did good, quality work. I still didn't completely trust him, of course—how could I? But I was at the point where I had to take some things on faith, if you'll excuse that expression when applied to breaking, entering, and pursuing feuds with powerful angels and demons. Wendell, Clarence, and the Amazons were what I had; without Sam, who still hadn't called me back, I had no choice but to roll the dice and hope for the best.

Oxana and Halyna reached me a few moments later, followed by Clarence. The stairway down was metal and full of echoes, so we took it slow. At the bottom I had to use the card again, but when the door popped open this time, we were in a service corridor at the outer edge of the North American Hall. I'd warned everybody about the workers just a few dozen yards away, so we all hurried through quickly, then continued through two more security doors (one of which I had to open the old-fashioned way, with lock-picking tools, sweaty fingers, and silent curses) until we were through and alone on the top floor of the Asia wing. We needed to make it through the "Oceania and the Pacific" collection to reach the stairs.

Yes, the place was borderline creepy. If you can think of any people in San Judas less likely to worry about haunted museums than me, I'd love to meet them—I mean, come on, some of my best friends are ghosts, and I've been to Hell. Still, even I have to admit that sneaking through pools of shadow and dim moonlight, between frowning ceremonial masks from Melanesia and life-size New Guinea ancestor fetishes with hair and teeth taken from dead people is in fact a bit unsettling. Kind of like I suspect things are at night in the *It's A Small World* ride, when all the little figures come to life and whisper about how they'd like to torture and murder all those screaming children and grinning grown-ups in the boats.

The collection here on the top floor also reminded me uncomfortably of Islanders Hall downtown, where I had spent an interesting night of sudden violence, blood, and lots of screaming not too long before. I hoped that wasn't an omen.

A lot of the creepiest pieces in the museum, by the way, were collected by Elizabeth Atell Stanford herself, which gives you an idea of what she liked.

Don't get me wrong. I've got nothing against Pacific Island culture, but when every time you turn around, you get a faceful of bulging, angry eyes and grinning dead-guy teeth, there's a strong tendency to believe that what happens in Oceania should stay in Oceania.

I checked my watch. If everything was on schedule, we had a good ten minutes before the guard finished his rounds of the floor below us. We wanted to get in as soon as he left, because that was the part of the museum we really wanted to explore, so we hunkered down near the stairwell and waited until Wendell, watching it all with the museum's own security cameras, sent me the all-clear. Clarence's man-friend had picked out some really nice communications gear, stuff Orban had accepted from a drug dealer who couldn't pay his armored car bill because of a slight downturn in the crack market. Halyna and Oxana both wore tanks on their backs, Halyna's part of an old Russian flame-thrower, Oxana's an industrial sprayer full of pressurized silver nitrate solution. The women were also sporting infrared goggles, which Clarence and I didn't need because we had angel vision; we can do a pretty good job at night without artificial help. Looking at the stuff we were all carrying—silenced assault weapons, coils of rope, grappling hooks, pry bars—you'd have thought we were carrying out a raid on an Al Qaeda stronghold in the Spin Ghar mountains instead of crouching next to a mannequin that was rocking a gorgeous cloak of bird of paradise feathers. (The cape actually looked really nice. I felt sorry it was so dark that I couldn't see the colors properly, even with angel eyes.)

When Wendell finally told us to move, we made our way quietly down the stairs, then waited at the bottom for his signal. The museum is laid out more or less on a geographic model, so we had to work our way across Japan, China, Korea and Southeast Asia before we reached the West Asian section where Edie had received those powerful impressions. Was the horn's hiding place something small, like a bootlegger's stash? Or, if it was something bigger, had the museum's bosses known about it from the start? It seemed like it would take quite a juggling act to steal enough space to add something that significant without everyone knowing, but who knew how far the archangelic power to cloud men's minds could get you?

We made our way quick-file through the cases of Tanagra statuettes and Chinese gilt-work. I looked at least briefly into every display I passed, not that I expected to see anything useful—even the craziest, most suicidal angel in Heaven would think twice about hiding a demon's horn in plain sight in a public museum, and Anaita had lasted a long time as a major player in a place that, at least for subtlety, made the Forbidden City look like *Sesame Street*.

"We're almost there, Duster," I whispered into the walkie-talkie as we reached the Western Asia section. "Do you copy? Where are the guards?"

"Not sure right now," came back the answer. "But I don't see any movement in your wing. Cash, you are good to go."

Now, I'm not totally a museum guy in the first place, and we were there in the middle of the night with malicious intent (not to mention in semi-darkness) and under clear threat from angry angels, but I still have to say the stuff in the Persian section was beautiful. Most of the exhibits dated from the heyday of their empire, about twenty-five centuries earlier—imperial drinking horns shaped like bulls, gorgeous carpets with repeating patterns of silver and gold sketched in silk thread, like John Coltrane blowing in full mathematical freefall, so intricate and charming that I wanted to stop and look at all of them. Not that we had the time—which was a big part of the problem. Now I was getting worried all over again.

What if the horn *was* here, but instead of stashing it in an office safe, Anaita really had stashed it in plain sight? There were hundreds and hundreds of exhibits just in this wing created by her donations, and at least half of them could have hidden something that size. Even if I limited my search to things that looked like horns, there were so many—animal horns, demon horns, drinking horns, hunting horns!

Worse, what if Anaita had stuck it downstairs in the back of the Iroquois Long House in the North American section, or in the pocket of a Boston whaling captain's jacket? I wished I could have brought Edie Parmenter along to help locate it, but endangering armed Amazons was bad enough without dragging in school children. No, our only real hope of coming away with anything useful was to find out whether there really was a hidden safe or stronghold and then get into it. So that was what we were going to do. It was only a matter of time until one of the security people did something unexpected, or one of the curators in the other wing suddenly remembered she needed a stapler that she'd left next to the Thai baskets. Or maybe the Angel of Moisture herself liked to pop in at night and look around at what her money had wrought. Wouldn't *that* just be perfect?

Which is when I noticed something very like Anaita standing right in front of me.

I will confess that even though I knew almost instantly it was only a mosaic made of glass and semi-precious stones, it still gave me a thump to the heart that I could taste in my mouth.

The panel on which it hung (because the mosaic was set in what looked like a delicate plaster matrix, protected by a sheet of glass or heavy plastic) stood against one of the side walls, near the end of the Persian part of the Western Asia collection. The goddess was winged and crowned, flanked by two fierce lions. The card said the mosaic was third century, from the palace of Bishapur. It didn't say it was Anaita, but I recognized my enemy instantly. The smile on her mosaic face was a bit disturbing, though: she had the serene look of someone who was three or four steps ahead of anyone who might be thinking about trying to take her down. Anyone like me, for instance.

Clarence, Halyna, and Oxana were creeping quietly through the exhibit hall, testing walls with a stud finder, looking for anything hidden. There were a few doors and a couple of small corridors that led to the public restrooms and the fire control equipment, and even a small curator's office. I carded the door to the office and went in, but though I checked every wall for hiding places or secondary doors, I couldn't find anything suspicious, and a search of the desk and cubbyholes didn't turn up anything, either.

As I got back out to the main floor, something clicked in my earbud.

"Cash, this is Duster. Copy?"

"Got you, Duster."

"Something . . . weird is going on." Wendell sounded calm, but there was an edge I didn't like. It was the vibration of somebody trying to hold it together when things were threatening to come apart. "There's a guard above you. Do you copy? I think it's a guard. In the Oceania exhibit."

"Shit." We had developed contingencies for this, so it could have been worse. "He's a little early, but we can hide in the—"

"No. Listen. He's down."

"What? Try that again, Duster. Did you say 'down'? What do you mean?"

"He's lying on the floor. I'm looking at him, and I can only see the bottom half of him, but he's lying on the floor near the stairwell where you came in. Did you do it?"

"What, club a guard? Hell no. Are you sure it's not just a shadow or something?"

"Cash, he is *down* and I think I see blood. A big puddle, getting bigger. Time to abort."

"Shit. Copy." I thumbed off the walkie-talkie and hurried to find Clarence and Oxana, who were down at the far end. I signaled for Halyna to come with me, but when I looked back she was still staring at the mosaic of Anaita. I knew she hated the immortal bitch, but this was a really bad time to be dwelling on it. I hurried back to get her.

"We've got a problem," I whispered. "We have to get out of here."

"Something is wrong with that picture," Halyna said as if I hadn't spoken. She took off her infrared goggles, stared at the eight-foot tall mosaic, then put them back on again. "There is a big cold place in the middle of it."

"We don't have time right now," I said. "We have to get to an exit. We may have to *make* an exit."

Halyna stepped forward, still not paying any attention to me, and began sliding her fingers up and down the slab, reaching up as high as she could, then down to floor level. She moved to the other side and did the same thing. She must have touched something hidden, because suddenly Anaita took wing.

Well, at least that's what it looked like when the goddess Anaita and her big kitty-cat companions rose into the air. They kept on until they'd risen six or seven feet straight up the high wall, revealing a door that had been hiding behind the mosaic slab. It had a card reader, but I was pretty certain that the poor slob of a curator whose information we'd stolen didn't know anything about this particular door and had no privileges for it. I slid the card in the slot several times, but I was right: no good.

Clarence and Oxana rejoined us.

"What's going on?" Clarence asked.

"Emergencies and craziness all over the fucking place," I said in a low voice. "Wendell says there's a guard down on the floor above us, and he thinks he can see blood. But look what Halyna just found."

"Is that . . . ?"

"It was behind that mosaic. What do *you* think? As for me, I think we've got about zero time left, but we're here, and I can't just walk away. How do we get this door open?" I got on the walkie to Wendell and told him what we'd found. "Any more information on that guard?"

"Nothing. He's still not moving. I've got a real bad feeling, Cash."

"So do I, Duster, but I'm making a command decision. Whatever happened to the guard, no one else has noticed yet. Are you still looping the security cam footage?"

"Yes, but maybe that's why he showed up. People notice eventually . . ."

"Any suggestions for getting this door open, Duster? Any magic passwords you've been keeping in reserve?"

"No. And I suggest you leave it alone. You can always come back."

"I don't think so. Not before shit goes completely vertical in my world, with me at the bottom. Cash out." I turned to face the others. "This is kind of like the Gordian Knot," I said.

"Is not what?" Oxana asked.

"History lesson later," I said. "Now, problem-solving." And then I pulled out my new suppressed Glock and blasted the shit out of that card reader with some of the special ammo Orban had thrown in with the silencer. The subsonics were impressively quiet—I doubted anyone outside the hall heard a thing. I reached in through the smoking wreckage and started pulling bits out, then grabbed the pry bar Clarence had strapped to his pack frame and put all of my not-inconsiderable strength to it.

Clarence was getting a bit panicky. The bullets had been quiet, but the pry bar was making noises like the world's biggest gopher chewing metal vegetables with metal teeth. "I thought we had to get out of here—shit, Bobby, I thought we weren't going to make a mess!" He really *was* upset. He hardly ever swore.

"Plans change, my friend."

I don't know what I did, but something shifted inside the door lock and the thing popped out. The door slid about six inches to one side, enough for me to feel a waft of cool, air-conditioned air rolling out. No wonder Halyna had seen a cold spot with her infrareds. I got my hands into the opening and started pulling. After a moment Clarence realized I wasn't going anywhere without getting past that door, so he leaned in to help, and together we dragged it open against the heavy inertia of the mechanism.

What we found on the other side was a dark stairwell. I went down it, and as I hit the bottom step a light came on above my head. The door in front of me was ordinary wood, with a latch but no electronic paraphernalia. Could it really be this simple? I clicked the latch down and pushed. The door swung open and a light came on inside. My comm-link made a scratchy, staticky noise in my ear, but I couldn't understand anything Wendell was saying.

I had about five seconds to look around before Oxana, who was closest to me on the stairs, said, "Bobby . . ."

"Just a second," I said. "We're in."

And in my earpiece: "Cash, this is Duster! Cash, please acknowledge!"

"Not now, Duster."

"The hell with that," Wendell was almost shouting. "Abort the mission! Abort the mission!"

"What are you talking about, Duster?" But I couldn't raise him again—the signal was all noise now. I assumed the guards were coming, but I was damned if I was going to run when I had finally found what we were looking for. I'd think of some way to stall them. "Duster, please repeat . . ."

"*Bobby.*" Now it was Clarence calling to me from the top of the stairwell. "I really think you'd better come up here."

I was losing my shit. "Will everybody just give me—"

"*Now!*"

I'd never heard that tone from Junior before. I legged it back up, pushed past Oxana and then stopped, amazed, beneath the mosaic that hung over the doorway.

The entire floor of the West Asian hall was alive with Nightmare Children. Dozens of the swastika-shaped things, hideous and hairy, scurried around and over the exhibits toward us like they were army ants and we were made of sugar.

"This is bad," was all I could think of to say. Not my most original line. I'll try to do better next time I'm about to be devoured in a museum in the middle of the night by a couple of hundred monstrous, spidery crawlers with babies' fingers.

And another thing. When a bunch of them got together, you could hear the Children breathing. They hissed quietly, like poison gas spewing from the vents at Bergen-Belsen.

twenty-nine
jam today

"**O**XANA!" I shouted. I should have been using code names, but since it was in the heat of the moment and we were about to be overrun by hand-spiders, I think I can be forgiven. "Hurry up and *spray that shit!*"

The first burst of silver nitrate solution came out in spatters, but the results were instantaneous. The Nightmare Children nearest us erupted in flame, like origami in a grease fire, and the air was suddenly filled with a howling so high-pitched I could barely hear it, like dozens of microscopic dental drills. Sadly, though, the swastikids were too basic or too brutal to be deterred by their burning comrades; the rest kept coming, although they avoided the bubbling wreckage of those the spray had hit.

I hadn't necessarily expected to see the little bastards again, but I'd wanted to be ready for surprises, both human and otherwise, which was why the silver spray. In the seconds after the first wave had melted into puddles of hair and twitching fingers (making an entirely new, astoundingly foul odor I'd never encountered before, even in Hell) I had my machete out of its sheath, and I was wading into them. I'd economized by only having Orban silver-plate the edges of the blades, but they seemed to do the job just fine that way. Every time I managed to hack into the body, another of the creatures fell into burning, jiggling bits. Even when I only got an arm, it crippled the little horrors nicely.

Clarence had his machete out too, and together we were able to keep a clear space open at the top of the stairs, but the army of scurrying things seemed endless. Oxana sprinted back and forth along the wall so she could spray the contents of her tank across the hairy, skittering wavefront. It was like napalming them, but I knew that she couldn't keep doing it forever. Even if it didn't clog, the tank didn't carry that much because the silver nitrate made it heavy as hell. I could only pray that no more of the things would show up.

Even as I was swiping away with my blade at the nasty, faceless creatures in front of me, tiny fingers clawed at my pants leg. I reached down and grabbed the nearest wire-haired squirmer and ripped it off me like a starfish off a rock, then threw it as far as I could. The exercise in clearance was pointless, because even as I pulled another away several more climbed the back of my legs. Within a second or two I could feel the terrible little fingers clawing at my neck.

I'm not a squeamish guy. You've probably guessed that by now. But being swarmed by those things brought me very near the screaming-and-running-in-circles stage. I was distracted from my growing fear when a great billowing cloud of flame rolled across the main force of crawlers. As they blackened and shriveled, the little monstrosities sent up an even higher-pitched chorus of inhuman shrieking that made my skull ache.

"No, Halyna! Save it!" I yelled. We weren't really in terminal danger, not yet anyway, and I didn't want her to set off the fire sprinklers, for oh-so many reasons, not least of which was the priceless works of art. I also didn't know if Wendell had remembered to disable the fire alarms or not.

By now Oxana's tank was spitting out little more than drips of silver solution. The Nightmare Children were still coming, but I thought I could see the end of them and felt pretty certain that we could hold them off at least long enough to escape the museum. Of course, it raised some questions—why were the crawling horrors here in the first place? Did Anaita use them too? And were they the only thing we had to worry about?

I was still making like Conan the Haloed Barbarian, hacking and slashing with my silvery sword, when I heard a wrenching noise from just above me, louder even than the shouts of my friends and the boiling-lobster squeals of burning swastikids. I didn't dare look up, but I didn't need to, because three seconds later several hundred pounds of living blackberry jam crashed through the vent in the ceiling and tumbled out of the air duct on top of me.

"Bird bug!" shouted Oxana.

While still thrashing around on top of me, the rubbery mass hit Clarence with a flailing appendage and tossed him across the room. He skidded and crashed into a display case with a noise like a grenade going off, flinging glass and irreplaceable ancient knick-knacks everywhere. As I writhed beneath what seemed to be at least two bugbears, I saw more large blobs force their way out of the ceiling through the ruined vent. You may remember that one of those bugbears by itself damn near killed me, and now it looked like at least a half-dozen were paratrooping in. Oxana vigorously blasted the newcomers, but their shiny hides only dimpled and blistered a little. Then the spray ended, and I knew her tank was empty. One of the hanging mucus-monsters swung at her like a pendulum, and although it didn't hit her square, it still knocked her spinning into the near end of the Asian section. She slammed into a case containing a Buddhist *thangka*, fell, and lay motionless. Clearly, she had been knocked cold, but it looked like she was crouching at the Buddha's feet. *Yeah, Existence is Suffering*, I thought. *Stop. I get it, already.* Oxana wasn't an angel, and she wouldn't get issued another body. I prayed she wasn't hurt too badly.

Bugbears aren't Hell creatures, I'd learned since the first encounter, but something older and stranger. They can be summoned and put to work, as some demons and most fetches can, but they have very little mind of their own. That means they're limited but also fairly foolproof, since they're not actively trying to figure out how to eat their summoner. The average bugbear really is about the size of a smallish bear, but beyond that the likeness is pretty shaky. They're made of something heavy but soft like jelly, can stretch and even break apart before reassembling themselves, and wrestling with one that's wrapped itself around you is like trying to pull apart a car tire by brute force.

So are they constrictors, I hear you ask? Shit, I wish that was all they did.

See, the weirdest thing about bugbears is that they can harden selective bits of their gummy selves, as I'd already discovered while fighting for my life inside my late Datsun 510. A blobby hole of a mouth can suddenly grow sharp, jagged edges; a flabby, fingerless paw can sprout hornlike claws. The only reason you know it is because the bit that's hardening goes from the usual near-black to a sort of purple-white. But even if you chop those harder bits off, they just turn back into the rubbery dark stuff and then flow back to the original, which is why even in this extreme situation I wasn't bothering to waste bullets on them.

So, General Dollar's battlefield report: one unconscious Amazon, Clarence at least momentarily out of action, Halyna (and her flame-thrower) somewhere in the darkness behind me, hacking gamely away with her own silver-edged blade. Which left me struggling by myself against two bugbears the size of young hippos, with more jelly on the way. The one nearest my face had gone toothy as a hagfish and was armoring itself with pale purplish spikes like a giant rubber sea urchin, but it was the one coiled around my chest that was squeezing me breathless. I got my machete into it and cut off as much as I could (which was about as much fun as sawing through old chewing gum that hates you and wants to hurt you) but at last it fell away. I staggered back a few steps, doing my best to saw away the parts of the other one that were biting me. Nightmare Children were still swarming me too, but I could only deal with one shrieking horror at a time.

You could slow the bugbears down by chopping them into pieces, but eventually they'd pull all their bits back together. Fire worked, but Orban had reminded me several times that Halyna's flamethrower only had three good bursts in it, and she'd already used one.

I had the strange experience of watching my machete pass through what would have been the face of the bugbear trying to eat my head. I almost cut my own nose off, but twisted the blade and managed to do enough damage that the thing slid off me and dropped to the floor, already repairing itself.

I backed toward Halyna so that we could protect each other while we fought. Clarence (who was proving to be pretty darn tough) had recovered, and although he was limping and dribbling blood from his cuts, he picked up unconscious Oxana and then dodged and slashed his way through the swastikids and bugbears to join us. The three of us put our backs to each other and waited, weapons raised. For a moment it almost looked like a stalemate, except for the fact we were clearly losing. Three or four more bugbears oozed out of the ceiling and plopped to the floor, then raised themselves up on pseudo-legs so they looked like larger, hairless versions of the Nightmare Children. This was turning into an evil-jelly jamboree, and I really didn't like the odds.

"Save the fire, Halyna," I said as she aimed the nozzle.

"Why? They will kill us!"

"Trust me. It's the only thing we know that works. We may need it to make an escape route."

"Escape route!" Clarence's voice was hoarse, and he sounded like he was close to losing his composure. Fighting supernatural creatures can do that to you. "That's a good one."

"Hang in there, Harrison. We've still got blades. I've still got a bunch of silver bullets and so do both of you. I'll tell you when to go to the guns."

And then the nearest bugbears suddenly rose up like cobras, spreading themselves at the top as they surged toward us, humping up and down like fast and furious caterpillars. I slashed at the leading attackers with my machete, but the bugbears were wedged together so tightly it was like trying to chop the top off an entire ocean wave made of putty—I'd get through one and the blade would get stuck in the next, or the next. Also, the silver bothered them, but it didn't kill them like it did the Nightmare Children.

We gave ground, but they were forcing us back against the nearest wall. I grabbed the first shieldlike object I could find, a broken Chinese screen, and used it as a bulldozer blade, trying to shove a way through them so we could make a run for it, but although it kept the nearest of the rubbery creatures off my face, the screen was too flimsy. One of the bugbears just reared up and flowed over the top of it like an octopus pulling a crab out of a hole. The monster's weight nearly collapsed everything on top of me, so I let go and scrambled out of the way. A few seconds later the Chinese screen broke and disappeared under a mass of rampaging jelly.

Just when the wave of purple-black death had risen up so high in front of us that I was about to let Halyna buy us a few more seconds (because long-term planning takes second place to short-term not dying) the bugbears around us started to erupt in flashes of fire, a stitchery of sparkling little explosions that blew them instantly into smaller pieces, some of which continued to burn. A man-sized figure was running toward us through the flailing, smoking blobs. Our savior wore a shabby overcoat, and waved a pistol with a big silencer on the end. No, not just big, immense. I mean, it looked like something you'd see in specialty porn.

I confess to being surprised. "*Sam?* What the—?"

"Sam!" yelled Clarence. He sounded like a kid spotting his dad in the Little League stands.

My old buddy leaped over a bubbling pile of bugbear glop. Watching Sam jump is a bit like watching a rhino trying to fly, but I have to admit he got pretty good air, even though he didn't quite stick the landing. "Talk later," he said as he skidded to a tumbling halt beside me, almost knocking me over. An ugly, rubbery tentacle had wrapped around my leg, and I was busy hacking it off before its owner could get a more intimate grasp on me. "I've only got one more clip of these incendiaries," Sam said, panting as he climbed back onto his feet. "If I'd known you were fighting the fuckin' Shmoos I would have bought one of those crazy-ass drum magazines."

I cut myself free, then got out my backup blade, a big old Bowie, and handed it to Sam. God, it felt good to see him, even if it just meant we were going to get fatally slimed together. "Silver-edged. It's great on the spidery guys, not so much on the jellies. Give 'em a little more fire when you're ready, and we'll make a break for it."

"I told you I'd try to make it to your party," he said.

Even in the midst of the ongoing nightmare, I was irritated. "You did no such fucking thing! I left you about a hundred messages."

"I wasn't talking to you, I was talking to the kid."

"Thanks," said Clarence.

I decided to let the matter slide for now. "Let's get going before we destroy any more of our priceless cultural heritage, people." I wasn't really making a joke—what had happened to the West Asian collection was pretty horrifying,

Oxana was still unconscious if not worse. I unbuckled her empty silver nitrate tank, then lifted her. She let out a moan of discomfort as I threw her over my shoulder, so at least she was still alive. "Light 'em up!" I shouted. "We're getting out of here."

Sam swung his Glock toward the thinnest part of the wall of ugliness before us. I don't know what kind of suppressor he had on it, but for something that looked like it should be mail-ordered from the Big Jim Steele catalogue, it worked damn good. Even right next to him, I could hardly hear the sound of the shots, but I could see what they did, and I liked it. When they went off inside the gelatin-monsters, the monster blew to bits. Some shots cut through the nearest bugbears without exploding, but then blew up others farther back. Blazing jelly was flying everywhere, and some of it landed among the remaining Nightmare Children, who scurried away in flames.

I was heading us toward the nearest exits through a minefield of squirming swastika-monsters and quivering Jell-O bits trying to reform even as they smoldered. Keeping our break-in secret was now a lost cause, but I was still hoping to get out without setting off any alarms, just to improve our chances of escape. That said, there was no way I was going to fight all the way back up to the top floor. I still had bullets in my automatic: if worse came to worse, we'd blast our way out through a ground-floor window.

Sam's Glock began clicking on empty chambers when we were only halfway across the room. Several bugbears were following us, hunching along the floor like elephant seals or waddling on distorted legs like mutant turtles, wide and low to the ground. The remaining Nightmare Children were also massing again, this time at the far end of the hall, spread between us and the exits. I was hoping that Halyna's flamethrower would be enough to get us through the whole mess, but there was still another short hallway to cross before we would reach the door, and I didn't think we'd make it past all those obstacles even if we had enough diesel fuel to set the entire museum on fire. I was using my own gun to try to clear some space in front of us, but the silver-tipped bullets weren't very effective against so many enemies. I wished I'd thought of incendiaries like Sam had.

Swastikids began to drop down on us from the ceiling. Halyna screamed that one of them had got between her tank and her back.

In other words, things were really looking shitty.

Then three human-shaped figures stepped out of the shadows of the hall beyond, right in our path, but on the far side of the bugbears and the way-too-many Nightmare Children. These newcomers had guns—big ones, military assault rifles—and they were pointing them right at us. I put Oxana down so I would have my arms free.

"Drop your weapon," said the tall one, pointing that wicked barrel not at me but at Halyna. It was my neo-Nazi Norwegian friend Baldur von Uruk von Dickhead, of course, dressed in some kind of formal black commando wear, wearing a massive medallion that, with his high collar, made him look a little like a Nehru-jacketed swinger in some old movie. So, all the time the creatures Sitri had taught him to control did his dirty work, the bastard had been waiting to step in when things were safe. I wished I'd killed him back at his little racist storefront.

"Drop it now, Robert Dollar, and do not try your disappearing trick again or I kill your girlfriend." His two chums Timon and Pumbaa were with him, done up in some kind of homemade stormtrooper drag. They looked excited enough to piss themselves, but their barrels were steady, and I didn't doubt they could take us out pretty easily. Four or five more Black Sun stormtroopers stepped up from the shadows, all armed with automatic weapons. That made more than half a dozen of them all together, and with much better guns than we had.

I didn't want to risk Halyna getting killed just so this cheapjack, would-be Hitler could make a point. I held my Glock out carefully so he could see it, then tossed it away.

"And your sword, too. All of you. Throw away the weapons."

I dropped my machete, then kicked it away. Sam and Clarence and Halyna followed suit. I was hoping von Reinmann would forget Halyna's flamethrower, admittedly a long shot, but he made her take it off. Timon carried it back out of range, then he and Pumbaa looked it over like a couple of kids inspecting a video game they'd heard of but never seen.

"Now, Mr. Dollar," said BvR, "the horn."

"I told you, I don't have it."

"We are going to search you, anyway." He nodded to Pumbaa. Instead of coming to me, the blond one grabbed Halyna and shoved her stumbling toward von Reinmann, who put the muzzle of his weapon against her head. "And do not be cute, Mr. Dollar."

"You know, I just can't help it," I said as Pumbaa returned to frisk me. "Cute is part of my nature."

He made me take off my backpack and kick it over to Timon to inspect. Timon found my backup gun immediately and slipped it into his own pocket, the little fucker. I'd had that .38 revolver for a long time, and the idea that some fascist punk was going to walk off with it burned me almost as much as anything else that was happening. Then Timon patted me down and removed a couple of more blades, some mags, and once again the cosh sewed into my sleeve lining. He slit the jacket and squeezed it out, waving the little cylinder for his friend to see, like he'd found gold.

"Man!" Timon announced as he found my last sharp thing, the razor blade in my boot heel. "This guy thinks ahead." They'd clearly decided not to skip my shoes this time.

"Too bad you don't," I said, "or you wouldn't be knee deep in felonies and probably selling your immortal souls in the bargain, just to push some tired old Nazi bullshit."

"The Nazis were well-meaning amateurs," declared Baldur. "We have bigger goals. But I am not bothering to explain to you. Where have you hidden the horn?"

"We didn't hide it. We don't have it."

"Really? We did not give you time to find it? You are disappointingly slow, Mr. Dollar." He looked at me for a long moment. Our Boy Baldur had very shrewd, very intense eyes. If you'd passed him on the street you wouldn't have given him a second look, except for his height, but I'd seen enough of him now to recognize the gleam of real madness. "Then you will find it for me now, because I know that is what you came for." He looked across the room to the hidden stairwell beneath the mosaic, now visible to all. "What is down there? That is not on the floor plans."

I was disgusted. The bastard knew almost as much about what we were doing as we did. "Nothing," I said. "It's an office. We didn't find anything."

"Well, then," he said, "you will not mind searching again, Mr. Dollar. Because we are very keen—that is the word, yes?—to find that particular item. We have a buyer who will pay us with something much better than money."

"And what if we won't help?"

"Then you will watch your companions killed one by one—starting with the young women. You see, I know something about you, Mr. Dollar. I know what you are. But I wonder, do all your companions have the same unusual background you do? I think not. And I think you will find it painful to watch them being shot to death, one at a time. So I suggest you get to work."

I hesitated, trying desperately to think of a way to stall them, to confuse them, or just distract them long enough for us to try and get away. But I came up with exactly nothing. Zero. Which seemed like a pretty good indicator of our chances.

"All right," I said. "You're the boss. For now."

"Oh, for much longer than that." He laughed as if he was really enjoying himself, but the gun never wavered from where he held it against Halyna's head.

thirty
death by porcelain

VON REINMANN and his cronies herded us toward the stairwell that led to Donya Sepanta's secret office. These fuckers had been watching us for awhile, it was clear, or more likely their demon minions had done it for them. It was an object lesson in the power of selling your soul. They'd reached out to Prince Sitri, Eligor's rival, and from the depths of Hell he'd sent them what they needed. Just as any jumped-up punk with a gun instantly becomes a threat, anybody with infernal backup becomes a monster.

"How is getting hold of this horn going to do you any good?" I asked von Reinmann. I already knew what his plan was, of course, I was just stalling. Half a dozen guys were pointing serious guns at us, but assholes love to talk about themselves.

"You wouldn't understand," he said. "You think only of small things—your woman, your boss, your job."

"I haven't thought about my job in years, von Rhinemaiden. Only a dick thinks everyone else is a dick."

"And the small-minded always think they are the measure of all things. They cannot understand those who have bigger thoughts, larger aspirations . . ."

I let him blab, hoping he'd work himself up into a mighty we-will-rule-the-world froth. I was close enough to Sam now to whisper and trust to my old buddy's angel ears.

"Do you still have that glove thing?" I asked in my quietest back-of-the-classroom voice. *"The one you wear to do shiny stuff?"*

"The God Glove?" That was Sam's nickname for a very powerful object Anaita had given to him to help him perform his Third Way job. *"Yes, but I don't think it's a good idea."*

"I'm not really interested in good or bad ideas, right now," I whispered. *"Because as soon as we're in that little room down there, it'll be a kill zone. The moment they're done with us—rat-a-tat-tat."*

"No, I'm telling you, B, it's a really bad idea!" Sam wasn't whispering any more.

"I don't care! Do something!"

". . . But I see you are not even listening," said von Reinmann. "You think you will distract me until you think of some plan. Go down the stairs now, Mr. Dollar. By yourself. If you are not back with the horn in two minutes, one of your companions will die." He chuckled. "My choice. Probably one of your girls."

"Fuck it yourself, you Norwegian bitch!" said Halyna, which I didn't think helped the tenor of the conversation. "We are not *girls*, we are fucking Scythians!"

Clarence reached out and grabbed her arm to try to shut her up. At their feet, Oxana was finally stirring.

Von Reinmann smiled and looked at Halyna, then his watch. "So. If Dollar is not back in . . . one minute and forty-four seconds, you will be the first to be shot, whore."

"One thing I don't think you boys from the Black Sun understand," I said, stepping in front of Sam to block their view of him. (I prayed he was doing something worth blocking.) "You are only children with guns. But we . . . we are angels of the Lord!"

Von Reinmann looked at me with zero fear or concern. Apparently he'd figured that out already. "So? You have bodies full of blood and organs. We have guns. We win." He looked at his watch. "One minute and twenty-two seconds, now."

"No, I said," and I made my voice louder, "we are *angels of the Lord!*" Still nothing happened, except me looking like an idiot shouting at men with AR-16s, so I screamed, *"Sam! For fuck's sake, don't leave me hanging here!"*

A great white light burst up and outward from where we stood, bright as a Saturn rocket lifting off, a blinding radiance that made the neo-Nazis stumble back. A second later the light faded to a fierce glow that only burned at the end of Sam's uplifted arm. Timon and Pumbaa found their courage and stepped back toward us.

"Aren't the bad guys supposed to die or something, Sam?" I asked.

"Shut up," he said. "I'm working."

"I have grown tired of your silly shit." B von R looked a little shiny—in fact, everything in the museum hall suddenly looked a little shiny—but he sure as hell didn't look blasted by angelic fire, or even mildly singed by angelic lukewarming. "Shoot all of them," he told his men. "Except Dollar and the red-haired girl."

I didn't even have time to dive for the floor. The guns roared, coughing flame. Bullets that would rip us to pieces rushed toward us at twice the speed of sound, far too fast for even an angel to see . . . except that I *could* see them. And they were slowing down rapidly. In fact, the closer they got to us, the slower they went, until they stopped and then fell to the ground like tiny, exhausted lead birds. *Ping, pingety-ping-ping, ping.* Dozens of them, rattling to the museum's tile floor.

"Wow," I said. I could see the astonished faces of the neo-Nazis only yards away, but except for the sort of prism-like glow around the edges of them and everything else, all looked normal. "Nice one, Sammy boy."

"Just . . . hurry up . . . and figure out the next part," Sam gasped, face dripping sweat, arm radiating light like a live-action Statue of Liberty. "Because I can't do this . . . too long . . . and we're going to have . . . *real* trouble soon."

The neo-Nazis were trying to shove their way through our God-Glove barrier, but having the same problem as the bullets. They would shove forward a little way, but then the emptiness seemed to thicken before them. Veins bulged on their necks as they tried to force their way toward us, but they couldn't get closer than a seven- or eight-foot radius, and when they fired again, the bullets didn't make it any closer to us than before, sometimes barely getting out of the barrel before slowing and falling.

Still, we had no guns inside the Glove's hemisphere of light, and I was having a difficult time thinking of what we'd do when Sam couldn't manage it any longer. Oxana had finally recovered enough to get onto her hands and knees. Halyna was kneeling beside her, and

Clarence was trying to help her stand. I hoped they were also explaining about the bad men trying to kill us, and that Oxana wasn't too badly hurt, because whatever happened, I was pretty sure some strategy on the order of *run like motherfuckers* would be in order very soon.

In the middle of this intense five or ten seconds of panicked thought, a memory wafted up. I threw myself down next to Oxana and began to pat her clothing up and down.

"She is okay!" Halyna protested.

"Good," I said. "But that's not what I'm doing."

I looked out past Black Sun commandos trying to pierce our ring of protection. Von Reinmann had withdrawn to a display area at the top of a couple of steps, like a cat seeking out the highest place in a room, but it didn't look like a retreat. He took off his gaudy medallion and held it in his hand. As I frantically scoured Oxana's jumpsuit pockets for a weapon, since she was the only one who hadn't been searched, I saw him hold the medal out before him, swinging it on its length of chain like a prop in a bad hypnotism act. Then he began to chant.

I'd say my heart sank, but my second-favorite organ (just in front of brain, just after you-know-what) was already huddled down at the bottom of my rib cage, and had been there ever since the Nazis-with-guns element had been introduced. Because I recognized the chant, if not the language von Reinmann used. It was a summoning, like the one we'd seen on the flash drive footage. I could only pray—and I mean that literally, because I am a goddamn angel, and sometimes I have to do it—that he wasn't calling Sitri.

Please, God, I know I've been a pretty bad servant, but there are people here who are actually almost entirely innocent . . .

"Angel! You think you are clever!" von Reinmann shouted. He had apparently finished his invocation. A cloud of mist was now rising before him, making the already prismatic light shift and writhe like tendrils of transparent kelp. "You liked my goblins, my *marrerit*? Then you will truly love the Nøkken!"

I wanted to say something, if only to keep my own spirits up, but so far Oxana's pockets were a dry well, and every time I looked over my shoulder, the horrible mess coiling at Baldur von Reinmann's feet was getting bigger and more real. Things I thought might be tentacles lifted and swayed, except one of them had a glassy flower at the end that swung toward me, displaying a mouth like the biggest, ugliest lamprey you ever saw, surrounded by fringes and tendrils that seemed to move in some unfelt current. The tentacles grew and spread and lifted high, wreathing von Reinmann's triumphant figure. He held the medallion up like the prize for a grueling race. The Nøkken was both substantial and insubstantial—transparent and watery, but its massive, growing coils now smashed the nearest display cases into powder. The head-tentacle rose up ten, twelve feet in the air, questing for prey, and when it saw us it seemed to swell even larger, the central limb, or neck, as big as a redwood trunk. The mouth gaped so wide I could have pushed a wheelbarrow down it and never touched the sides.

I darted a look at Sam. His eyes were squeezed tightly shut, and his face was as pale as death. I only knew he was still alive by the movement of his lips as he silently mumbled what looked like the same phrase, over and over.

I thought it might be time to start mumbling myself, and I had just started, "Our Father, who art in Heaven," when Oxana finally caught hold of my hand—apparently she'd been trying to get my attention while I was staring at the hydra-thing—and pushed it into her shirt-front.

She had a sheath strapped between her breasts, with the handle of a knife right against her sternum. As my hand closed on the weapon, I cried out in relief and then shouted, "Let it go now, Sam! Let it go!"

He hesitated for a second or two. The Nøkken began to draw its coils together to slither toward us. Something that strong, that nasty, would chew through Sam's fading defense like a kid's pup tent. Sam opened his eyes, saw it coming, saw me, and then suddenly the strange rainbow edges on everything just vanished. Sam's barrier gone, the gunmen who had been pushing against it now tumbled forward at our feet. Sam collapsed too, dropping exhausted to the floor like a pile of damp laundry.

I had the blade properly now. It was a tactical knife and not the best for throwing, but I wasn't shopping, I was doing my best not to die. The nearest of the fallen Black Sun commandos was crawling after his gun with the obvious intent of shooting me in the near future, so I pulled the knife back behind my head and then flung it, end over end, hard as I could.

By the way, throwing a knife hardly ever works. I'm also not very good at it. Leo, my old top-kicker in the *Lyrae*, used to tell me, "Boy, I hope you always carry a big gun, because you're useless with sharp stuff and you're even worse at hand-to-hand." And you know what? He was right.

I didn't hit what I was aiming at, which had been the best and biggest target, von Reinmann's torso. The tactical knife flew wide, and if he hadn't turned to watch his hideous water-beast do whatever it was going to do to us, it would have flown right past him and probably skidded all the way to South Korean Textiles. Instead it hit him in the forearm, blade first. It didn't hit straight enough to stick, but it gouged his arm deeply just below the wrist. The medallion flew from his hand and landed on the ground several yards away. He grabbed his bleeding arm and looked at me with such hatred that if Norwegian Death Stares really worked, I'd be playing banjo in the backwoods of Hell right now. Then he realized that he didn't have the medallion anymore. And so did the Nøkken.

The translucent thing was on him like a snake taking a mouse, so quickly that I barely saw it happen. One moment Baldur was standing there looking like I'd butted ahead of him in the Express Check-Out lane, the next moment a giant column of pulsating transparent muscle and goo curled down and swallowed him from head to chest. I could see von Reinmann's eyes bulge, his mouth open helplessly, but then the swirling interior of the thing made it hard to see as it gulped more of him inside. The Nøkken began to change, growing less clear, more smoky and obscure, so that within moments I could only make out a dark shape spasming at the center of it, still fighting for a breath it would never get to take.

I was snapped out of my mesmerized stare by the sound of a gun firing right beside me. Clarence had picked up an AR-16 a Nazi had dropped after falling through the vanished barrier, and he was proceeding to blow the shit out of everything within reach, including (nearly) me. I retreated a few yards to get out of the kid's line of fire. The Nøkken had now almost disappeared, and finished doing so as I watched, leaving behind only a greasy residue and one of Baldur von Reinmann's expensive black Oxfords.

Halyna quickly found a gun too, and within seconds the remaining Black Sun guards were running for their lives. I kneeled beside Sam to see if he was okay. He was, but just barely, his chest hitching like he had tuberculosis. I tried to get him onto his feet, but he was fighting me.

"Cut it out, you dumbass," I explained. "I'm trying to help you!"

He put a hand on my face and, with surprising strength for someone who looked like he'd been run over by a cement truck, shoved my chin around until I was looking back across the hall.

The Nøkken was gone now. The Nightmare Children were fleeing, literally running up the backs of the escaping neo-Nazis. Some of them got tangled up together; a few of the swastikids were stamped into bloody, arm-waving pelts, and some of the neo-Nazis went down under swarms of panicked Nightmares and never got up. But the bugbears hadn't gone anywhere. In fact, they were moving back in on us, as though all of this had been preliminary to the real fun starting.

I didn't have time to worry about it, but in the back of my mind I was also wondering why the museum guards or even the cops hadn't come swarming in after all the ruckus we'd made. Turns out that von Reinmann and his stormtroopers, far less interested in secrecy than I was, had rounded up all the museum workers and tied them up, except for the one poor guard upstairs who'd surprised them. They'd also used some kind of barrage-jamming device to make sure no alarms or phone calls went out. That was when we'd lost communication with Wendell.

"Shit," I said. "Shit, shit, shit!" Oxana was on her feet, still woozy but looking for a weapon. Halyna and Clarence fired into the advancing jelly-blobs with no huge effect except to scatter bits of them, which promptly started inching back to their mother-blobs. Sam was trying to get up.

"Halyna, throw Oxana your gun," I shouted. "You find the flame-thrower!"

To her credit, she only looked at me like I was crazy for about a second, then turned and flipped the AR-16 to Oxana, who scrambled across the floor under our not-too-effective covering fire, grabbed the clunky ancient weapon, then crawled back to us.

"You've got two bursts left, don't you?" I shouted to Halyna over the intermittent rattle of gunfire. She glanced at the tanks and nodded. She looked terrified but not panicked, which I admired as much as I could at that moment. "Okay, everybody, try to herd those things toward the wall there." I pointed to an empty spot beside the open doorway to the hidden office, about five feet from where the huge mosaic of Anaita still hung high on the wall, watching the whole thing with what appeared to be divine amusement. I ran to the spot. "Push them along with the first burst when I tell you to!" I yelled. "But save the second burst, Halyna—save it! Now, the rest of you, force them over here where I am!"

I watched as Clarence figured out he could get the bugbears to follow by charging at them, firing, then retreating again. I called to Clarence and the others to change their angle so they'd be driving the jelly-slugs toward me.

"Halyna, now! Light 'em up!"

Fwooooossshhh! A great billow of greasy flame exploded from the rifle-shaped nozzle. The half-dozen bugbears flinched back and then retreated, moaning in anger and distress so deeply that the few glass cases still unshattered now vibrated and cracked. Some of the nasty blobs were burning like Christmas puddings covered in brandy. I turned and reached as high as I could, then opened a Zipper right in front of the wall, from a couple of feet over my head down to the floor. Then I did a sensible thing and got the hell out of the way.

I knew Halyna couldn't see it, so I shouted again, "Now give them the second burst! Drive them right toward me! Force them all the way to the wall!" I was taking a huge risk, of course, because I had no idea whether or not anything as weird and inhuman as the bugbears could be pushed through a Zipper and into no-Time on the other side, but it was all I could come up with.

The flamethrower belched its last blazing plume, dripping fire and shedding black smoke. Sam understood what I was doing. He came roaring in from the side, holding the God Glove in front of him. I didn't think he could have mustered the force to knock over a child's punching clown at that point, but he made it blaze like a magnesium flare. Caught between Halyna's wall of flame and Sam's bewildering white glow, the jelly-things hunched and slid as quickly as they could toward the Zipper. At the last moment, as the flamethrower ran out of flame, I sprinted toward the herd of Boneless Ones myself, screaming like an idiot and adding to the general chaos. The flabby things began to pile their way into the opening to escape the flames, tumbling into Outside. It must have looked to Halyna and Oxana as though the jelly-monsters were disappearing into thin air.

The flames fell away. The last bugbear, still sizzling and covered with blisters like hubcaps, hesitated in the opening and began to slop back out again. I grabbed at it, trying my best to ignore the feeling of my hands burning, then shoved with all my strength. It teetered there on the edge of nothingness for a moment, then Sam was beside me, and we forced it through. I reached up and closed the Zipper. It held.

"What happen?" Oxana asked. "Where they go?"

"I'll explain later," I said. "We have to get finished and get out of here."

"We have to get out of here, period," said Sam.

"*No!* Not when we're this close. Use the glove, Sam." I grabbed his arm. It was shaking badly. "I know you're a mess, and so am I, but I need you to use the glove again. I have to find that horn if it's hidden down there."

"Are you fucking nuts?" Sam pulled away. "Do you have any idea of the shit that's going to hit the fan in about two minutes? She's going to know someone's using one of her God Gloves."

"Anaita?" I steered him toward the stairs. He seemed overwhelmed, or I wouldn't have been able to do it, because Sam's a big guy. "Look, even if she knows that you used it and *where* you used it, I've been to her house! She lives miles and miles away—fifteen minutes from here even if she's got a private helicopter. Hurry up, and we'll be out of here in five!" I turned to Clarence. "Keep Oxana and Halyna here—they're both pretty banged up, and Oxana can barely stand. We'll be right back."

Sam was still arguing as we hit the bottom of the stairs.

"Sam, just use the Glove, please. Tell me if there's anything in here that feels like serious power. Edie Parmenter said it had to be here, and the less we talk, the sooner we'll be done. Come on, man, I never ask you for anything!"

"You are shit and you are a liar," he said, but he thrust the glowing hand out in front of him. The light was so much dimmer now I could see the actual shape of his fingers inside the sphere of radiance, and the light itself pulsed weakly, like a dying fluorescent bulb.

"Well?" I asked.

"Shut up. You're right, there's something here. I don't know what it is, but it's definitely . . ." He closed his eyes, then moved his hand slowly through the air.

I'd hardly had a chance to look at the room before, but it was a very nice office, which made it even stranger that it was completely secret and hidden. A large desk made of some dark, shiny wood dominated the space, and behind it stood a high-backed chair made of the same dark wood, amply decorated with gold. There were Oriental rugs hanging on the wall and objects of brass and silver, oil lamps, bowls, vases set on shelves in tasteful clumps. The sumptuous carpet beneath our feet was probably worth enough to pay the salaries of the entire museum security staff, including the widow of the dead guard, for twenty lifetimes.

Sam swung around, letting his hand drift sideways, moving it along the walls and up toward the ceilings, sometimes toward the floor. He kept rotating until he faced a rectangular piece of stone on the wall at the opposite end of the office—white marble carved with letters in a script I didn't recognize, something so plain and simple in design that it looked almost like modern art. He hesitated for a moment, then swung past it and continued around the room again. Then he turned back to the marble rectangle.

"That," he said. "But it's not the horn."

"What are you talking about?"

"The horn isn't here. What else do you want me to say?"

"What else could Edie have felt? She's *good*, Sam. How can you be sure it's not here?"

"I know because I know. The glove makes me . . . feel things differently. Like hot and cold spots, or air currents, but that's not it." He shook his head. He looked ten years older than the last time I'd seen him, when he cursed me out at the restaurant. "I think it's a door."

"Door?"

"Shit, is there an echo in here? Yes, Anaita's door to Kainos."

"You mean the Third Way?"

"Yes. The only magicky, angel-y thing in this room is that slab on the wall, and it's a Kainos door. If you want to understand better, *you* wear the glove."

I hadn't thought of this. "Can I?"

"Oh, sure, if you don't mind your hand bursting into flame without the protection I get from being the rightful owner." His face darkened. "Rightful for now, anyway. Let's get out of here. It's a bum steer, B. The horn's not here."

I didn't know what to say. After all this, after the blood and the flames and the armies of horror we'd just fought. "I don't believe it. Try again."

"Don't you get it? We don't have any *time*—!"

"*Sam, Bobby!*" It was Clarence from upstairs. "Get up here!" A second later his voice rose in pitch. "Quick!"

"Shit, what now?" I hurried up the stairs with Sam limping behind me. When I got there, Clarence was staring at a spot near where I'd Zippered up the bugbears, and for half a second I thought they'd somehow gnawed their way back out. I should have been so lucky.

What the kid was pointing at, and what Halyna and Oxana were also staring at, faces pale and slack with fear, was the huge mosaic of Anaita that had covered the door to her secret office. The mosaic was sparkling. No, it was sparkling and *moving*. Ripples of animation made the whole thing seem to vibrate, blurring its edges.

"Get out," I told Clarence. "Hurry. Now."

"What . . . ?" He couldn't look away from the mosaic, so I shoved him in the back. Hard.

"Get the hell out of here now, Harrison! We need you on the outside, because this shit has gone as bad as it gets." If I could have sent the Amazons away too, I would have, but they were both hobbling, Oxana quite badly, and Clarence never would have made it carrying the two of them.

He opened his mouth to say something, but I shoved him again. He finally got it, although he looked like he didn't want to, and sprinted off across the Asian Hall.

I turned back in time to see the entire flat figure of glass and stone and porcelain tiles step off the wall in one piece and float to the ground. A moment later two porcelain and gemstone lions leaped down beside it.

"Fifteen minutes by helicopter," said Sam. "Right."

She was eight feet tall and made of glass and stone. Her eyes glowed like coals. Her flat, crude face smiled. Suddenly a whirlwind seemed to whip through the hall, knocking me sideways, lifting bits of glass and stone and priceless gems from the rubble scattered across the huge room. The glinting vortex whirled past me, its outside edges cutting and scratching my face, and then settled around the living mosaic. The mad wind died as quickly as it had arisen.

She had a shape now. She had three dimensions, and she glowed from within as if constructed from the most beautiful stained glass windows you ever saw. She was still eight feet tall, though, and the lions weren't much smaller. Their gem-encrusted tails lashed.

"Well," Anaita said in a voice like molten silver. "Doloriel. We meet again."

"Oh, come *on!*" I muttered. "This is some kind of bad cosmic joke, right?" I mean, after everything we'd been through, we could barely stand, let alone fight a living goddess. This sucked worse than . . . well, than suction itself.

"Perhaps the universe does indeed have a sense of humor, little troublemaker," said the queen of rotten angels. Her lions moved toward us, making *click, click, click* noises as their sparkling stony claws met the floor. "But I'm afraid this is a joke only I will enjoy."

thirty-one
ragtag

"WHY?" I asked, although I didn't really expect Anaita to tell me. As usual, I was simply trying to find time for my brain to function. It takes a while to get into gear when you've just barely escaped death by jelly monster and then find out you're about to be eaten instead by large cats made of broken glass. I mean, seriously, who else has shit like this happen to them? "Why?" I said again. "What have I ever done to you?"

She looked more human now as the glass and stone and bits of enamel tile began to blend together into something more like the woman I had met in her fortress home, but she was still so clearly far, far beyond me that I couldn't even imagine a way to fight back. She'd just traveled a minimum of several miles in a few seconds by projecting herself into her own goddess-sculpture, complete with matching glass-shard lions. No wonder she'd been able to send Smyler all the way to Hell after me—Anaita must have been burning through reserves of energy like a collapsing sun. But how long could she keep that up without someone in Heaven noticing?

Long enough to take care of a small irritation like Bobby Dollar, apparently. She loomed above me, shining like a fever dream, and she was *terrifying*.

"Why?" Her voice somehow both thundered in my ears and dripped with sweetness. I could hear the childlike tones she favored in Heaven and her deep goddess voice at the same time, as if they spoke in perfectly measured harmony. "That is what your kind always wonders. I have my reasons, but they are not for such as you." She looked very calm, a half smile tilting one side of her mouth, the Mona Lisa of divine vengeance. "Be assured, though, you have earned what is coming many times over."

"And what's coming to you?" Sam said, stepping forward. "What have *you* earned, Anaita? Or should I call you Kephas?"

Well, my buddy had finally accepted the truth, just when we were both going to be dissolved into random atoms. That was something, I guess.

"You need call me nothing. You are no longer useful."

She sounded grave, not triumphant, as though she really would rather have solved the whole thing with a civilized discussion over tea and little sandwiches. I couldn't help wondering, after so many thousands of years of identities taken up and discarded—goddess and angel and the Highest alone knew what else—whether a true Anaita even existed anymore. What happened when an immortal forgot what she'd been? Was that madness?

She raised her hand and the glass cats snarled, a sound like someone cutting stone with an angle grinder. "You are a traitor, Sammariel, and you will be dealt with just as summarily as Doloriel."

"Traitor? What about the Third Way? What about building Kainos so humankind had a hope of something better after death than more slavery?"

For a moment the cool mask slipped a little, just the tiniest bit, to show the furnaces behind it: Anaita didn't like being called on her own hypocrisy. Her eyes narrowed to jeweled slits. "You know nothing, *angel*. You understand nothing. You have no right to question me." Sam fell to the ground, holding his head and groaning as though a terrible noise was screeching in his ears. Then she turned toward me.

"Now, Doloriel." I braced myself, ready to leap toward her, determined to at least bite her a couple of times before I got euthanized like a mangy old stray. I shouldn't have bothered. She lifted a hand, and I couldn't move—could not fucking move an inch, as if I had suddenly been embedded in the clearest, cleanest glass you can imagine. Thank God I'd just taken a deep breath, because I couldn't take another. Only my heart and brain seemed to retain their functions.

"Let him go!" Oxana shouted. "You fat Persian fuck bitch!"

"Really?" said Anaita, looking at me. "This is your army? A pair of mortal Scythian whores and Sammariel the traitor? You truly have scraped the bottom of the barrel to assemble this ragtag, Doloriel."

"*Повія з Ectabana!*" Halyna shouted. No, I don't know what it meant, either. "Not afraid of you! We will—!" She didn't finish. Anaita waved a hand without even looking, as if dismissing a bad joke, and both Amazons were flung backward, skidding through the rubble to lay tumbled and silent against the far wall.

I could only stare as Anaita glided toward me, bleeding light in all directions, hand held out as if to bestow a blessing. She was beautiful, inhuman, and so far out of my league that I had been an idiot ever thinking I might have a chance. Instead, the Blue Fairy was simply going to take back Pinocchio's misspent, marionette life.

Caz, I'm sorry, was all I had time to think.

Her hand touched my forehead, and I *burned*—a cascade of electrical fire from my skull down through my spine, all the way to the ground like a bolt of lightning. My muscles all pulled wire-tight in an instant; I could feel them trying to tear loose from the tendons. It was as bad as anything that ever happened to me in Eligor's torture factory. I wriggled helplessly, like a live fish tossed onto on hot coals.

But I didn't die.

Anaita's hand was freezing cold and scalding hot at the same time— but not in a physical way. It was as if she'd reached directly into my soul and meant to yank it out by the roots. The pain was incredible, but as it blazed something came to me, a semi-coherent thought that made its way up past the clamor of my shrieking nerves, my panicked, dying thoughts.

Why is it taking so long? In some weird way I could sense that pain wasn't the point of what was going on at all, merely a byproduct. Because Anaita wasn't killing me. She was *changing* me.

And this, for no reason I can explain, felt a thousand times more frightening than simple suffering, or even death. I didn't want to be made into some mindless, happy angel, just another placeholder in the divine plan—*anybody's* plan, let alone Anaita's. But I could feel it happening, feel things inside me shifting and becoming almost liquid, my thoughts finding new paths like dammed rivers forcing their way into fresh channels.

I wanted it to stop. I wanted that more than I'd ever wanted anything, except maybe to have Caz back again. I wanted it to *stop*. So I tried to stop it.

I'm telling this now because I'm still trying to make sense of it, but in the moment there was no sense—there was no *time*. What was happening had always been happening. I was lost in a swirling river of color and light and flashes of understanding, all as disconnected as leaves caught up by a powerful current, sloshed together then pulled apart again with no sense or meaning. I could feel Anaita's hand where it burned coldly against my skin, but I could feel more of her than that, as though somehow she was also inside me, rearranging the things that made me what I am—Doloriel, Bobby, the *me* that rides inside and thinks these thoughts and gets the rest of me into trouble time and time again. And as I tried to fight back against Anaita's terrible, intrusive tampering, I experienced other things too, things that were part of me but not part of me. Visions more real than any of my other memories. Sacred pictures. Nightmares and echoes.

Dust swirling, and sky and sun lancing down through it.

Fallen rubble. More dust. Something heavy, pressing me down, trying to stop my heart.

A woman's face, not Anaita's, far more human, smeared in dust and dirt-caked blood, eyes half-closed.

And, distantly, the cry of a child, the hopeless, hitching wail of a child who cannot be comforted.

There's no way to explain this without making it even more confusing, but I felt as though I'd been in a dark room for years, then for just a second someone had finally opened the curtains to let in the fierce, startling, all-revealing light of day. I knew I was feeling *truth*. It was something greater than power, greater than the glory of Heaven itself, and I wanted more of it. It wasn't just bits of unremembered memory, I knew. It was Truth.

But Anaita sensed my resistance and pushed back, and that access to bright reality, a reality I'd never felt before and would always hunger for afterward, suddenly vanished.

With it went hope. For a bare moment I'd thought I had the strength to defy her, to beat back the things she was doing to me, but I had been wrong again. Her anger was as ancient and cold as pack ice, and she handled my soul like it was an ugly, broken toy. My very essence was being squeezed into oblivion. Nothing subtle now, no rearranging, no changing, just the pressure of oblivion, growing greater and greater as she crushed what I was, compacting what felt like the very molecules of my being until darkness began to bleed through everything, light and sound and thought dying. I was gasping for air and getting none, thoughts roaring with blood-red light, then fading into a black as silent as zero.

I could not speak, but I knew enough to call her what she was.

Liar! I thought. *I know you now!*

But I didn't. I had already forgotten. All the bright truth that for an instant had seemed so clear had been sucked away into the vacuum of nothingness.

Nothing.

Then light and noise rushed back in on me, as though I had popped up from beneath an ocean of tar, back into the world. Alive!

Anaita lifted her hand. Her face, beautiful and terrible with living light, was twisted into a grimace of something stronger than surprise: sudden rage made her eyes blaze almost red.

Something had changed. Something black was now throbbing in the middle of Anaita's chest, the swing of a metronome, a needle on Eternity's dial, vibrating, slowing.

An arrow.

I turned my head, which seemed to take years. Halyna stood some twenty feet away, covered in the powdered remains of a fortune's worth of antique statuary, tactical crossbow in hand. Everything was moving so slowly! Oxana limped up beside her lugging one of the AR-16s—those brave women, so brave!—and the flames from the gun's muzzle unfolded like flowers, bloom . . . bloom . . . bloom . . . I saw the bullets stitch their way along the wall as Anaita actually staggered back, again with aching, unhurried gravity, like a building toppling. One step—her other hand came up—then another, and then she bumped against the wall beside the bare panel where her mosaic had been. The moment seemed to hang. The Angel of Moisture extended her arms toward the Amazons, as slowly as paint dripping in the sun, and I couldn't do a thing.

Ten thousand shards of glass leaped away from her, flying across the intervening distance like a horizontal ice storm. They ripped into Halyna, the closer of the two. Oxana dove to the side, but I saw glass tear into her as well, freeing tiny rills of blood that lifted and spread like more flowers blossoming. It seemed to take half a minute before Oxana hit the floor.

Then suddenly everything was moving fast again. The glittering lions snarled and fell back beside their mistress, troubled for only a split-instant in the real world. Released from the power of Anaita's hand, I had stumbled and almost fallen, but I caught at the wall and kept myself upright. For an instant I was confused, because I had been in that spot along the wall, that same spot, only moments earlier, as if time had looped around. But why did that seem so important? Why couldn't I remember?

Anaita yanked the arrow from her chest, dislodging bits of glass and stone, and threw it away. Sam still lay sprawled on the floor, and both Amazons were down. In an instant Anaita would send the lions to finish them off, then turn back to me. I had resisted to my utmost, but it hadn't been enough. And now she was angry.

The thing I needed to remember came to me then. I took a staggering step along the wall, reached up to where I thought, hoped, prayed it would be, and opened the Zipper I had closed only minutes earlier.

As I dove to the floor, angry bugbears spilled out of their prison, exploding back into the real world in great stretching globs of purple black, as if a dam had broken and released a river of animate goo. They flowed down onto the floor and over the nearest stone and glass lion in a second. They flowed over Anaita as well, and for a moment I hoped she too might vanish for good under a heaving blob, but instead I saw light and heat lance out through the pulsating waves of jelly. If there had only been one or two of the creatures it would have been over right then, but all the bugbears were out of the Zipper by now, furious at their imprisonment, and they followed the others in what looked like a feeding frenzy. The translucent glob that had swallowed the Angel of Moisture stretched and bellied out, and I could smell the hideous stench of burning bugbear, but they were old, strong things and they weren't so easily beaten, even by someone as powerful as Anaita.

But she *would* win, that I was sure. We had seconds at the most.

I scrambled across the floor to Sam, dragged him to his feet, then staggered toward the Amazons. Oxana was on her hands and knees trying to get Halyna up, but one look told me that it was too late. Halyna was pin-cushioned with pointy shards of glass, many in her chest and throat, and had lost so much blood that it spread for several feet around her.

"It's no use," I said, dragging at Oxana, but she fought me.

"Halya!" she screamed, a heart-piercing sound. *"Вставай!"*

We had no time. I put my fingers to Halyna's throat where the pulse should have been, but it was only for Oxana's benefit. "She's gone. I'm sorry, but we have to get out of here." I grabbed Oxana again, held her tight. "Come on!"

She wasn't crying, but her face was lost, just lost. "No. Not go. Only with her!"

It was pointless—I could tell Halyna was already dead—but I knew it would be impossible to get Oxana moving without bringing her friend's body. The burning smell was getting stronger. I scooped and levered up Halyna's limp weight, then slung it over my shoulder.

"Where?" Sam asked. He looked as bad as the women, bloodied and ghostlike with dust.

"The door down in the office. The door to the Third Way."

He shook his head. "She can follow us!"

"She can follow us anywhere else just as fast, but that door will get us out of here quicker. Come on!"

Stumbling through the shambles of smashed exhibits, skidding on broken glass, we waded past the seething, burning, bruise-colored swamp that was Anaita swarmed by bugbears. Something as bright as the flame of a welder's torch was burning inside the mass, and I could tell things were going to get ugly in this particular vicinity real soon.

Halyna's limp weight almost tipped me over going down the stairs, but I made it somehow. Sam was standing in front of the marble rectangle, the God Glove on his hand. He said, as if to nobody, "You realize if she's locked it somehow, we're fucked."

There was nothing to say to that. We were already fucked so many ways they could have dedicated an entire revision of the Kama Sutra just to us.

As Sam gestured, the line down the middle of the marble rectangle glowed, but only for a moment, a seam of pure white radiance. Then it was gone, as was the wall and everything else, replaced by what I can only describe as a froth of bubbling light. Sam shoved Oxana through, then followed her. I took a deep breath, clutched Halyna's body close to my chest, and leaped after them.

*   *   *

Grass. That was the first thing I noticed as I fell forward, grass beneath my feet, then I tumbled, and it was against my chest, my head, all of me, even up my nose in spiky, tickling profusion. When I stopped rolling, I dragged myself to my knees. I seemed to have lost Halyna's body on the way through, but in the first moments that absence barely registered because of what was all around me.

One of the strange things about being me is the way "beautiful" and "horrible" keep squishing into each other. Only seconds beyond what had seemed like certain destruction, we had landed in paradise.

We were in a forest glade, but what was around us was as far beyond the usual state park picnic area as Heaven was beyond Hoboken. The vegetation was so vividly green it seemed to have been freshly painted. There was never a sky so blue, so triumphantly skylike, and even the gray mountains I glimpsed through the trees seemed to have been constructed specifically to give people a reason to use the word "majestic." Some extremely eccentric gardener might have watered everything with pure psilocybin, just to grow these beautiful, heartbreakingly realistic hallucinations. But they weren't hallucinations. This was real.

I would have happily stood there for hours, drinking it all in. But I had just realized there were only two of us in this magic place. Only Sam and me.

"This way," my buddy said. "Hurry. We've got to get rest of the Third Way people moving, get them hidden. Who knows what she's going to do now we got her really mad?"

Even in the middle of all this perfection, I was suddenly empty and hopeless. "They're gone. The Amazons, Sam. They didn't come through."

He stared at me, then slowly turned and looked all around. "Shit. They're not angels. Of course, they couldn't pass through to Kainos."

"But other souls came here, all your volunteers . . ."

"Souls. Not bodies."

"But Halyna . . . she was dead, Sam."

"Then her soul's somewhere else. Being judged." He started through the trees. "It's shitty luck, but now we have to save the ones we can, the rest of the souls here."

"No, Sam. I can't just leave them."

He spun and came back to me. "One of them is dead, Bobby. You just said so." He wasn't angry, just confused and hurting.

"That doesn't matter. You don't leave a soldier behind if you can help it. You know that. Can you open that passage again?"

Now he *was* angry. "You want to go back to that museum? To Anaita?"

"Just open the doorway or whatever it is. Oxana and Halyna have to be somewhere. Maybe I won't have to go all the way back. Maybe they're . . . in-between, somehow. I don't even know what that means, but I have to find them."

He only thought about it for a second. "I can't come with you, Bobby. I owe it to the Kainos people to stay and help them."

"I know. Just do it."

"I can't just open it, or it'll dump you right back into the museum, so I'll try to open the far end somewhere else. But I've gotta warn you, I've never tried anything like that. And after everything today, I don't know if I've got the strength." He lifted his hand, closed his eyes. A moment later a shaky vertical shimmer of light appeared beside me. "I don't know how long I can hold it, or exactly where it's going to take you. I'm hoping it doesn't just drop you into—"

"Don't say it. I'll find out in a minute, anyway." I took a quick last sniff at the clean air of this brave new unfamiliar world. Why do I only get these fleeting glimpses of happiness, these moments, then they're ripped away again? "Hang in, Sam. We're not beaten yet." But my buddy looked pretty damned beaten, and I had no doubt I did too. "Remember our motto—confusion to our enemies!"

Then I left paradise behind and climbed back into the light.

thirty-two
sad and beautiful music

A CTUALLY, I still don't know why I didn't wind up back in Anaita's museum office, especially with Sam in the kind of condition he was in. Maybe there's more kindness to the universe than I ever guessed. Maybe instead of being one of the world's unluckiest angels, I've actually been a bit more fortunate than I realize sometimes. Whatever the case, Sam's God-Glove doorway didn't drop me into the middle of the Anaita-versus-Jamblob death match, for which I can only be grateful. Extremely grateful.

Back in the way old days, when people believed (or wanted to believe) that the Sun and the planets revolved around the Earth, one of those old Greek guys proclaimed that the universe had built-in music, that the very existence of everything was underlined by cosmic sounds, and that even distances like the Earth to the Moon were measures of this "music of the spheres," the *musica universalis*.

Later on, that kind of fell apart, especially when Galileo was all, "The Earth revolves around the sun instead of the other way around," and then the Vatican was all, "We're about to go seriously Inquisition on your ass if you don't shut up," and Galileo was like, "Okay, you win," but under his breath he was all, "But it still totally revolves around the sun. Dicks."

Anyway, I give you this short history update to prepare you for what I heard when I stepped back into the door of light Sam opened, which was either the actual music of the spheres or an extremely convincing simulation.

I was surrounded by, or maybe engulfed in, what seemed not just white light, but different *kinds* of white light—not different colors, just different intensities. And as I tried to make sense of my surroundings, I heard something I'll never forget.

Now, mind you, I'm a guy who's heard the singing of the celestial choirs in Heaven, and screams wafting up from the deepest pits of Hell. I'm no rookie. But what I heard when I crossed back through, what surrounded me like the breathing of some immense creature the size of a galaxy, was unlike anything else I'd experienced. It was as different from any other sound I'd heard as day is different from night. It was deeper than the deepest rumble, but it had edges—harmonics, I guess a musician might say—that stretched beyond my ability to hear or even perceive, and yet somehow I could still feel them. I was in the heart of the greatest living thing that could ever be, as if I were only a cell in that body—no, as if I were a single electrical impulse in the endless nerves of the Highest, God Himself. The sound, the music, the vibration, whatever you call it, it was all around me and everywhere. I was nowhere at all, but I was also everywhere, and that was right where I needed to be.

This all washed across me in far less subjective time than it takes to describe, then my rational mind (no jokes, please) finally showed up, took my mental hand, and kindly led me back to current reality.

It was literally a sobering experience. The beautiful chaos hardened into something less diffuse, and the different tones of light resolved into a three-dimensional structure of sorts. I stood in an endless white corridor of glowing motes, like billions of tiny bubbles, but each one different, each one shining with its own tiny white fire, some brighter than others, but none of them dark. Everything around me, the floor, the ceiling, the walls, was made of these shining white cells, like the packing material out of the box the cosmos had been shipped in.

I sat up, and in doing so I realized that I was wearing my Earth body, and that until I made it move again it had been lying in a crumpled heap. Also, close by me, somebody was crying.

I turned, the white scintillations around me smearing into streaks, and saw Oxana, just as I had last seen her, her face buried in Halyna's red hair. Halyna was just as pale and lifeless as she had been when I carried her in my arms.

"Oxana?"

She jumped, or at least she tried to, but the cellular glow around us was nothing so simple as a floor: when she moved she seemed to be swimming in something viscous, and a scatter of tiny lights drifted up around her like startled fish.

"Oh, what is . . . ?" In the midst of so much sparkling brightness, Oxana's eyes were muddy holes. "*Ja ne rozumiju.* Don't understand. You are alive, Bobby?" A tiny glint of hope crept into her stare, but when she looked down at Halyna's body, the glint died. "No. Not her, just you." Tears filtered her eyes. "What is this? What place?"

"I'm not sure. I don't think either of us are supposed to be here—especially not you. But it's okay. I'm going to take you back."

Her eyes got big. "Back where? Not there! Not where Halya . . ."

"No. God, no, not to the museum. We're going back to the apartment." At least I hoped that was what Sam had managed to arrange, but I wasn't going to share my concerns with her unless I had to. She'd already suffered too much for my mistakes.

I stood, struggling with the strange surfaces, the oddly thick air. My feet sank into the cellular material of the tunnel, but the resistance was uneven. I couldn't even make any sense of what I was standing in, whether it was one big thing or a billion tiny things, but the white glow made everything feel relatively safe, if not exactly cheerful.

"No, Bobby. I don't want it." Oxana, clearly driven past what any sane person should have to endure, slumped back down beside her friend's body. "I want to stay. With my Halya."

"We can't. This place isn't meant for people—not living people, anyway." Remembering what Sam had said, that only angels and souls could pass through, I wondered if we were inside some kind of lining for the universe we knew, a placental barrier to keep things out that should stay out and keep in that which was appropriate. Certainly the living, vibrating vastness of it felt more like some kind of organism than any artificial construction.

It took a while to convince Oxana. I was beginning to worry that Anaita herself might pass through this place on her way to Kainos, and when I told her that, Oxana finally got up onto her hands and knees and then onto her feet, shaky as a newborn foal. "Where we take her?" she asked.

It took me a moment to understand she was talking about her friend and lover, Halyna. "Nowhere," I said. "I think we should leave her here."

"No! Never!"

"Halyna's gone, Oxana, believe me. This isn't her, this isn't the woman you love—it's just a body. The reason I came back but she didn't is because she *died*. Now her soul has gone somewhere else. If anyone knows that, I do."

A sudden, new worry struck me like cold water—what would happen when Halyna's soul was taken to Judgement? Like everyone else, she must have had a guardian angel. Now that she'd died, the authorities would know everything, including every crime of mine that Halyna had witnessed. And wouldn't they find out about Anaita, too? She was the cause of Halyna's death, after all. How could even Anaita interfere with such a basic function of the heavenly system?

As had been the case far too often lately, I could only shake my head. Too many questions that even an angel couldn't answer. "Come with me, Oxana," I said. "After all we've been through, all my fuck-ups, I'm afraid you still have to trust me. This part of Halyna will stay here, maybe forever. I think somehow this is the body of the universe itself, or at least, as much as we can understand it. The most important part of her has moved on, Oxana, but her body will be safe here. It won't be any different than burying her in the earth, just . . . cleaner."

"No!" Oxana would not look at me. "No. We don't go." I was close to carrying her out by force when she added, "Give me small time. To say goodbye."

She bent over Halyna's body and arranged the limbs, placing the young woman's pale, freckled hands on her chest, drawing her legs straight. She brushed a coil of glorious red hair back from the bruised face, stroking Halyna's skin, and murmuring to her in Ukrainian. At last she sat up.

"I wish she had weapon. We bury Scythian with weapon."

"God will know she was a warrior," I said. "I have no doubt about that."

"She was. She shot the Persian bitch! She hurt her."

"She did, and it saved my life, I think. All of our lives." I kneeled down and touched the corpse's bruised, pale cheek. "Thank you, Halyna. God loves you. May your journey be a good one and may you find the reward you deserve."

Oxana and I walked along the glimmering, soap-bubble corridor until the light closed behind us like a shining curtain, and we could no longer see Halyna's body. Oxana seemed nearly catatonic, but even for me it was like pacing through a dream. I wish I could explain that place better, but I've never experienced anything quite like it. I don't know if I will ever see it again, feel the musical air and the all-blanketing light (which tells you nothing about the weird physicality of the place) but I know I'll remember it until I finally stop thinking.

We had been walking awhile when I noticed everything around us was getting darker, as if twilight had begun to creep through the not-world. We seemed to be moving through a duller sort of light now, drab and colorless compared to what had surrounded us before. We continued on in silence through this dimming world, but it slowly became clear that the dimness was not uniform: patches of lesser light were followed by even darker stretches, then back to the dull twilight. Gradually these dim passages became alternating bands of dark and darker.

Some time later, we moved from a corridor striped with black and near-black into a few moments of total lightlessness. I felt Oxana's hand reach out and grasp mine, but I couldn't reassure her because I didn't know myself what was going on. Then a few seconds later, with little sense of transition, we were no longer inside something but outside, walking down a suburban street lined with trees and streetlights.

I had my phone in my pocket again. That and the street signs told me that we were back in San Judas in the early morning hours of the day after we'd broken into the museum, still a couple of hours before dawn at least. After everything else that had happened, clever, heroic, exhausted Sam had somehow managed to land us in the eastern part of the city, only a half a mile from home.

When we finally staggered into the apartment, and because I couldn't think of anything else to do for her, I made Oxana a cup of tea. A few minutes later she fell asleep sitting up on the couch, drink untouched. I took the teacup and dish off her lap, tilted her sideways and covered her with a blanket. Then I went back out.

It was a long walk to Stanford, but I needed to get the taxi back. Part way there I caught a bus full of the living dead you always see on buses before the sun comes up. I must have looked right at home. I'd washed myself and doctored my cuts and abrasions as well as I could, but I hadn't taken time to change clothes. My pants looked like I'd just been fired from Pit Bull Obedience School for incompetence, and I had a couple of weird, large, purple-black splotches on my shirt that would have stumped just about any forensic chemist you could find. Also, I felt dead inside. Empty like you can't even imagine.

I got off the bus on the Camino Real and climbed over the campus wall. I moved slowly and extremely furtively through the extensive wooded areas until I was close enough to the Elizabeth Atell Stanford Museum to get a good look.

No lights, no cop cars, in fact no sign of anything out of the ordinary. Which was good. Not that I was planning to go back in there, no fucking way. But if the crime had been discovered the cops would have locked down all the main gates by now and be checking anyone trying to leave.

The cab was still sitting in the auditorium parking lot, by sheer luck next to another couple of cars taking advantage of the lot on a weekend, which made mine less obvious. I drove back across the campus, neck-hairs standing up the whole way in anticipation of police lights in my rearview, but nothing happened, which probably meant the mess at the museum hadn't been discovered yet. The guard at the gate barely looked up, just thumbed the button to open the barrier, then I was through and back out onto the Camino Real. I stopped at a bakery to buy some stuff for breakfast, then ate half the pastries on the drive back to Caz's place, as if the bodily hunger of an exhausting, adrenalized night of horror and pain had lagged a little behind me but had just caught up.

Oxana was still asleep on the couch. I'd bought a bag of almond pastries that I knew she liked, and I left them for her on the coffee table, then took a fast shower and tumbled into bed.

Somewhere in the next few hours, the door to the bedroom opened. I came half-awake, the adrenaline flooding back, but it was only Oxana.

"I can come in?"

"Sure," I said. I held up the blanket and let her crawl in beside me.

I was more than slightly aware that she was wearing only a tank top and underpants, but I was too tired to care. She pushed up against me, and the trembling that ran through her from top to bottom was enough to tell me what was going on. I put my arm around her and let her get as close as she needed.

"I follow her," she said. "Halyna." I thought for a moment she meant she was going to die, too, but before I could say anything she spoke again. "I follow her because I love her. I know her when we are girls in school. To me, she is the bravest there is, like a kite."

"Kite?" I said softly.

"No, not kite. Ka-night."

"Knight. The ones in armor, who ride horses, yeah?"

"Yes, knight. To me, she is the bravest, the most beauty. When windy, her hair is like flag. I want to . . . to marry her." For long moments she couldn't talk. I held her while the sobbing washed through. When she calmed again, she said, "Halyna tell me I am too young for her. That she is the bad news and that she likes boys, too. I don't care! And when she goes to join the Scythians, I promise that I will do, too." Oxana put her head on my chest, as if she liked the sounds of her words better reverberating up from inside me. "And I do. Two years, then I leave from school and go. And I love it. All the fighting practice, I get strong, and Halyna still is the most beautiful—so strong compared to me! And so smart. She knows all about the world and the politics."

I had never heard Oxana speak so long and had never heard her use English for more than a few sentences at a time. I tried to ignore the physical nearness of a warm, healthy young woman and just become a pair of ears and a brain, because that's what she needed, but it wasn't easy. I may be an angel, but I was lonely too, and my body is just mortal as hell.

"And then after while, my Halya, she loves me also. Still she has other love, other girls, but she loves me best, she tells me. That is best ever for me. She call me . . . she call me . . ." Oxana's voice hitched again. She had to ride this one out like a bad storm, gripping my chest with her arm and pushing her head against me, an animal trying to burrow down into the safety of earth. When it passed, she said in a tight, calm voice, "She call me *Hoduločnik*. That is bird with long legs that walks in water. She says that is me. *Hoduločnik*!" The storm took her once more, and this time it went on so long that I fell asleep, still holding her closely.

Later, probably in the first hours after sunrise, I woke again. Oxana was still in the bed with me, but she was wrapped around me in a much different kind of way, her groin pressed against my leg, her breasts against my arm, and she was pushing me, nudging me, making soft, muffled noises. Her nipples tented her thin shirt as she pressed them against my skin. She dragged them across my upper arm and groaned, but so quietly it was like something happening in another room.

Oxana was asleep, I'm sure she was, dreaming of her lost Halyna. I tried to move away from her, but she made a whimpering noise and held on. I had been dreaming of Caz and was already half hard, but the rhythmic pressure of Oxana's mons pushing against me, the little sounds of need and pleasure, had given me a painfully full erection. I didn't know what to do, except I knew that I had to get out of that bed. Oxana didn't want me, she wanted something she couldn't have, and I didn't want her, or at least my heart didn't, and I certainly didn't want to take advantage of her, whatever my crude and ignorant physical plumbing might have thought was a good idea.

I turned a bit more to the side to keep her out of contact with my throbbing self, and as I was preparing to clamber out of the warm bed and into a cold chair, for the good of everybody in the room and at least one person who wasn't, Oxana gave a strangled little gasp, then her thighs tightened on my leg so hard I thought she might break my femur. I mean, that woman had some muscles. She lay there breathing deeply for long moments, then said something I couldn't hear, in a voice completely muddled by sleep, before falling back into even deeper unconsciousness.

I just lay there for a long time, trying to get back to sleep and not having much luck. I was missing Caz in every way a man can miss his beloved, plus a few new ways I hadn't even thought about before. Eventually all my blood flowed back to where it was supposed to be, dispersing to various useful tasks, and I could slide into darkness again, this time to dream of endless white corridors with no way out.

thirty-three
rabbit hole

I DON'T KNOW about you, but when I've spent weeks planning something and then it crashes and burns, bringing futility, horror, and death, I like to start planning something else right away. You know, so I don't lose that winning momentum.

Of course I was gutted, and would rather have been drinking and trying to forget the terrible mistakes I'd made, but I didn't have that option. I had to figure out what I was going to do next, because "next" was going to happen whether I wanted it or not.

The morning news, at least in the San Judas area, was full of the results of our expedition (*Attack At Stanford Museum—Vandalism Or Political Protest?* in the Courier was pretty typical) but to my immense relief, I saw no mention of bodies. Apparently the guard who'd been downed was going to survive, and the absence of other victims in the reports suggested the Black Sun had taken their wounded with them when they fled. I was pretty sure some of those wounded had been the kind we would label "dead, actually," but I was relieved that their impulse toward tidiness meant it wasn't going to turn into a murder investigation. It's always about ten times harder to stay out of trouble when it's a capital crime, I tell you with the sad voice of experience. How I longed for the days when I was still in good with my bosses, and I could have just called the cleanup crew from Heaven Central like I did for the Black Sun mess in that upstairs apartment. Still, I suppose even the heavenly cleaners would have had trouble trying to cover up the fact of neo-Nazis breaking in and tying up all the museum employees.

Still, the blowback from the museum disaster was going to be quite enough to destroy me anyway. Not only had I made my beef against Anaita very clear to her, I'd slapped her in the face about as hard as it was possible to do, but I still hadn't found the horn. In other words, I'd made her angry without hurting her a bit.

When I finished with the newspapers, Oxana was still asleep and looked as though she might be for hours, which was fine with me. It's one of the only things the truly bereaved can do, and I didn't know how much support I could give her in my current situation. In fact, I was thinking pretty seriously about taking her out to the airport immediately and putting her on a plane to somewhere, just so I didn't have to protect her from the shit that was going to go down. Actually, considering how much of my budget I'd already blown on the disastrous museum venture, I'd probably have to take her down to the County Transit hub and put her on a bus. Budget-wise, I could probably get her to Salinas.

Failure? Me? Only in *this* space/time continuum, bub. There must be tons of alternative realities out there where Bobby D is still The Man.

I went out to the courtyard to make some calls, but was distracted by something thrashing around loudly in the bushes beside the path, like a cat trying to upchuck not just a hairball, but an entire other cat. After some investigation I found a nizzic—*the* nizzic, the new bat-winged, read/write model—tangled deep in a juniper bush. I guessed it had gone looking for shade when the sun came up. Hell-creatures like it hot, but they also like it dark. I unhooked it from the clinging branches as carefully as I could, then took it inside, but it was still trembling and making little barfy noises, so I put it under a bowl on a cookie sheet and set the over for about 250 degrees.

After ten minutes or so I put on the potholders and brought it out. The little demon-creature looked happier now and was already reciting its message. I turned off the kitchen lights and listened to the rest of it, then let the winged messenger cycle through the whole thing again.

"I suppose this is one of the reasons I fell for you instead of just destroying you in the first place, like I should have—your psychotic inability to compromise

or do the smart thing. I'm so used to people who only care what's best for them that there was a certain charm in someone who couldn't take the sensible way out even under threat of torture and death.

"You were right about the gypsy story I told you our first time together— you wouldn't have done what Korkoro did. You would have charged up that mountain to attack the Fog King, and the whole thing would have been even worse for everyone, and all for a principle you're not even sure of yourself.

"Oh, Bobby, I can't tell you how much I want to fuck you right now. I want you all over me, pressing me down with your weight, holding me like I was trying to get away. But I wouldn't be. Because I know about being held against my will, and I also know about being held because it's exactly what I want, and I definitely know the difference between the two. What a ridiculous, night-mare world this is, my lover, where two people who just want to be together would have to turn the whole universe upside down to do it.

"Maybe we shouldn't talk any more, at least for a while. I thought I could handle it, but I don't think I can. All those years I lived in London, I should have learned from the English, because they have the right idea. The only way to deal with people, living or dead, is at arm's length.

"Don't tell me anything that will make me cry, Bobby. If you send a mes-sage back, just be funny. Be sweet. Otherwise I can't do this."

I wasn't ready to answer her, not just that moment. Too much stuff boil-ing in my brain. You know when you're a kid and you're so sad and angry that you just start crying? Like that. Instead of crying, though, I tucked the nizzic back into the warm bowl, blanketed it with a couple of my dirty socks (which I thought should make a little demon feel right at home) and stashed it in the back of one of the pantry closets so it wouldn't startle Oxana if she got up. Then I made a cup of coffee so strong it violated several workplace safety laws and took it back out to the courtyard to make some calls. The first was to Clarence.

"Bobby!" he said when he picked up. "Thank God, you're alive."

"Yeah," I said. "So's Sam and so's Oxana. But Halyna, she didn't make it."

The kid was genuinely sad and outraged, which shows you that someone picked the right person to be an angel. In fact, he seemed to take it harder than I had, not that I didn't feel sick about it. But in my case it seemed like it wasn't the loss of Halyna herself that burned as badly as my failure to keep her safe. Clarence the Rookie Angel, like any decent person, reacted first to the loss of the woman herself and its effect on Oxana.

After I'd given him the full battlefield report, the kid told me that he and Wendell had gone back to work as though everything were normal and that, so far, they seemed to be pulling it off.

"But what are we going to do now, Bobby?"

"No 'we' this time. So far, you're still clear, or you seem to be. Let's keep it that way, especially since I don't have the slightest idea of what I'm going to do next, short of complete surrender. You and Wendell just keep on keeping on. I'll contact you if anything changes."

"But, Bobby—!"

"No buts. I appreciate what you've done. You're a good man, and I was wrong about you, but I don't want to take anyone else down with me."

I hung up then. I wasn't being dramatic or selfless, it was just becoming clear to me that I was running out of options, that maybe this was not going to be a story that ended happily, no matter how much I'd hoped it would. After all the death and destruction, I couldn't quite imagine a way it *could* end well. Even Caz was beginning to seem like a phantom. She had been my dream once, but now she was only a voice, farther from my reach than ever.

I had only one piece of good news for anyone, so I passed that along next via a message on Fatback's voicemail, letting him know his days of being haunted and burgled were probably over, at least at the hands of the Black Sun Faction. Baldur von Reinmann was messily, monstrously dead, and Timon, Pumbaa, and any remainder of the local troop must be running for the hills by now. Or Argentina.

As I considered my next step, I nursed my coffee and tried to keep thoughts of Caz at arm's length. The sun rose higher in the sky, turning the dank, gray December morning into something almost cheerful. Birds scuffled through the leaves that littered the concrete patio all around me, then leaped into the air whenever I set my cup down or re-crossed my legs.

Why had I been so certain that I'd find what I wanted in the museum? I'd thought I was going at the problem in a systematic way, but the more I looked at it now, the more I saw what I felt sure was the real Bobby Dollar—a creature of reflexes and reactions, following whatever the most recent stimulus had been, half the time getting it completely wrong, the other half getting things right mostly by accident. But when you were fighting out of your weight class—*way* out of my weight class, with Eligor and now Anaita—hoping for dumb luck was not a viable strategy.

The feather, the horn, everything in the whole grim mess came down to the bargain Anaita had made with Eligor to create a place outside of Heaven, Hell, and Earth, a home for Kainos, her pet project. But why had Anaita been so interested in creating a Third Way? And why had Eligor taken a huge risk just to help a powerful angel, one of his sworn enemies?

I had a sudden urge to talk to Gustibus again about Eligor's possible motivations, but his phone only rang and rang—no answering machine this time, no semi-helpful nun. What could he have told me, anyway? Follow the money? There was no money, or at least the money was never the point with beings as powerful as Anaita and the Grand Duke. "Powerful"—yeah, that was the word, that was all that type cared about. I didn't need to follow the money here, only the power.

Something clicked. It wasn't a very loud click, but it was enough. That was what I'd been missing. *Who gained from all this? And what did they gain?*

I felt I had grasped something important, but I needed more coffee to shake the sense out of it. I went back inside and found the kettle still hot: Oxana was up and had made herself a cup of tea. She was wrapped so completely in a blanket she looked like a Bedouin tradesman, and she glanced up from the ghastly daytime show on the television only long enough to meet my gaze with a very dull, miserable one of her own. I gave her an awkward, one-armed hug, then took my coffee and went back outside. At the moment I felt pretty sure she didn't want to do anything except stare like a zombie at people that she didn't know on a screen.

The thing was, although it had almost taken over my life in the last year, I had no idea what Kainos was *for*, why it even existed. The official version handed out by Kephas/Anaita had been that it was an alternative to the present either/or of Heaven and Hell, which could be true for all I knew. But why would the Angel of Moisture want to create such a thing, and why would Eligor help her? It was hard to imagine either one of them getting misty-eyed over the rights of souls, and from everything Sam had said, an incredible amount of work had gone into making the Third Way real. Could I square the idea of Anaita as a sincere reformer with the creature who had now tried several times over to destroy me and the people I cared about?

Actually, I thought it was entirely possible. Maybe she really did think of herself as a do-gooder. Nearly every revolution, even the necessary ones, spawns a great deal of pointless bloodshed, revenge killings, and show trials of the insufficiently committed. Most of what Anaita had done to me had been in order to cover her own tracks, so I could accept, at least for now, the possibility that she'd set out to do exactly what was claimed, then panicked when the feather went missing—the feather that proved her guilt in conspiring against Heaven's order.

But Eligor was another story, of course. Whatever Anaita's motives might have been at the beginning, I found it impossible to believe that the Horseman had any interest in reforming the system or changing anything that didn't benefit him personally. So why would he play along, and even take a huge risk, by giving his horn—which wasn't really a horn, but a token of his essence—to Anaita to keep as potential blackmail fodder?

Trying to figure out the motivations of Hellfolk was like going down Alice's rabbit-hole. I put it aside to concentrate on things that I had a better chance of answering.

Don't worry about anything else, I told myself. *Follow the power.* I couldn't yet answer the questions about who benefited and why, but there were still plenty of other things to consider. I'd been fairly sure that the horn was hidden at the museum because Anaita had gone to a lot of trouble to conceal something there. If it hadn't been the horn, if it was only the entrance to Kainos, why? Why hadn't she just built the doorway into one of the many rooms in her giant, fuck-off mansion?

Because she needed to hide it, had to be the answer. Anaita wanted ready access to it, but not in a place obviously associated with her. Heaven didn't like the Third Way. Not at all. And it probably took a great deal of power to get there and back, or at least enough to be noticed by Heaven's higher-ups. That might be why the doorway to Kainos was hidden far from Anaita's own house. Perhaps that was also why she hadn't followed Sam and I through it when we got away from her—she'd expended as much angelic might as she could manage to disguise.

If so, then the only real weapon I had against her was her fear of discovery. But that still didn't tell me where Eligor's horn was, and without that, everything else was pretty academic, because eventually Anaita was going to catch me and blot me out like an unwanted spill on the kitchen counter. She had more resources than I did—a lot more. "Oops! I seemed to have crushed a Doloriel," she'd say, and everyone would say, "Tsk, tsk, too bad!" Then they'd go on as though it had never happened.

My new cell phone rang, startling the bejabbers out of me. The ringtone was some horrible European disco crap, and I throttled it into silence as quickly as I could.

"What?" I said into the phone, a little sharply. I assumed it was Clarence.

It wasn't. "Bobby," a male voice said. "I need to speak to you. In person."

My heart got a little jumpy. Nobody had one of these phones except Clarence, Wendell, Oxana, and Halyna, and Halyna was dead. "Who is this?"

"The person who took you for a nice drive in the Baylands. Remember?"

Temuel. But since he hadn't used his name, I wasn't going to, either. "Yeah, I remember. In person where?"

"How about the place we met before you went on your sabbatical? Do you remember that?"

By "sabbatical" I guessed he meant "trip to Hell," so he was talking about the Museum of Industry up in the Belmont district. I was a bit tired of museums, as you might imagine, but I also knew that the Mule wouldn't have called me unless it was important. "Same spot? Give me half an hour."

"Take the Camino Real. Traffic isn't too bad today."

I suppressed a smile. Some angels can't stop angel-ing. It's like an addiction. Or a reflex. "I'll be there."

I retrieved the nizzic from the pantry, listened to the message from Caz one more time, then burned some white camphor in a spoon and blew the smoke at the little monstrosity. The nizzic slumped a bit, and its head wagged slowly from side to side, like a cruise ship passenger who'd had one mai tai too many.

"Pay attention," I told it. "Otherwise it'll be silver salts instead of camphor, and you won't like that."

"I can't just be funny and sweet, my beautiful Caz, even to make you happy. You told me once you didn't do tender very well. I don't do friendly chitchat very well, because I usually only use it on people who worry me or bore me. Right away I get out the sharp stuff and start looking for a weakness.

"The fact that it's my own weaknesses I usually find is beside the point.

"So I can't do that shallow stuff with you, not after where we've been and what we've done. I want you so badly, Caz. I dream of you. I replay our one night together over and over in my head like I was some sad little film fan watching Casablanca for the tenth time, hoping against sanity that this time Rick actually gets on the plane with Ilsa. I can still taste the salt of you, the sweat, the tang of your juices. I can still hear the sounds we made together like they were happening in the next room. You want to fuck me? I want to fuck you so much that if someone opened a door to Hell right now, I'd walk right in and start the whole thing over again, just for the chance to get near you.

"I'm never giving up. I'm never giving up. Have you got that straight yet?

"Never. Giving. Up."

I put the re-messaged nizzic outside under a bush to wait for dark, then I gave Oxana some money in case she needed to go out and get anything. I was pretty sure she wouldn't. She'd found a bottle of wine and was systematically polishing it off while she watched people argue on TV about paternity tests and other unimportant things. Just as I was leaving she called me back, then raised her eyes from the screen long enough to kiss me carefully on the cheek, like I was Dad and she was my college-age daughter home for the holidays or something. It was weird but not entirely bad.

I took Temuel up on his suggestion and went by the Camino Real instead of surface streets. I had to change lanes frequently to keep moving, but otherwise the traffic wasn't too bad. The cab handled like a speedboat in tapioca even at the best of times, but I didn't mind. I was in no hurry. Even with all the stuff thrashing around in my brain just now, and a strong urge to look closely at every driver I could see in case they were planning to kill me on Anaita's behalf, something else had begun to bother me, though it took me most of the drive to put a finger on the problem.

My boss Temuel had called me on my Serbo-Croat Spinksphone. But Temuel wasn't supposed to know about the Spinksphones. That's why I'd bought them from Cubby Spinks before the museum break-in, so that the Amazons, Clarence, and I would have a private method of contact that neither Heaven nor Hell knew about. This was the second time Temuel had done something like this to me lately, and neither made sense. He'd known when I called out for a cab, too—the very cab I was now driving. He hadn't told me how he'd done that trick, and now he'd pulled another one. He really was keeping tabs on me, probably tapping these new phones too. But why? Was he really so concerned for my health? Or was it just his own ass he was covering? That made more sense, but it meant that things would change very quickly if our interests ceased to coincide.

Another thought struck me as I approached the museum. Why tell me to take the Camino Real unless he knew exactly where I was driving from in the first place? If I was hiding out in the hills or down by the Bayshore, the Camino would be a pointless detour. But that meant he didn't know only about my new phone but also suggested he knew where I was staying, and I had made sure none of my associates ever, *ever* talked about Caz's apartment on the phone. Even the Amazons had known and respected that rule.

For a moment real fear rose up inside me. I almost pulled over to the curb, ditched the cab, and made a run for it, but a moment's consideration showed me that even if he knew a lot more about my life than he was letting on, Temuel certainly wasn't trying to keep it secret from me, or he would have kept his mouth shut about the Camino Real. No, something else was going on. In fact, it almost seemed like he was trying to tell me something, give me a warning. But why not just wait and do it in person, since he was meeting me anyway? Would it actually be Temuel waiting to meet me, or had someone else made him call?

Thinking about Heaven and its ways really made my head hurt sometimes.

The Museum of Industry is a crazy place that used to be a rich family's mansion in the Belmont neighborhood of North Jude. The centerpiece is an odd fountain made of the plumbing from an old building that once stood on the property, but minus the building itself; a phantom edifice of pipes that sprinkled water from every joint during the warm months.

I could see a figure I was pretty sure was Temuel as I walked onto the museum plaza, a small figure huddled by itself on the bench. That made me feel better. The sun had given up an hour ago and sloped off behind some clouds, leaving a cold, gray afternoon. Nobody else was in the area except a couple of women in business clothes just departing on the opposite side.

I waited another minute, watching from the shadows of one of the museum's wings, but Temuel only sat. He didn't talk on the phone. He didn't look around. ("He" is perhaps a little misleading, because this time, he was a she: Temuel appeared to be wearing the older-Hispanic-woman body I'd seen once before. The archangel liked disguising himself, but this time he hadn't bothered to fashion a new one.)

At last I took a deep, calming breath and started across the open plaza. Temuel looked up as I approached. It was indeed the same body he'd worn once before, the one Young Elvis had so charmingly referred to as a "cleaning lady."

"Doloriel," he said as I got near. "I'm glad you made it."

For some reason, this plunged me right back into paranoia again. Because we'd met several times outside of Heaven, and during all those visits Temuel had never, never, *never* called me by my angel name—only "Bobby." I slid my hand into my pocket, so I could feel my gun.

He gave me a look of mild disappointment. "Don't do that, please. It's not going to help anything. Look, I'm putting my hands up." And he did, lifting them slowly into the air, those brown, hard-callused, working woman's hands. Then he slowly dropped them again, but this time they left trails of burning fire down the air.

Two angels stepped out of the Zipper on one side of him. Three more stepped out of the Zipper on the other. All five had the cold, serious look of Counterstrike veterans, and all of them were pointing serious-looking weapons right at me. They had been there all along. Temuel must have hidden them Outside before I arrived.

"Please, don't do anything foolish, Advocate Angel Doloriel," my boss said. "Just let them do what they have to do."

I could barely talk, I was so angry, so miserable. "And what if I don't?"

"Then they'll shoot your body to pieces, I expect—but your soul will still be going with them." He gave me a look that I could not read for the life of me, flat and emotionless. "Please, don't, Doloriel. It's a waste of materials, and you know our department is always up against budget constraints."

Before I could think of any reply to this amazing statement, someone grabbed my arms from behind and someone else stuck something sharp into my neck. I had time to open my mouth, the words *"Fuck you!"* forming on my lips, but I never got to say it before nothingness came and swallowed me.

thirty-four
deep inside it

*S*HE WAS *sitting beneath a tree in a patch of filtered sun, the gold of her hair so pale it looked almost . . . almost . . .*

I felt like I might cry. "You're so beautiful. Oh, God, you're so lovely, Caz."

"Trite," she said.

I laughed and dropped onto the ground beside her, leaves and fallen evergreen needles crunching beneath me. I kissed her cheek, then down to her neck and the curve where neck met shoulder in an expanse of smooth skin.

"Don't bite!"

"Sorry." There was indeed a small drop of blood where I had been too fierce, too careless, a glitter of red. "I got carried away."

"You're so right." She pushed me back.

I didn't understand why she was upset with me—it was just a little blood. "Come on, don't take it that way. Come back."

"Forget it. You're tight." And suddenly she was walking up the slope, leaning forward a little to keep her balance. The sun falling on the hill above her seemed too strong, too powerful. It wasn't the sun at all, it was something else, something blinding.

"Caz? I haven't had a single drink all day. Come back. Don't be silly."

"I don't want to fight," she called.

I got to my feet and scrambled up the slope after her, but already I was having trouble seeing where she'd gone. A mist rolled slowly downhill toward me, a great, ground-hugging cloud.

"Caz?"

"Something's wrong with my sight!" Her voice rolled down the hillside, this time with a note of terror in it, but I couldn't tell the direction.

I was stumbling over stones that blended into the gathering fog. I fell and got up. "Caz? Caz, where are you?"

Her voice was fainter now. "I think it's turning to night."

But it wasn't getting darker at all. Rather, the mist was rising up all around, stretching itself like an animal just awakened from hibernation. I was lost in a sea of cottony nothingness. "Caz?"

"Bobby, I'm getting really fright—!" Something cut her off in mid-cry. I shouted her name again, but no reply came. I charged uphill, but something went wrong, and I was staggering downhill instead, far too fast. I swung my arms to keep my balance, but I was out of control. It was no longer just mist that surrounded me, it was something colder. Snow. Flurrying, whirling, making everything the same, turning everything . . .

Where was she? Had the Frost King come to take her back? Or had that only been a story?

And all around me, silence. All around me, nothing but . . .

White and more white.

"Where did you go?"

Nothing but white.

"Caz!"

Just white.

"Caz, come back!"

White.

It was like rising slowly through milk, or from the center of a pearl toward its outer edge. For a long time I didn't even realize I was awake, because the difference between the white dream and a real dream was so small. It was only when I realized I was thinking the same kinds of thoughts over and over that I finally knew I was actually conscious.

Still, it wasn't exactly the kind of consciousness you could stake a claim to, or build a house on. Nothing that satisfying. More like being an iceberg in a sea of other icebergs, the slow bumping of thought on thought, the unending and unchanging surroundings. I wanted to be alive again, to do things, to be something, but instead I could only float.

I'm in some kind of prison, I finally realized. At first I couldn't understand why such a cruel thing had been done to me, but then it came back—Temuel's betrayal, the needle into the vein, the darkness that had rushed at me like a silent storm. I tried to use my body to push against whatever held me, but I didn't *have* a body, or if I did, I was so disconnected from its workings that I might as well have been on a different continent, trying to operate it by trans-Atlantic telegraph messages.

White. I was in white so deep that nothing else existed, so complete that it was hard to think coherently. It reminded me more than a little of the between-place I'd gone after being tortured by Eligor, that gray, utter emptiness. It also made me wonder when Heaven's torturers were going to show up.

Days. Weeks. Years. Centuries. I floated like a fish at the bottom of a frozen winter pond and nothing changed. Nothing ever changed. Thoughts became more rare. I think I actually forgot how to think.

Then, after what seemed a thousand years or more of milky nothing, something disturbed the mindless calm. Stirring in my white dream, I waited, or at least I tried to remember what it felt like to wait for something. Gradually the disturbance became a presence, then a cadence, and then it became words.

"Angel Advocate Doloriel. God loves you." It was a low, sweet voice, a female voice, one I had never heard. Just hearing it pushed back the worst of my fear, but it also woke me to how far from life I'd drifted. I hadn't realized how lonely I'd been. *"Can you hear me, Doloriel?"*

I had to think carefully about how to turn all the emptiness inside me into words. "I think so," I finally said.

The presence settled closer, warm and comforting, like the mother I must have had once but couldn't remember. For the first time in longer than I could remember, I wasn't alone. I didn't ever want to be that alone again.

"I am Pathiel-Sa, Angel of Conciliation. Do you know why you are here?"

It came back to me then, at least some of it—Temuel, Counterstrike angels, a needle. "No. Where am I?"

"In Heaven. Do you remember nothing?"

My thoughts were as slow and clumsy as blind grubs. "I remember Earth."

"Yes, but you are not on Earth anymore. You have been brought here. To me. Are you afraid?" The voice was sweetly patient.

I told the truth without exactly meaning to. "Yes."

"*Try to let go of that fear. The Highest wants only what is best for you. That is a fact the entire universe cannot refute. Why are you frightened?*"

"Because . . . because I'm so small. Powerless. And there are bad things happening."

"*Powerless, you say. Are there things you cannot do? Things that are important to you?*"

"Left alone. Be left alone forever. In the white." I could barely frame my thoughts. I felt like a head-wound victim waking up after only partially successful surgery. "But they won't let me—" I fished for words, but deep in the cold white, even with Pathiel-Sa hovering comfortably close, they were hard to catch. "Try to be good," was all I could come up with.

"*And are you good, Doloriel?*"

I wanted her to stay. I wanted to tell the truth. My returning thoughts were like shivers, convulsing me without really warming me. I felt crippled by my long bath in emptiness. "Try. But it's hard. Maybe I . . . maybe I really am bad."

"*What do you think, Doloriel? Are you bad? Have you done bad things?*"

Why was I afraid? Pathiel-Sa wanted to help. I could *feel* that. I didn't think I'd ever felt anything so clearly. "I don't know."

"*Is that true?*"

Something deep inside shrilled at me to keep silent, but that voice was easy to ignore. All I really wanted was for this floating cloud of sympathy to stay with me. "Guess. I guess I have. I'm a good person, really. I try to be."

"*But you say you've done bad things, Doloriel.*"

"I didn't want to." But I had wanted to, at least some of them. I'd wanted to do some of those things very much. "Can you do bad things and still be good?"

"*Yes, good people can do things which are not good. But they feel sorry about it. They know they did wrong. Are you sorry, Doloriel? Did you do wrong?*"

Again a smothered part of me tried to pull back, but the rest of me reveled in the feeling of safety, of being known and accepted, and I was tired to my nonexistent bones of half-truths and outright lies. After the clean cold of the long white, I felt as though I had been living in a swamp of falsehood.

"I am sorry," I said. "I tried. I tried to do the right things."

"*Oh, Doloriel, it makes me glad to hear that,*" said Pathiel-Sa. Her voice might have been her wings enfolding me, protecting me. "*And it pleases the Highest, too. It pains Him when His children are in pain or error. But most of all, it pains Him when the good do not repent of their mistakes. He wants to love you, Doloriel, but He wants to love you for who you truly are.*"

The thought of God's love swept through me like a tropical current, so warm that for a moment it pushed away the deep chill of the white. Something like happiness spread over me. I had forgotten how good that felt.

"*But you cannot hide anything from the Highest,*" Pathiel-Sa added, and the warm current dissipated. The cold washed back in, dulling me, diminishing me. "*That is the one thing that He cannot abide. Do you understand that, Doloriel?*"

"I . . . I do."

"*And it is wearying to harbor secrets. It is wearying to lie. It is wearying to wear one face for some and then change it for others. Do you see that?*"

I did. Just then, it seemed the clearest I'd ever seen anything. How could I ever hope to do God's work when I could not even live in Truth? "Does the Highest despise me?"

"*Never, Doloriel. The Highest misses you. The Highest wishes you to return to His love and the happiness it gives. Like a father who watches his little child do wrong and is unhappy only because the infant does not know better, He wants to show you the way to live in His Love. Do you want that?*"

"Of course. More than anything." I climbed into that certainty, huddled in it, anything to bring back the warmth. "But how can I be forgiven? After all I've done wrong?"

The Angel of Conciliation did not speak again for long moments, or so it seemed. In my slow way I was terrified, thinking I had driven her away in disgust.

"*Are you truly good, Doloriel?*" she asked at last. "*Truly?*"

"Yes. I think so. Oh, God, I want to be!"

"*But things have happened—things you did not plan but which forced you into difficult choices. Isn't that true?*"

"Yes." And I could plainly see it now, see the course of my angelic life laid out like the map of a journey, but the ways I had traveled were complicated, dangerous, many of them completely unnecessary, as was now clear. "Yes, I made choices. Some of them were bad choices."

"How did that come to be? You meant well, did you not?"

"I did, but sometimes things are complicated. Sometimes things that seem simple *get* complicated."

"The Highest is not complicated. He is simple. He is love."

A deep sense of failure gripped me. Pathiel-Sa was right, of course. Every step of the line there had been a proper path—I could see it now so easily—and yet so many times I had chosen the wrong direction. How could the Highest forgive so many mistakes? I thought that I had chosen love with Caz, but how could it have been love when it was against the Highest's own word? Even if she had loved me too, she was a tool of the Adversary. I had put all Heaven in danger because I thought I knew more than the Highest and his most trusted angels.

"You are thoughtful, Doloriel."

"I don't understand why I did some of the things that I did."

Pathiel-Sa seemed to come closer then, or at least the whiteness warmed once more, her presence wrapping me like a blanket around a shivering body. *"Of course not, Doloriel. Because you did not mean to do what was wrong, and it was not clear to you at the time. Or did you put your own judgement above God's?"*

"I don't know. Probably." I had the strangest feeling of wanting to cry, but instead of tears from my eyes, something larger but even less solid wanted to burst out of my soul, wanted to free itself even if the escape killed me. "I wish everything had been different!"

"It can be. Heaven is forever, which means there is always enough time. But you must see your errors before you can do better. You must admit your mistakes before you can forgive yourself. The Highest has already forgiven you, but you still hold yourself in a prison of regret."

That was exactly right. A prison of regret. This cold, white nothing was a prison of my own mistakes. And there were so many of them!

"You must think about it," said Pathiel-Sa. The quiet sincerity of her tone as reassuring as sunny skies after a storm. *"You must consider your mistakes. You must see them before you can escape them. Where did you step from the path of the Highest, Doloriel? Where did you stray from His love?"*

So I told her. I brought out everything I could remember, from my first moments of doubt back at Camp Zion to the very last secret I had hidden from Heaven before Temuel gave me up. I told her about Caz, and about Sam and the Third Way, and about the lopsided war I had fought with Eligor the Horseman. I even described my journey to Hell itself. The only thing I didn't tell her was that Anaita was behind so many of those things, even though I hadn't always known it at the time. In fact, I didn't mention Anaita or even think of her.

Only later did I realize how strange that was, since Anaita had been front and center in my troubles for a long time, and one way or another had been responsible for many of my worst crimes against Heaven. But as I poured out the contents of my soul to Pathiel-Sa, Anaita might never have existed.

As the Angel of Conciliation listened I described every single ugly thought I had entertained against Heaven, every petty act of defiance against my superiors. At times I wept with the horror of what I'd done. At other times I felt a fire of joy kindling deep inside me as I shed myself of these old, sick fears, of my countless petty crimes and insubordinations, the lies I had been forced to live, the fellow angels I had betrayed with my falseness. Pathiel-Sa barely spoke, but I could feel her quiet approval. When she asked me a question, I could feel that it came from love, which made me answer all the more fully. She loved me—the Highest loved me—and more than that, she understood me. She saw the good underneath the mistakes, the benevolent impulses that had turned bad, not through evil intent, but through clumsiness or bad luck. Pathiel-Sa loved me. I never wanted her to leave.

It seemed to take days, but at last I finished. The Angel of Conciliation thanked me and assured me for what might have been the thousandth time that God did indeed love me. Then she was gone and I was alone in the white—floating, calm, relieved. I had cleansed myself. I was empty, ready to be filled once more with God's light and truth.

I am good, I told myself. *Despite everything. She knows I am. And the Highest knows I am.*

It was only later, after many more centuries surrounded by endless blankness, that I realized I had met Heaven's torturer after all, and that I'd surrendered to her every last detail of my own certain damnation.

thirty-five
gag order

THE NEXT time I surfaced, I felt more like my regular self. Which means that I was angry, because it was clear that I'd been dunked in angelic glamour, then skinned and scraped clean by the Angel of Conciliation. I'd given up my every secret, so whatever happened between now and my sentencing would be nothing but a formality. I'd thought I could stand up to the big boys and girls, but I'd been embarrassingly, painfully wrong. Any way you look at it, I was in a bad mood.

"Do You Know Where You Are, Advocate Doloriel?" a voice asked me. This one was male, but although familiar, I didn't immediately recognize it. I might still have been a little groggy from too much white.

"It depends on where 'here' is," I said. "If this is Carmel, I'm probably here for 17-Mile Drive and the expensive souvenirs, because I've never been much of a golfer."

I had the satisfaction of a clear moment's silence before he answered. *"You're In Heaven, Doloriel."*

"Okay, then I'm guessing it's because of that 'Kill everyone' thing I put in the suggestion box."

Whoever he was, I was confusing him. *"Are You Disoriented?"*

"No, I'm making jokes. You haven't left me much else to do, seeing as I have no body, no way of leaving, and no option to discontinue this interview. Unless I do. Do I?"

"I Am Chamuel, Doloriel, Principality Of The Third Sphere And One Of

Your Ephors. Do You Remember Now? You Are Here Because You Are To Be Judged. Are You Aware Of The Sins That Have Been Ascribed To Your Record?"

"Well, 'pain in the ass' is probably one of them, as you've noticed." It wasn't Chamuel I was mad at, particularly, not compared to Anaita or even the deceitful creature Pathiel-Sa, but I was furious that they had bled me dry of information so easily, that Heaven's Ephorate had made me jump to their tune like rich folk teasing a lame beggar.

"These Are Serious Matters, Doloriel." Chamuel's mellow voice took on a subtle but distinctly disapproving tone. *"You Have Been Charged With Grave Sins."*

Yeah, and already found guilty, I silently added. I knew this was all just for show. "Let me guess—Attempting to Overthrow the Order of the Universe? Questioning That Which Cannot be Questioned? Blowing my nose on my sleeve?" If I was going to get burned at the stake, I was at least determined to go out with, if not class—I know, way, way too late for that—at least some spunk. And I was determined to take a bunch of other angels down with me, Anaita first and foremost. Oh, I was going to make plenty of noise, believe me.

However, the next thing Chamuel said pretty much knocked all the grit out of me.

"You Must Answer These Accusations." He sounded like Newscaster Delivers Sad News, which is even half a notch grimmer than Newscaster Contemplates Disturbing Trend. *"You Are To Be Judged For Your Part In Creating The Place Called Kainos Or Third Way, Which Is A Terrible Crime Against The Highest, And For Numerous Interferences In The Work Of The Highest, Including Seducing Souls From Their Proper Path To Heaven And Hiding Them From The Heavenly Host In That Illegitimate Place. Do You Understand?"*

Did I understand? Suddenly I didn't understand *anything*. I'd confessed enough secrets to the Angel of Conciliation to condemn an army of saints, so why was I being bum-rushed for the Third Way, something I didn't actually have much to do with, except after the fact? My only crime in that case was neglecting to arrest my friend Sam, who *had* been involved. And what about the things I'd really done? Falling in love with a high-ranking demon? Traveling to Hell, for goodness' sake? Making deals with Grand Duke Eligor, one of the Bad Place's major Ring-a-Ding Boys? My list of crimes would go on for a long time before it ever got to the stuff like Falsely Phoning in Sick and Failure to

File Proper Reports, but I was still more guilty of those than I was of the Third Way bullshit. So what was going on?

"What rights do I have in this judgement?" I asked. I couldn't see Chamuel—or anything, for that matter, except white and more white. I was getting a little bored with the view.

"Rights?" His voice was still calm and kind, but I thought I noticed a little edge in it. "That Is Not A Word That Applies Here, Doloriel. You Are A Piece Of The Highest. Does A Drop Of Water Ask What Rights It Has Against The Greater Ocean? Does The Cell Of A Mortal Body Ask What Rights It Has To Dispute The Needs Of The Entire Organism?"

I wasn't going to be sidetracked. "Call it whatever you want. What kind of trial am I going to get?"

"You Will Be Judged By Those Of Us In The Ephorate Already Assembled To Examine This Affair."

Great. So now Anaita and the rest of the Fab Five were finally going to turn thumbs up or thumbs down on me for good. I was pretty sure which way the thumbs were going to point, if only because Anaita was going to be working behind the scenes like a busy little bee to make sure I got stung. But she must know I wasn't planning to go quietly.

"What if one of the ephors is actually . . . ?" I began to say, but didn't finish. It was strange, because I wanted to finish, but the words went crooked and slipped away from me.

"What If One Of The Ephors Is What?" Chamuel's patience seemed a tiny bit strained, but I was desperately trying to find a way to talk about the real subject at hand—how I was being set up for something I hadn't done.

"What if . . . ?" I began, but again it didn't come out right. In fact, it didn't come out at all. I decided to take another approach. "What if the angel being accused is actually being . . . being . . ." I really wanted to say "framed," but that didn't seem to be the right word either. Don't get me wrong, it was the right word, I just couldn't say it. Something was extremely wrong. Fear grabbed me, then—very big, very cold, and very, very strong. I tried just to blurt out, "Anaita is the one who made the Third Way," but as soon as I thought it, the words (or the part of my thoughts where the words were forming) just fell apart. If I'd had a heart, if I'd had a heartbeat, it would have been rattling like a two-stroke engine with the throttle cranked. Something was wrong with me. I couldn't even mention Anaita's name.

"Doloriel?" the ephor asked.

"What if . . . ?" I struggled to find a work-around. "What if I wanted to say something about my guilt? Something that would . . . surprise the ephors?"

"What Might That Be?"

"That I'm . . . I'm . . ." I wanted to say *being manipulated,* and side-step Anaita's name entirely, but it still came out as "I'm . . . not sure."

"I Don't Understand You, Angel Doloriel."

"I don't understand me, either." It was hard to keep the bitterness out of my voice. I was fairly certain I sounded crazy or worse. "I've been . . . I'm being . . . I can't. . . ." I took a breath, tried to go blank. "Anaita is . . ." *There!* I'd finally managed to say the bitch's name. I did my best to stay calm, to not think too carefully about words. "Anaita is . . ."

"Yes?"

"Anaita is . . . one of the ephors."

"Yes, That Is Correct. You Have Met Them All Before."

If I had been wearing flesh I would have been sweating like a pig and gasping for air. It had been that hard even to use Anaita's name; trying to say anything meaningful about her was impossible. It was like pushing the wrong ends of two strong magnets together: something invisible just wouldn't let it happen.

"Is There Anything Else You Wish To Tell Me, Doloriel?"

Yes, I wanted to shout, *this whole thing is a joke, and I'm being set up by a monster who makes the Whore of Babylon seem like Marge Simpson,* but even thinking of Anaita choked off my words.

Now I knew what she had done to me in the library. She hadn't bothered to destroy me because she had a much better use for me: I was going to take the rap for her entire crime-spree. I could feel curses boiling inside me until it seemed they would blow me apart, but not a murmur came out, because Anaita's face was at the center of it all.

So I gave up, at least for the moment. "Do I get a mouthpiece?"

"I'm Sorry, I Don't Understand."

"A lawyer. An advocate—the same job I do for humans? Do I get someone to argue for me?"

The coolness in the voice told me before I heard the words. *"This Is Not An Adversary System, Doloriel, Such As We Have With The Opposition. The Object Is Not Victory, The Object Is Truth."* I could hear that damned capital T like it was printed ten feet high on the emptiness in front of me. If Chamuel had possessed a face at that moment, I would most likely have punched it, because Truth was clearly the one thing that was not going to play any part at all in this farce.

"And so the five of you are going to decide whether I live or die?"

"*Nobody Dies, Angel Doloriel.*" Chamuel's tone told me he had finished with me for the present, and was glad of it. "*That Is The Good Word We Of Heaven Know And The Good Word We Speak. No Soul Is Ever Truly Lost. It Is Only A Question Of Where—And How—You Will Spend Eternity.*"

Then he left me alone in the white again.

The next time I came back, it started with points of color. At first I thought I was hallucinating. I'd been doing a lot of that, although, in that odd situation, the difference between hallucinations and regular old dreaming would be hard to define. Here and there in the vast, depthless, edgeless white, I noticed what seemed like miniature rainbows, disturbances that had color and even movement. I had been drifting, thinking about my archangel Temuel and how stupid I'd been to trust him when he had obviously planned to throw me under the heavenly bus at the first sign of trouble. But partway through an elaborate fantasy of ratting him out and letting him spend a few thousand years in his beloved Hell, singing "Kumbaya" to demons, I had begun to realize that the way Temuel had given me up didn't quite make sense. In fact, he'd gone about it in a very complicated way that I needed to consider more carefully. Then the slow swirl of colors distracted me.

The colorful spots became brighter, first gleaming, then actually shining, and with that shine came a certain form. No, five forms. Five shining lights. My judges, my jury, and probably my executioners, the Ephorate.

As they became more substantial—although calling these ephemeral, vaguely human shapes made of light "substantial" is stretching it a bit—I could even recognize them, but only because I'd seen them all before—Terentia, the leader, Raziel, mysterious as a locked box, Chamuel, the color of a dying sun, and Karael, the only one who had ever seemed like he thought I was more than a bug to be splattered on God's windshield. And of course my old friend, Anaita, the monster who was going to walk away clean while I flame-broiled in Hell. Oh, how I wished I'd dropped a dime on her while I still could, before she got into my mind and soul and neutered me.

"Doloriel," said the cool but somehow benevolent glow that was Terentia. *"God Loves You. You Have Had Time To Contemplate The Charges Against You, And To Consider The Health Of Your Immortal Soul. Is There Anything You Would Like To Say Before We Begin?"*

Just as an experiment, with no real hope it would succeed, I tried to say *"Yeah, Anaita over there is framing me,"* but it only came out as "No." Just "no." So that was definitely how it was going to be. "Let's get on with it," is what I said next. That came out fine.

"Your Judgement Will Take Place Before The Assembled Hosts Of Heaven," Terentia said.

"Sure. Wouldn't want anyone to miss this much fun." No problem with those words either—even the fine edge of sarcasm was left intact, because it was useless to me and harmless to Anaita, of course. I wondered how tight her control over me might be. Was it active? Was she hearing everything I was thinking before I said it? Or were there blocks in place, like some kind of automatic censorship program?

"Terentia, The Hosts Are Waiting." If Chamuel had been a man instead of a glowing, man-shaped hole in the pearly emptiness, I would have said he seemed to be irritated that this was taking so long, but since this was Heaven and angels famously don't give a shit about time, I must have been wrong.

"Yes, The Moment Has Come." Terentia's radiance widened, as though she raised her arms or spread her wings. *"Come, Doloriel. And Fear Not—God Truly Does Love You."*

"Yeah. I'll try to remember that." It wasn't entirely sarcasm this time. A part of me still hoped, like a very young child hopes, that Somebody really was going to step in and save me. Because minus divine intervention, these good, kind, all-knowing angels were going to hang me. What made it really upsetting, though, was that they were going to hang me for the one thing I actually hadn't done.

So they paraded me through Heaven.

Of course, just by saying that, I've given you the wrong impression. They didn't literally put me in a tumbrel and wheel me through the shining streets like a French aristocrat going to the guillotine. I could barely tell it was going on, except for the fact that it actually took time to reach the High Hall of Heaven's Judgement. Normally when you go somewhere in Heaven, you just leave the place you were and arrive in the place you're going; there's no more sense of transition than a film dissolve. But instead I could perceive myself moving past and through the hordes of Heaven, and could feel them all reacting to me. As with so many things up there, it's not very easy to describe. I felt like a soap bubble in a tub full of suds: I traveled not so much by actually moving as by sort of sliding from being one bubble to being the next, as though I was not even a bubble but some color or bit of surface tension that could slip from one connection to the next without disturbing the whole. But still, I felt the curiosity of Heaven's citizens as I moved past them and through them, and more than a little of their discomfort at what was happening. Everybody's happy in Heaven, but there are gradations; wherever I passed on my way to judgement I could sense a little ripple of less-than-perfect happiness spreading outward behind me.

A smart guy once said, "Writing about music is like dancing about architecture," and trying to explain Heaven is the same way: words just don't do it. Words have to come afterward, and usually they're very bad tools for defining what actually happens Upstairs.

Anyway, I slipped, I slid, I lingered long enough in some spots to become a fact and briefly enough in others to be only a feeling. Whatever else they were doing, most of the angelic throng gave part of themselves to the spectacle, following me and communicating among themselves about it. Almost none of them knew me personally, of course, but by the time I reached the Hall of Judgement most of them felt they did. My anonymity—the anonymity of most angels, individual happiness bugs in a giant, joyful hive—had changed. I was more than a single angel now, but also something less—an Idea, perhaps, or a Concern. But what I felt pretty sure Heaven actually wanted me to be was an Example.

I too had experienced things like this and had even participated, during the innocence of my earliest days in Heaven. I remembered being certain that justice would always be served, that no matter how odd or confusing the situation, the hand of the Highest was guiding the proceedings. Because it was Heaven, truth had to win out. I guess I'd lost a little faith since then.

The Hall of Judgement was full, not with physical bodies, but with presences. I don't know how many angels were there to see what happened to me close up, to learn what I'd done and what would be done with me, but I could feel them and even sort of see them all around me, filling the vast space like a billion dandelion puffs. The great Paslogion loomed over us, a sort of clock tower (that's my best guess) which dominates the hall, a huge, powerful *something* made of translucent layers of transparent wheels. As far as I knew, it measured the reality of everything that ever was or ever would be. The shining tower reminded me now of what a small thing I was in the larger scheme: my trial and my inevitable sentence would be no more significant to the eternities the Paslogion studied than the pinging of a single subatomic particle.

And that's where you and I came in together, remember? Where this story began, with me in the dock, as they used to say in old English murder mysteries, and five judges getting ready to hand down a guilty verdict. Of course there were a few formalities to be observed first, like the trial.

What seemed hours of discussion passed solely in laying out the charges, but I won't bore you with that, or the even longer parade of "evidence" that followed. As I had been told, the charges boiled down to, "All that Third Way shit was Doloriel's fault." But the fine points of heavenly justice had to be observed, and each block in the false edifice of my guilt had to be carefully crafted and put into place. I answered all questions to the best of my ability, usually honestly, because the crimes of which I was accused weren't mine. But since I could never name the truly guilty party, I didn't help my own cause much. Basically, the case against me was that Sam and I had connived to overthrow the Heavenly order. Yes, that was the claim: the two of us low-level angelic schmuckos had come up with a plan to create an entire new reality all by ourselves, and then found a demon lord (to help us get around the Tartarean Convention agreements between Heaven and Hell) to build the place. And with no Sam and no mysterious Kephas-angel present in the courtroom to say otherwise, nobody bothered to disagree with this preposterous nonsense.

So that was me, apparently: Bobby Dollar, king of the rebel angels, the greatest traitor since Lucifer demanded his own key to the executive washroom. And this time I'd be the one to get the brimstone para-chute.

The Great Frame-Up started with the fact that I'd been on the scene when the first Third Way soul disappeared, the now infamous Edward L. Walker. Of course, it had been as big a surprise to me at the time as anyone else, but as they piled on other guilty-looking things I'd done, such as letting Sam escape me at Shoreline Park, it wasn't hard to see that my participation would seem pretty obvious to anyone who didn't know the whole truth. The odd thing I noticed after a while, though, was that other than the Walker disappearance, they weren't using any of the most damning evidence against me—the things that had actually happened.

For instance, it's a Bobby Dollar Fact that I'd coshed junior angel Clarence with the butt of my gun out at Shoreline so Sam could get away (because at the time, Clarence was working undercover for our bosses) but that little bit of assault wasn't even mentioned. It would have been a perfect example of my obvious guilt, but apparently Clarence hadn't told them. I was glad to know even at this hopeless stage of things that the kid really was my friend, even though it wasn't going to make any difference in the verdict—just one less "crime" to consider when they already had quite enough to measure me for the gallows-drop.

That wasn't the only strange omission, either. The ephors knew I'd been in touch with demons—they mentioned it about ninety times—but for some reason nothing at all was said about my actual trip to Hell, which was an extremely major crime and one I'd actually com-mitted. I had to assume they simply didn't know about it, because it sure would have made a nice piece of evidence of my total guilt. I mean, even demons only go to Hell because they have to.

And even weirder, they didn't mention Caz at all, at least not any of the things that would have really put the last knot in my noose, like the fact of us having vigorous angel-demon sex, or me pledging my undy-ing love to her in front of the Ralston Hotel (the hotel Eligor would blow up about ten minutes later). Now, since Temuel, the guy who handed me over to the heavenly authorities, had been deeply involved in me getting to Hell, it seemed like the Ephorate should know all about my little trip, but not a word was said. Maybe the ephors were just protecting their archangel minion, but it still didn't seem quite right. It would have been easy to claim Temuel was acting under orders when he helped me—that he had just been giving me enough rope to hang myself. So why no mention of Hell, which was a slam-dunk fact?

No mention of Hell and no mention of Caz, either—the reason I'd gone to Hell in the first place. Both of them would have been perfect additions to the case against me. The only reason I could imagine was a strange one: Temuel hadn't told them about any of it.

Was the Mule protecting his missionary work in Hell? Or some swindle of his own? Or had he genuinely been trying to help me? I couldn't hope to figure it out while on trial, and there almost certainly wasn't going to be a later—at least not a later where I'd have leisure to think about stuff like that, because I'd be too busy trying to breathe burning sewage while getting pitchforked repeatedly in the ass—so I let it go.

I have no idea how long the trial went on, because, you know, Heaven. The questioning itself was generally formal and straightforward, and there wasn't much open debate between the angelic judges, at least not so the heavenly public could hear, but I was pretty certain that a great deal of conversation was going on between the five of them. I could almost sense their thoughts buzzing back and forth through the heavenly ether like overexcited electrons or some game of multihyperdimensional Pong. I sometimes thought I could get a glimpse of the argument in the tone of their voices when they did speak, and the colors that flickered through their flames. Anaita took the lead in a prosecutorial sense, and generally, Chamuel backed her. Terentia and sexless Raziel were more careful and asked more general questions, as though trying to better understand what happened. And Karael, although he seldom spoke up, tried to keep the evidence against me from being overstated, balking at exaggerations like the bluff, military type he often seemed to be. He wasn't exactly on my side, but he didn't seem intent on bundling me into the Down elevator as quickly as possible, either. I decided if I ever had another afterlife in which to do it, I'd thank him for his open-mindedness.

One thing I did learn, which I hadn't known before (and hadn't particularly wanted to know, either) was that Anaita had more clout with the others than I realized. In fact, she was apparently the ephor closest to being anything as simple as "in charge" of San Judas and all its earthbound angels, and I understood for the first time how she could have gotten away with something as big and crazy as the creation of Kainos. Which raised another question: Had Temuel been working for her all along? Maybe that was why nothing that would make him look bad had come up during the trial. Maybe she'd picked me out as her sucker from the first and had used Temuel to lead me right up the ramp into the slaughterhouse.

That still didn't feel quite right, either, and, as I said, I had other things to worry about just then. Still, there were some angles I definitely didn't understand about the Mule's role in my downfall.

"I Sense That There Are No More Questions Relating To The Accusations," Terentia said at last when the examination had slowed a bit. I could feel a bodiless stir of anticipation pass through the countless spectators, wherever they might actually have been, at the signal that the end of this whole sordid affair was near. Now it was time for Justice, or so they thought. *"Does Anyone Wish To Add Anything?"*

And then Karael, warrior angel and hero of the Fall, said something that, for the second time in my otherwise bi-incurious life, made me want to wrap him in my arms and just smooch the holy heck out of him.

"Actually," he said, *"I'd Like To Hear Whether The Accused Has Anything Else To Say In His Own Defense."*

"Why?" asked Anaita in her sweetest little doll-baby voice, but I thought I could feel the fury she was hiding. *"Has This Doloriel Not Been Given Ample Chance To Respond Already? Instead He Has Mocked The Proceedings At Every Chance, Avoided Direct Answers, And Trifled With This Ephorate's Generosity By Making Unnecessarily Snide Remarks."*

"I'm Afraid I Agree With Anaita, Our Blessed Sister," intoned Chamuel. *"The Only Value To Heaven This Angel Retains Is That Of A Bad Example, And We Will Not Receive Any Value For That Until He Has Been Sentenced."*

"Raziel?" Terentia asked. *"What Say You, Comrade?"*

The mystery that was the fifth ephor didn't come any closer to revealing itself, but did add (after a long, deliberate silence that would have made me sweat bullets if I'd been wearing a physical body) *"I Would Be Willing To Listen To What The Prisoner Has To Say."*

I almost cried out with relief, though my doom had probably been postponed only by a few seconds. Now it was down to Terentia to cast the deciding vote. Her glow dimmed just the smallest bit, and I felt a sense of growing fear that she would deny me this one, tiny chance. Because I had an idea. Yes, it was a bad one. Many of mine are, especially when I'm nervous because someone's about to destroy me, but it was the only idea I had and the only chance I would get.

"I See No Harm In It," she said at last. *"Doloriel, You May Speak."*

I knew that if I said anything that implicated Anaita, the safeguards she'd put in place would stop me before I got it out. I had to be careful. I'd only have one try.

"Thank you, Masters and Mistresses," I said. "Instead of making a statement, I have something to ask—a request. I ask you to consider it carefully." Anaita's manipulation wasn't just passive: I could feel her hovering over my thoughts like a fearful miser, ready to snatch back anything useful before I could speak it. My only hope was that I'd surprise her by taking a different direction, so I took a deep, metaphorical breath before plunging in.

"We Are Waiting, Doloriel." Terentia sounded like her patience was fading.

"Very well. I respectfully request that you delay your judgement in this matter until all the facts are known."

"What Can This Mean?" demanded Chamuel, like a grumpy old man kept up past bedtime. *"Facts? We Have Uncovered All The Facts!"*

"If you will delay judgement, and free me temporarily . . ." I began.

Suddenly I could feel Anaita clamping down on me with the talons of her thought, trying to crush what I was about to say before I could manage it. For a moment I thought she'd stop not just my words but my entire existence—I was smothering, though I had neither mouth or lungs—but I'd learned a little during our struggle back at the museum. I fought back against her assault, struggling to keep a small part of myself free. If I'd been about to name Anaita herself I wouldn't have managed, but my intent seemed to surprise her long enough for me to get it out. "If you'll free me, I'll bring you Advocate Sammariel, the one who brought me to the Third Way, and he knows all the answers I can't give you. You've never been able to catch him. Free me for just a little while and I'll hand him over to you."

"And How Will You Manage That?" asked Terentia, clearly surprised. *"If We Can't Find Him With All The Power Of This Ephorate, If We Can't Reach Him In This Heretical Place Called Kainos, How Will You?"*

"Because I know how to get there. And because he trusts me."

I admit that I've had prouder moments.

thirty-six
bobby wins again

FOR ME, there was little or nothing in the way of transition back to Earth, although the five ephors must have discussed the arrangement a bit. The next thing I knew, I was standing in the middle of the main quad of the Museum of Industry where the Mule had handed me over to the Counterstrike unit, by the same bench near the fountain. I was dressed in the same street clothes. My gun was even back in my coat pocket. Crazy, right?

Even crazier, I hiked over to the parking lot and found my taxicab right where I'd left it, shiny with recent rain like a healthy young banana slug. Who had cared about me enough to put me back next to my ride? And why was it still sitting here, instead of being stripped and searched for evidence in some heavenly impound garage?

After all I'd been through, I was as nervous when I got into the cab and started it up as one of those anti-Mafia judges in Sicily. It didn't go ka-boom, though, just coughed into life with what might have been a bit of a fuel-mixture issue. When I backed out, it left a dry spot in the parking space, as if it hadn't been moved at all.

Same bag from El Gran Taco on the floor. Same Coke cans that the Amazons had left in the back seat. Everything in the cab seemed untouched, although I would have been a fool not to suppose it had been stuffed full of tracking devices.

Still, the condition of the cab was another piece of minor weirdness I didn't have time to think about just now. Time was short. I was dragging a barely suspended death sentence like a ball and chain, and I had things to do and best friends to betray. I drove until I spotted a pay phone—not that easy these days—and called Oxana on the shielded, rerouted landline at Caz's apartment.

She picked up right away. "Bobby? That is you? Where you go? I am so worrying!"

"I'm sorry about that. I'm not going to talk about it on the phone, but I'm okay." Which was a wild exaggeration, but whatcha gonna do?

"How about you?"

"I am fine. Was food to eat. But I am worry when you go out and don't come. All night!"

"All night? Hang on, what day is today?"

"Is," she had to think about it for a bit, "is Thursday."

"Thursday? Like, the day after I went out? You saw me *yesterday?*"

"Yes, Bobby. Yesterday."

Wow, I thought. *The spirits did it all in one night.* Except Ebenezer Scrooge's spirits had saved him, but mine had just pissed me off. "Okay. Well, I've got an errand I need to run. I'll be home by dinner. Don't go out and don't open the door for anyone. Remember, you're getting on a plane day after tomorrow."

"I don't want to go."

"We'll talk about it. But you're going."

It was another cold, foul day as I sped over the hills to the coast. No CDs with me, and the cab's radio didn't work very well up in the Santa Cruz Mountains, so I had nothing to listen to except the slap, slap of the wipers and the hissing of the tires on the wet road.

It was a lot easier finding Casa Gustibus the second time, and soon I was rolling up the gravel road and around the promontory. I'd left so many messages without reply that I almost expected to find the house simply gone, like something out of a story, but as the road curved back in toward the hill I saw it, facing out toward the cloudy, rain-lashed ocean just like last time.

It might even have been the same sister who came to the door, or a slightly different one in the same hat, but since I'd left my copy of *Audubon's Antique Nuns of North America* at home, I'll never know. She beckoned me in before I'd even finished introducing myself.

"Dr. Gustibus is in the middle of something important," she said.

"He will see you as soon as he can." She poured me a glass of water and decorated it with a lemon slice, then left me in a sitting room by myself with nothing to look at except old pictures of architecture and engineering projects. I got up and wandered around a bit, but the photos were all of *things*: there wasn't a person or an animal to be seen in any of the images. I still had no idea who this guy was, or even *what* he was. In any other circumstances, trusting him for important information would have been frightening. But I wasn't in any other circumstances. I was in bad, bad trouble, and I needed any help I could find.

I'd been reduced to playing games with my lemon slice when the nun in the hat shaped like a Quaker Oats box finally came back and said, "Come this way, Mr. Dollar," her accent light as a thin smear of mustard on a sandwich.

Gustibus was waiting among his tables of books and oddments. He was dressed in the same filmy white vestments, and had his hair pulled back in the same white ponytail. He smiled briefly when he saw me, but didn't put down the thing he was examining by magnifying glass. It appeared to be some kind of clay tablet. At last he set them both down on a nearby table.

"Sorry to keep you waiting, Mr. Dollar. I gather you've had a busy week." He said it like I'd missed the bus twice and received an unexpected parcel.

"Yeah, you could say that. Why, what did you hear?"

"About your trial? Nothing specific, except that a verdict wasn't brought in. I gather you found a way to—what do they say? Plea bargain?"

"It's more like I found a way to stall them a tiny bit longer." But I didn't want to talk about the choices I'd made with this unworldly character, who seemed to have no concerns more pressing than which organic vegetables to eat that day. "I've been trying to get hold of you."

"I've had some busy times myself," he said with that almost annoying offhandedness. "What do you need?"

"Information, of course. And I'm willing to trade for it." I looked around to make sure the Low-Flying Nun had left the room. "I need to know things about horns. And feathers. The trial didn't end, it's been postponed, and I don't think it's for very long. I'm running out of time."

"Ah." He beckoned me to a chair, and I remembered that he said he never sat. "And you need . . . ?"

"I need to know how the objects themselves work—how they travel, I guess, for lack of a better word. How they manifest. Where they could be hidden."

"I'm surprised you didn't ask the last time we spoke."

"Didn't think of it. I tried to call you later." For some reason I was finding his distant, benign vagueness a lot more irritating this time. Maybe because I was literally down to my last life in this particular video game. Maybe because a young mortal woman that I'd cared about was dead, and her lover was going to be mourning for the rest of her life. "Look, do you want to help me or not?"

He gave me a searching look, almost as if he could hear echoes of my thoughts. "I apologize. I didn't mean to upset you, Mr. Dollar. Let's get right to it. What are you offering to give me?"

"I didn't tell you about my trip to Hell, last time. It was a long, long trip. I saw a lot of the place and had a number of . . . well, 'adventures' isn't the right word. 'Fucking horrifying experiences' is probably closer. I could tell you about that."

Gustibus shook his head. "I'm afraid that's not really up my alley, as they say. I specialize in Heaven. Hell holds very little value for me, at least as far as my work goes. Oh, I find its minions useful as sources of information, but it's what they can tell me about Heaven that interests me, not their own sordid home."

I kind of wanted to smack him. Shit, I wish *I* had the freedom to pick and choose what I learned, instead of having all my new projects announce themselves by trying to shoot me or gnaw off my face. "Then what *do* you want?"

"What happened to you before the trial? When you were imprisoned?"

"What? You mean in the white? I don't know what else to call it."

"That might do, if anything happened. It's a part of the process I don't know much about."

"I got jobbed by the Angel of Conciliation, Pathiel-Sa. That humiliating enough to pique your interest?"

He smiled. "That might do very well. Go ahead and tell me, and then I'll do my best to give you good value in return."

So I described my time in the white emptiness, the things I'd felt and heard and (sort of) seen, with an emphasis on how it ended up with me spewing out every secret I had. Gustibus spent most of the time listening but not looking, staring out the window at the sullen blue-black ocean and the prison-gray sky.

". . . And I don't really remember," I finished, "but I'm pretty sure I told them all about you, too, because I told them just about everything."

He didn't appear too bothered. "Did Pathiel-Sa ever directly ask you, or even order you, to confess?"

"No. I did it because I wanted to. God, I needed to. It felt like it was the best thing I'd ever done." I paused and took a breath, because the memory made me want to shoot something, and there weren't any acceptable candidates in the vicinity. "Now, does that do it for you? Is it payback time?"

"What you told me is fascinating." He turned from the window. "What do you need to know?"

"The horn. Since the last time we talked I broke Anaita's civilian cover and researched her movements. She poses as a Persian-American philanthropist named Donya Sepanta, and she's been in San Jude for about thirty years or so. She seems to have first met with Eligor at the Stanford Museum, where she's a major donor, but that's just a guess, and it isn't where she's hidden the horn. We found that out the hard way. What *is* there is a hidden doorway to Kainos."

"Ah. The heretical Third Way, as the authorities in Heaven call it."

"Right. So for all I know she and Eligor could have made their deal decades ago when they first met, or only recently. And there's a jillion places where she could have hidden the horn just here in San Judas alone. What happened in the museum tells me I can't afford another confrontation with her until I find where it is for real. I mean, that damned horn could be literally anywhere, couldn't it? If she could do what my friend Sam did with me when he hid Anaita's feather in a kind of time-pocket . . . well, the horn could even be here in this room, and I wouldn't have a chance of finding it." And as I said it, I realized how arrogant I'd been from the start, how incredibly self-absorbed. An object perhaps the size of a cigarette lighter, that could literally be made invisible and hidden outside of the flow of time itself, and I'd cheerfully set off to find it, as certain of success as the only grown-up at an Easter egg hunt.

"And that's the problem," I said when I was done hating myself for the moment. "The more I search, the less I know. How could a demon's horn or an angel's feather get from one world to another, anyway? I mean, humans can't cross over from Earth to Heaven without dying, right?" Like Oxana, stuck in that timeless nowhere between worlds with only her lover's body for company. "How does travel between places like Earth and Heaven or Hell even work?"

Gustibus nodded. "How does it work? That is indeed the question, and one I've been puzzling over for longer than you can imagine. Are you comfortable?"

I shrugged. "Reasonably."

"Good. Because this may take a while." He folded his hands behind his back and looked down, like a schoolboy getting ready to recite his times tables. "Very well. Here is what I know, or have enough evidence to guess at fairly confidently. For the purpose of this discussion, remember we are not bodies, but souls."

Which was a weird thing to say—"for the purpose of this discussion," like it wasn't always true—but I ignored it and tried to focus. My previous experience with Gustibus had been that he liked to take people for Socratic roller-coaster rides.

"Now, angels and demons are nothing *but* souls. That is, although they can inhabit bodies, they exist primarily as bodiless spirits. However, in that state they can experience very little of actual life and certainly nothing that you would recognize as ordinary earthly pain or pleasure. A rather arid existence, I'd call it." He nodded. "Humans, while they live, are bound to a physical body. When they die, the soul is free of the body and can then leave what we call the Earth and pass into other places like Heaven and Hell. When they reach those places, the soul will be re-embodied in a form that is more fitted for that existence."

"I already understand all that."

A small frown. "Please don't hurry me, Mr. Dollar. Now, as I mentioned, angels and demons—and certain others—are not bound to bodies and so can enter and leave them at will, and in fact, if they want to appear and function on Earth they *must* take on earthly bodies. Yes? That is clear?"

I nodded.

"Good. Now, if an angel, let us say, wishes to use part of his or her earthly body as a token of agreement—a feather, for instance—then it is not enough simply to hand it over to someone. A feather on Earth, even an angel's feather, is only a feather, a part of an earthly body—an earthly thing. It is of no probative value whatsoever."

I raised my hand. "Probative?"

"It proves nothing. So in order for that token to *mean* something, it must be invested with at least a tiny bit of the essence of the angel who gives it away. Some of that angel's soul must enter that article, and I've never heard of it happening by accident. The same would be true for a demon and his horn."

I thought about this. "So the reason it was so obvious that Anaita's feather was an angel's feather is because she *made* it an angel's feather?"

"Yes, more or less. She had to release something of herself into it when she gave it away. Similarly, Eligor would have had to imbue the horn with part of himself."

"Okay. But what does that mean for me?"

"It means that the object itself is not the important thing, although the essence of it is. And because it is in truth an essence, like a soul, it is not confined to the earthly realm but can go anywhere the angel or demon in question can go. Do you understand?"

The only thing I understood was that my impossible task had just become even more so. I had single-handedly discovered a previously unmapped realm of impossibility—Bobby wins again! "So, basically, I'm fucked. The horn could literally be anywhere, and there's no way to tell. I'm just massively, totally, permanently fucked. Is that what you're saying?"

He might have shown the ghost of a smile. "Knowing the truth is always better, Mr. Dollar. You're still in the same situation but better informed. And I haven't finished."

"Oh, it gets better?"

"That depends on what you make of it. But the first time I met you here, when we discussed Anaita and her motives and history, set me thinking. Something else came to me later that I think could be important."

I was almost too depressed to reply. "I don't have anything left to trade."

"You'd be surprised—but this is, how do you say it, a bonus? I am throwing it in. Yes, Anaita could have hidden the horn anywhere she could go herself. But remember, she has that horn for a reason. It is her protection against Eligor's informing on her. They are sworn to mutual destruction if either one breaks faith. Now that Eligor has recovered the feather, his horn is even more important to her."

"So?"

"So she will not hide it anywhere it would be difficult to reach. She might be able to hide it somewhere in the Holy City itself, but that would only make it difficult to recover it in an emergency, especially because Heaven and Earth sometimes move through time at different rates. The chances are, she will have it somewhere available to her at a moment's notice."

"I'm sorry, but I don't get it."

"I am not intentionally tormenting you, Mr. Dollar. I don't have the answer myself, but I feel that the answer can be found, and what I've just told you seems likely to help you do it."

I stood up. "Well, that's helpful, then. I guess." But what I actually felt was helpless. I hadn't thought I was Mr. Lucky after escaping judgement by the width of an angel hair, just Mr. Delayed Doom, and now I had fallen all the way back to square one, or even square zero.

"One last thing," said Gustibus. "Remember this, too—Anaita is not an angel who happened to have once been a goddess. She is a goddess who became an angel. She is not like most of the rest of her heavenly peers. She may have existed before humankind, as with the rest of the angels, but she was not as they were. She became what she is because humans worshipped her."

"What does *that* mean?"

"You'll have to ponder that yourself, I'm afraid, Mr. Dollar. I've enjoyed seeing you again, but I have promised to make dinner for the sisters tonight, and the kitchen awaits me."

Part of me wanted to thank him for his time, another part wanted to pick him up and kick out his window and hold him over the rocks and the foaming waves until he told me why he was always being such a mysterious dick. I don't handle the Socratic method well, I guess.

I got back in my car instead and drove home through the wet, green hills, listening to the monotonous percussion of the December rain.

thirty-seven
cleaning house

I'D PLOTTED, I'd planned, I'd wriggled like a worm on a hook, but my enemies were simply stronger than I was, and Anaita had outmaneuvered me all down the line. All I'd bought myself with all my tricks was this final chance to pull off a miracle, or it was going to be an express ticket to Hell for me, where more than a few folks would be thrilled to have me back in soul-biting range. I had no idea where to find a miracle in San Judas and didn't know where else to look. Most of my allies were out of the game, and one of them was dead. Since the odds for my future didn't look good, I decided I might as well take care of some unfulfilled obligations.

I still had about two thousand bucks left, give or take a hundred, from the money I'd earned selling my late, lamented Matador Machine. A whole lot of the rest I'd given back to Orban to buy weapons, which kept some of us alive but hadn't done a damn bit of good when it came to either saving Halyna or to getting my hands on the horn. I wasn't going to solve my current problems by chucking money at them, anyway, so I'd have to do what I could with what I had and hope that good, old-fashioned stubbornness counted for something.

Step one—in many ways the worst of all, since it was an admission of guilt and massive failure—was to get Oxana out of Jude. My struggle with Anaita was only going to get more desperate as the clock on my suspended sentence ticked down, and I'd already got Oxana's lover killed. I couldn't even think about what it would be like to have both of them on my overloaded conscience.

She fought me, of course.

"No. How I go when Halyna is killed by that . . . Persian *blyat*?"

I wasn't sure what a *blyat* was, but I could tell by the curl of Oxana's mouth that it probably wasn't "sweetie-pie."

"I go when the *koorva* is dead."

"You don't understand. That whatever-you-called-her used to be a goddess, but now she's an angel. She's *connected*. Do you understand that, Oxana? Like the Russian Mafia. Even if we could kill her, which we can't, someone else would come after us instead, and then another, and then more and more. You can't just attack Heaven, even if it's only one important angel, and not expect Heaven to hit back."

"I not care." She threw herself down on the couch and gave me a fierce look that only made me feel more responsible. This young bad-ass, for all her weapons training and soldierly determination to right ancient wrongs, was an innocent. If I had known things would get this serious this fast I would never have involved either of them. I'd expected that Anaita would have some defenses set up at the museum, not that the Angel of Moisture would make an appearance herself. That was a miscalculation I would live with the rest of my angelic life (although that was beginning to look like a very short-term problem).

Still, I wasn't going to make the same mistake twice. "I don't care if you don't care, Oxana, because you're going. I can either get you a plane ticket to Kiev and drive you to the airport, or I can call U. S. Immigration. What's Ukrainian for "La Migra"? Because the government will definitely deport you, but only after you spend a couple of months in those fucked-up cells of theirs, plus probably get de-loused and go through about nine or ten body cavity searches. Wouldn't you rather just skip that and go straight to the Diet Coke and a package of peanuts while you watch some horrible Adam Sandler movie on a nice, fairly clean plane?"

Well, it was like telling your teenager that she absolutely, positively wasn't going to go to that party, of course. Tears, shouting, the whole ball of wax. I'm not making light of it, it was the result of a tragic situation, one that I was personally responsible for, but I was at a point where I didn't have much patience left. In fact, I didn't have much of anything left.

Eventually Oxana locked herself in Caz's bedroom, and I took advantage of the calm to track down a ticket online for about eleven hundred bucks, a one-way flight leaving in two days. I left my angry Amazon a note to explain what was going to happen and, in an attempt at repairing the relationship, suggested that she and I stay home that evening, and I'd bring some burgers from Junior's. Honestly, it really was almost exactly like having a grieving, trained-killer teenage daughter. Well, at least how I imagine that would be.

Still, getting Oxana the hell out of a war zone was only Item One on my ambitious schedule, so after I finished the note I hopped in my Yellow Bobmarine and headed downtown. Yeah, I just can't stay away from that part of San Judas. The Bible says, "As a dog returneth to his vomit, so a fool returneth to his folly." (By the way, thanks for sticking that image in my head, King James and friends.) And I had more than a few follies to deal with.

It was definitely a Delta blues kind of day, I decided as I drove across gray San Jude in a pelting rain. Son House was singing "John the Revelator" as I reached my old neighborhood, scene of so many interesting events. "Singing" isn't quite the right word for Son House, because that's kind of like calling what Jimi Hendrix did "strumming" or saying that Michael Phelps was "pretty good at not drowning." I've been to Heaven, and I've been to the other place, and listening to Son calling on the blues to keep him sane can give you a genuine a taste of both.

Anyway, the rain was still thumping on the car roof as I parked on a nearby street. The song was just ending.

Who's that writin'?—John the Revelator.
Tell me who's that writin'?—John the Revelator
Tell me who's that writin'?—John the Revelator
Wrote the book of the seven seals.

Most of the time when you listen to a song like that, even if you know that the "book of the seven seals" is from Revelations, they're just words. The seals themselves are seals that, when they finally get opened at the End Times, release the Four Horsemen, and eventually lead to the trumpets blowing and the world going *pfffft*. Hey, I'm actually an angel, and most of the times I've heard the song, I was only thinking about what an amazing artist Son House was. But today it all seemed a bit different, and it wasn't just because my personal End Times seemed closer than they'd ever been. I'd been in tight spots before, but things seemed different this time. Maybe it was because I'd seen the rock of Heaven lifted a little, and had seen some of the things that had scuttled out. It's one thing to know that there's a lot you're not being told, it's another when it starts crawling all over you.

But even though I was doing a potentially very stupid thing coming back to the Tierra Green apartment at all, there was no sense in making it even more stupid by lingering in the area. I shut off the engine, made sure my gun was loaded, and then pulled up my collar and headed for my old digs.

Just opening the door of that apartment was like walking into a museum of the last nights I'd spent there—some of the furniture was still lying on its side from my attempts to capture the four-legged horror I'd found in the closet, and I had never washed the dishes in the sink after I'd got the first message from Caz, because then Sam and I had our argument, and the next day I moved out. Only a couple of weeks had passed since all that, but it already had the feel of ancient history. Not the good kind, either, more the Curse of the Pharaohs kind where you immediately wish you'd just left the damn tomb alone. But I had things to do. I intended to clean house, literally as well as emotionally, but I didn't want to take all day about it. I was pretty certain nothing significant was left of the Black Sun Faction, at least in San Judas, but it still wasn't a good idea for me to linger around any of my known hangouts.

The first thing I did was retrieve my stereo. Caz's computer was adequate for playing music, but the stereo was the only nice thing I owned other than some guns and knives, now that the Matador was gone. It was compact, and it had a very nice subwoofer I'd spent some serious money on and never really got to use because I was always living in apartments and motels. I might be in danger every moment I lingered in my old place, but I was damned if I was going to leave my subwoofer there for some punks to steal.

The stereo equipment just about filled up the front seat and floor of the cab. I put three boxes of CDs in the trunk, then cleared my meager wardrobe out of my closet and draped it across the cab's back seat, trying not to add wrinkles to the wrinkles that were already there. I looked at the boxes of car magazines I had been dragging around from place to place and felt a huge tide of weariness roll over me at the thought of lugging them down the stairs too, so I left them for anyone who wanted them. I threw the rest of my toiletries into a bag, bundled up my blankets and sheets (such as they were) and, once I'd thrown all of that into the trunk, went back upstairs for a final look around the scene of so few happy times.

As I was examining the living room one last time, noting the bullet hole in the wall and various bloodstains on the carpet (it was looking pretty certain I wouldn't be getting my cleaning deposit back) I remembered that I had a small stash of weapons in the hall closet. You know, just some fun-size stuff—blades, a cosh, some spiked knuckles. I hadn't ever had to use them in this place, although I'd been tempted by some people trying to get me to accept copies of *The Watchtower*, but that was no reason to leave weapons behind for some kid to find and brutalize his little sister with.

The board that covered the hole where the Nightmare Child got in was still nailed in place and covered with duct tape. As I stood remembering that strange night, I heard something skitter across the floor of the closet. I stepped back and saw movement in a pile of old t-shirts I used for oil rags, so I kicked them out of the way. Something low and hairy scuttled out and darted past me.

"Oh, shit," I said. "Again?"

I followed it toward the living room. "Darted" may not have been the most accurate word to describe the thing's movement; now that it was out of the dark closet, and I could see it better in the gray afternoon light, I think "hobbling" might have been closer. It was one of the Nightmare Children, all right, but it didn't look well. In fact, it looked terrible.

My sense of alarm, whose needles had all redlined when I first saw it, began to ease back into more normal territory, because this thing wasn't much of a threat at all. One of its legs was shrunken like a deflated balloon, and its baby fingers were no more than shriveled curls, as if the creature was slowly collapsing in on itself. I didn't know how long the little horrors could live out of whatever netherworld or parallel dimension they came from, but this one clearly was nearing that limit.

The Nightmare Child wobbled from closed door to closed window like a broken toy, then scuttled under the couch, but I wasn't having that. The nasty little thing might have been all but dead, but I still didn't relish the thought of getting down on the floor to try to yank it out with my bare hands or poke it out with a broom, so I hefted the couch up on end. The thing made another limping break for it, but wound up in a corner with nowhere else to go. As I walked toward it, it waved its useless leg at me as if asking for mercy, and it was so clearly not a threat that I almost felt sorry for it. Almost. Then I thought about the little bones burned in the fire upstairs, the innocent lives snuffed out so Baldur von Demonfucked and his SS fanboys could summon this thing into our world, and instead of finding something silver to dispatch it quickly, I lifted my foot and ground it into the carpet. Crunch. Pop. Splurt. Imagine crushing about five or six hamsters tied together like sausages, plus add the little whistling noises it made as it died. The Nightmare Child may have been scientifically and even theologically impossible, but it went out like regular old disgusting.

When I was finished I took off my shoe off and sprayed the sole clean under the kitchen faucet, then wrote a note for the landlord and left it next to the splatter-with-three-and-a-half-legs.

Dear Mr. Avilsi,

I've moved out. Conditions were not optimum. You also might want to call an exterminator. This apartment appears to have nightmares.

Yours,

B. Dollar

I finished up at the apartment, then drove down near Shoreline Park and hiked out across the wooden walkway to the ruined amusement area in the middle of the windblown bay. Sam hadn't answered his phone or returned my messages since Heaven had let me walk, which I assumed meant he was stuck in Third-Way-Land, so I left a note for him on the funhouse mirror in the abandoned park. I didn't want to make it too obvious, so I just wrote "Showtime, tomorrow. At your last stiff one." I hoped he'd figure it out.

Then I headed back downtown to the Compasses to buy a final drink for any friends who were there. Or maybe two. After all, my customized Matador was gone, Caz was still a prisoner, Halyna was dead, Oxana was flying back to Far Amazonia, and I almost certainly had a seat reserved on the next shuttle down to Hell's intake ward. I honestly couldn't think of a single reason not to spend my last few dollars and perhaps my final earthly hours on a potentially suicidal evening of getting blasted and telling lies with the old gang. Can you?

Right. I didn't think you could, either.

thirty-eight
showtime

YOU MAY be wondering about the message I left for Sam on the Crazy Town mirror. "Showtime" was breakfast—a joke on "fast break," as in basketball, and specifically the Lakers teams with Magic Johnson that had earned the "Showtime" nickname. "At your last stiff one" meant "at the site of your last drink," and in Sam's case it had been a bit spectacular, since it had killed him.

I could spend a lot of time telling stories about Sam and drinking. Most of the stories are pretty funny, even some of the horrifying ones, but Sam wouldn't approve. Not because it would embarrass him, but because he hates drinking stories. "It's a kind of bragging," I remember him saying once. " 'Oh, I'm such a badass because I turned myself into an animal and lived through it.' It's bullshit." I think he also never wanted to listen to other people's drinking stories because they just didn't match up to his, and he didn't want to repeat his own because he'd decided that whole part of his afterlife had been stupid and was best ignored.

I didn't know back then, but part of what was going on was his growing disgust with what he was expected to do as part of Heaven's Counterstrike force. All I could see was a guy who meant the world to me systematically turning into someone I couldn't even recognize. Don't get me wrong—Sam wasn't one of those angry drunks who becomes a monster, at least not the ordinary sort. He didn't pick fights, which was good because he's a big, strong dude. He didn't rage at people, although there were definitely rages. But knowing him then was like watching somebody drown in slow motion. Every time I looked at him, the Sam I knew so well—the guy with the sense of humor like a prison shank, honed and sharpened until you could hardly even see it—seemed more unfamiliar. He looked like Sam Riley on the outside, but the real Sam, my friend, was slipping further and further away. Sometimes I thought I could still see the real one staring out from behind those bloodshot eyes like a prisoner.

These were the days before we became heavenly advocates—I joined up because of Sam.

We didn't hang out at the Compasses in those days. We spent our time at another angel bar, a place called Barnstorm over in the Mayfield District. It wasn't much like the Compasses at all: the owner was one of us, but most of the clientele were ordinary mortals. It was a big, loud place, and Sam and I drank there for a couple of years, continuing even after I left the Harps. We might have kept doing it for years more if it hadn't been for Carlene. She was a waitress, and although quite astoundingly pretty, tall and red-haired, she was a human woman. The problem with her wasn't that she was a waitress, either, but that she was a waitress at some other joint who only came to Barnstorm to drink. That was the problem: Carlene liked to drink, just like Sam did.

Sam and Carlene hooked up, and for a long time things seemed to be going in the right direction. He didn't tell her at first what he was, and after he fell hard for her he was scared to do it. He might have been right. She was a strange girl, country-raised somewhere out in the Central Valley, a trailer-park Baptist with a crazy mom who'd fed her kids Oreos for breakfast and potato chips with ketchup for dinner. Carlene had a history of falling for big cowboy-type guys—she said Sam was the first one who didn't hit her. She also had a terrible self-image, because pretty as she was, what I found out later (and Sam found out sooner, of course) was that she was so pale as to be nearly albino. Her hair was so light that she dyed it red, and she even painted on eyebrows; otherwise, as she put it, "I'm just a ghost." She was always referring to herself as a freak, and it didn't make anyone smile indulgently when she said it, because you could tell she was serious. And all the drinking didn't help. No, that's bullshit. The drinking made everything much, much worse.

I still don't know exactly what happened on the night they broke up, but judging by how much booze Sam was putting down afterward, it must have been ugly, because in those days he had already become little more than a method for alcohol to move itself out of bottles and onto the sides of various roadways.

Then Carlene went home and killed herself.

And Sam got the case.

Any sane angel would have asked to be let off—would have demanded it. At that point, however, my friend Sam was lots of things, but sane wasn't one of them. Again, I don't know what happened, because Sam would never talk about it, but it can't have been good. When it was over, he came back to Barnstorm and started drinking again. It was something like what they say about Dylan Thomas's last binge, I guess— Sam just called for Rudy the bartender to set up a stack of rye whiskeys on the bar, then he poured them down his throat, one after another. He'd been drinking since sundown, and it was one in the morning.

When he finished, he was going to order another set, but I knew it was only a matter of time until somebody played "Queen of Hearts" on the jukebox (because that had been *their* song), so I somehow convinced him to come outside with me, I think under the pretense that I needed to buy some smokes and the Barnstorm's machine was empty. Sam insisted on bringing his last shot out with him. He set it down long enough to bend over and yank a parking meter out of the ground—it took him some work, but it was still pretty fucking impressive—and then he threw it end over end down California Street, scratching up a couple of parked cars. He retrieved his drink, swallowed it, set the glass down, then stretched his arms high into the air like a monster.

"*Goodnight, Tokyo!*" he bellowed. At the far end of the street a couple walking toward us turned around and headed in another direction. "*I will fuck your buildings and shit in your harbor!*" It could have been funny, in a different world. He took a couple of staggering steps and just dropped onto the pavement in front of Springtime Dry Cleaners like a puppet with its strings cut.

He was dead before the ambulance got there, or at least his earthly body was. The official verdict was heart attack, but the fact is, Sam Riley took the strongest body Heaven could provide and pretty much systematically drank it to death.

*   *   *

Barnstorm was gone, but the location was still a bar, something called Mike's Corner Pocket. Springtime Dry Cleaners, however, was still there, as if all those years hadn't passed. I was peering in the window when I felt Sam behind me. I pretty much always know. I tell him he's got a heavy shadow.

"You thinking of going into a new profession, B?"

"Yeah. I figure this angel thing can't last, but people always need clean clothes." I turned and got the morning sun in my eyes. That's another thing I hate about that time of the day. The sun is completely fucked up and jumping out at you unexpectedly all the time. "Too bright—why does anyone go out of doors? I think there's a coffee shop down the street."

There was, and we slid ourselves into a corner booth. "Sorry to bring you back here," I said. "But neither of us can afford to go near downtown, and I couldn't think of anything else without spelling it out for anyone who might be following me."

He shrugged, but I wasn't sure that was really what was going on for him. "No big deal."

"Everything all right on your end? Did you-know-who show up in you-know-where?"

"No. But she will. And you? Has the shit started raining down from our little museum visit?"

He apparently didn't even know I'd been picked up, let alone put on trial. "Don't you get any news there at all?"

"In Kainos? Shit, B, the Third Way is like another planet, remember? Everything we used to get came from Ke . . . you-know-who. Speaking of, why haven't you been squashed like a grape by the folks Upstairs?"

It wasn't an idle question, I could tell. Sam isn't stupid—far from it, although he'll ride that Andy Griffith, aw-shucks routine as far as it'll take him. "Oh, trust me, it's been interesting. I'll give you the details later. But I want to find out if that invitation you gave me is still open."

"To our place? The you-know-where place? You finally ready to come and join us?"

"I'm beginning to think I don't have much choice. I'm in trouble, man."

"We all are."

I shook my head. "Thanks for showing up at the museum. That meant a lot."

"Didn't do it for you. Did it so you wouldn't get Clarence killed."

As was sometimes the case when he was in a bad mood, I couldn't tell for certain whether Sam was kidding. "Yeah, I notice you two have been close. Anything else you want to tell me?"

"Huh?"

"Now that Clarence has come out. Anything you want to share?"

"What do you mean? Did you just figure that out?"

"And you knew?"

"Since before the kid did himself." Sam waved impatiently and a grizzled-looking guy in a spotty white shirt came over and took our order, which heavily featured caffeine and grease. "Man, someday they're going to learn how to deep-fry coffee," said Sam, "and I'll never have to look at a menu again."

"Look, moving past Clarence and his lifestyle choices for a moment, how did you finally figure out about you-know-who?" We'd avoided saying her name so many times now it was beginning to feel like a magical necessity.

He gave me a very dry look. "You mean, how did I finally figure out that you were right?"

"Okay, I'll take it that way too."

"Fuck yourself, Dollar. It didn't just come out of the blue. Some weird shit had been going on. First she told us—well, didn't know she was a she, then—that we weren't going to be getting any more souls for a while. That the project was on hold, or in hiatus, or some other bullshitty bureaucrat's term. Then the Magians started kind of disappearing."

"The Magians? You mean the others like you?"

"Yeah, the other angels she'd recruited. That she'd tricked." For a moment I had a glimpse of the anger he'd been hiding, and while I didn't think it was the only thing that bothered him, it was certainly part of it. "First Nistriel, then Tehab and some others. At first we thought they were on some kind of extended missions, but then one of the others ran into Nistriel on Earth and said she'd been wiped."

"Wiped?"

"Yeah. Like what you said happened to Walter Sanders. She had no memory of the Third Way or anything. So we began to wonder which way the wind was blowing. Then you gave me your big speech, and it made so much sense that I didn't want to hear it. But I couldn't *un*hear it afterward. I started thinking things over, putting a few questions to some of the other Magians, and it didn't take very long until I could make sense of a lot of shit that hadn't been making sense before that. It's a long boring list."

"The whole thing sucks. And it still doesn't make any sense. What did she want if she didn't believe in the Third Way?"

For a moment he looked angry again, then the expression settled into something sadder and more resigned. "Maybe she did, at least to begin with. Fuck, who knows, B—I can't spend any more time on the whys and why-nots." He shook his head as the food arrived. "So what next?"

"You mean what are we going to do to protect ourselves?" I paused with a whole sausage impaled on my fork like a harpooned pilot whale. "I wish I knew. I mean, I have a couple of ideas I wanted to bounce off you."

"Oh, yeah, you are definitely the idea man." The remark sounded a bit strained. "Go ahead."

So I told him what was in my head, or at least part of it, as well as some of the ideas I was considering. He listened, asking questions from time to time, and made a few suggestions that made me look at some of the problems from different angles. It was pretty much what I hoped for, and it's one of the things about Sam that I've always valued: he didn't take things for granted. If you said, "I've got a plan that will make us rich," he'd probably ask you, "Do we really want to be rich?" And he'd be right to ask—that was something you needed to know before you started.

After about half an hour and three or four cups of coffee each, we had a few preliminary ideas scraped together into something that, while not yet deserving the name "plan" or even "desperate stopgap measure," at least gave me a starting point and a foundation for more thinking. I paid the bill while Sam used the restroom, then we walked outside. The wind had stiffened a bit and the skies were cloudy. Christmas decorations swung on the wires overhead like hardy winter blossoms.

"How do I get to Kainos?" I asked.

"Depends," he said. "How much notice can you give me?"

"Who knows? Maybe none. I may have Heaven and Hell both on my backside when the moment comes. I sure don't want to have to leave a note and arrange a rendezvous like this time."

"Well, I could just stand there for days and days, waiting for you to be ready."

That had been more than just grumpy. "What's up with you?"

"Nothing. Bad week." He scowled. "Look, I'll get back to you on how you can cross over. I have a few things to do while I'm on this side. I'll call you before I go."

"Every phone I have is tapped, Sam."

"Then I'll be sure to keep it top-secret and hush-hush. I'll think of something, don't worry." He turned and started in the opposite direction from Mike's Corner Pocket, which was a relief. From his weird mood, I'd been afraid he might have been falling off the wagon, or thinking about it. "Oh, and thanks for breakfast," he called back over his shoulder.

The landline rang a little before two in the morning. I'd fallen asleep on the couch, so it took me a minute to get myself oriented. Oxana was watching some movie on television, her suitcase packed and sitting on the carpet beside her, as it had been for hours. She was still pissed at me and had hardly said a word all evening. She was obviously not going to answer the phone.

I crawled toward the desk and picked it up. At first all I could hear was a lot of dull roaring, like I was holding a big seashell to my ear. Then I heard someone's voice, although it wasn't talking to me.

"Sam?" I asked.

"Yeah?"

"What's up? Where are you?"

Something was definitely weird, but it took me a moment to figure out it wasn't the connection. "Just been thinkin'," he said.

"I can hardly hear you. Did you say 'thinking'?"

"And I wanted to say something." There was a long pause. "Tell you something."

My heart was icing up. I knew this Sam. I hadn't spoken to him in a long time, but I definitely recognized him. "Are you okay?"

"Fine. Fine, fine. With some friends. Say hello, friends." Somebody laughed in the background, and somebody else shouted something I couldn't hear. Country-western music was playing far back there somewhere.

Oh, shit, not now, was my primary thought. It was pretty clear that Sam had fallen off the wagon, and fallen hard.

"Do you want me to come pick you up?" I asked. "You need a ride?"

"Fuck no! A ride? I got wings, man. Magical angel wings, remember? No, I just called to tell you something, man. Because, you know, I was thinking today that I needed to tell you. About some shit, some *important* shit. And I wanted to, I really wanted to. But then I kept thinking, why should I tell that motherfucker anything when he sold me out?"

Ice. Ice in my chest so cold it burned. "Sam, I didn't—"

"Get fucked, *Bobby*. Do you think I don't know anything? You don't think I have any friends expect . . . no, *except* you? No friends except you? So I wouldn't know you totally sold me out?"

"I didn't intend to actually *do* it, Sam. You have to believe that. I had to offer them something so they'd let me go. Shit, they were just about to pass judgement on me!"

"Yeah, oh, yeah. I get it. Completely. You weren't really going to do it. That's why you didn't even tell me." For a moment his voice threatened to break. "Didn't even tell me . . ."

"Sam, I would have, but we got talking about all that other stuff—"

"And you know, I said I'd get back to you about how to get to my place? When they come for your lying ass? And so I'm getting back at you." He laughed like something badly broken. "No, getting back *to* you, sorry. Sorry. So when you need to come along to my place, when you really need to . . . you just take a flying fuck at the moon, okay? Okay? That'll do it, baby, that'll . . . do it."

Then there was nothing on the other end of the phone at all. No people talking and laughing, no country-western music, and no Sam.

thirty-nine

narwhals and empanadas

I COULDN'T GET back to sleep, of course. I lay on top of the blankets on the couch for about three hours, feeling like a couple of unpleasant animals were fighting to the death inside my stomach. At some point Oxana had given up on television and sloped off to the bedroom, but I hadn't even noticed.

Finally I couldn't stand it any longer. I got up, poured myself a drink (with full awareness of the irony) and called the only number I had for Sam. His message was the same: Sam, growling in his best Robert Mitchum voice: *"Go ahead. Arouse my interest."*

"Look, man, I'm not even sure you're going to hear this," I said to his voicemail. "I hope you're in a motel somewhere, and that you made some sleeping arrangements before you started your evening's adventure.

"First off, don't be a fucking idiot. Whatever you think of me, it's not worth what you just did to yourself. But it's done, so now you have to start over, that's all. You fell off the wagon before. Remember that thing with the kids who died in a fire? Man, I thought you were going to drink another body to death in a single week that time. Didn't help them, though, and it didn't help you. And you puked all over my only suit. Three different times.

"And here's another thing. Don't bullshit yourself. You're angry at me because I wasn't a very good friend, and you're right, but not because you really believe I was going to turn you over to the Big Happiness Machine. Because if you think I was going to hand over the guy who let himself burn to death to show me not to be afraid—you still remember that, don't you? Even with a nasty-ass hangover and a gut full of angry feelings, you remember that, right? If you think that I was really going to do that to you, that's some kind of weird self-hatred trip. And okay, yes, a lot of this was my fault. I was scared to say anything because it does look bad and it made me shitty even pretending. It does look like I was going to sell you out. I was embarrassed. But I never thought you'd actually believe it. I didn't say anything because it felt to me like I hadn't stuck up for you in front of our bosses. Ex-bosses, I guess.

"Okay, maybe it was also because I didn't know how you'd take it. I don't really know how to deal with a world where I'm not sure what my friend Sam is thinking. You spooked me bad by not telling me about the whole Third Way thing, and I've never quite got over it. It wasn't because you kept it from me—I can understand that, we have freaky jobs, and you have to be careful, and other people were counting on you. But it spooked me because I never thought you'd get so serious about anything that didn't automatically include you and me staying friends. Yeah, I know, I sound like a wife or something. Live with it. You were knee-deep in your future happiness while I was still home doing the dishes. Fuck, I don't know, make your own metaphor. I haven't slept all night."

Jesus, I thought, *is this thing even recording all this shit? What if it cut off five minutes ago?*

"Anyway, that's really all I wanted to say. When you hear this, I hope you're already sobered up. And if you still hate my guts, well, that's just something I'll have to deal with. But don't ever try to convince yourself that I was really going to sell you down the river, 'cause that wasn't going to happen. Couldn't happen. I was a prisoner of war, and I said and did what I had to to survive, and that's all. You're my best friend. I love you, man, even when you call me in the middle of the night to tell me I'm a traitor, and I should fuck off and die. Because that's how it works."

I put the phone down then. I finally managed to get a couple of hours of sleep.

San Judas International was built south of the city on reclaimed tide-lands in what was, at the time, a largely unused portion of southern

Sunnyvale (before Sunnyvale joined up with Jude, one of those hive-of-scum-and-villainy backroom deals that people still swear about). It's on the edge of the bay, and only about twenty-five or thirty miles south of San Francisco's airport. I've always thought it was a bit strange to have three major airports in such a small area as the SF Bay, but if we had more bridges and tunnels and stuff, we probably wouldn't. As it is, the bay keeps everyone separate and each of the major metroplexes wants their own landing strips.

Hey, I wouldn't mind my own airport either, but you don't hear me whining about it.

Because of the Celtic knot of freeways around the airport itself and the edge of the bay down there, what we could have probably managed in about an hour on bicycles took just as long on a weekday morning in a car. However, I discovered one cool thing about my otherwise stone-ugly ride—I could use the cab lanes. I mean *legally*, unlike the way I usually did.

I'd never had the slightest dealings with LOT, the Polish airline, so I decided to do the advised three-hours-early thing for international flights. But when we got there it looked like they weren't exactly fitting customers onto the plane with a shoehorn, so instead of Oxana hurrying through security, we found a coffee shop and had a second breakfast. I wasn't that hungry myself, but even in mourning, Oxana was a very healthy young woman. She plowed through pancakes and bacon and toast and jam and a couple of coffees while I nursed a tomato juice and said a silent prayer that the Bloody Mary Fairy would appear from nowhere and dump bitters and vodka into it.

I could have just ordered one, sure. That's the great thing about airports, nobody knows what time zone you're in, so nobody bats an eye when you order booze at nine in the morning. But for a zillion reasons I felt like I shouldn't. Magical fairy intervention, however, would have meant it wasn't my fault, see?

Give me a break. It'd been a long week. A *very* long week.

Oxana was still angry with me, but she had the good grace not to make a big thing of it, so I didn't have to look like some old guy ditching his young girlfriend, or worse, somebody sending his wife-by-mail back to Mother Russia because he was pissed she had the wrong color hair or something.

"But how will I know what you do?" she asked. "If you die or no?"

"Well, that depends, but since you gave me your address I can always write to you. Or even email. You guys have email in the Ukraine, right?"

She gave me that look young women always give embarrassing older men, no matter what we've said or done. "Yes, stupid. We have car and email and even airplane."

"No, you don't, or I wouldn't have to send you out on a Polish carrier."

"You are head-butt."

Once she'd finished eating, we still had a while to go before I could put her through security with a good conscience, so we took a last walk around the concourse. San Jude doesn't have quite as many tourist attractions or sports teams as San Francisco, so the gift shops always seem a little impoverished by comparison. We had the Cougars, of course, who had been there forever, but they were a minor league baseball team. We were going to get an NHL franchise next year, and a contest had already been held to pick the name. The winner had been "Narwhals," which I wasn't quite sure about, but the shops were already stocking merchandise in the team's projected purple, green, and gold; the stuff with the official logo, a narwhal smashing up through ice, and the less official stuff, like a cartoon narwhal on a t-shirt I saw that said, "I'M HORNY. PUCK ME!"

SJ International's also got the usual airport array of weird local foods—you can mail frozen empanadas to your friends back home in Kansas!—and other odd businesses that only grow in airports, like vending machines full of overpriced phone chargers and earbuds and whatnot. Oxana actually bought a couple of these things (I'd given her a few hundred bucks for the road, to make sure she could get transportation back to the Scythian camp in the mountains.) She and Halyna probably would have enjoyed a trip to Bender Electronics or one of the megabox stores, I realized now. I felt bad I hadn't taken them there instead of the gun warehouse and the fucking fatal museum.

Airports are weird places. Actually, they remind me a little bit of Heaven—not, God knows, because they're so lovely, but more because everybody's kind of off on their own little trip, surrounded by their own bubble, like the cheerful but not particularly chatty souls Upstairs. I'm sure people meet and make lifetime friends in airports, but I can't imagine it happening to me. Too disconnected. Too . . . airport-ish.

After we walked in glum silence for a little while, I led Oxana to the security gate and hugged her, then watched until she'd gone all the way through the scanners and out the other side. I wasn't treating her like a child—more like a hardened criminal. If I'd just dropped her off at the airport she would probably have traded in her ticket, turned right around, and the next thing I heard of her would have been the bombing of some local Iranian Community Center. She didn't want to hurt any Persians except the goddess herself, of course, but she *really* wanted to bring some pain to Anaita. As it was, I wasn't a hundred percent certain she wouldn't sneak out again once I'd left, but short of flying to Kiev with her, I'd done all I could, and I was desperate for some private thinking time.

My phone rang on the way back, but I was busy trying not to get crushed between a very large furniture truck and someone entering the Bayshore right in front of me at about thirty miles an hour. A couple of miles later I pulled off the freeway and parked at a gas station to check the message.

It was from Sam. You know the expression, "death warmed over"? He sounded like death had been warmed until it caught fire and had to be extinguished with a tenderizing mallet. Like a man who'd been gassed in the World War One trenches and had only just learned to talk again.

"I hate myself, Dollar. More than I hate you. Fuck you and your friendship and good sense and seeing the other side of things. Fuck alla that. You're still a rat bastard. Remember when you ate all my Baja Nachos while I was in the restroom that time? Yeah. So fuck yourself. Head for Neverland. Write your name on the mirror in blood. Yes, blood, asshole. Then step through.

"I'm going to go shoot myself now. I just remembered that the worst part of drinking is the sobering up. Did I already tell you to fuck yourself? I hope so, 'cause my head hurts too much to say it now."

And then he'd hung up.

Believe it or not, this was a good thing, despite the death's-door sound effects. This was Sam forgiving me, in his own Samlike way, and telling me how to join him in Kainos. Which was good, because a plan I'd been thinking about for the last few hours was beginning to take practical shape, and I really did think I was going to need to visit Sam's compromised paradise. The plan was a completely crazy one with almost no chance of working, but time was running out. So, as far as useful ideas, well, let's just say the new one didn't have much competition.

The more I thought about it as I made my way south on the rain-slicked freeway, the more certain I became that I was either a genius or the biggest idiot ever to tape a "Just Kill Me" sign to his own back. And not only was the idea itself astoundingly dangerous, every step on the way to implementing it was crazy suicidal, too. But it was the first decent possibility that had occurred to me since we'd escaped the Stanford Museum, bloodied, beaten, and carrying nothing but the dead body of a young Ukrainian woman.

Look, let's be honest, I don't have that many ideas. I don't have *any* good ones (as Sam would be the first to tell you) but even if you ignore quality, I don't have that many of them, so I wanted to start putting this one together. Unfortunately, I realized as I was passing the first of the San Judas exits, I needed one major component to make it work, and that wasn't going to be easy to get. It would require me striking a bargain with someone who might be even stronger than Anaita, and who had certainly proved that he hated me as much as she did.

Yeah, you see where this is going, and yeah, you're right. It was stupid in dozens of different ways. Suicidal, too. But it's not like I had a lot to lose. One way or another, someone was going to rip my soul out of my body soon—mainly just a question of who and when and how official it would be—so heading for Five Page Mill to visit Grand Duke Eligor was just giving the executioner a choice of weapons.

That doesn't mean I wasn't terrified, of course. Doesn't mean that at all.

forty
devil you know

I HADN'T BEEN inside Five Page Mill since my first meeting with its owner, which had ended badly (with me being dragged out by the police) but much less badly than it could have, since only a few minutes earlier I had been dangling in the neck-grip of a very, very angry archdemon, Eligor the Horseman. And now I was going back. It would have been questionable strategy even if I hadn't had several encounters with Eligor since, including a long stint in Hell as his prisoner, during which he tortured me continuously for what felt like months, burning me, shredding me, feeding me to things I couldn't even describe, and resurrecting me each time to start over again with something new. So now I was going to visit him again. See what I mean? Would you like yours Regular Stupid, sir, or Extra Stupid? But beggars, choosers, blah blah blah.

I'd gone in stealthy the first time, and it had turned out very badly. Today I was going to try something different. In fact, the only thing I did by the normal Bobby book was leave my hideous yellow ex-taxicab out on the Camino Real, since I didn't want my current ride to be known to every creature in San Judas with a picture of Satan on its office wall. But once I'd reached the front walkway I just moseyed inside and went straight to the main reception desk. It was now behind bulletproof glass, which was probably because of me, but that didn't keep the young man behind it from giving me a pleasant smile.

"How may I help you?"

"I'm here to see Mr. Vald."

He gave the smallest hint of a surprised look, but for frontline office cannon-fodder, he coped pretty well. "Let me just check. Do you have an appointment, sir?"

"No, I don't think so. But he'll want to see me."

"I'm afraid you'll have to arrange it through Mr. Vald's executive assistant."

"No, you'll do that for me." I put one of my cards through the slot, the kind that only has a name and a phone number on it. I don't think that number even works any more. "Tell them it's Bobby Dollar to see Ken Vald. I'll wait right here."

And I did. The receptionist's phone conversation, which I observed from a discreet distance, looked a bit heated. My guess was that the person on the other end had started out, "Who?" and then quickly got to, "What the fuck is *he* doing *here?*"

When the kid hung up, I strolled forward again. "Shall I go up?"

His smile was sickly, but he was still doing his best, bless him. I hoped he was a regular human and didn't know who his boss really was. He seemed like a go-getter. "If you'll just wait a moment, Mr. Dollar, someone will be out to see you."

"I'm sure," I said, returning his smile with more confidence than I actually felt. But that's how it works when you're on Hell's home ground, even if it's just an embassy on Earth. You have to stay confident, or at least seem that way. You cannot flinch. You definitely do not want to panic, because they really do smell fear.

It was a minute at the longest before a dark-haired female security agent appeared out of one of the lobby's interior doors. She was attractive, if you liked faces hard as stone temple carvings, and wore the same black suit as the male agents, but with a buttoned collar and no tie. Her nametag said "Kilburn."

"Mr. Dollar?" she asked. "Bobby Dollar?" You'd have thought from the way she said it that I'd announced myself as something filthy. "I think you'd better come with me."

"I think first you'd better tell me where, Officer Kilburn." I gave her my best array of charm-teeth, my friendliest grin. "The last time I was here, I had a bit of a misunderstanding with security. I'd hate that to happen again."

Zero amusement. Less than that, actually. If a cold fog could reach out from someone and suck the enjoyment out of others, that's what she was emanating. "I'm sure you would, Mr. Dollar. I'm taking you to my supervisor. Come along."

She turned and walked back toward the door. She didn't look to see if I was coming, and didn't seem to care if I did. I followed her anyway, since that was why I was there.

A whole complex of narrow halls and rooms lay hidden behind the lobby wall, almost a second building inside Five Page Mill, like a piece of pipe shoved inside a larger pipe. She led me down a corridor that must have run more or less parallel to the lobby's inner walls, then stopped outside a door no different than the half dozen others we'd passed. She opened it and indicated I should go inside. "Mr. Felderscarp will be with you in a moment."

I stepped inside. She closed the door. It was a small, unremarkable office—a desk, chairs on either side of it, no pictures. Just as I'd figured out that Felderscarp must be Fiddlescrape, Eligor's latest demon bodyguard, replacement for the very much unlamented Howlingfell, the door opened again behind me. I turned in time to get hit so hard in the stomach that I thought someone had fired a rocket launcher right into my gut. I slammed back against the wall and for a second everything went black. Then the little sparkle-lights appeared, and I could hear well enough again to detect the sound of someone strangling to death trying to swallow a porcupine. That was me, I realized a couple of seconds later, trying to get some air into my body.

Something very large stood over me, flexing giant claws. It seemed to tower yards and yards above me—not possible in that small office. Only as the first of the new oxygen got into my cells, and my brain coughed back into more or less working condition, did I realize it was only tall Fiddlescrape, with his huge fists and his small head, which made my perspective from the floor even stranger.

Of course, sheer reflex already had me planning how to bring him down—a kick in the knee, hard as I could, to be followed by crumpling his cantaloupe-sized head with the chair I'd knocked over on my way down—but I reminded myself I wasn't going to let things get out of hand the way I had last time.

I did my best to fill my lungs. I wasn't ready to get up yet. "Hello, Fiddlesticks. Nice to see you again. How are the wife and kids?"

He just stared at me.

"What's with the sour expression? Seems to me if I hadn't got Howlingfell killed, you wouldn't have this nice white-collar job. Is it really worse than being back in Hell hacking pieces of petrified shit into smaller pieces, or whatever you used to do?"

"Why are you here?"

"Duh. To see your boss, as I already explained at the front desk. Of my own free will. No socking people in the breadbasket required."

His head was certainly strange, almost normal in profile, but too narrow across the front, and about eighty percent of the proper size, although with the right haircut and clothing he could just pass for a normal human. He didn't really have the right haircut, though. The small span of his face and the slightly outturned eyes made him look more like a horse or a fish than a person. Still, he at least knew how to tie a double Windsor knot. That's kind of a dying art.

"Why shouldn't I just beat you to a bloody, dead mess right here?" he asked.

"First, because it wouldn't be as easy as you think it would. Second, because I'm an angel, so I wouldn't be dead anyway, just waiting briefly for a new body so I could come back and gut you like a large-mouth bass." I should have stopped there. "Oh, sorry. Smallmouth bass, in your case." I was lucky that he didn't seem that sensitive about his appearance, but I'd almost sent the whole thing off the rails. "And third," I said quickly, in case he just hadn't figured it out yet, "because I have an offer for your boss that I know he'll want to hear."

He looked angry and bewildered—not a good combination on any-one, much worse on him. "What the fuck are you talking about?"

"It's not hard, Fiddle-me-this. I want to offer the Grand Duke some-thing. He'll want to know about it. So if you and I get to ripping pieces off each other, and he never finds out what it was until it's too late . . . well, he'll probably send you to Doctor Teddy."

This hit home. Doctor Teddy was a hideous little thing that worked for Eligor in his house in Hell, inflicting inventive kinds of pain on the grand duke's enemies. Fiddlescrape gave me a worried look and stood there for a moment, rubbing his huge hands together. I took the op-portunity to lift myself slowly from the floor until I was standing. Whatever else happened, he wasn't getting another free shot at me like the first one.

He growled at me to stay put, then stepped out of the room again. I heard the door lock with a very definitive click, then heard his steps moving away at the same time as I heard him speak to someone, presumably on a phone. I righted the chair I'd knocked over, sat in it, and calmed my breathing, trying to slow my heart. I can't tell you how badly I'd wanted to put my foot up Fiddlescrape's too-tall ass. It's a lot harder being smart than it is being stupid.

A minute or two later he came back. He beckoned and led me out into the hall, then nudged me along it, past another half-dozen unmarked doors and into what looked like a freight elevator at the end of the corridor. We went up. The stories ticked over until we'd reached the forty-fourth, then the door opened.

"Office is at the end," said Fiddlescrape.

"You're not coming with me? What if I start to litter or unreel the fire hose or something?"

"Office is at the end," he said, louder this time.

"Well, it's been fun," I said as I stepped out. I'd been in this corridor before, knew the dark green carpets and expensive wainscoting. The entrance to Vald's office was at the far end. The door of the elevator hissed shut behind me. Then the lights went out.

But I hadn't been hit this time, or if I had, I hadn't noticed it. I was still standing, though, could still feel my body, could still hear the elevator murmuring down toward the lower stories, but I couldn't see a damn thing. Until the fire came. *Whoosh!* Flames all around me, blossoming from the walls, ceiling and floor like huge wavering flowers. It had to be gas jets—that was all I could figure, but I could already feel the fire licking at my clothes, shriveling my lashes and eyebrows to ash, so I jumped forward into the dark space before me.

Whoosh! More flames. What had at first seemed like a built-in crematory just outside the elevator on the executive floor expanded into a cascade of flames that stretched away in front of me, as if the oven had just become a long fiery tunnel. I couldn't find the elevator now, let alone get back into it, and the skin on my hands and face was beginning to burn. *Eligor*, I had just enough time to think, *you are such a shit.*

Then I began to run, telling myself that it couldn't last any longer than the twenty yards or so down the hall to Eligor's office door. I could barely see the narrowing of the flames ahead of me, but I put my head down and did my best not to bump into any walls, or—God forbid—to fall down, because then I'd be roasted like a chicken dinner.

The pain had already gone past the point I can describe. Fire had engulfed my clothes and was burning the skin right off my body. The only thing that had kept me alive this long was the fact that my body was from the heavenly warehouses. I could feel my eyes glazing, cracking, my lungs smoking as they shriveled into chipotle peppers. Every nerve in my body was giving its death cry, a shrill, continuous screech of pain that felt like it would kill me long before the actual damage did.

I ran for what must have been a hundred yards without finding anything but more fire. The burning corridor went on and on forever. Which meant I wasn't in Five Page Mill anymore, or even in San Judas. Which meant I was in . . . no, not Hell. Not that fast. If Eligor could have managed it so quickly and easily the first time, I never would have survived to be here now. I wasn't in Hell, I was stuck in my own mind.

Not that it did me any good to know that. It took everything I had to ease my crazy, dying sprint, because every second that passed meant I could feel the skin and muscles blackening right on my bones. But running wasn't going to do it—I had to find my way out. Physically, I felt pretty sure I was still in the corridor on the forty-fourth floor.

I slowed to a walk. It really was one of the hardest things I've ever had to do—it went against the desperate, dying alarms of every nerve ending I had, against pain like nothing you could understand unless you've been through it. But I had to do it that way. I reached out my hands, putting them right into the jets of flame as I groped along. I was feeling actual walls beneath my touch while simultaneously feeling the bones of my fingers char and turn into ash and flake away. I don't know why I wasn't screaming like a madman. Maybe I was.

At last I felt a bump as I trailed my fingers over a doorframe—fingers that my howling senses told me had already been burned away. It felt like my actual brain was exposed in a scorched skull, and that everything they always said about no nerves in the brain was a horrible fucking lie. I found the doorknob then and turned it before I had time to think about what I was going to do if it wouldn't open.

It opened. Into nothing. Then I was falling through blackness—tumbling, waving my arms and kicking my legs as I plummeted down into depths I couldn't see, couldn't even imagine. For half a second the air sawing across my exposed bones and meat actually felt like a cooling relief, but then it began to feel like all that raw Bobby-area was being sandblasted. This wasn't lost-in-emptiness blackness, this wasn't floating-in-nothing blackness, this was a hole that went down so far that I was plummeting like a meteor out of space. I'd plunge forever, burn up, or hit the bottom and burst into a million pieces.

I opened my mouth against the shrieking winds of my fall, but almost couldn't make a noise because the breath had been blasted out of me. When I did, it was little more than a squeak, the noise of a mouse dropped out of the space shuttle.

"Cute," I said, the words suck-snatched by the uprushing air as they came out of my mouth. "This is cute, Horseman. And so *mature*."

I hit bottom. It wasn't like hitting bottom from high orbit, though, it was more like I did an ordinary pratfall thump onto an expensive office carpet, then lay there gasping. I had fallen out of darkness into cool fluorescent light. Kenneth Vald, six feet and something of handsome, tanned, blond billionaire, watched me from his office chair. He held up a small object I couldn't quite make out, because my brain was still rattling in my skull.

"Want a Pez?" he asked.

I struggled up onto my knees. The little plastic tower in his hand had the face of Jesus in his death agonies. Eligor thumbed the head back and a red lozenge of hard candy slid out of the neck like Christ's throat had been slit.

I shook my head.

The grand duke took out the little candy and waved it at me. "You sure?" When I didn't reply, he flicked it with his fingers. It shot at me like a bullet, hissed past so close I could feel the wind, then ricocheted off four walls (there may have been a ceiling-bounce in there somewhere) and back toward him. Eligor didn't move, just opened his mouth a tiny bit and the Pez flew in. He crunched it up with gusto.

"Yum," he said, "Tastes like Daddy Issues."

I staggered erect, found a chair and sat down. I didn't speak because I didn't trust myself not to squeal like a wounded pig or simply burst into tears. Eligor hadn't needed to remind me that he could fold me up like human origami and throw me away if he wanted to, but that's the thing about Hell's high rollers: they really enjoy their job.

"So, what brings you here, Doloriel? I can't say I'm pleased to see you. You weren't thinking of revenge, were you?" The Kenneth Vald face, famous from many newspapers, magazines, and websites about

What Rich People Do, looked almost ordinary. Only the spark of scarlet gleaming deep in his eyes, a tiny reflection of the fiery passage I'd just escaped, made it clear that what was looking out from in there was a lot uglier than the shape it was wearing.

I sat slumped in my chair. You probably think I was acting beaten to disarm him, but I wasn't acting. I'd been beaten by Eligor a long time ago. "I've got an offer for you," I said at last. "Are you a gambling man?"

He laughed. I mean, he sounded genuinely tickled. "Oh, dearie me. A 'gambling man'? Do you really think the house is going to stake you for another try, Doloriel? What's your idea? Double or nothing to get the Countess back? I thought you'd learned your lesson by now. Since I have everything I wanted from you, I was actually going to leave you alone—at least for a while."

"But you don't have everything you need," I said. "Anaita's got your horn. She can still blow the whistle on you any time."

He didn't speak for a moment, but the embers in his eyes flared. "Why would you annoy me by reminding me?"

"Because I want to make a bargain with you—or rather, kind of a wager. Demons love to bet, right?"

"Not interested, little angel," he said. "And getting bored now, too. Would you like another swim in the eternal fires?"

I took a breath. I couldn't let him hurry me. I had nothing on my side but whatever calm I could muster, as well as a smidge of stubbornness. And I thought I might know one thing he didn't. "No thanks," I told him. "Not that it wasn't interesting. It reminded me of when I visited you at Flesh Horse."

"Ah," he said with a faux-wistful smile. "Yes. Good times, good times." His face went flat again. "But I just really enjoy burning the shit out of you. So why shouldn't I start again?"

"Because you haven't even found out what my bargain is. And that you're not the only person interested in getting hold of that horn."

Now his eyes narrowed. I felt myself falling toward him, falling into those fires that blazed at the center of each pupil. The falling wasn't real, I told myself, but it was still very, very dangerous. I forced myself back into the present reality.

"What do you mean?" he asked at last.

"Sitri," I said. "Remember him? Fat guy, prince of Hell, hates you as much as a ham hates Christmas? He's looking for the horn. In fact, he's gone to some impressive lengths to try to obtain it."

"What the fuck are you talking about? Sitri? That crude, miserable slug wouldn't dare—"

"I suggest you watch this," I said as I took my phone out of my pocket. I clicked on the video of the Black Sun's little séance and set it in front of him.

He watched it through to the end, his face getting stonier and stonier. When it was finished, he didn't say a word as I picked up the phone and pocketed it again.

"Well?" I said at last. "You going to put me back in the oven? Or do we talk?"

Now the handsome Ken Vald face looked like something stretched over a rack, an uncomfortable fit and a poor disguise for the beast beneath. "You have five minutes to pitch your so-called bargain, Doloriel," the grand duke said. "Five minutes to arouse my interest, or you'll never see sunlight again."

forty-one
straight on 'til morning

BY THE time I got out of Five Page Mill, a wet afternoon had become a wet early evening. I didn't really have much left to do now. Unless Oxana had squeezed out of the boarding ramp and made a run for it, she was on her way back to the land of Scythian warriors. I'd had my last knees-up at the Compasses, and I'd spent pretty much all my money. I'd even put a final check in the mail to George, a bonus, with a note telling him to use it to hire himself a part-time back scratcher (because I was pretty sure it must be itchy living in a pig sty). And I couldn't take anything where I was going, either, so I gathered up all my stuff and stowed it in one of Caz's closets, then gave the apartment a cleaning, just in case she came back one day. The Amazons, bless them, had left candy bar wrappers and potato chips bags in some very unexpected places, along with chocolaty fingerprints on several of the expensive draperies, so it took a while before I was satisfied. I don't like tidying up much, but once I start, I can't stop until everything is damn well *clean*.

I also sent a letter to Clarence care of Chico at the bar, thanking him and Wendell for the risks they'd taken on my behalf. I didn't want to tip the kid off too early.

I took a last look around Caz's windowless, Arabian Nights apartment. It was so full of memories now that it was harder to leave than anywhere else I'd ever been. I don't get too attached to places, usually, at least not the places I sleep in. But Caz and I had fallen in love here, and for a few crazy days during the last weeks, with the Amazons and Harrison/Clarence/Junior around, it had begun to feel like a home. I'd never really had one of those, at least not during my afterlife. As to what my earlier, non-angel life had been like . . . well, if I hadn't been sure I had no future, I would have spent some of it finding out who I used to be. The visions I'd experienced under Anaita's influence in the museum had seemed more than simply real, they had seemed profound, even crucial in some larger way. I couldn't ignore the possibility that she'd manufactured them somehow, but in my gut they'd felt genuine. Normally I'd have been fired up to learn more, but I had simply run out of time: Judgement Day was here, and I had pretty much reconciled myself to exiting this afterlife with unanswered questions.

As I took a last turn in the courtyard garden, I heard something fluttering. A moment later a tiny, crooked shadow dropped to the ground in front of me, extended its four wings, then folded them back up. I kneeled beside it.

It was a new nizzic, smaller than the last, kind of a cross between a bald hamster and a dragonfly. What it said was quiet and the message was short—by the time I picked out a few words, it had finished. I had to hold the creepy little thing close to my ear to hear properly when it started again. The voice was Caz's, but weaker and more distant than before, as if she broadcast from a distant galaxy.

"This nizzic can't be reset. This will be the last message, Bobby. I can't stand it. It's too hard, waiting to hear from you. These little sips of foolish hope only delay the inevitable. I'm sorry, my love, it's my fault. If anyone should have known better, it's me."

I left the miserable little thing in the courtyard, locked up the apartment carefully, then climbed into my ugly yellow chariot.

I'd discovered something interesting about the cab while running my errands, another odd-shaped piece in the small puzzle that had been my relationship with Temuel. See, Heaven was definitely trying to keep an eye on me, and they had to know about the taxi, but they didn't seem to be able to keep a direct trace on it. I knew this because in the few days since my trial, I'd already managed to lose several tail cars. Also: Heaven's spies didn't seem to know where the apartment was, either. I'd clocked several suspicious vehicles in the general vicin- ity of Caz's place, but they seemed to be unable to narrow down my whereabouts past a good-sized sanctuary. Heaven's Finest didn't even seem sure which side of the freeway the place was on. How could that be? I had to admit that it seemed like it might have something to do with Temuel getting me to come all the way across town before he handed me over to Counterstrike.

Heaven may not have known exactly where I started my trip, but they latched onto me within a few minutes after I left the apartment. I was on the Bayshore, a mile or so south of the University Avenue exit, when I spotted the tail car, a nondescript Ford minivan. Actually, it was almost *too* nondescript, without bumper stickers or even dealer plate- frames. Female driver and male passenger were also wearing sun- glasses, although it was now after six at night and the sky was getting dark. I was almost insulted until I decided they were just the *obvious* tail, the ones who I was meant to concentrate on and maybe even lose while the real tail followed me at a distance.

I took a circuitous route, pretending to try to lose the minivan, but I didn't really want to lose them, so I didn't give it my best shot. I took them on a long, irritating ride through the south end of town, up San Antonio Expressway and through a dozen cross-streets, then down Shoreline toward Stone Fruit Mall. It was interesting to see how much more modern the buildings were at this end of the city. The center of San Judas was moving, at least the economic center, leaving the dear old downtown behind. Out here, Silicon Valley's current wave of well- to-do immigrants were building a big toddler town for themselves, full of zippy restaurants and coffee shops with sidewalk tables and aw- nings, and office buildings with the fancy, brushed-metal look of ex- pensive bathroom fittings.

How did I get to be such an old man when I've only been alive twenty years or so? I must have been a real curmudgeon in my previ- ous existence. But you probably already guessed that.

I pulled into the new parking structure at the Stone Fruit Mall. If you ask an old local, they'll be happy to tell you that much of this part of San Judas (and the rest of the lower peninsula, too) was once the world's fruit basket. I'm not sure I'd want that nickname myself, but I guess large rural areas can't be choosy. Anyway, the massive four-story shopping center was built on the site of what had been one of the biggest apricot orchards in the state, which only survived now in the name, the blossoming branches on the mall logo, and probably expensive dried fruit packages in the mall's many gift shops.

Now came the tricky bit. I parked in one of the outermost stalls on the second level, left my phone in the taxi (because let's face it, we all know it had to have been bugged as hell after the trial) along with my car keys, stashing both under the seat, then made my way into the mall's vast front atrium. You could look up several stories once you got inside, and the storefronts were nearly all glass—a huge faceted jewel of commerce. People wandered through the place like they were in Oz, some even bobbing their heads to the piped-in music.

Never listen to mall music. It will put you in an apocalyptic mood. But maybe the mood was only mine. The customers seemed happy— modern shopping malls are like a small (and somewhat brainless) world of their own. A guy I know who used to work in the Stone Fruit said that in the summertime, lots of parents just dropped their kids off in the morning with money for food and a movie at the theater, then came back and got them at closing time.

I figured that however many people were tailing me, some would stay outside to keep an eye on the cab while others followed me in. That meant I had to make my move quickly, before the inside tail found me, so I grabbed an elevator and shot up to the third floor, in and out of The Gap, then immediately shuttled back down to the second floor boutiques, up to the fourth, then down to the food court and across the mezzanine to the elevator on the opposite side, which I took down to the underground parking lot, where I was greeted in the elevator lobby with a large "Coming Soon: Target" sign. Dodging up and down that way was how I'd used the lifters in Hell to confuse the demons hunting me, and it had worked pretty well. I was pleased to see it seemed to work on angels, too.

I didn't go near my own vehicle, of course. The elevators ferried shoppers back and forth to the main building, but at the far end of the garage was a set of stairs that led up to a bus stop and taxi stand next to the parking garage. I climbed the stairs, walked as fast as I could to the main doors, and then hailed the first passing taxi.

Yes, that was my plan in miniature. Leave one cab behind, get another. Everything else was just hand-waving for distraction. It was a lot simpler than trying to lose my surveillance on some breakneck, movie-influenced car chase. In fact, the best plans are usually always simple. Why don't I remember that more often?

The driver let me out about a quarter of a mile from the Shoreline Park footbridge. After I paid him I had about twenty dollars left, so I gave it to him for a tip. In return, he warned me not to hang around too long after dark—because, he said, some real weirdos were out in the baylands at night. He clearly didn't know he was talking to one of them. As he drove off, I pulled up my collar against the stiff bay breeze and started walking.

I thought I'd handled it all very neatly, so I was embarrassed as well as disturbed to see a solitary figure standing beside the beginning of the footbridge across the bay. The only thing I hadn't got rid of was my gun, so I kept my hand on it as I got closer. The guy didn't look like he was going to move, so I slowed to check him out.

"Come on, hurry up, would you?" he shouted at me. "It's freezing out here."

"Clarence? What are *you* doing here?" The kid was wearing a long overcoat—playing James Bond in his imagination was my guess—and looked every inch the mysterious contact in a dangerous foreign spot.

"Waiting for you, obviously. And you seem to have forgotten my name again."

"Yeah, sue me. Why are you here? You couldn't have got my message yet."

"What message?"

"Shit." I stood in front of him for a few seconds, staring. I hate surprises. "It's been a long month, kid. Why are you here?"

"Because I'm going with you."

I don't feel good about this, but I confess that my first thought was to smack him unconscious again like I had last time we'd been out at Shoreline, because I just didn't need this shit. I knew it was wrong, though, and I also had a suspicion I might not get away with it as easily as I had on the first occasion. The kid had been running and working out, things I should have been doing myself if I hadn't been so busy trying not to get killed by demons and Nazis, and he was looking pretty fit. "No, seriously, why are you here?"

"Look, Bobby, don't treat me like an idiot, whether you think I am or not." He was flushed, and I didn't think it was just windburn.

"You've been on your farewell tour for days, anybody with any sense could see that. You slow-danced with Monica Naber right in the middle of the Compasses a couple of nights ago. You got drunk and sang "Carrickfergus," for goodness' sake, and you're not even Irish."

"I might have been."

"Yeah, but now you're just a self-important jerk. A jerk who's planning to sneak off and do something stupidly heroic, or heroically stupid, probably get charred black like Cajun food, and leave the rest of us in the dark."

I was mildly impressed by the Cajun cooking reference. The kid was working up better material. "And what if I am? I don't think I'm under any moral obligation to get you and Wendell killed, too."

"I agree. Wendell doesn't need to be involved any more deeply, so I didn't tell him. But I'm a different story, Bobby. Now, are you going to pistol whip me again, or are we going to go see Sam?"

It finally caught up with me. "But how did you know I was coming *here?*"

He smiled, clearly pleased. "A lucky but educated guess. When Sam told me what really happened here that night with the *ghallu*, he also told me about the portal or whatever it's called. He never mentioned another one until you found Anaita's in the museum, and I thought it was pretty unlikely you were going back there again. Anyway, I was coming over to your place to talk to you about what we should do next when I saw you leave, so I followed. You were being tailed by a white van . . ."

"I know."

". . . and I figured you knew and you'd ditch them somewhere, and probably ditch me too without realizing. I took a chance that you were on your way out of town already, and that meant here." He grinned. "And I was right!"

"Yeah, congratulations. You win an all-expenses-paid trip to see 'Revenge of the Bitch Goddess'." I slumped a little. "So I'm going to have to knock you out to get rid of you, is that right?"

"Hey, it could have been worse. I might have brought G-Man." He produced his phone. "I could still call him."

I considered it for a moment. "You win," I said at last. But I would be damned if I was going to thank him.

We turned into the wind and walked out onto the footbridge, the long wooden causeway that led across the bay to the abandoned park. The railing was only about waist high. The wind got colder as we neared the middle. I couldn't help remembering a night on this same walkway, with a giant, molten-hot thing running after me and Sam, determined to disconnect my important bits from my other important bits. I tried to cheer up by reminding myself (and Clarence, when he asked what I was moping about) that I hadn't really believed I would make it through that one, either.

"So maybe there's a greater purpose after all, kid. Maybe there's a reason all this shit keeps happening to me."

"There's nothing sadder," said Clarence, "than an angel getting religion."

"Wow, kid, that sounded just like something Sam would say."

"Thank you."

We stepped off the bridge and onto the rising ground of the man-made island. The south side of Shoreline Park, which had once been a picnic and hiking spot, and was the original purpose of the landfill island, had gone completely feral in the nearly twenty years since the place had closed. It looked like the Jersey Pines, like the kind of place the Cosa Nostra would dump inconvenient corpses. We cut across the island toward Happy Land, the old amusement park, a collapsing museum of the grotesque that has been involved in more low-budget movies than Roger Corman, usually as the background to some kind of post-apocalyptic zombie/mutant/alien freakout. You could almost hear the screams of overacting extras in the wind.

Crazy Town, the funhouse, was on the far side, looking out over the bay and the ferry lanes. It was amazing to think that just a short time ago, even by California standards, the old Ferris wheel had painted colored circles of light against the sky every night and the place had been full of visitors and music and the excited shrieks of the roller coaster riders. All over now, baby blue.

The funhouse stank like you'd expect with a place that had only been visited in later years by crackheads and the last-stage homeless. We stepped under the pitted aluminum roof, and for a moment I considered hiding my gun there somewhere, since I was pretty sure it wasn't going with me when I journeyed to Kainos but decided against it just in case something nasty jumped out at me from somewhere at the last second.

"Third mirror from the left," I said to myself, then finished the joke I'd made to Sam the first time. "And straight on 'til morning."

"What's that?"

"From *Peter Pan*, more or less. The road to Neverland. That's how Sam taught me to know which mirror."

"Now what do we do?" Clarence was looking at the place a bit nervously. It's one thing to brave almost certain death to help a friend, another thing to wade through broken syringes, shattered bottles, and human excrement at the very beginning of the trip.

"Sam gave me instructions." I picked up a piece of glass, then spit on the tail of my shirt and started to clean it.

"What are you doing?" The kid's eyes were big.

"I need some blood. Don't worry, I'll use my own."

"And you're going to do it with *that filthy thing?*" He was horrified. As I thought about it, I realized it wasn't too smart, really, not if by some odd chance I ever wound up back in this body again. "Here, use this." Clarence fumbled in his pocket and brought out a little bottle of hand sanitizer gel. "Use a lot. I can get some more."

"Not where we're going." But I cleaned the sliver of glass and was secretly grateful that the kid was there. Now that I thought about it, I really should have brought a razor blade or a pocketknife or something clean.

Which did not in any way detract from the neat magnificence of my mall-taxicab-switcheroo, of course.

When I was finished scrubbing, I picked a part of my hand that wouldn't inhibit me too badly, the ball of my left thumb just below my palm, and made a small slice. ("Incision" doesn't feel like the right word when you're using a shard of a Southern Comfort bottle as the scalpel.) When the first drops of red appeared along the cut, I put some on my fingertip and wrote "DOLORIEL" on the third mirror from the left, which was a mirror in name only, because the metal surface was so pitted it looked like Freddy Kruger's backside.

Nothing happened.

After we'd waited a few moments, I had a sudden idea. "It's a mirror," I said. "It doesn't look like it now, but it's a mirror."

"So?"

"So maybe I need to write backward." I dabbed my finger in my blood again, which was beginning to puddle in my palm, and wrote LEIROLOD.

Still nothing.

"Well, this sucks," I commented.

"What did Sam say? I mean, exactly?"

"He said write my name on the mirror in blood."

Clarence gave me a look that I swear was full of pity. I rethought the don't-hit-Junior decision for a moment. "What?"

"Does Sam ever call you Doloriel?"

I looked at him hard for a couple of seconds, just to let him know I could have figured it out without his help, then went to the bloody inkwell one more time and scrawled "BOBBY" on the pitted metal. The place was beginning to look like Jack the Ripper's washroom, but this time we had only a moment to wait before a glowing line appeared in the air in front of the mirror—a Zipper, or something similar, but foggier and less distinct. I'd seen one like it before.

"Step through," I said.

"You first, fearless leader," said Clarence, and so I did.

And stepped out again into a cold, winter forest. But this wasn't anything like what I'd seen the first time I'd come through, when we escaped the museum. When you hear the word "forest," you usually think of trees, but the only treelike thing about the scorched pillars standing all around us were their half-exposed roots in the black, ruined ground. The devastation extended as far as I could see along the hillside where we stood—devastation, corruption, destruction. From where I stood, I could not see a single living thing.

"Anaita's already been here," I said. "This isn't good. It's not good *at all.*"

"Damn it, Bobby, I hate when you say things like that." Clarence turned in slow circles, staring at the ruined forest like a child who has just realized he's alone in a supermarket and his parents have disappeared. He took a step and little puffs of ash rose into the air around his shoes. The sky seemed bleached almost white. We were surrounded by silence. "Because you're usually right."

forty-two
wrath

IT WAS a place I'd barely even seen, a place whose connection to my own life was mostly negative, and yet as we made our way across the devastated landscape of Kainos, I was on the verge of tears.

Oddly enough, part of my reaction came because the destruction was limited: I could still see the unsullied mountains and the pristine sky. Looking at those I had the same sense of wonder, of connection to something deeper and more real than reality itself, something that had struck me so hard on my first, brief visit just a couple of days earlier. It made the destruction seem even more pointless.

But what upset me the most was that it wasn't simply devastation, all the scorched trees and gouged earth, but *fury*. The destruction was vengeful, and it was personal. This was no act of nature, despite the rifts in the land twenty feet wide and unguessably deep, or the burned trunks of huge trees scattered in all directions as if by a hurricane. This was the work of a very, very angry, very powerful being. An enraged goddess, I felt sure—an avenging angel who had thrown off the restraints of Heaven.

Almost swimming in deep black and gray ash, we finally crested the nearest hill and could look down on a valley at the outer edge of the devastation. It was sickening to see the wreckage of the forest on this large a scale, but that wasn't what first caught my eye. On the far side of the field of char that had once been a rolling meadow, bisected by a river that was now only a blasted, empty ditch, stood the house I had seen twice from afar, once in person with Sam and once through the door in the fun house the first time Sam had opened it in my presence. It sat like an unwieldy spacecraft on the top of a hill that could have been the scorched, blast-cracked launch pad of some abandoned ruin of the Soviet space program. But the house itself was completely untouched.

Clarence and I stood staring, surprised into silence. It seemed like a mirage that might shimmer and disappear if we made any noise.

As I stood there, staring at something that shouldn't exist—or at least not looking like it did, like a nice house in the hills in a real estate add—I realized for the first time that something else odd was going on: Clarence looked just like Clarence.

Now, normally when you're standing next a person who looks like that person, it's no big deal. But when you get to Heaven, you always look like an angel. And, as I discovered, when you wind up in Hell, you look like something that belongs in Hell. So why was Clarence standing beside me wearing his button-collar shirt, and his windbreaker that looked like he ironed it, and his suede shoes that always looked like they belonged on the feet of a rich old European man? (I accused him once of wearing Hush Puppies, and he was really insulted. "These are Ferragamos!" he said, I guess the same way I might say, "It's got a 426 Hemi engine!")

I looked down at myself and saw I was also wearing basically the same thing I'd worn during the trip through Shoreline Park, except now with a layer of ash and dust—my jacket, a black t-shirt, a pair of dark jeans, and the work boots I like because a) they're black, b) they're not half bad to look at, and c) you can kick the shit out of someone with them if you have to. I tell you not to compare my wardrobe to the kid's, but because finding myself wearing *exactly the same clothes* in an entirely different reality was hard to figure. Remembering my gun, I checked my pocket, but it wasn't there. So, same clothes but no other objects.

"Are you wearing a belt?" I asked the kid.

"Yes."

"And you were wearing it before we got here?"

He gave me a puzzled look. "Yeah. Why?"

"We'll talk about it later. Meanwhile, we have to figure out what to do. And I have. We're going to go check out the house."

Now his expression changed from puzzlement to Seriously Contemplating Mutiny. "No way. You're joking, right? Because if that's the only place around here that doesn't look like a bomb dropped on it, then the person who did this is probably inside."

"I don't think so."

"Oh, then let's go, sure. 'I don't think so' is all the assurance I need to risk whatever we're risking here. What *are* we risking here, by the way? Just our bodies, or our souls, too?"

I laughed, but it wasn't because I found anything very funny just now. "Let's put it this way—if there were such a thing as soul insurance, I'd be calling my agent."

Clarence looked pale—no, he looked pale green. There's a difference. "And we're going there, why?"

"Because it's there. Because it didn't get blown to shit and matchsticks. And because we're trying to find Sam, and it's the most obvious place he'd leave a message, or at least a clue where he is."

"But it's so . . . *exposed.*"

"And so are we, standing in the middle of all this nothing. Let's get to getting."

It would have been an odd house even if it stood in the middle of nice neighborhood instead of the remains of downtown Hiroshima. It was too tall, for one thing, four or five vertical stories in a box only about half as wide as it should have been. From this angle the tower at the top was much more visible, and looked less like a cupola and more like a steeple.

It set me to thinking, but I kept my thoughts to myself because Clarence was like a spooking horse, all nerves and eye-whites. Of course, that was really the only sane reaction to trying to sneak up on an angel, a genuine Warrior Queen of Heaven, with nothing but our bare hands. Hell, my own mouth was so dry that if Anaita had appeared in front of me, I couldn't even have spit at her.

Up close, the ring of devastation looked slightly less complete. I could make out the remains of a couple of paths and the ruins of more than a few outbuildings, although "ruins" was a stretch, because what we really saw were only the scorched outlines and ordered ash where buildings had once been, before the firestorm. A ghost of a grassy verge still fringed the place, like the hair of a dying monk, but the grass had turned gray, and when I reached down to pick some it crumbled to dust in my hands.

"Shit," said Clarence in a whisper. "She just burned and burned and *burned*."

I almost warned him to keep quiet, but of course if Anaita was in there and listening, she'd probably heard us long before that. It made me wonder again how much power she had used here and how she managed it. That's one difference between the higher angels and the schmuck angels like me and Clarence: We were limited by the physical fact of our bodies, the bodies that Heaven gave us. (People are limited that way, too—it's called "being mortal.") But the important angels, as well as bigtime demons like Eligor, could channel a much larger amount of power than I could ever hope to. It still wasn't unlimited, though, and that reminded me of the line from Gustibus that I'd modified: *Follow the power.* Not like now, where we were walking across its effects, but in terms of figuring out how the whole mess worked. Clearly, Anaita was very strong here; as powerful as she'd been on Earth, probably more so. When we'd met on Earth, she hadn't been able to do anything like this, or she would have just grabbed me for my brainwashing, then evaporated everyone who followed me into the museum. Not to mention that she wouldn't have been anywhere near as occupied by the closet full of bugbears I'd dumped on her. But here, maybe second only to Heaven, she could call on the energies of something like a force five hurricane.

That was bad news for us, of course, although it made me feel better about not having a gun. (Because it would have been as useless as a cock ring for a Ken doll, I mean.)

But if the battle plan I had begun percolating, back on Earth, was to have any chance of succeeding, we definitely could not afford to get into a shooting war with the Angel of Moisture—a pretty good joke, now that I thought about it, since I was wading through gray dust and black ash as dry as corn starch. We had to outsmart this superior being. Somehow.

Clarence hung back a little as we got near the house, but I had already decided that if Anaita was around she'd know we were here, so I decided on the direct course. I walked up the steps, leaving little ashy outlines of my shoes on the otherwise unblemished wood. The house wasn't painted, but it didn't look like it ever had been, and the ruination all around didn't seem to have touched it: the wood was the color of Philippine mahogany, healthy and solid, with no sign of damage. It gave me a mental picture straight out of *The Wizard of Oz*, with Anaita as Wicked Witch, standing on the roof and spraying death all around.

"Bobby . . ." Clarence said nervously, but I ignored him. I mean, I know people say I charge into things without thinking, but what difference was that going to make here? Should I have stood on the porch in the middle of that lunar landscape and called, "Yoo-hoo! Anyone home?"

I pushed the door open and found myself in the middle of what was clearly the main room, a large, high-ceilinged hall with several doors leading off it, like something that had once been a barn but had been converted into a family room for a very large family. The furniture was beyond rustic, rough and tied together with cords, not nailed, no paint or stain on anything. One wall was mostly taken up by a huge medieval fireplace. At the opposite end of the room stood a closed cabinet, simple but unlike the handmade objects everywhere else. In fact, it looked a bit like something that, in the old days, used to hide a television set, although I doubted they got cable here, or even satellite. There were also lots of tables and rough benches, but no sign of any people. To continue the children's stories theme, it looked like the Three Bears' had built a casino in the middle of the forest, and then gone out for one of their long walks before opening it.

"I don't think anyone's here," I called back to Clarence. My voice echoed. A furious, fiery angel made of broken shards of glass and pottery did not appear. I walked over to the big, square cabinet and pulled open its hinged doors. Light leaped out, startling me, but it was not the bright beams of a psychotic angel about to burn me to charcoal but the cool, misty light of Heaven, or at least as much of it as we ever saw outside of the real place, Upstairs.

What was inside the out-of-place cabinet was a cube of solid, shifting light—something I'd seen before. We had one in the advocate's office downtown, where it was kept under lock, key, and the grumpy, watchful eyes of Alice the dispatcher. The cube looked like it was made from a single piece of crystal, but it was a lot more powerful than even the wildest New Age imagination could grasp. It was used to communicate directly with Heaven. Sam called that, "Going to Mecca." I've never been the reverent type myself, so I only used the one downtown when I absolutely had to.

The problem with this particular cube was that it was almost certainly linked not to Heaven but to Anaita, and *only* to Anaita. I immediately shut the cabinet doors and moved away from it.

Continuing the investigation, I poked my head briefly into a large side room that appeared to be a kitchen, except the only appliance was a huge, beehive clay oven built into one wall. The ash in front of it was undisturbed. Whatever had destroyed the outside hadn't even shaken the floor in here. I headed upstairs to the next level. The stairs, like the walls and roof, were very, very solid. I was beginning to think the house had been brought here—or created here—as a whole, and then the cruder furniture had been added by Sam's Third Way souls as part of their new life.

But where were all those Soul Family Robinsons? And where was Sam? A nasty thought kept whispering that if I went outside and looked carefully, I might find ash outlines of more than just buildings—maybe even of something Sam-shaped—but I kept pushing that thought away.

The upstairs floors seemed to be mostly bedrooms, although that word is stretching it a bit. They were a lot more like the barracks at Camp Zion, with wall-to-wall bunk beds made in the same Tom Sawyer Island style as the rest of the furniture. These, at least, gave some sign of being slept in, the thin wool (and, again, very handmade) blankets tossed in disarray. It had clearly been something less expected than a military reveille that had got this group moving.

I was inspecting the dorms on the next floor up, trying to get a rough idea of how many people had lived here, when I heard Clarence call me from down below. He sounded a bit uptight, but why shouldn't he be? "Be there in a second."

"No, I think you should come. *Now*."

Oh, shit, was my first thought. *He's found a body.* I reached into my pocket out of habit, but there was no gun to be drawn. Usually I hate carrying them, because then I keep having to use them, but I hate it even more when I need one, and I don't have one. My gun control dilemma in a nutshell.

"Bobby!"

"Coming, Junior." I clomped down the stairs, making lots of noise so he'd hear me and unclench. "Just take a deep breath and hold your . . ."

I didn't finish the sentence, because as soon as I saw Clarence standing in the middle of the dining hall I also saw the guy who was aiming a drawn bow at him, a very wicked-looking arrow balanced on the string, pointing right at the kid's guts.

"Well," I said in my calmest voice. "What have we here?"

The man with the bow turned to look at me. He was whipcord thin, with a narrow face, somewhere between twenty and thirty years old, and smeared with ash. He also had a healing scar on his forehead that went through one eyebrow like the San Andreas fault, giving him an expression of mild surprise, but his eyes were cold and hard, and his mouth was set in a thin line that said, *"Don't push me, because I'd love to put an arrow into this guy's chitlins."* The weird thing, though, is that he looked somehow familiar.

"Who are you?" he demanded. It's always a bit hinky when you change astral planes, since everything sounds like what you're used to speaking, but I was pretty sure he was speaking actual modern English, despite being dressed like one of those guys in *Last of the Mohicans*, pseudo-Native-American gear of leather and fur and ragged cloth. (Okay, I didn't actually read it, but I watched the hell out of that movie.)

"We're not the ones who burned this place up, if that's what you're asking."

The line of his mouth stayed as taut as his bowstring. "It's not. I *saw* what happened here. Who are you?"

I wasn't quite sure if somebody who'd watched Anaita trash the area was going to be thrilled with more angels, and I didn't know what the rules here were as far as me and the kid dying painfully with arrows sticking through us. Would we come back? Not that I could afford to trust resurrection these days anyway. "Bobby. My name is Bobby. And this is—"

"Harrison," said Clarence, and despite being on the verge of kebab-hood, the kid shot me an evil look. "My name is Harrison Ely. We're not your enemies."

"Be interested to know why you think that's true," said the man. There was still something about his face that struck a chord, at least what I could see of it under the ashy pseudo-camouflage. "But I think I'd better leave the questions up to the rest." He moved the drawn bow off Clarence long enough to gesture toward the door. If I'd been close enough I might have tackled him then, but I wasn't. So I didn't. "Go on," he said. "You first. And make it quick—I'm not staying here any longer than I need to."

I won't bore you with a description of our entire journey, except to say that as we left the house and its charred perimeter behind, the scenery became increasingly impressive. No, that's a stupid, weaselly word. It wasn't impressive, it was stunning. Gorgeous. Transcendent, even; as affecting as the first time I'd seen it. As we made our way out of the grassy foothills and up into the lower reaches of the mountains, I again had the strangest sensation of being under the influence of psychedelics. I don't know if you've ever taken them, but the "is"-ness of everything becomes almost heartbreaking. Water is so unbearably transparent and yet full of color, and moves so strangely. Light is more refracted. Textures are astounding, and details you would otherwise overlook, like the pattern of bark on a tree, become as intricately fascinating as the most engrossing piece of art. And everything, simply everything, seems almost to glow from within, as if it has been constructed just for you to see at that moment and admire in its peak of perfection.

Kainos, once we got away from the site of Anaita's apparent hissy fit, was a lot like that. Not because we were on drugs, and not because it was somehow supernatural, but because it was sort of ultimately natural, like a landscape created to remind people that we were part of nature and nature was part of us. Each tree seemed to bask in a certainty of its place in the universe. The soil was pungent with the smells that soil can give you, and they were all, even the slightly foul ones, just glorious. Even the rocks seemed to have a presence, like fascinating people. But I think it was the sky that really did me in. It was just a sky—blue, high, and full of streaky clouds—but for nearly the first time in my life it felt like something that was truly the crown of creation, the milky sapphire that surrounded us, and in which we were all fortunate to live.

"It's a beautiful place," I said at last, because I felt like if I didn't say something the feelings would make my chest explode.

"It is," the stranger replied, and for a moment the watchful look on his face eased. "When I first came here, I'd just walk. Walk and walk for hours. Lie on my back and watch the clouds. Like being a kid again."

And then I recognized him. It was something in the light as he looked up that brought back a photograph I'd seen in his house, one that had been taken when he was about the age he appeared to be now, hiking up a mountain somewhere, looking young, healthy, and full of purpose. Completely unlike what he'd looked like when I'd first seen him in the flesh, in fact. He had been pink then, very pink, and very, very dead.

"Edward Walker," I said. "You're Edward Lynes Walker."

He turned so quickly I didn't even have a chance to step back. The arrow on the tight-drawn string was only about three inches from my left eye. "How do you know me?"

I considered telling him how his death and the disappearance of his soul had started me on a journey through a world of craziness, had nearly got me killed or worse a couple of dozen times, and eventually led me even into Hell itself, but I decided it could wait until I had a better idea of how things stood here. "I knew you when you were alive," I said, which wasn't exactly true, but I had spent a lot of time studying the living Ed Walker, so it wasn't a complete lie, either.

He wasn't content with that, but I drew the line and politely refused to say more until we got to wherever we were going. He threatened me a little, but I could see his heart wasn't really in it. He might have shot me if I'd tried to disarm him, or maybe even if I'd tried to run, but he was at heart a scientist and a humanist and couldn't quite work up the anger to skewer me in cold blood. At last, and none too graciously, he told me to get going again.

The journey lasted through the dying afternoon, and I had the pleasure of watching the sun setting in a world I'd never visited before. Except I felt pretty sure I had.

"This is Earth, isn't it?" I said.

"Bobby!" Clarence thought I was going to try to trick Walker, and he clearly didn't feel as confident about the man's unwillingness to murder as I did.

"Yeah, it is," Walker said. "Seems to be, anyway. An Earth without people. No farms, no cities, no dykes or canals or roads. Not even Native Americans stringing salmon nets across the river."

"Huh," I said. "Place looks a lot happier without us, doesn't it?"

"I guess so," Walker said. "Now, a little less chatter or someone's going to hear an unfamiliar voice and put some arrows in you, and maybe hit me by accident. I hate those kind of accidents."

I took the hint.

We hiked up what looked like a deer track, out of the scrubby oak forest and into something altogether more northern and more hoodoo. The air turned tangy with the smell of resin, and soon we were surrounded by redwoods and pines tall enough to block the light. I thought we must be getting close, since the cover was deep enough for hiding pretty much anything you wanted to hide, but I was still startled when a high-pitched voice out of the trees said, "Stop or you're dead."

"It's me, Sharif," Ed Walker called. "We've got company. Run ahead and tell them."

"Will do!" said the voice, which sounded like it belonged to a young boy.

A few moments later we reached a level promontory. Men dressed in the same caveman-chic as Ed Walker appeared from the shadows, quickly surrounding us. They all had homemade weapons, cudgels, spears, and more bows, so I kept my hands visible and tried to look harmless. Clarence was doing it too, like a new kid on his first day of school.

"Give them some room," a familiar voice called from back in the woods. Our captor walked us forward, through a good-sized crowd who had come to stare at us, until I could see a group of men and women around a small fire whose glow was almost completely blocked by the stones piled around it. Sitting in the middle, still wearing the tattered remains of the suit he'd had on the last time I'd seen him, but also wrapped in skins and rags as well, sat Sam. "That you, B?" he called. "Hey, and the kid, too! I was beginning to wonder if you were coming. Took you guys long enough."

"I just got your message," I said. "In fact, you were over in my neck of the woods, what, yesterday? So it hasn't been very long. You okay, man?"

"Yesterday on Earth. It's been a good bit longer here." Sam laughed—not the cheerful kind. "So, what do you think of the place? I hope you like it, old buddy, because I don't think any of us are going to be leaving."

forty-three
another fine mess

"**W**ELL, DAMN, Ollie," I said to Sam as we seated ourselves on a couple of the rocks ranged around the fire. "Sorry about this."

"It's one of your best, Stanley." He shook his head in his best Oliver Hardy style. Usually this is funny, sort of, even when we're in a horrible situation, but I don't think either of us was feeling very cheerful. Knowing how much water you've both seen go under the bridge isn't much comfort when the bridge finally collapses.

We all sat in silence and tried to warm our hands. Many of the Kainos-folk, who'd been watching our exchange like worried kids spying on the grown-ups, began to relax, or at least not to feel actively endangered. There were no real children, of course. Even the sentry Sharif, who in person turned out to look like a teenager, had probably lived a long full life, since that was the only kind of volunteer the Magians had recruited to come here, experienced adults willing to trade in the coin-flip of Heaven or Hell for a more nuanced afterlife. I imagine by now some of them were regretting the decision. Ragged, many of them bandaged, the Third Way pioneers looked a lot more like international refugees than the souls of the great and good enjoying their reward. A quick estimate of the number of campfires scattered through the woods told me there were probably only a few hundred survivors here in total. Not exactly an army.

The ground was hard and the air was raw and chilly, but at least whatever version of Earth this resembled wasn't in the middle of winter. That was a good thing, because the fire wasn't big enough to cook a single strip of bacon.

"How did everything go bad so fast, Sam? How much time's gone by here since I saw you?"

"About two weeks, I guess. But it happened pretty quickly. You-Know-Who showed up the same day I got back. Luckily, most of us were away from the settlement when she came. Man, that angel's not just ambitious, or complicated—she's insane, or at least she was when she got here. Some of our bosses are complete assholes, literally holier-than-thou, but her . . . there's something really wrong."

"Doctor Gustibus," I began, then realized Sam didn't know who he was. It was another small blow, since in the old days Sam knew everything I knew, but things were different now and had been ever since this Third Way thing started. "This guy I know, kind of a researcher, said that she's not like all the other angels because she was a goddess first."

"Yeah, and not the nice kind." Sam was bleak. "She came in here like gangbusters."

I shook my head in frustration. "But we still don't know why she built this place, what the whole thing is about. Why would she make such a risky deal? And what did Eligor get out of it?"

Clarence spoke up. "Is there something here she needs?"

Sam grunted. "What does a Heavenly Power need that she doesn't already have? Or can't already make?"

"This is horseshit," said a third, clearly angry voice. I turned. It was Ed Walker, who was sitting a few feet away, giving us a bit less respectful distance than the others. "We've got more important things to do than talk about crap like that. Like surviving."

"Simmer down, Ed." Sam turned to me. "I assume you've figured out who this is by now. He's a good man, but things have been a little difficult for all of us—"

"You don't have to apologize for me, Sammariel," said Walker. "We've got several hundred people here to protect, and she's coming back. She's coming back because of *you*." He spat. "You Magians, you . . . *angels*." It was a curse word. "You're the cause of this. And now your crazy boss is going to destroy us all."

"Or maybe your souls will go where they should have gone in the first place," Clarence said. "The Highest won't just let you disappear."

"I had years left to live!" Walker stood up. "We need to kill that monster or buy her off somehow, because we can't beat her. And if you can't think of a way to do either of those things, then we're all just wasting time here when we should be trying to get as far away as possible." He gave Clarence and me a nasty look. "And when we run for it, our chances will be a lot better if we don't take any angels with us—not even you, Sam." He picked up his bow, turned, and marched away from the fire.

"Don't mind Ed," Sam told me as he watched Walker go. "He's been patrolling night and day. He's tired and scared. We all are." But he looked bothered.

"How many people do you have here?" I asked. "And how do you keep them all fed?"

Sam actually smiled. "Fed? This was going to be a paradise, son! Souls don't have to eat here in Kainos, although they can. Some of the settlers eat fruit or edible roots and vegetables, just because they like to. And of course we use the plants to make things." He held up the blanket he wore over his suit coat. The coarse-woven fabric looked a lot like burlap. "There's a plant fiber that we've learned to weave. And there are sheep and other animals, so I'm sure we'll learn how to make proper clothing someday soon."

"We? You sound like you've gone native, Sammy-boy."

He didn't smile this time. "I've had to pitch in. After all, I'm the one who brought a lot of these people here. And there's plenty to learn—or re-learn, in a sense. Kainos has only existed for a few years, after all, and we recruited more scholars than farmers. That was Kephas's— You-Know-Who's doing. It's like she went out of her way to pick the philosophical over the practical."

"Yeah." Then something clicked. "Her enemies."

"What do you mean, Bobby?" Clarence asked.

I looked around, but with Walker's departure most of the other inhabitants of the Third Way had turned from us, perhaps because they didn't want to know what we were talking about. I could tell by their faces that they were frightened, that angels didn't mean many good things to them anymore. "I think that's it," I said quietly. "She wants to be *worshipped*. I think that's what Gustibus was pointing toward. As an angel, she was just one of many doing the Highest's work, however important she might have been compared to you and me. But I saw her in her home, and if you want to talk about a five-thousand-year-old Persian-American princess, that's our girl. And if she was going to be worshipped again, like in the old days, she didn't want lumps and idiots doing it, she wanted the best and the brightest. Like these." I made a small gesture to indicate the people around us. "She wanted the smart ones, the rationalists, the kind who back on Earth hardly even believed in Heaven."

"Really? All this—just to be somebody's deity again?" asked Clarence.

"You don't get the goddess out of your system that easily, kid. Yeah, it makes sense." I felt like a piece of the puzzle—only a small one in our present situation, but still a piece—had finally fallen into place. "Why else would she risk everything to build something like this? First of all, it takes balls, serious angel balls, to go against Heaven this way, not to mention bargaining with Hell. Why else would she strike out on her own and build what's basically a colony? Because she wanted worshippers again, her very own. That's what she's done here. But it's gone wrong, and so she's pissed off."

"Ha. Pissed off doesn't begin to describe it," Sam said. "She came in on a chariot of light. I didn't see it, but Ed Walker did—it's one of the reasons he's so angry. She came in on her chariot. It was pulled by those two lions, but they flew. They were made of light and diamonds, and they flew. She came in like a Phantom jet and she scorched everything around the house. You saw that, I'm sure."

"But she didn't burn the house," I pointed out.

"I think that's because the Going-To-Mecca cube is in there, but I'm not sure."

"Or because it's her church."

"Huh?" Sam wiped his hand across his face, wearily. "Sorry, say that again. Even us angels need sleep here sometimes, just like on Earth."

"Haven't you wondered about the way the house is built? Taller than it should be? That big tower? It's a stealth temple. It's where she expected to be worshipped."

Sam pursed his lips. "Maybe, but I'm doubting she expects much worshipping now. Not after what she did. Those of us who weren't there could still hear her, even from miles away, so loud her voice echoed in the mountains, demanding that we turn over the traitors." He looked at me. "By the way, those traitors are you and me, buddy—

but mostly you, I'm afraid. Still, I'm pretty sure she won't deal too kindly with me, either. Besides me, the last two Magians still here, Kelathiel and Phidorathon—we called them Kiley and Fred—were watching the settlement, and she vaporized them, along with a couple of dozen poor souls who happened to be there at the time. The only good thing was that she didn't stay long, that she didn't hunt the rest of us down and wipe us out right then."

"You're right, that's hopeful. It means there's some limit to her power, either here or because of something back in Heaven." I filed that one away. I still didn't think we had a snowball's chance in a game of Tartarus tennis, but I wasn't giving up without some kind of fight.

A little while passed in silence, not the peaceful kind of sitting with old friends so much as the exhausted kind. Clarence and I hadn't done much except to take a long walk, but seeing what Anaita had done to the place had hollowed me out, and I didn't have much left. Also, I truly didn't think we had much of a chance. It was a familiar feeling, in a way, like the hours before a major action back when I was in the Harps, especially after we lost our top-kicker Leo, and he didn't get resurrected. It was all there—the doubt, the fear, the feeling that what you really wanted to do was start screaming about how unfair it was and never stop, or even just pick a direction and start running. But in the Harps we never did, mainly because everybody else was in the same position, and if you buckled, the whole wall might collapse and come crashing down. But, damn, the wall sure felt shaky.

"Anything else I need to know about the physics of this place?" I asked Sam after a while.

"What, you mean like, 'You can avoid dying by jumping twice and then using your special Survival coin?'" Sam smiled sadly. "Ain't a video game, B. This is pretty much just like Earth. Superior force beats weaker force. We don't eat, and the souls themselves may not die, but they disappear and don't come back if their bodies die here. We found that out after You-Know-Who blew our asses up. As the kid said, I'm guessing that the ones who got killed went back into real Judgement." For a moment I saw the deep hurt he'd been keeping hidden. "God, I hope they did."

"Yeah, but she's got that wired somehow, too," I said. "Otherwise she wouldn't risk freeing all those souls. She must have some way to silence them about Kainos when they're being judged. Maybe the same trick she used on me at my trial. Or she's keeping them away from judgement altogether." I confess I shuddered a little. "What was it like here before everything went to shit?"

"How do you mean?"

"What was the routine? Did the wicked witch visit often, when she was Kephas?"

"I'm sorry about that, Bobby. You were right about her. I just didn't want to hear it. I'd put too much into the place. I let myself get conned into believing in something again."

"It doesn't matter now, Sam. I just want to know all the odds."

"You think there's something we can do other than just get barbecued like so much brisket?"

Clarence wasn't saying anything, but he was clearly listening. I had come to like him enough that I was truly sorry I'd got him into this not-so-fine mess. "Who knows?" I said. "But I live in hope, so please answer the questions. The Mecca cube, for instance. Does it connect to anything besides Anaita?"

"Just Herself, as far as I know. She used it to send us messages, instructions, back in the days when we all believed in this. And we could call her with it if we had an emergency. She didn't like that much— even then, when she was Kephas, she was kind of a pain in the ass about answering questions—but it always worked."

"Well, that's something, anyway. Do you still have your magic glove?"

He was a bit surprised. "Yeah. Tucked away in here." He patted his crude jacket. "But I don't think I can use it against her. In fact, I'm pretty damn sure of it, because Fred—Phidorathon—had one, too. All us Magians do. Walker said Fred tried to use it against her when she came. All that happened was that Fred burned up like a road flare, hand first, then all down him. At least it was quick. In fact, I might use it that way myself, if it comes to it." He laughed, and for a moment sounded a bit more like the old Sam. "Better quick than slow."

"Don't do anything stupid. We're not totally out of options."

He gave me a look, mostly cynical, but with just enough interest to make me feel like a real bastard, because even I didn't believe any of my half-baked ideas had a chance of working. Too many variables, especially variables as crazy as whether Eligor could be trusted. Yeah, that's what I said. If we had even the tiniest chance to survive this, it would be because the archduke of Hell, who hated my guts and had already swindled me several times, would decide to do something that would help me. He'd accepted the deal I offered him in Five Page Mill, but that meant exactly nothing. In fact, since even if he fucked me again, Eligor himself would stay fat and happy, the odds were distinctly against his honoring his promise.

"Options? Tell me," Sam said.

"Is it safe? Can all these people be trusted?" Clarence asked.

It was a fair question, but as I said, none of the Kainos-folk seemed to be listening. Still, I beckoned Sam and the kid to get up and move with me a little farther away from the camp. It wasn't until long afterward that I realized I never checked to see where exactly Ed Walker had gone.

"It's like this," I said when we'd settled ourselves against an outcropping some distance away. "We really don't have a prayer—no pun intended—against our goddess friend if we're just going to try to trade shots with her."

"We're not going to trade any shots, anyway," said Sam. "You may have noticed that other than the Mecca cube, there isn't any technology here that would make a medieval peasant scratch his head. We've got arrows, spears, clubs. Shit, we haven't even got around to smelting bronze yet. So how are we going to fight You-Know-Who? This isn't Kansas, but it isn't the Emerald City, either. You could throw the world's biggest bucket of water on her, and it wouldn't do a thing."

"I know. But I'm not just going to lie down and die, either. The bitch has been after me for months, sent that Smyler psychopath after me, brainwashed Walter Sanders and banished him to Hell—yeah, I know, kid, I haven't told you about that, but guess what, she did. Oh, and she murdered a really nice young woman who was a friend of mine. And now she wants you and me on a stick, Sam. You too, Clarence, since you're with us. She won't leave any witnesses."

"Harrison," he said.

"Huh?"

"You promised you'd stop calling me Clarence."

"Shit, yeah, I did. Look, if we survive, I promise I'll do better."

"That's so like you, Bobby," he said, but without too much heat. "Give a promise you know you won't have to live up to."

"The only kind worth making, my friend, the only kind worth making. Now, just let me spin out some stupid, hopeless ideas, and you guys can start shooting them down."

"I'm too tired," Sam complained. "Can't I just tell you now that you're full of shit, it won't work, and you'll get us all killed, so I can get some sleep?"

"Not a chance, big guy. We're all in this for the duration, but it may go down as soon as the sun comes up, so we need to do our talking now."

Sam sighed. "Shit. You probably won't stop talking even if you *do* burn up."

So, as the familiar and yet wildly foreign stars wheeled through the sky above us and the camp fell into silence and sleep, I explained to them the novel way I'd figured out to get us all killed.

Because who wants to die some boring, old-fashioned way?

forty-four
white on black

IT STARTED snowing during the night, swirling tiny white flakes that stuck in hair and clothing but never came thick enough to make drifts on the ground. Not until the wind rose, anyway. After that it all moved pretty quickly into what you'd expect in the hills in midwinter back home, and that's basically where we were, even if this was a California that hadn't known a human footstep until recently.

I was finding it hard to sleep, so I got up and wandered through the camp and out to the edge where I could brood by myself. As I stepped out of the last knot of Kainos-folk sleeping huddled together for warmth, I saw a lone woman standing sentry, several layers of cloth and skins wrapped around her, a spear in one hand and something I couldn't quite make out in her other. I could see it, of course, because I have Super Angel Vision (a bit better than human normal, not really x-ray eyes or anything) but it was way too weird-looking to be any weapon I could think of. The sentry watched me approach without saying a word, but she seemed to make a small, strange noise as I passed. It took me a moment to realize it was the sound of her teeth chattering. I turned back.

"You sound cold. Can I take the watch for you?"

She stared. "You're an angel, aren't you?"

I had the feeling that we weren't quite as popular as we used to be, but I told the truth. "I am. Doloriel." I stuck out my hand. "But back on Earth I'm called Bobby."

She nodded, clearly quite used to the phrase, "back on Earth," but she didn't look particularly thrilled to meet me. "An angel. Are you friends with Sammariel?"

"Years and years."

She nodded again. "He's from San Judas, same as I am. A lot of us early ones were, like Ed." Behind the very red tip of her nose was a young, intelligent face—everybody was fairly young here, at least in appearance—and a pair of dark eyes that looked like they'd seen things their owner wished they hadn't. "You know Ed?"

Now it was my turn to nod. "Only now, in the flesh, but yes."

"Yeah, everybody knows Ed. He's kind of the mayor. Well, not really—that's Nathalie Weng, but only because Ed said if we elected him he wouldn't do it."

I had become a little uncomfortable about Edward Walker. It was hard to reconcile the quiet, angry man I'd met with the well-known and apparently popular scientist and businessman whose life I'd studied. Still, there wasn't really any precedent for what he and the others had been through. "And you are?"

"Oh, sorry." She stuck her spear into the ground, butt-first, and extended a hand in a fingerless glove of the burlap cloth I already thought of as "Kainos cotton." "Lyra Garza—Lyra, like the star. My father was an amateur astronomer."

I couldn't help smiling a little at the coincidence. My Counterstrike unit had been the *Lyrae*, nicknamed "the Harps." "Where in Jude are you from? Because I'm from there, too."

"Small world," she said, then looked around. "Almost literally, at least the human population." She shook her head. "A few hundred of us, max, with a whole world to explore and build in. Then this shit happens. Sorry. I was at Stanford. I lived in Barron Park, over by the university."

"Downtown, me, usually somewhere within walking distance of Beeger Square. I've been meaning to ask you—what's that thing you're holding?"

She looked quickly from her spear to the weird, bulbous object. "Oh, this? It's a rattle. Dried oak gall, a big one, full of rocks. In case I have to wake everybody up. It's pretty loud." She squinted at me as she pushed a wisp of hair from her face. "You offered to take my watch, didn't you? That was nice, but no. I want to do my part, and I'm not going to be much of a fighter if it comes to it."

"I hope it won't come to it," I said. "At least not for you and the rest of the . . ." I trailed off. "I forgot to ask Sam—what do you call yourselves?"

She smiled, and for the first time I saw her as something other than a poor soul shivering on a cold hillside. "We argued about that a lot at first. We spoke lots of different languages at home, and now we're all speaking . . . well, whatever it is we're speaking here, and the words have different meanings." She laughed. "I'd love to study it, actually, this angelic language thing, and how it translates to all of us. That's a career study and more, right there. I was an etymologist—was, who am I kidding? Always will be. Anyway, you can imagine, lots of smart, freaked-out people. In the beginning we were much happier arguing than exploring or building, most of us. I think it was the . . . well, to be honest, the religious nature of what had happened to us that made us settle on 'pilgrims'."

"Pilgrims, huh? But you wound up being more the Plymouth Rock kind than the going-to-Canterbury kind."

"A little of both of those, I think. But we're also the going-to-Lourdes kind."

"Hoping for a miracle?"

"Well, we sure are now."

I took a long walk, thinking about what Lyra said and a million other things. I wandered until I would have worried about finding my way back if I was a normal human, but my sense of smell and direction were both pretty good, so I located the camp again without trouble. Dawn was still a short time away, but most of the pilgrims were up and getting ready to move. Getting ready to walk toward danger and maybe even destruction. Talking to Lyra Garza had made it even clearer to me that even if I hadn't been involved in bringing them all here, as Sam had, I still wanted badly to keep these people safe. And if that unlikely circumstance actually came to pass, it would be interesting to see what happened with this little colony of pilgrim souls starting over again on what was, for all purposes, Earth Two—The Reboot.

In the cold, windy dark, Sam explained to the pilgrims what he thought should be done to ensure their chance at survival. There were questions, of course, lots of them, but I was surprised and pleased by how practical most of them were. A few were adamant about wanting to keep running, that they didn't want to take the kind of risks Sam and I were talking about. We told them they could go, but only a couple of dozen actually left. That surprised me, too.

Shortly after sunrise we started out. At least we hadn't needed to feed everyone. They say Earth armies march on their stomachs, but ours could survive on heavenly righteousness alone. At least until the serious shit started happening. Then all the righteousness in the world wasn't going to save us.

Clarence was way too chatty for this early, especially in a world where I couldn't get any coffee, so I sent him off to talk to various folk Sam had picked out to handle different parts of our plan. Besides, I wanted to chat with Sam in private, and privacy was already pretty damn hard to come by, surrounded as we were by nervous pilgrims.

The private talk didn't happen right away. First Sam and I had to have a long meeting with Nathalie Weng, an Anglo-Chinese woman from Shanghai with the self-confident air of a tiny General Douglas MacArthur. I liked her, and I liked her deputy as well, a thin, thoughtful young man named Farber, who had lived in Freiburg while he was alive. I say young, but he mentioned how a bomb had flattened his house "during the war," and I don't think he meant the Gulf War since, as far as I know, that conflict never reached southern Germany. That was the thing about the Kainos people—they looked like the student-age counselors at a summer camp, but most of them had probably reached seventy or eighty before they died, some of them more.

Ed Walker stayed close to us but didn't actively participate. Still, he was a constant presence even when he was a dozen yards away, and it was clear that Walker had clout no one else did. Several times I saw Mayor Weng look over at him as if to make sure he agreed.

"Our people here are all hard workers," Weng told Sam and me. "All achievers, and they've got young, healthy bodies, but we're a little short on engineers and military folk."

"I'm hoping we don't need those things," I said. "Other than the special volunteers, we're not planning anything that requires real expertise, just labor. In fact, after we get set up there, I want all your people who aren't actually involved to move as far away as possible."

"You won't have much trouble convincing them," she said. "We're all pretty shocked by what happened to the others. None of us wants to die again so soon."

At last, all our mental lists cross-checked, Weng and Farber went off to do their own organizing and, I suspect, deliver a few pep talks. I finally had a chance to talk to Sam without an audience.

"What about the God Glove?" I said. "I asked last night, but you obviously didn't want to talk in front of Clarence."

"No, I just didn't want to get into an argument in front Ed Walker and all those the other people. Kinda sucks for human morale, to watch angels call each other names. Because I can't use it, B."

"It's the only real power we've got."

"I thought I already told you about this. We all had them, all of us Magian angels. And when she did her Wicked Witch number, Phidora-thon tried to use his glove against her. He burned up. Ed Walker was there—he saw the whole thing, but he didn't know what was really going on. He thought it was something Anaita did to Fred, but I know better. That's what happens when you try to use something like the God Glove against the Power that gave it to you."

I tried to hide my disappointment, but he could see what I was feeling. We've known each other too long not to know things like that. "Can it at least let me make one private call on the Mecca cube?" I asked. "Without Anaita finding out?"

"Don't know. Maybe. But she's probably going to know about it."

"Well, my idea would work anyway—not that it's *going* to work, but in a hypothetical sense it could all still work even if she intercepts the call. She'll still show up. But she'll be a lot harder to beat."

"I'll do my best, B." Sam punched my shoulder. It sort of hurt. "I say we think of it as an interesting challenge, a bunch of stone-age savages trying to take down a goddess."

"They're not stone age."

"But their technology is. *Our* technology, too, because that's all you and I have to work with. Let's face it, this is going to be one of those Butch and Sundance things."

"Yeah," I said. I hope I didn't sound as miserable as I felt. "I just hope the rest of these folks survive so someone will remember the cool things we said as we were blowing up."

"Yeah. Me too. I was planning on, 'Oh, shit!' How about you?"

"Well, now I'm going to have to think of a new one, since you're using mine."

*   *   *

It was a long walk through the hills back to the house, and although everybody was reasonably young and fit, more than a few had sustained injuries in their initial escape from Anaita's deadly tantrum, so the line got a bit strung out. If it hadn't been for the cold air and snow flurries, and if I'd been wearing something warmer than a light jacket and t-shirt, it might have been a pleasant winter's walk in the California hills. Except, of course, this wasn't the same California, and back in the real one, autumn wasn't even technically over yet. There was definitely a time slippage between here and Earth, and it made me wonder about some of the other differences.

"Not that much, really," said Sam when I asked him. "When we first got here, nobody died, of course. That's one of the reasons this group is so worried and fucked-up now. They thought of this as the afterlife, and afterlife usually means immortality."

"What do you mean, nobody died. Should anybody have?"

"One of the men, African guy named Chima, had a tree fall on him when we were timber-cutting for the new houses. See, after the first few weeks it was pretty clear we were going to need more housing, so we made hand axes and started cutting down trees to make log cabins. None of the people here have really done this stuff, and some idiot planned his fall wrong. Chima couldn't get out from under it. He should have died on the spot—that was a couple of thousand pounds of hardwood—but not only didn't he die, his bones knit back together in about a week, and he was up and around again not too long after that. He didn't even limp. I'd introduce you to him, but he was one of the people near the house when Anaita showed up."

"Shit. So he actually died three times."

"Maybe. That would probably be the world record for humans, but since he hasn't come back this time, I don't know how proud he's feeling about it."

"Anything else different here that we can use? People with odd abilities?"

"No. The mortals we brought here, the pilgrims as they call themselves, are just tougher than at home, but not stronger. Harder to kill— or they used to be."

"Damn, man, stop cheering me up so much."

*   *   *

The Kainos pilgrims started getting spooked even before we reached the great field of bare, devastated ground. I can't really say I blamed them, since I was feeling that way myself. I suppose I should have been thinking about my life, reviewing my failings and my (very occasional) successes, thinking about my friends and loved ones, but except for a simmering bitterness that I probably wasn't ever going to see Caz again, I could only focus on what was in front of me. It's a protective mechanism. Just do your job. Just put one foot in front of the other. When you see the enemy, pull the trigger—although there were no actual triggers to pull in this case. Boil everything down to staying alive, think about the other stuff later, that was my plan.

Except there was one other thing. I'd thought I hated Eligor, the archdemon, the all-time nasty fucker of the millennium, but it was nothing to what I'd come to feel about Anaita. Eligor, bad as he was, was my enemy. He was just doing his job, even if he enjoyed it way too much. In the Highest's scheme of things, at least as far as I could tell, he was doing exactly what he was supposed to. But Anaita, she was supposed to be like me, defender of the helpless, protector of the innocent, instead of what she was: an astonishing, gigantic, fucked-up pile of evil.

Whatever happened, I was praying I'd at least get to hurt her somehow. That alone might be enough to make it worthwhile. I wanted to be the mosquito that gave her a big ugly bite just before she was throwing a chic party for the other VIPs. I wanted to be her pimple on prom night.

We reached the charred ground shortly before the house itself rose into view above us. Considering it sat on a hill in the middle of nothing, you'll have an idea of how much territory Anaita's snit-fit had destroyed. We crunched across the cinders. Faint, windblown drifts of snow were accumulating, but not enough to cover the destruction, only to stripe the burned ground with undulating streaks of white, like lines of cocaine on a black light poster. We hiked across this great circle of ruination, the pilgrims scattered and trailing behind us, and I couldn't help thinking about some of humanity's other death marches— Bataan, the Trail of Tears. The chill, the lifelessness of the terrain, the faces of the people we'd brought here, all worked to drag me down into hopelessness. Sam hated seeing those expressions more than I did, I'm sure, since he had personally recruited dozens of the pilgrims.

We got to the house and gave it a quick inspection, but it was just as we'd left it, empty as a bill collector's heart. A sifting of snow had accumulated beneath windows blown out by Anaita's attack. We found what we needed, then got to work inside and outside, toiling in the cold like medieval peasants, digging and chopping and tying knots. Mostly digging. We stopped to drink water occasionally, more for the feel of stopping than any real need for a break. Sam was right—the pilgrims were a hardy lot, and the grim but determined mood seemed to have infected nearly everyone. Only Ed Walker seemed opaque to me, doing his part but always as though in his mind he was somewhere else. But where? That was a question that worried me. He'd overheard us the night before, when we thought we were alone, and he'd heard enough of my plan to angrily demand answers. He'd never seemed very satisfied with them, but to tell the truth, I wouldn't have been either. It was a pretty damned desperate plan, and that was being charitable. Walker had reluctantly agreed, but he'd hardly met my eye since, which added to my feeling that the whole thing was too precarious to work, too crazy. And this was me, the guy who made crazy plans like clouds make rain.

At last, about an hour before sunset, we had done all we could. Sam called together Ed and Mayor Weng and Farber, her deputy. "It's time," Sam said. "Get your people out of here. I want all the noncombatants as far away as they can get in the next thirty minutes or so."

"Thirty minutes," said Farber. "Well, we'd better synchronize our watches." We all turned to stare at him. "It was a joke," he said, a little sheepishly. "Because, obviously, we don't have watches."

"I've actually been to Hell," I said. "And you know what? All the comedians there were German."

He gave me a look of mock recrimination that made me smile. It didn't last long, but it was a nice two seconds of humanity. I hoped it wasn't my last.

"So is it go?" I said.

Sam looked around. "Looks like it."

"God loves you," I said to Mayor Weng and her pilgrims. "And all of us, I hope. Now get out of here."

As they hurried away across the snow and drifting black grit, we sent Walker and his volunteers to get into position, then after a last check, Sam and Clarence and I went into the house. I let Sam open the Go-To-Mecca Box, which he did only after pulling on the brilliantly glowing second-skin that was the God Glove. It looked like the end of his wrist was one big sparkler, but I knew it was only a birthday candle compared to what Anaita could muster, and we didn't dare use it against her anyway.

"I think the cube is ready," said Sam. "But she may have noticed that I flipped channels, if you know what I mean, so make it fast."

I did. I kept my call brief and to the point. *"It's time,"* I said—just that.

When I'd finished, Sam hung up the cosmic phone and adjusted it back to its original setting, which was a hotline right to Anaita, Angel of Moisture and goddess of our personal ruin, then he opened the channel. I held my finger to my lips for silence until we crept a little farther away, then Clarence and Sam and I began to talk normally, as if we didn't even know our words were flying right to Heaven and directly to our deadliest enemy. We didn't have to wait long to get results.

It started when my ears popped, a sudden change in pressure like a cupped blow on both sides of my head. I looked at Sam, and he nodded then hurried over to adjust the Mecca cube one last time. No need to speak. The pressure increased, and with it came a definite tang of ozone and an electrical crackle that I could feel on the hairs of my arms and neck. We all took a breath and stepped outside.

She stood there in snow flurries that turned the depth of the background into flat black and white static, like a television transmitting only the last whisper of the Big Bang. No glass or potsherds now: she looked like something out of a classical painting, like Juno or Minerva stepped out of a frame and into the world of men, bigger than life size and unutterably, astoundingly beautiful. She had two cats on leashes, tiny compared to what they'd been when I last saw them, not lions this time but something long-eared and tawny. If it hadn't been for Anaita being more than seven feet tall, and the shimmering ripple of her garment, which was more light than fabric, she could have been a rich and gorgeous actress walking her exotic pets. Except we weren't in Beverly Hills, but at the end of an entirely different world.

"Doloriel." Her voice was honey, love, and regret. The anger of our last meeting was gone as if it had never been. "Why do you fight me? Why didn't you just do as you were told?" She turned to Sam. "All your friend had to do was bring you back, and we would have been merciful."

"We?" Sam asked. "You mean you and the person you pretended to be?"

She looked amused, almost. "Pretended? Do you mean the guise I wore to recruit you? There was no pretense, only secrecy. Didn't I do what I said? Isn't this world beautiful? Didn't I make it just as I promised, and give it to the ones you brought to me?"

"Then burned the shit out of it and killed a bunch of them," I said. "Not exactly what one expects from an angel. Not what usually happens in paradise."

"Yeah," said Clarence, but he didn't say it very loud. Still, he was standing in there. He hadn't faced her the first time, of course. Maybe that helped.

"Why are you such a troublemaker, Doloriel?" Anaita didn't sound angry. In fact she sounded exactly like a mother worried by a foolish child who won't learn. "You have been a thorn in my side since the beginning. So unnecessary."

"I didn't do anything to you. You sent that stabby maniac after me. You've done nothing but try to destroy me."

"And you've tried just as hard to destroy my work," she said, but still calm, still more in sadness than in anger. "You and that report you made. We should have had months more to build here, years of Earth time before the others found out about this place. Instead you upset everything, you silly little creature, ruined a plan whose glory and beauty you can't even conceive. You dare to complain to me about what I did? I should have incinerated you the first time you interfered with my project. In fact, I should have done it earlier. At the very start."

Which made no sense, since other than the report, which I had to make because of the heat I was getting from my superiors when I found out about Ed Walker's missing soul, I'd done nothing to her. Seemed to me that my involvement had caused trouble for Sam, who'd been the one to recruit Walker, far more than it had Anaita.

Or did she mean something else by that? *At the very start . . . ?* Not that it mattered now. I could think about it later, if I was still alive and my thinking parts hadn't burned up. "Look, just leave these people alone, leave this place and Sam alone, and I'll go back with you."

She looked at me for a long time—it seemed long, anyway, as we stood in the fluttering snow—then let out a laugh like a bird's song, haunting, sweet, and very, very brief. "Imagine! You're going to offer me a bargain. You, Doloriel, who have done so much to spoil triumphs you are too ill-formed to appreciate."

I suddenly remembered something Heinrich Himmler had once said in an address to his SS men, who were weary and horrified by implementing the Final Solution. *"That we should have to do such things and still remain decent men,"* he told them, *"that is true heroism."* Anaita really was insane. I had never thought an angel could be, but she was. She believed herself to be so obviously right that everything else no longer mattered. In fact, everything else barely registered.

"Fine," I said. "No deal. So come and get me."

"As you wish, Doloriel. But I will not dirty myself again with you. I don't want your filthy blood staining my raiment." She dropped the leashes.

The cats leaped forward. By the time they had taken a couple of steps they were growing, and as they raced toward us across the snow and ash they kept on doing it. Eyes like glowing amber, big as lions, then bigger, they sprang across the ground so quickly I could scarcely have counted to three, even if I had enough air in my lungs and spit in my mouth to do it. The nearest one leaped, a huge, gray-brown shadow, even as I took my first stumbling steps backward. It crashed to the ground in front of me, skidding through ash. Then it was gone into the black, rectangular hole we had dug. As it fell onto the sharpened stakes at the bottom of the pit, the cat's initial snarl of surprise exploded into a maddened howl of agony.

The second cat was already in midair. It jumped easily over the exposed trap, but when it landed it was slightly off to the side, so instead of the second trap swallowing it, the covering of boards stolen from the house, along with scavenged branches, fell inward as planned, but the monstrous cat still had enough solid ground under its paws to scramble to safety. Safety for *it*, of course. Not so safe for me.

Those were the only two pits we'd had time to dig.

I wasn't thinking much about pits or digging at that moment, though, because the second cat leaped again as soon as it found its footing, something like a thousand pounds of claws, teeth, and rock-hard muscle flying through the air toward me. I couldn't even get my spear into the dirt to brace it before the thing hit me. We rolled over and over, and although my head hit the ground so hard that, for a moment, I didn't quite know where I was, I could definitely tell that a mouth full of sharp teeth was about to tear my face off, and that I no longer had a spear in my hand. Then the massive jaws snapped down, and the world disappeared into a deep, foul, and extremely slobbery darkness.

forty-five
how a world ended

OKAY, BEFORE I explain to you what happened while my face was being chewed off by *felis mythicus giganticus*, let me tell you the good news: I was certain now that Anaita's power really did have limits.

Knowing that wasn't a lot of help right then, what with the fangs and the drool and the huge jaws crushing my skull, but it meant that we actually had a chance. Not a good one. Not even a statistically significant one. But a chance.

See, nobody (at least nobody like me) actually knows where the high angels get their power. "Direct from the Highest" is what we're told, and that may well be true, but I'm pretty sure there's more to the story. The power is rationed, apparently by rank, and the higher up the ladder you go, the more pure force the angels in question can bring to the dance. Someone like Anaita, one of the chief powers of the Third Sphere, could bring a great deal of it to bear where she wanted, on Heaven, on Earth, or even here on Kainos. In fact, she had a great deal more freedom to use power on Kainos because the place pretty much belonged to her. But this was the kicker: she didn't have the *right* to that power.

So Anaita could call on far greater resources than she needed, far more than Sam, Clarence, and I could ever hope to match: if angelic power were water, she had a fire hose the size of the Holland Tunnel, and we had squirt guns. But just like someone using a fire hose, the water had to come from somewhere, and so did whatever heavenly reserves she was drawing on. More important, she had to disguise the fact that she was using it, because any massive deployment of angelic force was going to attract notice Upstairs.

I'd been suspicious that she destroyed such a small portion of Kainos during her scorched earth hissy fit. Yes, she wanted to preserve the place, but she never really found out whether I was there or not, and she hadn't managed to capture Sam either, who was at least as much of a threat to her secrets as I was. That suggested that she didn't dare use that level of force for very long. Yeah, she could come down and rain destruction like a helicopter gunship, but only for so long before someone back in Heaven was going to start wondering what she was doing.

Which explained why she'd mostly worked through others, sending Smyler after me instead of just obliterating me with a snap of her fingers, and using Sam and the other renegade angels to do the groundwork of populating Kainos.

The big cats were the final giveaway. The monsters were the manifestations of Anaita's power, yes, but she was using them because they were a comparatively thrifty way to get rid of us. Create something with hunting instincts, muscles, talons, and fangs, then turn it loose, and you get much more bang for your buck than just vaporizing everything in front of you. The fang-toothed kitty tasting my face at that moment might have been nasty, but it was actually a sign of weakness. Anaita was trying to take us down on the cheap, because she needed to keep what she was doing hidden from Heaven.

I promise you, I didn't spend as much time thinking about all that at the time as I just did describing it.

The cat-beast had me down, but it hadn't yet found a way to get its jaws squarely around my skull, and I was doing my best to hang onto my facial features, hitting, kicking, squirming, rolling. Still, several seconds of that hadn't done me any good, and I was already running out of strength. I pulled the knife I'd stashed in my boot, wishing really hard that it could be something longer, stronger, and sharper than a leaf of flint with string wrapped around one end to make a handle. I knew I wasn't going to make any major puncture wounds with it, so I just started slashing at everything I could reach, trying to cause pain. This might have been the imaginary sort of giant cat, but until I learned otherwise, I was going to assume that its nose and mouth and eyes were its weak spots, like almost any other predator.

Sadly, I seemed to be learning otherwise, or else I was just pissing it off. It bit down on my hand hard enough to make me drop the stone knife, and when I punched its nose with my other hand it only reared back, mouth wide and teeth very obvious, ready to go for my throat. Then something hit it.

Crock! That's the noise it made, like someone throwing a large rock against the side of a concrete building. The cat reeled and stumbled back a step, one half of its face suddenly a different shape and oozing gray stuff that might have been blood. Clarence swung his club again, a stone the size of a volleyball tied into the fork of a thick branch, but only managed to hit the beast on the shoulder this time. It shook its head and snarled.

One of its eyes was gone, or at least lost in torn tissue and broken bone, but the cat was nowhere near dead. Clarence tried to yank me away by my collar and only yanked me onto my ass instead, but I'd found my spear, and just managed to lift it high enough to pierce the creature's throat as it came at me. The force of its leap knocked me over again, but the spear had struck home. The cat twisted and contorted itself, trying to get a paw on the stick wagging in its neck.

I grabbed at the spear, got lucky, then braced myself and tried to force the beast toward the second pit, but even with half its head crushed and a spurting hole in its windpipe, Godzilla-Garfield was still intent on killing me.

One rear paw slid over the edge of the pit into empty space, but the thing began to push back hard against the spear, as if it knew what I planned. So I let go of the spear and threw myself at the giant cat, hitting the creature low in its body, right in the ribs. My weight and momentum pushed it flailing and snarling over the edge. I went with it, but most of my body landed on the rim of the pit, and Clarence caught my leg.

It may not have been a real cat, it may have bled gray, but it died just like any desperate, angry living thing on those sharpened stakes at the bottom of the hole. Not that I spent long watching it.

"Where's Sam?" I gasped as I used Clarence's arm to pull myself back to safety.

"In the house." Clarence had reached some kind of battle clarity, exhaustion and fear canceling each other. His voice was like a robot's.

"Then let's fucking run," I suggested.

I stole one look back at Anaita, who did not appear too upset by the destruction of her pets. Made sense if they were things she'd just made, but it didn't help my plan any: I wanted her angry. Not to the point of burning down the house and all the rest of us with one pissed-off gesture, but close to it. Clarence and I dug across the drifting snow and black ash toward the building. Luckily for us, Anaita felt no need to hurry.

"Duck!" I shouted at Clarence as we burst through the door. I grabbed his head and bent him down to keep him from getting tangled. "She's coming!" I shouted to everyone else. Not that they needed to be told. The door we had dragged shut behind us simply flew apart, with a *snap-snap-snap* chorus of broken timbers and a *whuff* of displaced air, then the Angel of Moisture glided through—right into the web of ropes and rattles the pilgrims of Kainos had strung in the entranceway. As she thrashed her way angrily through this minor distraction, several Kainos men and women stood up from their hiding places on the second floor landing, screaming wordless battle cries (okay, shrieks of pent-up terror) and letting their arrows fly. None of them had been living in this place long enough to become marksmen, but enough of the wooden arrows struck Anaita to make her cry out in rage. She ripped loose those that pierced her, flinging them away as though they were no more than burrs and stickers from a walk in the country.

As the archers fired, others all over the house began pounding on the walls with tree limbs and shaking their rattles, making so much noise that even I lost track for a moment of where I was and what I was doing. Then a chance arrow struck Anaita right between the eyes.

If she'd been human it would have killed her, but of course she wasn't. Still, it got her attention. She turned to look in the direction of the archers, her face contorting in a mask of fury; then the stairs leading up to the second floor simply flew apart, like an explosion without the explosion. The pieces of wood hurtled in all directions. One of the larger fragments hit Clarence in the leg and knocked him flying. Several of the Kainos pilgrims went down and didn't get up.

But Anaita's sudden attack on the screaming archers and other noisemakers had snapped me back into gear. Even as stair boards turned into wooden shrapnel, I dropped to my knees and crawled across the main room toward the wooden box where the Mecca cube—

and something else—was hidden. This was the crucial bit, and if the thing wasn't there waiting for me, well, Anaita would have the leisure to shred us into component molecules and spread us around her invented world like dandelion seeds in a tornado. And I would go wherever angels wind up when a very powerful, very angry higher angel decides to dispose of them.

Still on my hands and knees, with broken boards raining down all around me, I reached up and opened the doors of the cabinet, then felt along the inside, just in front of the Mecca cube. It was there.

Anaita had brushed aside the distractions of the doorway like they were cobwebs, shredding the hand-carved rattles and the rope curtains knotted full of sticks and clattering stones. She was crackling with energy that bent the air around her, and she had a look on her face that I wouldn't have wanted to see on a five-year-old having a tantrum, let alone on one of the most powerful beings in the universe.

"Wait!" I shouted, and scrambled to my feet.

She turned to me and the anger simply vanished. She became cold as a statue. "You." That was all she said.

I knew I had perhaps a second, maybe two, so I held up the thing I'd taken from the cabinet. "Just thought you should see this first," I said, showing her the horn.

Cold as a statue? No, colder. Like an ice storm turning the sky black. Like the front of a glacier just before it rolled over you and ground you into the earth. "What," she said, "is *that?*"

"This? Come on, you know what this is." I hefted the bloodshot ivory thing in my hand, bounced it once or twice. It weighed a little more than I would have expected—not as much as a curved, four inch piece of ordinary horn, more like a petrified souvenir. The whole universe had come down to something the size of a paperweight. "This is Eligor's horn. I found it. And he's coming for it."

And just like that, Eligor was there. No burning line in the air, no dramatic blast of light and smoke and brimstone, he was just . . . there. In his Kenneth Vald face and body, dressed as though he was going to receive the Entrepreneur of the Decade award from some grateful civic body.

"Greetings, Angel of Moisture," he said.

Anaita looked at him, then at me, then at the horn I held cradled in my hand. "What nonsense is this? What are you doing here, Eligor?"

"Don't I have a right to be here?" He smiled. "Didn't I help you build this place?"

She didn't smile back. "You and I made a bargain, Grand Duke. Would you interfere now? Are you very certain you wish to do that?"

"Who's interfering? I've just come to have some of my property returned. Angel Doloriel? I believe you have something of mine."

"Impossible." That was all she said, but there was a lot going on behind that single stony word and that mask of chilly indifference.

"Right here." And I flipped him the horn. I watched it spin through the air toward him. Every living creature in that big room watched it too, all the pilgrims cowering on the stairs, even Anaita herself. He caught it with the ease of a man reaching out his hand to see if it was raining. Then it dissolved into a cloud of starry light, and Eligor absorbed it.

For half a second everything seemed frozen. Anaita hadn't moved, but it seemed like something was heating up inside her. I could feel a pressure beating out from her, a force that could devastate everything in the church-shaped house. "Impossible," she said again, but she sounded less certain now, maybe even confused. "Conspiracy!"

I held my breath. The next few seconds would tell. If everything went right, then maybe, just maybe . . .

"Don't, mistress! It's a trick!"

Ed Walker half-ran, half-tumbled down the stairs from the second level. He caught the string of his bow on a newel post and instead of untangling it, simply let it go. The bow sprang back, swung hard around the post, and clattered to the steps just as he reached ground level and threw himself down on his face in front of Anaita.

"Ed, no!" someone shouted from the upper floor, a cry of genuinely astonished horror.

"Mistress, *you* built this place for us, not these others!" Walker's words came fast and breathless. "Not these so-called angels who've brought us nothing but death and destruction." He looked at me and glared. "Don't fall for their tricks. Don't take our home away because of them. It's not true—that's not the horn you had, that's Eligor's *other* horn. He and the angel worked this up together. It's a trick!"

"You shit," I said. "You treacherous little shit."

"Shut up." Walker didn't even look at me now, just stared up at Anaita. She seemed even more like a statue now, something impossibly fine and rare, with supplicants appropriately arranged at her feet. One supplicant, anyway—Edward Lynes Walker, the unofficial leader of the pilgrims, the man who hadn't liked our plan from the beginning. "Spare us, mistress. Spare us and spare Kainos."

"Dear me," said Eligor. "You seem to have rolled snake-eyes, Doloriel."

I'd done everything I could. There really wasn't anything left but to fall down on my knees. I'd wanted to do that for a while, anyway. I was exhausted, a bloody mess from the wounds the big cat had given me, and I'd kept going this long on pure adrenaline.

"Okay," I said. "You win."

Anaita looked at me. I swear, she had never looked more beautiful than at that moment, a frozen, perfect immortal beauty. It was hard even to look at her. If she'd been a huge rock, mariners would happily have steered right into her, foundered and drowned while singing her praises.

"Of course," she said. "There was never any doubt. Did you really think I was foolish enough to hide the other horn *here* on Kainos?"

I was so very tired. "I admit it did cross my mind."

"You must have thought you were quite clever. I can imagine your logic. Where would she keep it, this oh-so-important object? In Heaven? Of course not. In Hell or on Earth? Why make it easy for her enemies to search for it? Ah, but here on Kainos, the place that can only be reached with her permission—"

"Or mine," said Eligor. He sounded like he was enjoying this.

"You may go away now, Horseman." Anaita wouldn't look right at him. I don't know if that was because she was scared of him or because she was trying to resist the urge to blast him into sparkly cinders. "Unless you mean to challenge me. As you already conspired against me."

Eligor laughed. "My dear, you give yourself too much credit. Challenge? Without the permission of our masters? That would violate the Tartarean Convention and several others. As for conspiracy, my little friend Doloriel asked for a favor. I granted it to him because it amused me to do so. I, of course, had no idea what he planned to do with my horn."

"Of course." Anaita bit the words off and spat them at him.

I couldn't do anything. This was going all kinds of bad, and I was helpless to change it. The two of them were *talking!* Like they had just bumped into each other in front of the laundromat and were catching up on old times.

"Seriously, though," said Eligor, "that horn must have been a worry. I had the feather in my safe in my office. Couldn't have been more protected. But someone took it away from me anyway. And I had the devil of a time getting it back—if you'll excuse the expression."

"So, the horn isn't here," I said, forcing myself into their little tête-à-tête. "So I guessed wrong. It was worth a try."

"There were moments I almost had respect for you, Doloriel." Anaita had returned to her calm, emotionless voice. The weird thing is, I could still hear bits of the childlike tones that we all knew, that soothing, sweet voice still submerged in the goddess persona, like a toddler fallen down a well. "But ultimately, you were a mistake from the beginning. I should never have let you continue to exist." She shook her head. "Did you really think I would keep the horn somewhere you or some other sneak-thief could reach it? Hide it in my house? In a museum? Or here?" She laughed, and I heard something then that I hadn't heard before, even in her rages—the sound of something that had nothing human in it. "Since the Grand Duke and I made our bargain, the horn has never been out of my keeping. Never! An army of angels could not have taken it from me—or an army of demons." She placed her hand over her heart. The spot began to glow. "You, with your sad little tricks. Sammariel hid my feather in a hidden pocket, folded into time! How clever! Did it never occur to you that if he could perform such a trick with a mere fraction of my power, I might be capable of things you could not even grasp?"

And then she reached into her own chest, as effortlessly as reaching into a coat to pull out a wallet. A moment later, she withdrew her hand. Sparkling, shining with a sickly pale glare, the horn lay in her palm. All I could do was stare at it. If I hadn't been yards away from her I might have been able to reach out and touch it, but it was hopelessly beyond my grasp. "Here, annoying angel. Is this what you wanted? To buy back your demon sweetheart?"

"Why?" I said. "If you knew—if you knew all this already—why go to so much trouble to frame me?"

"Frame you? You have not been accused of half of what you've actually done, Doloriel. And as for what you've done to *me*, by my divinity, if you spent eternity in the lowest pits of Hell, you couldn't possibly pay for that. You've spoiled so much. Even when you were alive, you were a thorn in my side."

My eyes slowly lifted from the horn to her face. "When I was alive?"

"But now, the loose ends will be cut off, or burned away." She lifted her other hand, the one without the horn. It had a strange waviness to it, as if I saw it from several directions at the same time, or through thick glass. "Horseman, you have no business here, so depart. You have my feather. I still have your horn. Our bargain is still in place."

"I'll be going, I promise," said Eligor, grinning. "But I confess I find this fascinating. I'll watch a bit longer, but I won't interfere."

"As you wish." She looked down at Ed Walker, still prostrate on the floor. "And you have done well, little pilgrim. Kainos will survive. But you will behave yourselves from now on, and treat me with the respect your creator deserves."

"I knew it." I said it loudly.

Anaita turned just the slightest bit toward me. "Silence. You are no longer important, Doloriel. You are the first loose end that will be trimmed." She lifted her hand toward me, spreading her fingers, so I started talking fast.

"Yeah, whatever," I said. "I knew it would all come down to the same old shit. It's not even real evil—it's just selfishness." I pulled myself up into a half-crouch. I was still too far away to do anything but get burned to ash, but if you gotta go, you might as well do it upright. "You actually think that what you want is more important than what anyone else wants, and you think that having power proves it. The last important angel who fell, the Adversary—that was what he thought, too. People act like it's some kind of terrifying, incomprehensible evil, but it's not. It's the same greed you see in a sandbox full of children. 'Give me that! I want all the toys! Mine!'"

"I told you to be *silent*, Doloriel." A little heat crept back into her voice. "You cannot even grasp what I've created here. The mistakes of the Highest—I've fixed them. It was worth every death, every deception. With you and your friends gone, Heaven will never find this place. Little angel, spiteful little angel. You cannot grasp the beauty, the perfection, of what I've made!"

I stood. It was painful. "And you've failed to grasp a few important things yourself, my lady. For one thing, everything you've just said has gone straight to Heaven. Because the lines of communication have been open this whole time." I pointed to the Mecca cube, which had at some point begun to glow in its open cabinet, a thin but vibrant pale, pale violet-blue, like the first shift from dawn to daytime sky. "In fact, I believe that you've just made what's called a full confession."

Her entire face changed, twisting in fury that even Eligor might not have been able to match. "*What?*"

"Oh, and one other thing." I'd been wondering what had kept him so long, but there Sam was, standing just behind her. "This."

But instead of simply knocking the horn from her hand as we'd planned, Sam reached through Anaita with the God Glove. I shouted out in surprise—he wasn't supposed to use it anywhere near her—but my voice was lost in the sudden wail of anger and shock from Anaita as Sam's glowing hand forced its way through her body from behind, making her writhe like a hooked fish—no, an electric eel, sparking and discharging—then knocked the horn out of her grasp. It bounced across the floor, a simple object apparently obeying simple laws of physics, and landed only a yard from me.

"You!" she shrieked, turning to see Sam, still caught with his glowing hand sunken in her body. She did something I couldn't quite make out, lashing out with her arm; there was a burst of white light, a great crack of heat and sound, and Sam went flying across the room. She staggered, but pulled herself upright again, looking around as if for her real enemy, someone more significant than a mere advocate angel. "Traitors! Thieves!"

By now I had the horn in my hand. I turned to Eligor, who was watching the whole thing with a gleeful expression. "You want this? I want Caz!"

"Throw it to me."

"Not until I have her! Don't fuck with me now, Horseman! No tricks! I want her, the real thing, the Countess, just like you promised!"

"Little angel," he said, "you are no fun." A moment later Caz appeared, pale hair flying as she tumbled to the floor. She lay on her side, gasping. It sure looked like her, and there was nothing else I could do to make certain before Anaita turned us all into ashes. I tossed him the horn. It flew end over end across the room, but before it even landed in Eligor's hand it was peeling apart into flecks of light, being absorbed back into the Grand Duke's person. For a moment I thought I even saw his real face, horns now proudly in place once more. That's all I'll say about it. Then the Vald face returned.

"And now I'll let you have the rest of your fun," he said. "Because things are about to get crowded."

He vanished. Caz didn't. I couldn't really enjoy it, though, because a very, very unhappy Anaita was only a few feet away from me.

Suddenly light began to stream down from above. The roof and upper floors of the house peeled apart and began flying away, up into the sky, and as they rose I could see a thousand bright, winged shapes falling down toward us through the swirling snow.

Something hit me, smashed me to the floor. Anaita stood over me, her beautiful face now something else entirely. "First what you love—then you," she said, and every word was a serpentine hiss. She reached out her hand, the invisible air rippling and bulging around it, and then flung something toward Caz where she lay on the floor.

But something else got there first. Clarence, who had already been limping toward her, dragged my beloved out of the way just before the entire wall behind her burst into a foam of molecules. Clarence, bless him, didn't even glance back, but kept dragging her out the front door. I saw Caz look up just before she slid out of sight, and for the first time she saw me. Her eyes went wide.

Then the room was full of moving lights, of whispering, half-visible wings and beautiful glowing shadows. I heard Anaita shriek, and then I heard that shriek get smaller and smaller. I turned. Where she had been, a dark unreflecting shape like a huge dark gem now stood—a prison, I supposed. A casket, I really, really hoped.

The entire room was swirling, becoming unstable. There was so much light! I could barely see to crawl through the blinding, directionless glare to the spot where Sam had fallen.

He lay curled on his side in the splintered wreckage of the wall. The arm that had worn the God Glove was gone, only a blackened stump left below his shoulder. He was bleeding from a dozen wounds, red streaming out onto the floor.

"I see the cavalry showed up," he said, but he was forcing air through his lips by sheer effort of will.

"You'll get help, Sam. You're an angel, you're tough. Hang in there."

"Oh, yeah. All . . . the king's horses." He coughed blood.

"Why did you do it? Why did you use the Glove? You said yourself that she could control it!"

"Because even with Walker's trick and the other stuff, she wasn't confused enough. We couldn't . . . risk it going wrong." He twitched, then shivered all over, but without much strength.

"But, Sam . . . !"

"Heaven . . ." he stopped to cough, "was never going to let me back in. One way or another . . . I was gone."

I could barely understand him. I'm pretty sure his jaw was broken. Clarence and Caz staggered up. She dropped down to my side—I could feel her, smell her—but she was carrying a handful of snow from outside and wasn't paying any attention to me. She squeezed it over Sam's mouth, trickling water onto his tongue. He tried to smile. "Come on, B." His voice was very faint. "A last drink without . . . without a proper toast?"

"I don't think there's any booze here," I said. I don't even know why I said it.

"Why ruin . . . fourteen days of . . . sobriety?" He grinned. Damn, he was strong. There was blood between his teeth, and red bubbles forming in the corners of his mouth. "Water's f-fine. Just fine."

"Sam, I . . ."

"Shut up. I've been . . . grooming the kid . . . to keep an eye on you."

Clarence didn't say a thing. He was crying. You don't see angels cry much.

I couldn't see so clearly either. "Sam . . ."

He lifted a hand, struggled for a few seconds before he could form a word. "Confusion . . . !" The hand fell back.

". . . to our enemies," I finished, but Sam wasn't listening any more.

forty-six
bobby's blessings

I CAN'T REALLY tell you what happened next—well, not much of it, anyway. I remember Caz wrapping her arms around me. I remember turning to put my face against her neck because losing Sam hurt so much that I didn't know what else to do. Just as the fact struck me that she was *actually there*, Caz herself, the woman that I loved enough to go to Hell for, we were surrounded by astonishingly bright light. I couldn't hear anything but the beating of wings and something that I swear to Jiminy Cricket was the sound of the world's biggest, most spiritually committed choir. Then everything flew up into the air, or at least I did, we did—Caz was still there, sort of, but we were both fractured, flying apart, breaking up like light shattered by a prism. And then nothing.

I woke up in my apartment. Not Caz's apartment—mine. The one that I'd moved out of because of the infestation of swastika-shaped occult creatures, among other reasons. That apartment.

I had about three seconds after consciousness rolled in when I could lie there and tell myself that none of it had happened—that Sam was still alive, and Caz hadn't been snatched out of my arms yet again. I wanted to believe it. God, how I wanted to. But although I was in bed, I was fully dressed except for shoes and yet not even slightly hung over. Something was definitely out of whack.

I jumped up and ran out of the apartment, then down to the street, stepping on sharp things I could feel through my socks and not even caring. I was desperate to know what day it was, and I got halfway down the block, stumbling and staring and probably terrifying the shit out of the other pedestrians before I thought to check the phone in my pocket for the date.

December 11th. Time *had* passed. It had been five days since Clarence and I stepped through that mirror smeared with my blood and into Kainos. Which meant that everything I remembered had actually happened. My world really had ended, and now I was alive again in some pathetic imitation place where everything I cared about was gone.

I returned to the building slower than I'd run away. I didn't bother to go check the apartment where the Amazons had been. I was pretty sure the cleanup crew from Heaven had scrubbed away all forensic traces. It was probably even rented again. Heaven is thorough.

I found my most recent gun, a Glock 17, stashed in my sock drawer, along with several of my favorite knives. Like I said—thorough. They could do everything except put my heart back in my chest.

I got on the phone and called the office. Alice answered. "It's me, Bobby," I said.

"Oh," said Alice. "Hurrah."

Everything back to normal. Except it wasn't, and it never would be. "What's my current status?"

"Don't worry, Dollar. I'm happy to drop everything just to answer a question that you should already know the answer to." I heard a wrapper crackle, then the sound of Alice eating something crunchy while she searched the official database, or pretended to. "You're currently on compassionate leave, whatever that means."

"I want to talk to Temuel."

"So go talk to him."

"I want him to call me. Give him a message from me, tell him that."

"I live to serve, Master." Crunch, crunch. "Done. Any other ways you want to annoy me?"

I couldn't think of any just then, so I hung up.

It was interesting to discover that I could have my insides torn out and still keep functioning as if I actually cared about living. While I waited to hear from Temuel, I called Clarence, just to see what the kid had to say. Ominously, his outgoing message, after a few formalities, continued, *"And if this is Bobby, please let me know when I can call you. We really need to talk."* I didn't leave a message, but I checked my own voicemail. Sure enough, the kid had left several over the last couple of days, all variations on a theme of "Call me," but I just didn't want to. Clarence had come through the disaster with flying colors, and I was pretty sure he was missing Sam just like I was, but I couldn't bear the thought of one of his optimistic chats right then. I'd talk to him later, if I went on living.

While the Mule continued not to return my call, I wandered around the apartment like a depressed robot, checking things out. Heaven's cleaners had been hard at work. The paint was new, the carpet was new—hard to get out those squashed-swastikid stains, I guess—and there was even food in the refrigerator, although it was laughably un-ready-to-eat. Somebody had badly misread my personnel file if they thought I was going to make a stir-fry from scratch. However, some brilliant soul had also left an unopened bottle of vodka in the freezer. Good stuff, too. So after another hour or so of waiting for a call from my archangelic supervisor and trying to find some music in my collection that didn't make me feel like I wanted to bash my head against the wall—even *Kind of Blue* made me jumpy, which should tell you something—I gave up and opened the bottle. My kind superiors had offered me a first-class ticket to oblivion, and the only alternative I could see was to stay sober and sit around thinking about Caz and about Sam and about the big empty that had once been my afterlife. I decided it would be rude of me not to accept Heaven's invitation.

A day later, give or take a few hours, after a long drunk and a series of nightmares so bad I'm not even going to talk about them, I was back on Planet Apartment, a bit hung over but more or less sober again, and in need of something to do to avoid going seriously, permanently crazy. It wasn't like the heartache I'd had the first two times Caz had been snatched away from me. I didn't have the strength for that, I guess. Maybe I had finally accepted the fact that the universe hated me. I felt like I was in a car with the fuel tank almost empty, the engine sputtering, still moving, but pretty soon all the momentum would be gone, and I'd coast to a halt in the middle of big, big nowhere. Until that happened, though, I couldn't think of anything else to do but keep rolling forward, even though it was all but pointless. There were still some things I didn't understand, and I figured I might as well satisfy that curiosity while I still had a little strength.

I called the kid and told him to meet me at the Compasses, hoping he'd have a few answers. I still didn't know why I was even alive and free instead of banged up in Heaven's equivalent of a supermax detention facility. Our bosses usually don't like loose ends, and I was about as loose as they came.

To my shock and horror, I discovered that although everything else had been fixed up for me and returned to normal (as if such a thing was even possible), when I checked the parking spot for my apartment I found the same horrible yellow thing I'd been driving, Temuel's taxicab. Apparently the universe was still having a few laughs at my expense. Just looking at it depressed me, so I decided to walk.

Clarence was waiting when I got there. Quite a few regulars were around as well, and it might have been my imagination, but it seemed like they were all trying not to make it obvious that they were watching me with keen interest. The only person who acted normally was Chico the bartender, who grunted in recognition, slid me a vodka tonic, then went back to cleaning glasses with a bar towel.

"I'm really glad you called me," Clarence began, but I held up my hand.

"Just a second." I downed half the drink. "Okay, better. You were saying?"

He gave me a look that had a little too much of Sam in it, except more disapproving. "You don't need to do that, Bobby."

"What? Drink? The fuck I don't. Look, just tell me what you know and don't slather it with happy-sauce." I lowered my voice. "What happened? Is Anaita really gone? Dead?"

"Not dead, but definitely in heavenly custody. They froze her in some big blue block of . . . I don't know what. Then they took her away. I've heard she's already been tried and convicted."

"What? Tried? You mean they had a trial already—the biggest one in centuries? Was it public?"

"In Heaven?" Clarence snorted. Some of my cynicism appeared to have rubbed off on him. "No. But everyone knows."

I looked around the bar where everyone knew lots of things that I probably didn't know. They looked like that didn't bother them, but it sure bothered me. "What about the Mule? Why won't he call me?"

Clarence shrugged. "Can't say. I haven't heard anything official about him, and I haven't seen him either. But he's still in charge of the San Jude departments, as far as I can tell."

"Shit. They're just going to sweep the whole Anaita thing under the rug, I bet. Did you make a report?"

"Report?" His smile was not a happy one. "I've been grilled by every fixer on Heaven's payroll, I think. They wanted to know everything. Everything."

"Shit. And shit. What did you tell them? Did you tell them . . . ?" I looked around. Nobody was paying attention except Monica's friend Teddy Nebraska, who, as usual of late, was looking at me like he wanted to say something. I didn't particularly want to be said-something-to, so I looked away. "Did you tell them about Caz?"

"No." He frowned. "And they didn't ask. I don't know why. They didn't ask about your trip to H-E-double-hockey-sticks, either. But they wanted to know everything about your . . . *conflict*, I think that was their word, your conflict with Anaita."

I stared at him. The thing with Clarence, I could never tell if he said things like "H-E-double-hockey-sticks" to be ironic, or if he really was some reincarnated youth minister. "Okay, let me try another one. Why the hell am I free? Why did the cleaning crew go to all the trouble of re-doing my apartment and even filling my fridge with fresh crap I'll never eat?"

"I don't know, Bobby. But I think it's out of our hands now. We just have to wait and see what Heaven decides."

"Waiting," I said. "I *hate* that." But Teddy Nebraska had apparently decided that he hated waiting, too, and now he was finally making his big move. Clarence and I watched him walk over to our table.

The kid stood up. "I'm going to go get myself another iced tea."

"Hi, Bobby," Nebraska said. "Can I talk to you for a moment?"

I was torn between wondering why Clarence would walk all the way across the room for a drink containing no alcohol and wondering what the hell Nebraska wanted from me. I didn't know him well, but of course I'd seen him a lot recently, with Monica. He dressed well, but with that faintly overdone look that suggested not too many decades back he would have been wearing a white Panama suit and a straw hat. "Yeah," I said. "Sure. Sit down."

"Thanks." He slid into the booth and then just sat there. I wondered if he too, like Walter Sanders, had been approached by one of our superiors about me and had only now worked up the courage to tell me (when it was way too late to make any difference).

"What can I do for you?" I asked at last.

"Well, I've always admired you, Bobby—"

"Please. Today of all days, that kind of shit just makes my head hurt. I'm sure you're a nice guy, Nebraska. Me, not so much. So please, just get on with it."

He took a breath. "I don't know if you know, but I've been seeing Monica Naber. Nahebaroth."

"Yeah, I know." If he thought this was the complaints department, I might have to pop him one in the mustache. "So?"

"So, I just wanted to . . . to make sure that was all right with you."

I stared at him. I honestly thought for a moment he was putting me on. "Let me get this straight—you're asking me if it's all right for you to date Monica?"

"I guess so. Yes."

I couldn't help it. I laughed. First time since the snow and ash and the end of the world. "You're joking, right? You and Monica set this up as a prank?" I pretended to look around for cameras.

Instead of being relieved or pleased, Nebraska seemed worried. "Does that mean it's okay?"

"You're serious—you want my permission? Did you tell Monica you were going to do this?"

"She thinks I'm crazy," he admitted. "But I didn't want you to think we were sneaking around behind your back. Everybody knows things have been tough for you lately."

At another time I would have bent one of his fingers until he told me all the things that "everybody" knew, but at this point my shit was so muddled up I didn't even care. "Look, Ted, Monica is a wonderful person. Well, she's a wonderful angel—I'm not sure how good any of us are at 'person.' But she can make up her own mind, and she can see whoever she wants. Neither of us ever had a claim on each other. Frankly, she deserved better than me, anyway. If you're the better, more power to you both."

He looked as if a weight had been lifted. "So we have your blessing?"

I nearly said something mean. It was just so silly. I even looked around to see if Monica was watching, enjoying the whole stupid conversation, but the Compasses was pretty much stag right then, just a bunch of the boys in various states of looseness. Daytime tends to be guys-only, not because women aren't welcome, but because most females have the sense not to spend the sunshine hours in a saloon. And as I looked around and realized I was really *back*—maybe not the same, but back on my home turf—a tiny bit of hopelessness lifted off me. Not enough, mind you. I still couldn't imagine living much beyond the next day without Caz and Sam, I still couldn't believe there was anything on this gray planet to keep me here, but at least I could see a little farther through the darkness than when I came in.

"You want my blessing? Then you have it. Monica's one of the best. If she sees something in you that she likes, I'm willing to believe you're a good one too, Nebraska. Be kind to her. Be kind to each other." I lifted my hand. "God loves you."

I wasn't completely sure God loved anyone, to tell the truth, but at that moment, for some reason, I was willing to accept the uncertainty.

The rest of my visit to the Compasses was spent getting what Clarence had said confirmed by pretty much everyone else: Anaita's fall was the talk of the angelic confraternity. It was known that the kid and I had been involved, and the fact that we were both walking around free suggested that the earlier bad things they'd heard about me had just been ugly rumors. I wasn't quite so certain myself. I had confessed a whole lot of bad stuff to the heavenly inquisitor, Pathiel-Sa, and things like that didn't just disappear. Heaven is forever, and that means the heavenly statute of limitations is at least that long.

But at the moment I was free—there was no arguing with that. I was free, and I was alive, and someone had painted my apartment. If I was going to find out what it all meant, it seemed I would have to stay alive a bit longer. I had already thought of an errand I wanted to run, and a few other matters had been nagging at me as well, although I hadn't been sober enough to hear them very clearly.

Still, despite having at least one more day left on my personal calendar, I turned down Clarence's offer of a ride and walked home. I also picked up another bottle of vodka on the way. These earthly angel-bodies are sturdy. You have to pour a lot of alcohol in them to shut down the kind of things I wanted to shut down, to silence the guilty, angry, lonely thoughts long enough to sleep.

I'm really not an alcoholic angel. I'm a self-medicating angel. I swear there's a difference, even if I couldn't quite put my finger on it just this moment.

forty-seven

pointed questions

THE OLD Bobby would have lain around a few days and then would have sobered up and started knocking shit over, trying to make something happen and get some answers. Because there were a lot of things that still needed answering.

Why wasn't anyone in power talking to me? What about my trial? Was I still all but convicted of treason against the Highest? My heavenly superiors had to know about Caz, and Eligor, and Hell, because I'd spilled my guts to Pathiel-Sa when they had me in custody. Not to mention all the bigger questions, like what Anaita had meant when she said she should have killed me "even before" I was an angel. And that vision I'd experienced when she was brainwashing me—vision, memory, whatever it was—still made my mind itch. It had felt so real—*realer* than real, if you get me. Was it a glimpse of my before-death past?

Questions and more questions as far as I could see, without the smallest hint of an answer. Now I knew how my friend George the pig man must feel—shoulder-deep in shit and pretending it was normal life.

Like I said, the old Bobby would have been making trouble all over town, trying to figure it out, but this time I couldn't get started. Despite the surge of vitality that had sent me out to the Compasses, I just didn't care enough. I felt like a party balloon a few days past the best-use date: nobody was holding my string anymore, but instead of flying I was sort of bumping along about halfway between floor and ceiling, unable to reach either the top or the bottom. Drifting and doomed.

It's not like I didn't think about ending it all. I mean, really, what did I have left? Caz gone, snatched from me again. Sam gone too, at least the Sam I knew and loved, probably forever. My bosses still with the guillotine blade hanging over my neck and not bothering to tell me whether I should get up and get on with things or just lie there and wait for the drumroll to finish and the blade to drop. But it wasn't that easy, anyway. As you've already seen, death and angels don't always go together—our fates are not in our own hands. The chances were good that no matter what I did to myself—even if I went to the Ephorate and insisted on making a full, public confession of every rule I'd broken—I might only be recycled into another body, this time with obedience reflexes more in line with current workplace standards, a bleating Bobby-sheep who didn't ask questions. But what if they recycled me, and I still remembered what it was like to be discontented in the pastures of the Lord? And couldn't do anything about it?

So the next couple of days dragged past, and I let them drag me along. Christmas, once only a vague nightmare, crept closer and closer, like a determined, tinsel-covered zombie. I drifted, bounced, drank, slept, and watched television with the sound off. Clarence tried several times to get me to come out, but I declined. I knew he'd try to talk me into something, and right now I couldn't handle something. I was having enough trouble with nothing.

Okay, here's the truth, embarrassing as it might be. When my archangel finally contacted me, I was walking back from Oyster Bill's and a late breakfast, and I was actually trying to figure out whether I should take the toast crumbs wrapped in a napkin in my pocket and feed them to the pigeons in Beeger Square or go home and watch *Maury*.

I had decided on the pigeons, because I figured at least somebody should benefit from my shitty life, even if it was flying rats, when I noticed a small, Middle-Eastern looking man walking beside me. It wasn't exactly the same body I'd seen before, but I was beginning to recognize the Mule's Earth-body-language, if you know what I mean.

"Bobby."

"Temuel." I kept walking. Beeger Square wasn't too crowded on a chilly December pre-noon.

"Don't be angry, Bobby."

"Angry? Me? Because you handed me over to my bosses to be put on trial?"

"You know that wasn't my choice. I *know* you know that."

"Oh, really? Funny, because I wouldn't say I know anything like that."

I picked the first bench that didn't have spilled milkshake congealing on it and sat down. Temuel sat beside me. As I unfolded the napkin full of crumbs, a particularly bold pigeon dove down to get first choice. Startled, I nearly took its head off. I still hadn't entirely recovered from being in Hell, even months later. I didn't like things jumping at me without warning.

"If you truly thought I sold you out, then why didn't you tell them about me?" Temuel asked. He looked exactly like the kind of harmless old guy, maybe a professor of Semitic Languages, you'd see sitting on a bench like this. I wasn't sure where I fit in, although the pigeons appreciated me for about thirty seconds, until the crumbs were gone.

"I did. I told Pathiel-Sa about you. I told that sweet-talking witch everything."

"That's not what I meant. You couldn't help that. But you didn't mention me to the ephors when you were on trial."

"Nobody asked me." Which was only partly true, of course. Even during the trial I'd begun to figure out something more complicated than mere treachery was going on with Temuel. In fact, in a few ways he seemed to have taken risks to protect my secrets—Caz's apartment still seemed unknown to the authorities, for one thing. I'd dropped by the place one day in a drunken fog and had a look around, but it had been too painful to stay more than a few minutes. Still, I'd found no sign that Heaven had been there.

"Okay," I said, "you did a few things to make sure I had something to come back to. Did you work something special with the cab, too? Because it doesn't seem to show up on the heavenly radar for some reason, so they have to follow me the old-fashioned way. I'm guessing that was something you arranged."

Temuel nodded, almost shyly. "I was wondering if you'd noticed."

"Yeah, I noticed. Thanks." But, strangely, I wasn't feeling very grateful at that exact moment. "So what do you want from me now? It's all over, right? Anaita got taken down and you seem to be free and clear, but I'm still waiting to see if I get the inquisition treatment. Did you want to know if I'd go on keeping my mouth shut about you?" I tried to see the answer in his face, but Temuel was giving nothing away. "I guess I'll do my best. But I spilled it all to the Angel of Conciliation already, so *somebody* in Heaven knows more than enough about both of us to drop us into the Pit for a term of forever-to-longer. It's only a question of why they haven't used any of it yet. In other words, if you're worried about keeping your wings, I'm not your biggest concern."

"No! That's not why I'm here." The archangel seemed a bit frustrated. "I can't talk about any of it yet, but I wanted you to know that I haven't forgotten about you. You have no idea how complicated things are right now, how . . . delicate." He patted my hand. It felt just like being patted by a human being.

"And that's all? 'Good luck, Bobby, I'd like to help you but it's complicated'? Okay, leave me out of it for a minute, then—what about Kainos and all the human souls living there? Did they just get disappeared?" *And my girlfriend along with them,* I almost said, but even now my habit of secrecy was strong. "What about Sam Riley and the other Magians who were betrayed by Anaita? Do they just stay dead? Or do they get recycled into something more manageable, angels who don't ask questions?"

"It's not that simple."

"You know, I've heard that before, and it's not really what you expect from friends."

"I've never been your friend." He didn't bother to make a reassuring face, but I must admit he at least looked sad. "Heaven, Hell, Earth, it's all too complicated for anything as simple as friendship, Bobby. But I've tried to do right by you, and I'll keep trying."

"So this whole visit was to tell me what? Not to give up?"

"I'm not worried about you giving up. I'm more worried about you pushing things too far when the time isn't right."

"What the split-level Hades does that mean? Time isn't right? I just brought down an angel who was running the biggest anti-Heaven scam since Satan tried to invent upward mobility."

"Funny you should mention that," he said, and for a moment I thought I might actually hear something useful. Then Temuel stood, ran a hand over his balding head, adjusted his glasses, and gave me another one of his wise-old-uncle smiles. I was really getting sick of that particular facial expression. "I have to go."

I couldn't even think of anything cutting to say. Like I said, half helium, half regular old air, dragging my string along the floor. I watched him walk away across the park. A couple of pigeons too stupid to know the crumbs were gone kept me company until I finally got up and headed off in the opposite direction.

If it had been a day like the last few, I would have gone back home and saluted the passing of noon with a drink or two. But somewhere in my subconscious I'd been waiting for Temuel to check in, one way or another, and now that he had (and had given me a lot of nothing), I couldn't turn off my unhappy thoughts. I wandered up and down the waterfront and the dark, narrow blocks around it—oh, sorry, the Pioneer District—and considered the differences between disappearing into a bottle and just doing the job properly by stepping off a dock and into the cold green waters of the bay. For a while I listened to a guy with a guitar playing an okay version of an old Slim Harpo song that people only remembered because the Stones recorded it. The guy wasn't that good, but he wasn't that bad either. Eventually the proprietor of the nearest souvenir shop came out and gave him five bucks to play somewhere else, a win-win for everyone.

Strangely, it was a message from Orban that pulled me away from the hypnotic green waters of the bay and my empty, uncaring mood. He called to say that he'd finished the sale on the Matador Machine to the guy in the Pacific Northwest and that he had the rest of my money.

So it was official. My car was gone.

I'd loved that car, had spent hours with it, searching for replacement trim and the right paint and upholstery, shoveling money into the pockets of mechanics to make it run like new, and now it was leaving my life. Lot of that going on. But where losing the Matador should have felt like a death, the actual news was more like a pinch, so much less than I'd expected that it hardly registered. Did I no longer give a damn about anything? Or had my priorities changed? Because as I walked along Parade through clusters of chilly tourists, I found I *did* still care about some things. I cared very much.

Caz had called me a wounded romantic, a self-destructive optimist, but I wasn't feeling either very romantic or optimistic. Still, there's a part of me that needs to get knocked down to remind myself of why I get up, and that part seemed to be awakening again. Heaven wasn't going to tell me anything. Temuel couldn't tell me anything, or at least that's what he wanted me to believe. Sam was gone, Caz was gone, and even the ephors who should have been grilling me like a Junior Burger didn't seem to give a damn.

But I still gave a damn. I still needed to know what had happened to me, and why.

I walked back to my place and climbed into that ugly-ass taxi, then headed west, over the hills and toward the ocean.

The surf was midwinter-impressive below the onetime nunnery. Half a dozen women in gray were dutifully hanging washing on a line outside the cabins down below the house, although I couldn't imagine that bedclothes and nun's habits were going to dry very fast in the biting breeze off the Pacific.

One of the nuns opened the front door and tried to tell me that Gustibus wasn't at home. I didn't care whether he was or wasn't, to be honest, because I wasn't going to leave that easily, and I didn't really have anywhere else to go. I said I'd wait, and made my way down the hallway toward the big room, which really upset Sister Kremlin or Sister Igor or whichever one it was, but she was apparently too Christian to get into a wrestling match with me.

I had scarcely found myself a place to sit in the midst of all those tables littered with books and papers when Gustibus appeared through a side door, tying the rope on his weird Buddhist Warrior Pajamas like I'd got him out of the bath. I could see the nun hovering in the doorway behind him (she was now holding a broom) but Gustibus apparently didn't think he'd need her help quelling the invasion; he closed the door gently but firmly behind him.

"Thought you weren't here," I said.

"Nice of you to drop by, Mr. Dollar. Perhaps next time you could call first?"

"Sorry. Old habit of mine. People who don't want to see me find it easier to avoid me when I let them know I'm coming."

"Perhaps. But I wasn't trying to avoid you."

"Didn't say you were. You still interested in swapping information?"

He looked me over, then went to get two glasses from a tray and poured water into both of them. "Some refreshment?"

"Sure. You had the glasses ready. Were you expecting someone? Like me?"

He gave me a look that was a little amused, a little irritated. "Why would I be expecting you?"

"Never mind. I'm here because I want to know more about a particular angel." I checked my notes. "Yep, that's all. Just some info on one little angel. I'll take hard evidence, interesting stories, completely dubious scuttlebutt—you name it."

"Oh? And what do I get in return, Mr. Dollar?"

"The inside information on how a major angel fell. You've heard about Anaita?"

"I confess that I have. In fact, even if I hadn't, the fact that you're still around suggested she was out of the picture."

"Yeah. Well, I was there when she was taken down. And it's an interesting story. What do you say? You game to trade?"

He drank his water, eyeing me over the rim of his glass. "And what angel is it you want to know about? Because that might make a difference. One of the ephors in charge of your case? Someone involved in the Magian movement, one of Anaita's dupes?"

"Nope. I want you to tell me all about an archangel called Samkiel."

I'm betting that name won't mean anything to you, but trust me, you've heard it. Gustibus recognized it, too, because he looked surprised. "Really?" He shook his head as though I'd offered to hock him a priceless antique for the price of a cheap bottle of wine. "Very well. Let's talk."

And so I told him about the snow and ash on Kainos—all the way up to the last moments when the angels came and my best friend died in my arms. I told him everything, even the things I'd rather have forgotten. When I didn't tell him enough, Gustibus asked questions— good questions, hard questions that I didn't always have the answers to myself. It really made me wonder about him, because it might just have been the hunger for truth of a true historian, but there were times when it seemed to go deeper than that.

When I was done, he answered *my* questions, and you'll hear about those answers soon enough. All together, it made for a fascinating afternoon, and for a long time it was just the two of us, one speaking while the other listened. The ocean beat against the shore like a lover at a locked door, and the wind plucked at the shingles and rattled the windows.

By the time we finished it was early evening. I stood up, stretched, then fumbled in my pocket for my car keys.

"Oh, one last thing," I said. "Just a minor question, not a trade. You don't have to answer."

He put his glass down and turned from the window. He, as usual, had stood during the entire time I was with him. "What might that be?"

"I was just wondering whether you might be someone else."

"I beg your pardon?"

"I know, it sounds strange. But I couldn't help thinking that if someone wanted to slip me information, even manipulate me a bit here and there, it would be nice if they had a cover as someone who knows a lot about Heaven while still being an outsider. Someone like you."

"Ah. And in this solipsistic view of things, Mr. Dollar—Bobby— who would I be?"

"Don't know. That's why I'm asking. One of the ephors? My boss Temuel? Some other angel I don't know? Heck, maybe not even an angel—there have to be lots of folks from Hell playing the long game up here, who wouldn't mind the combination of getting inside information and making trouble for Heaven."

His smile looked genuine, if a bit indulgent. "Should I remind you that you came looking for me, not the other way around?"

"Absolutely. Can't argue with that."

"And even if this conspiracy theory *were* true—although it most definitely is not—you know very well that such a mysterious double-agent version of Karl Gustibus would have to deny everything anyway. So the question is a bit pointless, isn't it?"

"I guess so." I got up. "Thanks for the briefing on Samkiel. I have a feeling I may find that very useful."

Gustibus didn't walk me out. The nun who'd let me in hours ago was still clutching the broom as I went past her on my way to the door, but at least she didn't take a swipe at me.

I had a lot to mull over on my way back through the hills. I put on Sonny Rollins' *Blue Seven*, good thinking music, and watched the trees swaying in what looked like the winds before a storm. The sky was dark. So were my thoughts.

I parked my gaudy yellow ride in the Tierra Green garage and headed for the stairs. I had decided to call Clarence, because I thought I'd better share some of this with somebody, and he was about the only person left who knew enough of the story to understand, not to mention that he'd handed me a major piece of it himself. But just as the phone screen lit up, and I started to put in numbers, something punched me in the back *hard*, knocking the wind out of me. I staggered, and it was harder to turn around than it should have been. I got myself swiveled just in time to see the pale, staring face of one of Baldur von Reinmann's minions—Timon, the dark-haired one. His eyes were wide with an almost sexual excitement, and I could see sweat beaded all over his face in the pale light of the garage's overhead light. He had a long, bloody knife in his hand, an SS dagger.

"The fuck!" I said, then he stabbed me again, this time in the belly. He grabbed me with his free arm so he could plunge the knife in several more times. My knees buckled and he let go of me.

"You killed him!" The words tumbled crookedly out of his mouth. "The most beautiful man, our leader! He could have been one of the world's masters!" Timon's dark hair hung in his face. He looked way too emo for a genuine murderer. "You ruined it!"

"No," I said, bubbling blood. "*You* ruined it." I was on my hands and knees, drizzling blood, trying to find a way not to shriek at the pain that had set the whole of my torso on fire, front and back. I was talking to distract him, but it felt like I was belching out fire and broken glass. I grabbed his legs with my hands and began to drag myself upright. He tried to pull away, but somehow it didn't occur to him to stab me again. "Dumbass," I grunted through clenched teeth. "You could have been a camp counselor. Or a Deadhead, or a fucking comic book fan, something decent." And there it was, tucked in his belt like a birthday surprise for me—my own sofa gun, the Smith & Wesson .38 that he'd stolen at the museum. "But you had to hook up with a bunch of miserable racist Nazi shits—!" I did my best to punch him so hard in the nuts that he'd die, but I was pretty weak and only gave him a mild thump. As he stumbled back, though, I managed to hang onto the butt of the revolver.

It took him a second to realize what I was pointing at him.

"I bet you wish you'd taken up golf," I said as his eyes grew wide. "Or collecting stamps." Then I emptied the revolver into the middle of him. Like a good little fascist, he'd cleaned and reloaded it, so he got all five rounds. I don't think the last two or three were necessary, but by that point I couldn't actually see anything, and even the healthy crack of the .38 Airweight sounded like the tap of a distant hammer.

I died pretty quickly after that.

forty-eight
one tick away

O KAY, HERE'S something you may not have known: apparently dead people dream.

How did I know I was dead? Well, unless it's ever happened to you (and you were an angel at the time, like I was) it's hard to explain. Basically, there was a brief moment when all the lights went out, the party was over, and I could no longer feel the breath of the Highest whispering in my blood. I can't explain it any better than that.

So I know for sure I was dead. What I don't know is how I came back to life in the same body. But I'll get to that in a moment. As for the dreaming part . . .

It was Caz, but somehow I was seeing through her eyes. And I thought she must be in Hell, because all I saw was fire and smoke and hopeless faces. She was stumbling past them and the owners of those faces kept trying to grab at her, to pull her down, but she fought past them and out into a swirling nothingness. Suddenly there was a line of fire in front of her, and then something else was there—something big. Something powerful. Something that had come for her and her alone. It raised its hand . . .

And I woke up. Shouting. Thrashing, trying to help her, save her, but I was restrained.

No. Only restrained on one side. And not exactly restrained, either. Somebody was holding my hand.

"Bobby. It's okay. You're in the hospital. Don't fight, you'll tear out the stitches!"

It took me a long moment to focus. Part of me was still seeing that sparking hole in the air, the huge dark shape stepping through to take Caz. "Clarence?"

"Shit." He almost smiled, but he looked worried. "I guess even almost dying isn't going to get you to use my real name, is it?"

"Almost?" I fell back against the pillow, or at least something shaped like a pillow, but with no actual pillow-ish qualities like softness or comfort. "Are you sure?" I couldn't understand what I was doing here. "Are you still holding my hand?"

"Does it make you nervous?"

"No, I was just checking. I'm trying to figure out what's what." What's what included a standard-issue hospital room with the window blinds shut and everything around me the same institutional beige color. "Why am I alive?"

"Because God loves you?"

I was tired already and wanted to go back to sleep, to drop into darkness where I could at least dream about Caz. "Could be. Or maybe it's more of a curse than a reward." I felt like the hacked remains of a Thanksgiving turkey. I swear I could feel places where the neo-Nazi bastard's knife had scraped the bones in my chest on its way to my vital organs. "The guy who stabbed me?"

"Dead. Very dead. Name was Geoffrey something. One of the Black Sun guys."

"Yeah. I recognized him." I was feeling waves of weariness now. "What's the news? How long have I been out?"

"A good while—several days. The doctors barely saved you. Monica and a bunch of others have been here a couple of times to see you, but you were unconscious, full of tubes, and not much fun. As far as how things are going, Heaven-wise, pretty much the same. Still the big hush-hush about you-know-who."

"I wish they'd give her a golden parachute. A real one. Let her try to use it from high Earth orbit." I changed my position on the bed. It hurt, but not so badly that I couldn't feel my body already healing itself. Soon I'd be back to normal in a world without Sam and Caz or any point at all. Fucking Heaven. They'd found the best way to punish me. Simply keep me alive and stupid and suffering forever.

Clarence squeezed my hand and then let go. "I'm so sorry, Bobby. About Sam. Do you think there's any chance he'll be back?"

"He sure didn't think so."

After a short silence, he said, "I miss him too, you know. A lot."

I almost said something sarcastic, but the impulse just evaporated. "I know, kid. He really liked you, and that wasn't all that common with him."

"Sam spent a lot of time with me in the last few months. It was like he was coaching me to take over for him. I think maybe he had a feeling. That something would happen."

"Coaching you to what? Say that again."

The kid looked embarrassed. "He knew you'd need a partner. Someone to watch your back."

I gave him a long look. Sam was right, of course. Sometimes I'm a half-empty balloon, but sometimes I'm a kite. It's nice to have someone around who knows when to grab the string and keep me anchored. "We'll see."

"Or, if you'd rather start interviewing other applicants, I'll let G-Man know."

"Fuck you. I'm not that happy about being alive, so don't you dare make me laugh. It feels like I've got stitches holding my stitches together. I still want to know why I'm not a corpse. And don't tell me it's because God loves me."

"Okay, I won't." Clarence smiled and stood up. "But you ought to at least entertain the possibility."

"You're dead to me, Harrison. Dead."

"And you're alive, Bobby, whether it's convenient or not. See you visiting hours tomorrow."

I almost let him get out the door before I remembered. "Hey, Junior."

"What?"

"Just wanted to check something. Samkiel, right?"

"Sorry?"

"The guy who sent you for training, an archangel. Samkiel, that was his name, wasn't it?"

"Yeah." He gave me a look. "What made you think of that?"

"Nothing. Next time you come back, bring alcohol."

"Not happening, B." He went out, closing the door quietly, as if loud noises might be particularly upsetting to the recently dead. Because I *had* been dead, or at least as dead as an angel ever gets, I was sure of that, but here I still was, and I hadn't even been recycled into a new body.

The things I'd been considering when the guy with the knife jumped me on my doorstep were coming back to me, definitely including my most recent conversation with Gustibus. But I was tired from being awake, worn out just from that little give-and-take with Clarence, so I didn't get much thinking done before I was asleep again.

I was standing in the middle of so much beauty that even the hardest of hearts would have broken, even the most stiff-necked would have bowed his head, but even in the middle of the Elysian Fields, with the shining towers of the Celestial City on view before me, I felt oddly hollow.

Angel Doloriel, a voice boomed, filling the green world with implied echoes, although only I heard the words. *You are wanted in Heaven.*

I wasn't surprised. I hadn't come here by my own choice, so I had been expecting a summons. I could have taken the slow way and appreciated the glory that was Humanity Beyond Death, the contented souls in the Lord's fields and the tuneful, heart-healing songs of the Choir Invisible, but I was tired—not body-tired, but soul-tired, which is deeper. I let myself be carried directly to whatever fate was waiting for me.

I found myself somewhere I'd never been before. From the way the light fell (or didn't fall—it's hard to explain) I was pretty sure I was actually within the Heavenly City, but it felt like a part where I'd never been before. For a moment I wondered if I'd finally made it into the Empyrean, the center of everything, forbidden to the rank and file, but I guess I'll never know. All I could say for certain was that it was a place that felt both indoor and outdoor at the same time, with the silence and solemnity of a crypt under a cathedral, but the airiness of a tent on a windy hillside. The walls even seemed to be some kind of fabric, light as cloud, moving in a breeze I couldn't actually feel. Except for the intimations of size and the heavenly light, it could have been the field headquarters of an important general. Which gave me a clue about who I was going to see.

"Angel Doloriel. God loves you."

I found myself facing a figure wrapped in brilliance. The angel was seated, but on what I couldn't see, and although I couldn't make out face or features, only a manlike shape of light and cloud, the voice confirmed my guess. "Lord Karael. You called me?"

"Come here, son." A moment later I was much closer, and also seated, but as with the Angel Militant himself, I couldn't tell if I was on a throne or a camp stool or somehow perched in midair. "You've been through a lot, haven't you?"

"With respect, Master, yes, I have."

"And now someone else has tried to kill you. How fortunate he failed. These mortals are stubborn things." Karael smiled. I don't know how I knew that, since he didn't really have a face I could make out, but I felt it like a curtain pulled back a bit to let the sunshine through. "Believe it or not, Doloriel, not everyone in Heaven is out to get you," he said. "Some of us admire your intelligence and your—how shall I put it? Your determination. And, of course, some don't."

"Anaita would be one of those, I guess."

A cloud rolled in front of the sun, or the curtain fell closed again. "We don't really need to talk about her. Nobody is proud of what she did or how far it got. But you don't have to take the blame for that any longer."

"I don't?"

"No, sir. You, son, are even going to be rewarded a bit. From now on, consider yourself restored to duty and cleared of charges. But that duty will only be half-time for as long as we need until you're back to your old troublemaking self. We'll make sure the San Judas central office has its caseload covered." He said it with such an air of generous, cheerful finality that he might have been God explaining to Adam about how this direction was going to be called "up" and the opposite would be named "down."

"Thank you, Lord Karael."

"You don't have to keep calling me "lord," son. I'm not the Highest. I'm just one of his faithful servants. Please, call me Karael."

"Okay. But can I ask a few questions?"

"Of course." He spread his glowing arms expansively, but with the kind of grace that reminds you why angels are angels. "You've earned it."

"What about my trial?"

"It will be as if it never happened. We've announced that the whole thing was Anaita's deliberate attempt to confuse and mislead."

"Wow. Thanks. That's a huge load off my mind. And Anaita herself?"

Karael went a little bit cloudy for a moment. He might have been shaking his head in sadness, not in anger. If he'd had a head instead of just a vaguely head-shaped glow, that is. "She will be punished, don't you worry about that."

"Yes, but did she explain why she did some of those things? Because a lot of what happened doesn't really make sense."

For a moment he seemed oddly still. "Like what, son?"

"Well, I don't want to waste your time. I know you must be very busy. Are you in charge of my part of Earth now that Anaita's out of the picture?"

"The division of duties in the Third Sphere is a great deal more complicated than that, but I suppose the simple answer is yes." A thin beam of sunshine. "I suppose I'm your boss now. But of course the hierarchy remains the same. You'll still report to—"

"Temuel," I said, cutting him off. "Right?"

"Right." He hadn't liked being interrupted. "So, if there's nothing more, Doloriel, then I will send you back and get on with some of that new business waiting for me."

"If you have another moment, sir, I didn't finish telling you some of the things that didn't make sense. See, it was all weird from the very beginning. Like when the souls first began disappearing—the ones we found out later went to Kainos? Edward Walker was the very first one, and I was there right after he killed himself. I was with Hell's prosecutor, Grasswax."

"Grasswax. The one who was butchered by Eligor over the feather."

It was very strange sitting with a powerful angel, discussing secrets that only a few days ago had still been getting people ripped to pieces or sent to Hell—or both. "Yes, that's the one, sir. But the weird thing was, when the first soul went missing, Grasswax and I weren't the only folks from our two sides who showed up. In fact, it was like someone pulled a fire alarm. Almost as soon as we noticed that the soul was missing, angels and demons were all over the place."

The airiness and light got a little roiled. "Hmmm. Interesting point. Why would Anaita do that? Why risk her entire plan by bringing in extra scrutiny and more witnesses so soon?"

"Exactly."

"I imagine it was Eligor," Karael said after a moment. "Just because he had a bargain with her doesn't mean he wouldn't try to make things difficult for her. He *is* a Grand Duke of Hell, after all."

"Good point, sir. Which leads me to the next question. I spent a lot of time thinking about how the bargain worked, Anaita's feather for Eligor's horn, and how Anaita kept it hidden, and what she wanted to do."

"Which was to be worshipped, to be simplistic about it." Karael's voice took on a tone of disapproval. "She never got past her origins. She didn't truly appreciate the Divine Plan."

"Clearly. But here's a question I've never been able to answer. What about Eligor? What did *he* get out of it?"

"What do you mean?"

"It's quite simple, my Lo . . . Karael. Sir. A powerful angel and a powerful demon made a bargain and went to great lengths to keep it secret. For instance, Anaita sent Walter Sanders to Hell and brought a serial killer back from the dead—*two kinds* of dead—and sent him after me, all to keep the lid on what she'd done."

"And what do you know about angels in Hell, Doloriel?" The cloudiness threatened a storm. I swallowed, or would have if I'd been on Earth.

"I think you know, sir. I think you know where I've been and a lot of what I've done. Anaita wouldn't have a reason to keep quiet about it, not once she was really in Heaven's power for good. And also I told Pathiel-Sa, the Angel of *Conciliation*, pretty much everything while I was imprisoned."

A long silence, and it *was* a silence. We might have been in outer space for all the background noise that wasn't. "Let's assume that you're right," the Angel Militant said. "That I know more about what you've been doing than is going to be officially admitted, Doloriel. And yet I'm still willing to let you go back to your normal job and even give you a few perks."

I had the distinct sense of a shiny lure bobbing in front of me, but I wasn't in the mood. "I hear you. And I'll be happy to do that once I've had a chance to finish talking to you about all this."

"You really are a very determined fellow," said Karael.

"So everyone tells me." I took an imaginary breath, the kind you take before jumping into the deep end. "Okay, so let's put aside the question about what was in this for Grand Duke Eligor, although I think that's probably pretty important. Help me out with one last thing. You know all about my partner Clarence by now, right?"

"Clarence?"

"Sorry, kind of a private joke. Haraheliel. Earth-name Harrison Ely. Sent in at first to keep an eye on Advocate Sammariel on behalf of management, then he later decided Sam was getting a bum deal and sort of threw in his lot with me. He was one of the souls picked up when you guys raided Kainos, but someone's put him back on the street again, kind of like you're offering to do with me if I stop asking questions."

"Ah," he said. "*That* Clarence."

"Right. Well, apparently instead of going through the normal training like Sam and I had when we joined Counterstrike, when Clarence was being prepared for his undercover assignment for the big bosses, he was sent somewhere different. Somewhere I'd never heard about before. Got schooled on guns there and all kinds of stuff."

"Yes? So? That was Anaita's play, son." He really did sound like a military officer. Just his serious tone of voice made you want to get up and salute. "She needed information about the Magians and wanted a source she could control, so she could stay quiet about them—or, if things went bad, she could manufacture an excuse that she'd been investigating them all along. But I never trusted her."

"That sounds exactly right, sir. And it makes a lot of sense. But the problem is, it's not true."

A very long pause this time. "What?"

"You heard me. It's not true. Do you want to know what *is* true? Clarence's training, that whole little mini-spy-camp of Anaita's, a kind of under-the-table Counterstrike unit not answerable to the heavenly hierarchy, was arranged by an archangel named Samkiel. And Samkiel's one of your oldest allies, I found out. Now why would he do that for Anaita? Unless you asked him to."

"Son, this is getting dangerously close to—"

"We both know what this is getting dangerously close to, Karael. Sir. And you can silence me any one of a thousand ways. But since we're both here, you might as well hear me out first." Yes, I knew this was ridiculously dangerous—I'm not *that* kind of stupid—but I couldn't stop now. I'd been waiting too long to put it all together. "See, the only arrangement where everything makes sense is that Anaita wasn't working alone—that she was never working alone. Somebody else must have known exactly when the first soul-snatch was going to take place, because only the folks involved would have been able to put out the alert so quickly and have angels and demons swarming all over Edward Walker's house like that."

"Eligor—"

"Didn't really have a reason to screw things up for Anaita when her plan was going to do Heaven more harm than it would Hell. Doesn't mean it's impossible, but it doesn't make a lot of sense."

"But why would some *partner* of hers want to 'screw things up,' as you so eloquently put it, son?"

"I'm not sure. A warning? Or just to get some things into the public records as quickly as possible—insurance that could be used later on? We may never know."

The silence hung thickly. "And?"

"And then the thing with Samkiel. Why would you approve him doing that for Anaita unless you were helping her out—or pretending to? Because if she wanted the protection of being able to claim she'd been investigating it herself in case things went bad, well, then her partner would want the same thing. And what better protection than being able to say, 'I sent her to my old ally Samkiel precisely so I could keep an eye on what she was doing. If I'd known she was involved in a crime against Heaven, of course, I would have acted immediately' and blah blah blah."

Karael's voice was even flatter than usual, and usually you could balance a full drink on it without spilling a drop. "You know that proves nothing, son. It's just speculation."

"This is *all* speculation, of course, sir. It's kind of what I do." I tried to sound more confident than I felt, but it's hard to be really brave when you know the person you're accusing of high crimes can extinguish you as easily as a birthday candle on a cupcake. "But it leads to the most critical unanswered question—what did Eligor want? Why would the Horseman risk his own standing in Hell, give his enemies the means to destroy him if they found out, just to make a deal with Anaita? Who we already know was a bit unstable, not as careful as she should be, prone to silencing allies, and not generally beloved in Heaven?"

"Tell me."

"Because he didn't really want a deal with Anaita—he wanted to make contact with someone else. Someone he could make a long-term alliance with. Someone who *didn't* make the kind of mistakes that Anaita made, and who would almost certainly become even more powerful after she was gone. Somebody like *you*, Lord Karael."

It was a magnificent silence, which gave me plenty of time to wonder what it would feel like to be erased from reality.

"So you're suggesting that I was involved with Anaita's madness from the beginning?" Karael said finally. "That she thought I was her partner, but in truth I manipulated things from behind the scenes all along the way, and then left her to hang when the time was right?"

"In a word, sir—amen."

"Then it's your turn to answer a question, Doloriel. If all this was true, why haven't I destroyed you, too? Why would I leave a loose end like you dangling?" The air of good-old-boy, drill-sergeant familiarity that always colored Karael's speech in my presence had abruptly disappeared. He was clipped, precise, and as calm as a deep, deep pond, but I could see the darkness roll through his glowing presence like a storm. "In short, why do you still exist?"

"That's the one thing I don't know," I admitted. "I don't believe bumping off witnesses is really your style, but I doubt that's the most important reason. It might have something to do with what Anaita said about knowing me when I was alive, but maybe that's not even true, or if it is true, it's irrelevant to the bigger picture." I had run out of tricks and revelations. I suddenly realized the next words might be the last I ever spoke. "I can only guess that for some reason, sir, you think you might need me someday."

The roil of darkness coagulated, and for a moment I was facing something from which no light gleamed, as though Heaven had tipped sideways, and I was looking down into a hole full of ultimate nothingness. Then, as suddenly as an eyeblink, it dispersed, and I was looking at Karael's misty but luminous shape again.

"An interesting guess, Doloriel. You will never know if it's right—in fact, you'll never know if any of this is right—but you will definitely know when I *do* want something from you. I'll tell you one thing now, and one thing only. I have ambitions. Ambitions that you couldn't begin to understand."

I couldn't help myself. "But why would you want to change anything? It's Heaven, right? Heaven is perfect."

Karael squeezed out the gleam that indicated a smile. I honestly could not tell you what kind of smile it was, amused or angry. He'd stopped pretending to be my bluff, gruff commanding officer and was now something much more distant and difficult to read. "We all have choices, Advocate Doloriel, whether we are angel or mortal. We make our own path by those choices. And since we are all different, it stands to reason that some of us make better decisions than others. Those who make the best decisions should be allowed to do so for the good of all. Do you understand?"

I couldn't tell whether I was hearing the plain, unvarnished truth or just another excuse for a fascist takeover. I came extremely close to pointing that out, but there was no question Karael was different from Anaita, and I really had no idea what he planned. Maybe he was right. Certainly the Highest couldn't be too pleased about how things had been running lately. So for once I kept my mouth shut.

He seemed satisfied with my silence. "Exactly. As for your being useful, well, you had better hope so, Doloriel. Leaving aside all this conspiracy talk, you are an angel who was a single tick of the great Paslogion away from utter destruction. I'd suggest that in the future you do what you're told. At least when I'm the one telling you."

And just like that, Heaven vanished and I was back in a hospital bed, full of hurt and stitches, but also—and quite remarkably—still alive and still in possession of my very own soul, however ragged around the edges it might be.

forty-nine

the station

I SPOTTED HIM from about a block away, on the corner of Broadway and Spring, last-minute Christmas shoppers flowing around him like a tall, sharp rock in the middle of a stream. Of course, in that long coat and Dickensian top hat he was hard to miss. My pale friend was doing a funny little two-step, of course, scarf fluttering in the brisk wind. Everything seemed back to normal.

"Mister Dollar Bob!" he said when he spotted me. He tipped his hat. "Such a pleasant thing to see! So happy to notice you are all attached, body-parts and such."

"Yeah, Foxy, same to you, I guess." My body parts were intact and connected, all right, but my knees were still wobbly from the previous day's interview Upstairs. "How's business?"

He performed a little samba-move, one hand pressed against his belly—*step, step, spin, stop.* "Very good now. Was a little worried. Foxy Foxy is not in the munitions field. He does not make bang-bang guns like your other friend Mister Orban. War is bad for business." He smiled, his teeth impressively white considering they had to compete with his albino complexion. "But now—no war! All happiness, all good things. So now Mister Fox is happy, happy!"

"War? You talking about Heaven?"

"Of course! When the folks Upstairs or Downstairs have a really big fight, all of us mousies hide in the grass." He laughed. He really did sound relaxed.

I wished I felt the same, but the cold, gray day really fitted my mood. I'd survived my face-to-face with Karael, but that, I felt sure, had been only because I was no threat to him whatsoever. In fact, I was totally irrelevant. I'd been through Hell, literally, lost everything I cared about, all to get some answers, but the only real answer seemed to be, "Meet the new boss, same as the old boss." And I wasn't even going to receive that last consolation of the stubborn idealist, a hero's death. I was walking around alive only because I didn't really know how to do anything else. And because I needed to leave the apartment occasionally to buy more booze.

"Yeah, well, I'm happy for you," I said. "Enjoy the holidays."

"Hold on, Mr. Dollar B. I have a message for you."

"Message?"

"A friend is waiting in the square. You might want to drop by."

I could think of a couple of possibilities, none of which I liked much. "I'm relieved to hear my enemies are now willing to wait politely to kill me, instead of pushing and shoving to get to the front of the line." Just thinking about it made me feel sour. It was one thing living in a self-induced alcoholic coma, another getting taken down like a punk in the middle of the Pioneer District, in front of God and everyone. I took a quick look around to make sure Pumbaa the Nazi wasn't crouching somewhere nearby, waiting to avenge his beloved Timon.

"You have a very unique humor, Bobby Money Man," said my dancing friend. "Everyone knows. It's fun! I wait breathlessly for the chance to do business with you again someday."

"I hope not too breathlessly," I said, but when I turned around again he was nowhere to be seen, gone like a white fox into snow.

I walked into Beeger Square carefully, eyes open and a hand in my pocket. The bench looked so cold and windblown that I almost felt sorry for the figure sitting there, but I'd seen that small, hunched shape before.

I walked slowly across the square toward her. Yes, "her." Temuel was wearing his little-old-Latina-lady body again. A battered shopping bag sat beside him, threatening to tip over and blow away any moment. I stared, not quite willing to sit.

"Well," I said. "Merry Christmas. Or close enough. What's a couple of days to an immortal?"

"You're still angry."

"Wow, good guess."

"Please, won't you sit down?"

I wasn't clutching my gun any more, but I wasn't feeling particularly friendly, either. "No, thanks. So you're working for Karael now?"

Temuel shook his head. Because of the body he wore, Fellini Peasant Lady Type A, I half-expected him to make the sign against the evil eye. "I can't talk about it—any of it. I told you it was complicated. Well, it *is* complicated."

"You know, hearing that isn't as enjoyable as it was the first two dozen times."

He pulled a thermos out of the shopping bag, unscrewed the top. "I'm sure it isn't. But what would you say if someone asked you the same questions?"

"What do you mean?"

He didn't answer right away but poured the cup full of something that wafted steam. "Coffee?"

I took it, sniffed, then sipped. It was strangely sweet. "What's in this?"

"Horchata. It's South American, I think. You're supposed to drink it cold but I like it in my coffee."

Normally I'd have run like hell to get away from sweetened, milky coffee, but the dank, sobering chill of the season had sunk through my clothes and skin, into my bones. I took another sip. "It's okay."

"You didn't answer me, Bobby. What would you say if I ask you the same sort of questions?"

"What questions?"

"The obvious ones. Why did you risk your life and soul for your friend Sam? Why did you travel to Hell? Why did you make a deal with one of the most powerful demons in existence and try to bring down a high angel by yourself?"

"I don't know. Because I couldn't see any easier ways to do it. Because the deck was stacked against me and I didn't have much choice. It wasn't an organized plan, that's just how it turned out."

"Or, in other words, *it's complicated*." Temuel held out his hand for the cup, which I discovered to my surprise I'd emptied. He screwed it back onto the top of the thermos. Then something clicked for me.

"You were working for Karael all along, weren't you?"

"Nothing is simple, Bobby."

"That's your excuse? Just like me, you did the best you could. Is that what you're saying?"

"I'm not saying anything." He stood up. "I'm giving you something." This time it was an envelope he pulled out of his tattered bag and placed in my hand. "But I can tell you one other thing before I go. You've probably noticed that I went out of my way a couple of times to keep information about you from my superiors." He gave me a tired smile, exactly the kind I'd expect to see on the face of an older lady who'd worked too hard all day for too little thanks. "But it wasn't to protect you, Bobby. That's beyond my capabilities."

I stood up too. "What's that mean?"

"I can't protect you from the major players. I don't have the power. If they want to hurt you, they can hurt you. No, I was just trying to protect your privacy. Sometimes we all need a little privacy." He nodded, then turned and walked away, shoulders bowed as if the tattered paper shopping bag weighed a hundred pounds.

"What the hell is *that* supposed to mean?" I shouted, but Temuel only raised a small hand and waved as he disappeared into the Friday afternoon crowd of workers heading for their cars, their homes, their lives. Real lives—the kind I didn't have.

What the fuck was he talking about? How had he protected my privacy? He'd handed me over to our employers easy as selling a puppy to a medical lab. Yeah, he gave me a car—a fucking ugly car, to boot—but private? Everyone knew about it. Hell, half of Heaven had been following me around as long as I'd been driving it. So what did he keep from them?

It was only then I realized I was still clutching the slightly soiled envelope he'd handed me. It wasn't that easy to get it open because my fingers were cold, but when I did, all I found was a single piece of paper. The words were printed and the note was unsigned, but I knew who it was from.

Your first assignment. San Judas main railway station at 6:15 pm. Track Eleven.

So my new boss—who I now felt pretty sure was also Temuel's old boss—had a job for me already. I should have been pissed off at being ordered around like a hired driver, and I was, a little bit, but I was also deep into a stretch of several long days of not giving a shit about anything. All I'd been planning to do tonight was get hammered and watch television with the sound off, anyway. Maybe Karael needed someone picked up. Maybe that's why Heaven let me keep the taxi.

Hurray—my new job! I wondered if I'd have to report my tips.

I was going to do it, of course. If it turned out to be too depressing, I could always throw myself under the San Francisco commuter express, which would at least liven up my weekend.

It was weird that the note hadn't told me what to look out for, but I was guessing it was going to be Karael himself, come down to earth for one of his infrequent visits. Maybe he was going to give me a personal briefing on whatever dirty work he wanted me to do. Well, I'd play along, but Karael was going to learn that he didn't have as much of a hold on me as he thought he did. See, I'd lost pretty much everything, so what did I have left to be scared about? Destruction? Don't make me laugh. At this point, an eternity of darkness and silence seemed like the nicest, most soothing thing I could imagine. I suppose Hell was the real implied threat, but even that didn't have the terror for me it once had. Torture no longer seemed like that big a deal. It was only pain, whether for a moment or an eternity. I've learned how to do pain.

Because I was looking for a tall, soldierly figure, the type Karael seemed to choose on Earth, I didn't notice the much smaller passenger at first, even though most of the other arrivals had already swept by me, bumping their luggage along and talking urgently into their phones. Then the announcer's voice, which had been reading a list of destinations over the public address system, suddenly turned into echoing nonsense in my head as the small, slender woman pulled off her wool hat and her straight, white-gold hair fell down onto her shoulders like a flash of sunlight on snow.

I should have run to her that instant, grabbed her before she disappeared again forever, but it felt too much like a dream—the weird kind where you can't make your body do what you want. In fact, I couldn't quite believe what I was seeing. There she really, truly was, wearing some ridiculously gorgeous skirt and coat combination, looking like a young Ivy League co-ed just arrived for the first time in 1930s Paris, and I could only stare, my heart somersaulting inside my chest.

Then at last my brain found the levers, and I could move again. I ran to her, grabbed her arm and spun her around. Her eyes flared open, a moment of fear before the gasp of recognition. Then we were holding each other so hard that it hurt. We kissed and kissed and kissed.

If you've ever had this kind of reunion, you know the frustration and the glory. You can't say what you're thinking, because the words wouldn't make sense. You can't do what you really want to do, because there are laws and things, and the police would come, and also you'd wind up in a dozen people's internet videos. So all the energy and surprise and sudden need went into our kiss. We had our mouths pressed so tightly we were breathing through each other. Caz was crying, ordinary tears of water and salt, not the icy flakes that had dotted her eyes the last time I saw her. I might have cried a little, too. I'm not usually the weeping kind, but it is a human body I'm wearing, you have to remember. I'm not a stone.

At last I loosened my hold on her; then, holding her lip with my teeth until the last gentle second, I ended the kiss. I looked hard, but I already knew. Even Hell couldn't make an imitation this good, this real. "It's really you, isn't it? Really you this time."

Her eyes were shiny. "I could hit you, if that would make things feel more ordinary."

I might have been laughing, then. Might have been crying again. "I don't have the words, baby," I said when I could talk. "But let's . . ."

"Oh, God, yes!" she said. "Take me somewhere. I don't care how squalid. It can even be your apartment. Just take me somewhere and fuck me until I faint."

Sexual need shook me like a terrier shakes a rat. I struggled for a second before I could string words together. "I have the perfect place, actually."

"Then let's go. Now! I only have the weekend, then I have to go back."

"Back?"

"To Kainos. The angel told me I have to go back Sunday night. Don't let's waste time talking about it, Bobby!"

I steered her across the station and toward the parking lot, our steps echoing up in the high ceiling with hundreds of others. For the moment we were just two people—two people who could do what they wanted, at least for a short while. "Sunday, huh?"

I was drowning in happiness even as I realized what a perfect trap

I had fallen into. I should have known Karael was too smart to make the kind of mistakes Anaita had. He had me in a way that fear could never accomplish. He was going to use Caz to keep me on a leash.

At that moment, though, I didn't particularly care. Did. Not. Care. If I was Heaven's dog, I was now officially the happiest dog on Earth, at least for the next forty-eight hours. I threw my arm around Caz's shoulder and pulled her to me, smelled the back of her neck and kissed her there, smooching and sniffing and biting until she squirmed.

"This perfect place," I said. "You'll like it."

"I'm sure . . . I will." She forced herself to concentrate on walking.

"A friend helped me hang onto it, through all the shit." I realized I could actually say it and mean it. "There was a *lot* of shit, as it turned out, but just enough friends."

She wasn't really listening. "Where's your car? That one? Oh, Bobby, not really!"

"No remarks," I said with what I hoped was a quiet dignity. "It runs. It will get us where we're going."

She turned, sweetly hiding the grin that had spread across her face. "No, really, it's lovely, Bobby—so yellow! But where *are* we going?"

"I told you, it's perfect. My friend helped me hang onto it and keep it secret, and I only just figured out why—so I'd have a place to be with you, with neither Heaven nor Hell to bother us." I grinned. "Don't worry, you'll approve of the furnishings. In fact, it's your own apartment."

epilogue

YES, I know you'd like details, but for once you're not going to get them. I mean, come on, don't you have any imagination? I will tell you this much: We barely kept our clothes on long enough to get inside the apartment, and we didn't make it as far as the bedroom. (Not until early Saturday morning, anyway.) We broke a couch, kicked over the coffee table, and pulled down a couple of very pretty silk hangings, and all that while we were just getting started.

Later, we were lying on the carpet, naked and shiny with sweat. I had an upended lamp pressing against my rib cage, which was a tiny bit uncomfortable, but I didn't have the strength to move. Also, I had my face buried in the side of Caz's neck, just behind her ear, so that I could feel her pulse beating against my cheek as it finally slowed to something approaching normal.

No offense to the Highest, but that is my true idea of Heaven.

"What are we going to do?" I asked when I could stop inhaling the fragrance of warm Caz long enough to form words. "What are we going to do when Sunday night comes?"

"We're going to do what we're told," she said. "You're going to put me on the train, and I'm going to magically go back to Kainos. Because then we'll get to do this again. And again. And again."

"But I don't want to let you go. I want you to live here with me, not go back to some cold, empty, wild place. I don't ever want to let go of you again."

She was silent for a long time, but it wasn't the dreadful kind of silence I'd been forced to endure so many times before, the silence of
hopelessness. "Actually, I've come to like it there," she said. "It's quite
beautiful. And there are still people. The Third Way pilgrims all
survived—thanks to you and Sam and Haraheliel."

"Don't you dare get the kid's name right. He'll expect me to do it,
too." I rubbed my cheek up and down on the back of her neck. "Do you
really like the place?"

"It's quiet. Oh, Bobby, after hundreds of years in Hell, that's such a
blessing. And the weather's real, and it changes. Changes! One day
sunshine, another day rain—and the rain is actual water. Clean water!"

"Yeah, I get it. I went through a few of the rainstorms in Hell. Like
an amusement park ride built around Montezuma's Revenge."

"But it's not just that. The people living there have a purpose.
They're rebuilding, and when they finish with that, they'll keep going.
They're making something new. Something no one's ever seen before.
And when I'm there, I'm part of it."

I wondered what the pilgrims made of Caz. They couldn't know she
was a demon, could they? "So Karael's just . . . letting Kainos be? Not
interfering?" I'd filled her in on what I'd learned earlier, when we'd
staggered to the kitchen at one point in search of water and food.

"I don't know. For now, anyway."

"Huh. Hearing you talk about it, I almost wish I could go back with
you." And thinking of her going back without me on Sunday evening
made me hold her even tighter.

She laughed. "I don't think it's your kind of place, Bobby. Not a
single poorly lit street corner or dive bar on the whole planet."

"Hey, there's slightly more to me than that!"

"I'm teasing." She reached down to stroke me, to show me she was
sorry. She held on and squeezed. She was clearly *very* sorry. "I'd be
happy to be anywhere with you, my beloved angel."

"He's not going to let me, anyway." I held her close, marveled at
how well we fit together, like two puzzle pieces that had come off the
lathe side by side but had been separated for years. "Karael doesn't
strike me as the kind of dude who does things for sentiment or even
amusement. He's kept me around for a reason."

"I know. That scares me."

"Why?"

"Because. Oh, let's just not talk about it. Let's pretend we only have this one time, this one weekend, and let's not waste a second of it."

Something chilled me then, and I half lifted myself off her. "Are you trying to tell me something?"

She looked at me in concern, and for a moment I thought I saw the old terror, but then her eyes widened as she understood. She smiled and I saw it was all right. "Oh! No, Bobby, I didn't mean anything! We'll do what we're told, and we'll see each other again and again. I just didn't want to waste too much time talking. There are better ways to communicate."

I saw what she was getting at, or rather I felt it. "Okay, you're right," I said. "You can't do *that* by nizzic."

She really was right. We had more important things to do than worry about what our bosses wanted from us or what came next. Only a fool walks into Paradise with a chip on his shoulder, searching for the ugliness behind the beauty. I'd been that fool for a long time, but now I'd earned myself a little time off. A vacation. "This is a holiday," I said, turning her toward me so I could appreciate her perfect nakedness once again. I leaned over and kissed her chill, soft mouth. "It means 'holy day'."

My demon-woman reached up to me. "You certainly talk a lot, Wings. I think it's time to stop talking again for a while."

She was right again, and I was right to listen to her. In fact, at least for these few, fleeting moments, all was right with the world.

That doesn't happen very often, of course, and those who know Eternity tell me it never lasts. We have to grab it when it's there and hold on as long as we can, because that's the only good we can know for certain. Everything else we are and everything else we do, whether it's born in our bones and blood or spawned from our restless souls, is only an act of faith.